The Liquidator

Iain Parke

For Pat – who didn't want to go in the first place...

Author's Note

All characters, places and events in this book are fictional and any resemblance to actual places, events or persons, living or dead, is purely coincidental. None of the views expressed are those of the author.

Pronunciation of written Kiswahili is phonetic. Thus, Mkilwa is approximately 'mm-kill-wa'; Bharanku is 'bar-ank-you', *vigogo* (big shot) is 'vee-go-go' and *npya* (new) is 'imp-ea'.

Kiswahili makes use of prefixes, so the root word 'zungu' appears in the book as *mzungu* (a white Westerner), *wazungu* (white Westerners), and if there was a single white European language, this would by extension be *Kizungu*. Similarly *wahindi* refers to East African Asians while *wananchi*, normally translated as 'citizens', is a term often used by black East Africans to describe themselves.

Confession

I took the newspapers out onto the balcony at the back of the apartment as I didn't want to be overlooked. She had bought stacks of the Citizen. It was about tabloid size, printed on rough cheap paper.

I sat in the warm sunshine with my back to the wall of the apartment and gradually over the next half hour or so, the pile of papers on the right became a heap of paper tubes on my left as I took each copy, rolled it along its length and wrapped some tape around it to keep it in shape.

Then I put a blanket in the bottom of a bin bag and packed it with a stack of the rolled up papers. Repeating the process I managed to make four full bags.

I put most of the rest of the blankets to soak in a bucket full of cooking oil.

The day seemed to pass slowly. It seemed an age before darkness fell as it always did at around six. I had about another two hours to wait until the disco at the back started up.

But now I could finish my preparations. I picked up the jerry can. The awkward weight felt heavy but familiar in my hands as with a clank I opened it. As I tipped the sloshing can into the first open bin bag the oily reek of diesel perfumed the night air.

The can shuddered and rocked in my hands as the oil poured with a soft gulping sound, soaking into the papers and the blanket. Once each bag had been doused, another blanket went on top, again to be soused in fuel, and I knotted them closed.

Carefully I closed the can with a snap and left it out on the balcony as I went in to wash my hands. I didn't want any accidents here, after all.

When I had first moved into the apartments, immediately outside the front of the block, but before the roadside shanty *dukas* and bars, there was a slowly spreading waste ground strewn with blackened piles of old bags, cans and bottles. This was the dump where all the apartments' houseworkers simply piled the trash and where once the heap was big enough one or other of them would set fire to it. Until one day, a lorry full of workers and breezeblocks arrived and at the end of three days, there was the pen.

It was a simple construction about two metres square. Three of the walls were about two metres tall whilst the fourth, facing towards the apartments, was half that. Gaps had been left between the breezeblocks at the bottom to let air in so it made for a relatively efficient incinerator. Now, instead of just dumping garbage at random, the houseboys and maids from the apartments dumped it all in the pen, which at least contained it all in one place until it was full enough to burn.

Carrying the first two bags down, I heaved them over the low wall and onto the stinking heap of tied up plastic shopping bags full of papers, vegetable refuse, potato peelings, scraps and all sorts of trash that had been accumulating in the pen over the last few days, together with some brushwood that had been cut from around the entrance to the car park and dumped earlier in the week. I was pleased to see it was so full.

As I added the second pair of bags a few minutes later I looked around carefully. There didn't seem to be anyone about.

I was quite casual about it. Undoubtedly many of the locals would know that I was going. The houseboys would all gossip together with the *askaris* every day. People around the apartments would be expecting to see rubbish being dumped as I cleared out, although they probably wouldn't expect to see me doing it obviously.

I could hear a soft hubbub of voices from the bars outside at the front of the apartments, but they were another ten or so metres down the road from the pen.

In daylight the front of the structure was clearly visible from the apartments. In the dark and in the shadow of the pen itself, I doubted that anyone could see me, even if they were looking.

Then there were my friends the *askaris*, but they all dossed out on the concrete steps in front of the cars at the far end of the car park that led to the path around the back of the furthest block of apartments. I would be unlucky if there was anyone watching.

No, it looked safe enough, or as safe as I could hope for at least. Now it was a matter of waiting.

As I sat there, just after eight, I heard the girls' voices coming from above, a little bubble of brightness and jollity disappearing down the stairwell; then the rusty creak as the ground floor grating opened, followed by the grinding complaining squeal as it was pulled to again and the jail-like clank of the moment the grating crashed shut with a reverberating clang that seemed to go on forever.

It was like the doors of hell closing.

2

Well, I thought. Time to go to work.

With the girls now out from the apartment above and the apartment below empty that only left the family on the ground floor, but they wouldn't probably matter too much. The shower room's window faced out to the back of the apartments so it was away from the blocks on either side which would be making their own noise anyway. At the back there was the short stretch of ground with the water tank which then gave over on to the road, on the other side of which was the big empty building plot and a large walled house which at the moment looked unoccupied. The disco seemed to be a couple of hundred metres further down on the right, it was shielded from view by trees but I would hear it clearly when it started to get going.

Most of the relevant bits of shopping were on the table.

Standing in the darkened living room I pushed the play button on the dusty black ghetto blaster before turning back into the room and reaching out for the clothes. As if in a dream I pulled the boiler suit on over my boxers and stuffed its legs into the tops of the Wellington boots. As the staccato guitar gave way to the crashing beat of the drums and the strangely echoing melody I felt that at home I'd have been afraid of it drawing attention, of having some neighbour come round to complain about the noise. But here it was normal. Mind you, at home I wouldn't be in this situation. I felt strangely distanced, disassociated from the present almost as though I was watching myself from afar.

I felt nauseous, and then a violent hot churning need to run back towards the *choo*. You're stalling, I thought to myself, slipping the elastic straps of the protective facemask over my head. You're finding all sorts of excuses the voice in my head went on. You've just got to get on and do it.

With an unbearable effort I took a first reluctant step towards the hallway. And then a second.

All of a sudden there I was, dusk mask and goggles in place outside the door as the familiar haunting voice growled its instruction.

I reached across to the unit on the shelf to turn up the volume.

I fitted the bar into the latch on the shower room door and opened it as the song crescendoed.

The shower room was dark, I hadn't bothered to turn on the light.

There was a sort of grunt and movement as I pushed the door open. He must have heard me come in.

For reasons I could never really explain I said, 'I'm sorry about this.'

With the tape over his eyes he wouldn't even have seen me as some massive shape, haloed by the light of the living room.

And then I fired.

There was what a colossal crack and the room was lit with a momentary flash as I felt the kick of the recoil.

Above the scream of the record there was a horrible hideous gurgling sound.

I quickly worked the pump and then in the darkness, I fired again, low.

I was coughing.

There was an acrid stench of cordite in the air. In the small room it seemed to bite and sting my eyes and then there was the smell of blood.

I stepped backwards out of the shower room and shut the door, shuddering and breathing deeply.

My whole body seemed to be going through hot and cold flushes. I don't know how long I stood like that, maybe ten, twenty seconds.

I felt as though I was going to shit myself. It seemed a lifetime.

And then... Well, I felt suddenly calm. I had done it. I breathed deeply. There was no going back now.

And that was it. That's how I committed murder as the song turned into a denial.

With a click I turned off the tape. My ears rang with the silence.

There was no going back now.

It was done.

I just had to get on with it. I picked up the shotgun again and taking a deep breath, opened the shower door and switched on the light.

He was lying huddled in the corner. Dead of course. No surprise about that. One of my shots, the first I guessed, had taken him just at the shoulder, at that range it had just about amputated the arm and smashed in the left-hand side of his chest. It was probably enough to have killed him instantly. The second had hit him full on, slap bang in the centre of the belly and had almost blown him in two. The sky blue mattress was now a sodden, purple black with thick oozing pools of blood.

I took a deep breath. My throat felt tight. I could feel my gorge rising, my hands gripped the gun, my knuckles were white. But I felt oddly calm, collected, controlled, I was on top of the situation. I knew what I had to do.

The problem with killing him had always been what to do with the body. I was living on a peninsula so my first thought was could I just dump him in the water? I had quickly discounted the idea as impractical. There were estuaries on either side and the sea was shallow and quite tidal, while other than the little headland at the end of *Mnazi Moja*, the coastline was largely beaches or mudflats so there weren't any cliffs off which I could reliably tip him into deep enough water. To use the sea properly, I would need access to a boat which I didn't have. The last thing I wanted was to have him found lying in the mud at low tide or washed ashore.

If I took him inland and could find the right place and wanted to take the risk, I could always dump him and trust the animals do the work. But it was a long way to drive with a body in the back of the Suzuki to turn him into hyena or croc meat. And I would have to get far enough away that circling vultures wouldn't be a giveaway.

Trying to bury him in a patch of wasteland somewhere on the headland would be a complete disaster. There were people everywhere, herding goats, living in little huts, scrabbling over discarded rubbish and litter to see what they could find of value. Either I would be caught in the act or he would swiftly be found.

The only solution was the obvious one. I would have to put him out with the rubbish. I would need to dismember him to fit him into the bin bags we had bought. I also needed to prevent him being identified if his remains were ever found. Ideally I wanted to prevent him being identified as human at all by anyone who came across any remains.

I had to make sure I did three things, well, four, if you include avoiding cuts and breathing in any blood that might be carrying HIV.

I had to cut him up small enough to be able to get his remains into the bin bags for disposal. Draining out anything that could be washed down the shower grate so as to lose weight would help.

Secondly, I had to ensure that any body parts that might by any chance escape the destruction process would be unrecognisable for what they were.

And thirdly, I had to combine the bits as I wrapped them in the oil-sodden blankets and put them into the bin bags, so as to best help the destruction process.

I plugged the extension lead into the socket in the corridor and turned the music back on but at a lower volume. I was going to need to use the chainsaw.

The legs were first, as the great ripping blade tore into cloth and flesh in a spray of blood, the whining tone deepening as it bit into the bone. Working quickly, I looped rope around each ankle and passed them up through the iron security bars cemented across the window, and back down into the room. Heaving on the ropes I hoisted each leg up the wall so that they hung like lambs in an abattoir to drain. They were surprisingly heavy things, huge lumps of muscle and bone. I was going to need to section them in any case, I thought, they were still too big.

I worked steadily and methodically with the axe and saw. The arms came off and I cut them down into smaller chunks and lumps, the flesh jagged and shredded at the edges. I took the fingers off to make the hands less recognisable.

I set his head down carefully on its side on a portion of the mattress in the middle of the floor. I wanted to deaden the sound as, standing over it, I pounded at it with the sledgehammer, smashing the skull, the face, the jaw bone. Without the flesh I wanted unrecognisable fragments of bone, if any survived at all.

I was careful to crush the jaw with direct blows. I needed to ensure I broke all the teeth. I had to do a solid workmanlike job. If there was one thing in my life that I had to do right, this was it. No cock-ups, no mistakes, because there was no second chance, no excuses in this situation.

The guts felt squelchy and hot through my rubber gloves as I scooped and ladled them into some of the bin bags. I was hacking the innards loose with a knife – the liver, the heart, the lungs. I was trying not to look, trying not to think about what I was doing. I was just reaching into the body cavity, pulling out handfuls of organs, hacking the sinews and connecting tissue to free the contents for disposal.

The rib cage would be distinctive. Luckily it was mostly gone on the left-hand side. I cut it into four strips, up the breastbone, up either side to each of the armpits, up either side of the backbone, chopping up and under the shoulder blades with the axe until I could wrestle sections free.

The backbone I cut into manageable sections, the pelvis was a huge lump that I thought would be very recognisable. It was too big for the sledgehammer so I used the chainsaw to cut it into two before pounding it as best I could.

I had finished the noisy bit now and ran the tap in the basin to rinse my gloved hands. There was a mist of blood in the room's air.

I didn't want to leave bloody footprints so I slipped my feet out of my boots to step into the main room and turn the tape off again.

I listened hard but the only noises I could hear were those of any normal evening drifting across from the dukas out on the road.

I used the blankets soaked in cooking oil to wrap his mortal remains in as small chunks as possible, before putting them into the bin bags. Once each bag was sufficiently full, but not so full it was impossible to carry, I dragged it out through the living room and kitchen to the balcony. As each shot had shredded the body it had also shredded the mattress beneath and so a mess of blood-soaked foam and pellets went into each bag as well. What bits of mattress were still big enough I used the saw to rip so that I could also stuff them into the bags. The shower room was a mess.

It's called the wick effect. I'd come across it drunk and alone late one night as I vegetated on my couch watching some crappy documentary investigating explanations for so called spontaneous combustion cases. It's been found to happen occasionally when someone's clothes catch fire. In principle, it's a bit like the way a candle burns, but where the wick rather than being trapped in the middle of the fuel, is a sheet of material wrapped around the outside of it.

As the wick burns it melts the body fat, which then soaks into the wick material around the body to burn, giving a very low and localised flame, but one that burns at a very high temperature for ages. They demonstrated it with a pig's carcass. It lasted for something like six hours, smouldering away, but eventually turning even bone to ash. At least he had plenty of fat on him, I thought, as I sloshed the last of the cooking oil into the bags for luck.

I had been careful with the diesel soaked papers that I had dumped out earlier. Just enough to get it going I judged, but not so much that my wick was burnt away before the process could start to work.

The clothes I was wearing would need to go in the bags as well so I had no real choice but to start to clean up now. I ran the shower for about half an hour while I hosed down the walls and floor and used bleach on the scrubbing brush to get the worst of the mess sluiced away. Caustic soda down the drains would help to chemically remove the evidence. I would need to have another go tomorrow. The cement walls were pitted and scarred with shot. The cement and paint would sort that and the damage in the bedroom out later on over the weekend.

I pulled off my sodden boiler suit and quickly ran my head, arms and feet under the shower, scrubbing vigorously to get rid of any obvious signs. I was surprised to find my hair sticky with blood and rubbed it furiously, trying to get it clean.

By now it was nearly ten o'clock. Out on the balcony I threw the clothes I had been wearing into one of the bags. Finally in went the bits and pieces, the scrubbing brush, the extension lead, the mask and the gloves.

I towelled myself down, dressed and looked out the front of the apartments. It all seemed fine. There weren't too many cars in the car park and as normal the *askaris* seemed to be asleep on the step down from the hard standing. The little row of *dukas* were shutting up for the night and as ever there were groups of two and three people picking their way around the puddles as they wandered away.

I decided I would leave it for half an hour or so to let the *duka* owners go home.

I made myself a cup of coffee and thought about it as I drank. I wanted the trip to the pen to be over as quickly as possible and I now had a lot of fairly heavy bin bags sitting out on the balcony. Getting them down the stairs would take a while, as would coming in and out of the building.

I tied the top of each one shut and looked out over the balcony. If I carried them down I could put them behind the water tank, between it and the fence. They would be out of sight there while I fetched and carried from the apartment or from there to the pen.

I just brought the last of the bags downstairs when I realised I had been a complete idiot. I had forgotten the matches. So it was back upstairs, to open the grille, open the door, collect the box, close the door, close the grille and head back downstairs. I was just about to go out through the back grille when I heard a clanking behind me. It was Mr Chavda, coming out for his evening stroll.

He was a pleasant enough old stick. I liked him. He did like a bit of a chat though. Especially with *wazungu* because then he could indulge in a bit of a moan about the *wananchi*.

'Bloody Africans, no civilisation, no culture, they are just always so noisy. I hear from Dinesh that you have been over to complain to the apartments next door. I've been over to complain as well before. No consideration.'

We stood there in the hallway for a few minutes. I winced inwardly but nodded when he said he had been going to go across to complain about the banging earlier on but he hadn't been able to work out where it was coming from. It was only a couple of minutes talking to him but it felt like an hour, just one of those times when you want to get on and do things and you feel time ticking away. At last he said goodnight and walked off around the corner.

The moon was out, a pair of crescent horns sticking up over the top of the trees, and as I stepped away from the pool of yellow light and its dancing moths at the exit from the stairwell, there was a delicious blue silvery sheen which belied the velvet warmth of the night. I started to transfer the bags across to the pen. I kept my head down and walked, did not run. The *askaris* were lying on the steps, asleep on their long coats. The last thing I wanted just at the moment was for one of them to wake up and volunteer to help. As I carried the second set across Daisy came snuffling up.

'Go on, shoo,' I hissed. She stopped, looking up at me, hesitant. Normally I was friendly. 'Go on, off with you.' I swung the bag at her. It was so big and heavy and slow it was never going to connect, it was more an indication and she backed off, almost shrugged her shoulders, and trotted on by me towards the back of the apartments.

I walked across the car park and out of the gate towards the pen, thinking, It's absolutely normal, nothing to worry about, nothing to notice, just a *mzungu* putting out rubbish. I lifted the first bag up and dumped it on the pile, then the second to join the other black bin bags sitting there. Just a few more to go, I thought, as I wandered back.

As I came round to the water tank for the last time I could see something moving. So that was where she was off to.

'Shoo Daisy, shoo. Go on get out of it.' I was waving my arms as I came up to the tank. She darted off the other way before I got close. I picked up the last two bags and tramped back towards the pen.

The pile of rubbish was quite high now and stank to high heaven of rotting food and veg. I put one of the bags down in order to use both hands to lift the other one on to the top of the pile. I brought my hand underneath it, lifted it to chest height and then up and on to the pile.

I turned and stooped to pick up the last bag and grabbing the neck with my right hand, as I lifted it up from the ground I straightened and swung my left-hand underneath to repeat the operation. The underside was wet and slimy.

I looked down, this was odd. I had done this with all the other bags. Had I put it in a puddle or something? I lifted the bag to chest height and there, staring me in the face, was a huge tear in the bag. The wet sliminess was blood. For a moment I was frozen with panic. All I could think was, Christ, Christ, Daisy, it had to be Daisy. She had been round by the tank.

I could dump this in the pen but if I had dropped anything on the way from the water tank, had I just left a trail of blood between here and there? It was dark. I couldn't tell. I forced myself to think calmly as I shoved the bag on to the top of the pile.

Between the tank and the corner of the block I had come across the grass. I had walked on the paved path just along the side of the block and then had cut straight across the grass in the middle as the most direct route to the gate. So the only places I could have dripped blood where it might be seen would be on the path and across the car park. But the car park was sufficiently dusty and dirty with tyre tracks and oil stains that nobody would notice anything, so that was OK. I lifted the torn edge of the bag and peered quickly inside. Daisy had obviously been after something, had she got anything? If she had pulled something out could other things have fallen? I knew she had a den in amongst some old water tanks dumped in the back corner of the site. I would never find her there now in the darkness, but as I walked back I would just have to check the ground to see if there was anything obvious, check the back of the apartments around the water tank and just trust to luck.

The first thing to do was just to get this away before anybody caught me. I chose a likely looking selection in the corner nearest to me and another on the far side. I glanced around but there didn't seem to be anyone in sight. I fumbled with the matchbox. The first two sticks broke and I muttered, bloody shitty matches, to myself, they were Kharatasi of course. The next one struck and I had to duck to avoid being burnt as the paper in the bin bags took with a whoosh of flame.

I stepped sideways around the corner of the pen to be out of the direct light from the fire as it roared into life and then walked smartly, but carefully, back through the gate. I tried to trace the route I had taken with the bags, my eyes on the ground. I crossed the car park. I couldn't see anything; down the steps on to the grass, it was hopeless here. Behind me flames were just starting to dance over the top of the wall of the pen, the flickering light casting shadows from the parked cars across the field. The moonlight was bright but the light of the flames and the dancing shadows made it difficult to see. I had been carrying that last bag in my left hand so as I had come around the side of the building it would have been the one nearest the wall and would have been directly over the paved surface whereas the other would have been over the grass. I stopped at the corner of the building and looked. It was far enough away here that moonlight ruled again. I couldn't see anything. There was nothing which looked obvious. I would just have to wait for daylight.

The girls arrived back about twenty minutes later.

'Hope you're feeling better,' Clare said, as I opened the door to Sam. 'You missed a good night.'

'Yes, we went to Rooftops, did the barbecue,' said Sam looking pained.

'Looks like somebody is putting on a show here,' said Clare, nodding at the raging fire which could now be seen blazing in the pen as we turned and looked through the sitting room and out of the balcony windows. 'They don't usually burn it at night, it's a bit spectacular though, isn't it?'

I turned and we all looked out at it for a moment. It really had caught, it was roaring now, all furnace oranges, reds and bright yellows, as flames licked up into the sky while puffs of exploding sparks crackled and snapped as a stream of hot red embers and sparks rushed up in to the night air with the hot billowing smoke.

'Yes,' I said, 'it is spectacular. I've been standing here watching it.'

1 The appointment

Six months earlier

Slaves don't need cultivating, Tippu Tip, the most terrible of the traders told Livingstone. *They just need harvesting.*

By day the city was an island citadel of narrow canyons between towering limestone cliffs, a mysterious labyrinth of sandy connecting alleys creeping amongst the blank walled old merchant princes' *riads,* their thick iron studded double doors locked shut against the merciless sun. Nothing stirred as the silent houses sought shelter in the quiet cool of their inner facing sinks and once richly tiled courtyards. It was a secret sun-bleached and faded, self-sufficient place, built on a history of blood and power more recent than many cared to remember.

Waiting out the hours until dusk I lay in the gloomy tranquillity of my room, insulated by the thick stone walls and propped up with my book. And as I read on, I could feel with the pleasure of appreciation the age and terrible beauty of the city. Bharanku was old. For centuries its trading lifeblood of slaves had come across the open water of the lake from its sister city Mkilwa a hundred miles away on the far shore. Thousands of men, women and children a year, bound by the marauding Arab slavers, or their venal African hunting and trading partners, to be sold in the markets of Bharanku, before starting their long march down across the T'chame plains to the Bahari ya Hindi coast at Boma or Kigoyo, the beach of tears, and over the seas to Zanzibar, Arabia or beyond.

Now at the setting of the sun the eerily beautiful air raid warning cries of the Muezzins' calls to prayer keened through the air from a dozen mosques' amplifying PA systems, the alarm spreading out across the city in waves as each one took up the call to the faithful. I shut the thick history and swung my long lanky frame off the bed. Sitting on the edge between the mozzie nets, I ran my hands through my close cropped hair, rubbing my face and satisfyingly short bristly beard before reaching under the bed for the scuffed DMs I had been wearing daily for the last two years. It's time, I thought.

Leading Chuck out into the alley a few minutes later I felt the familiar exciting entrancement of my senses. As the first breaths of the light breeze began to come in off the lake, all around the rapidly falling turquoise darkness was coming to teeming life in the everyday magical transformation of dusk.

'You really love it here, don't you?' observed Chuck.

I shot him a surprised look, momentarily taken aback at the closeness of the comment. 'Well, sometimes it's fun, yes.' I recovered myself.

While I sure-footedly navigated our way through the darkened maze towards the outskirts of the old town, I could taste the familiar overwhelming exotic sense of the place through every pore. But Chuck was right, I had to admit to myself. I did love it here. I could lose myself in the tropical night's perfume of spices and the rich aroma of roasting coffee and cloves mingled with the smell of paraffin. I was a comfortable appreciator of the murmur of the thousand quiet conversations that were gently growing on all sides of us as the *dukas'* brass oil lamps flickered into dancing naked yellow flames, while the warm orange glow of light began to spill from shops that were opening like bright night flowers from behind anonymous bleached and faded shutters.

Except as we emerged suddenly from the edge of the medina by the police station. It sat in a pool of darkness at the straggling end of the old Arab stone town. The building's two single storey wings pointed like an arrow at the corner of the junction and out over the causeway that had once been the landward start of the great slave road across the lagoon, out onto the vast African plain and down to the coast.

It was a fifties-built, breeze block construction with a corrugated iron roof that was just too low to be a true edifice. Uncared for, its khaki paint dingy and peeling, it jutted from the shoreline of buildings behind it, not filling its allotted plot exactly, as though shoved violently outwards by the town whose back was turned against it, until it had dug its heels in facing the reclaimed water, now a park, flat as a millpond and pitch black in the sudden tropical night.

Outside a lanky flagpole next to a broken bus shelter was the only thing standing rigidly to attention, year in, year out.

As we turned the corner, I saw in through the doorless gap, up two chipped and worn concrete steps from the sandy sidewalk, to the empty reception area lit by the harsh bright light of a hissing pressure lantern that gave out a ghostly illumination.

We were just past the end of the building when we were caught in our stride by a shuddering scream that ended in a suddenly strangled gurgling sob. And then, silence.

'My God!' said Chuck, whipping round to look up at me in

13

shock, his eyes suddenly wide 'My God. What the hell are they doing in there?'

I could only shake my head wordlessly as I stared back towards the dark barred windows of the police station. There was no movement in any of them that I could see, but I was in no doubt that was where it had come from.

We stood, shocked into immobility. I could hear voices now, normal and bantering in tone, coming from the reception area just a few yards away at the corner we had just turned.

And then the scream came again, seeping from the very fabric of the building, oozing out from under the iron roof, urgently connected to it, but seemingly divorced from the building's activity and from everything else around. Primeval in its power, it seemed to grow of itself until it filled both the darkness surrounding us and my head. I could feel it reaching deep inside me, tearing me for a moment between an overwhelming reflexive animal urge to heed this terrible warning of danger, to turn and flee away in terror; and a fierce instinctive pack desire to rush forwards, to help, to fight, to rescue this unknown voice.

As an act of will, I held myself still to listen, but there was nothing that seemed to be connected with the scream that I could hear. There was no interrogator's voice raised in question, no sounds of threats, no thud of blows, no shouted angry denunciations, nothing.

Just the scream of a soul in agony.

'That's pure terror,' said Chuck.

I glanced quickly back down the street through the darkness as I wondered what to do. The first warm sanctuary glow of light from a *duka* was a hundred metres away and the faint noise of chatter from the road beyond it. We seemed cut off, isolated in a pool of night with the now fading scream echoing round our heads.

Then to my horror, I heard Chuck say, 'C'mon,' and step forwards, towards the police station. As he did so, I reached out and caught him suddenly by the shoulder.

'Hey Chuck! What the hell d'you think you're doing?'

'What do you think I'm doing?' he said, spinning round surprised to face me. 'I'm going in there. You coming?'

I looked towards the building. No one seemed to have noticed us, yet. 'So what are you going to do?'

'Do?' Chuck seemed puzzled. 'I'm going to go in there and find out what's going on, that's what!'

'Now do you think that's sensible?'

'Hey let go of me.' Chuck insisted, staring to squirm free of my grasp. 'We've got to do something, say something.'

'What are you going to say?' I demanded, holding on to him. 'You're going to march in there and do what? Ask a question? "Excuse me are you torturing someone?" So where's that going to get you?'

'So what do you think we ought to do?'

I hesitated for a second. Was he right?

'Don't get involved,' I insisted determinedly. But wasn't that what my ex-wife always accused me of? I remembered disconcertingly; refusing to let my guard down, keeping my distance? Until she left me of course; now who's not involved?

'What can we do?' I demanded. 'It's nothing to do with us and what good is it going to do apart from getting us into trouble?'

There was a moment of silence that stretched out while we waited. And waited, and looked at each other. What, I wondered, were we waiting for? For the scream to come again? For us to have an excuse to do something?

'Hey don't forget we're *wazungu*.' I thought I heard a note of contempt in Chuck's voice. 'What are you afraid of? We can't just disappear you know.'

'Oh sure, but we can get slung in jail can't we?' Chuck seemed to shrug at this and twisted in my tightening grip to face the police station again. 'Have you ever been in an African jail?' I demanded, my voice rising angrily in return.

'No.'

'Well neither have I and I've got no intention of going now!'

Chuck hesitated. 'Hey, they wouldn't dare!' He exclaimed, but now there was a trace of doubt in his voice. 'The embassy would come and get us out.'

'Oh yes? And how long would that take?'

'Well…'

'Come on. I know what you want to do. You don't think I felt it too? But there's nothing we can do,' I urged. 'You know that.'

'Well I guess so,' he conceded reluctantly.

'It's just, it doesn't feel right.'

'No it doesn't but…'

'But what?'

'It's what we have to do, so come on!'

As we waited, the stillness was disturbed by the sound of a car as a beige Landcruiser drew up outside the entrance and a *fundi* in khaki fatigues jumped out to open the rear door. A moment later a huge policeman carrying an officer's baton, his polished Sam Browne belt shining in the light from the doorway, came waddling down the steps. There was a murmured greeting as the officer squeezed himself into the back of the car, the *fundi* saluting as he closed the door respectfully after him, before jumping back into the front seat to let the car draw away.

Chuck swung round to face me, his face hesitant, I looked him calmly in the eye. I was right and he knew it, even if it didn't feel good.

And in the pressing slow silence I felt Chuck give way as his shoulders slumped and he shook off my grasp. 'God you're a cold fish.'

I smiled blankly as I released Chuck and shrugged my shoulders. 'Way of the world out here I'm afraid.' She used to call me that as well, I thought.

We turned, and hesitatingly at first, and then more confidently as if breaking free of a spell, we started to walk on.

*

Chuck was a geologist; he and I hardly knew each other really. We had met in Mkilwa a couple of times during my year up at the lake on the Kharatasi job and tonight found ourselves staying at the same hotel, while travelling in opposite directions, Chuck across the lake to Mkilwa and up country for a final tour, me back down to the coast and the office in Boma.

By the lakefront a generator was roaring, chained to drunken iron railings as crowds milled in and out of the traders' electrical stores.

We ate on the terrace of a second floor restaurant above the throng. The choice was fish curry, vegetable curry, or goat curry, the Ndovu beer was barely cold so we ordered plenty of rounds and talked expat gossip and work.

'Off up to the gold mines again?'

'And the rest,' Chuck said, turning to wave at the waiter for another beer. 'Hell the rift valley's been so volcanic over the last few thousand years that just about everything you can think of is up there in the hills if you look for it. It's just a question of which deposits are rich enough to be worth digging up. I tell you, you'd be surprised at some of the stuff that comes out of the ground up there.'

We shared something in common. We were both leaving.

'I'm outta here,' Chuck announced. 'I've had enough, home to a hole in the ground back in Idaho in the good old US of A.'

'Any particular reason, other than the obvious?' I asked.

'It's got a bit dangerous around here for my liking. I don't want to find my hair falling out, if you know what I mean.'

'I just keep pulling mine out with frustration,' I agreed, surprised that Chuck thought things were that bad even with the camps by the border and the election coming up. All the mines had a reputation of a robust approach to security with no holds barred.

'So if you're off, what are you doing heading back up?'

Chuck shrugged took another pull at his beer.

'I really don't know. It's that crazy *wahindi* bastard I work for. I told him that if I've only got a fortnight left, the best thing I could do was get the paperwork sorted out back at the office, tidy things up and brief my replacement. But no, I've got to get my ass back up to the border for one last session. I mean c'mon, hey, it's not like I'm going to get a whole lot done or find a great new deposit in less than two weeks is it?'

I shrugged sympathetically. 'Wants his last *shillingi npya*'s worth does he?'

'I guess so. Can't think of any other reason.'

'So who have they got coming in to take over from you?'

'Oh some *wahindi* kid.'

'Any good?'

'No idea. I just suppose the old bastard wants him because he's cheaper than a *wazungu* like me. He seems to have stepped straight off the boat from someplace and doesn't seem to speak much English. Nice enough though. Just keeps grinning at me every time I try to talk to him.'

Sunday, 4 September, Jijenga

And now, only a month or so later, Chuck was dead. Killed in a helicopter accident in the mountains my assistant Iain had heard down at the yacht club. It was a shock of course, but really, I thought, I hardly knew him, so it actually wasn't anything to do with me.

It was six-thirty in the evening as I unlocked the security gate at the foot of the apartment's grubby white stairwell and headed out into the warm inky black night.

I dropped the T-lock's hefty clasp onto the empty passenger seat as the Suzuki's engine caught straight away and a moment later I headed out on to Siad Barre in the white tin can, the little four-by-four bumping over the recently regraded but rapidly corrugating sand and gravel until I hit the first rotten tarmac at the crossroads just before the International School. There I slowed down for the first of the speed humps, viciously narrow pipes concreted across the road. Long ago they had been painted stark white as a warning, now they were pale, ghostly bands. I saw hands outstretched into the beam of the headlights, urgently fanning at the road as if telling me to slow down to avoid some terrible accident, only to swiftly change to pairs of pleading cupped palms dipping in supplication.

There were three of them at the side of the road, standing apart from the bustling night time crowds further back, their faces hidden above the level of the lights and the blinding glare from the full beam of a bus coming the other way; but out of the corner of my eye I caught a glint of flashy jewellery and smart, well pressed trousers. As ever, I ignored the hitch-hikers as I thumped over the humps and into potholes with a spine jarring crash, and I knew that they would give up when they saw I was a *mzungu*. I headed away, past the little wooden shack *dukas*, on towards the Ghandi Road crossroads at the other side of the school and the harsh white light from the lanterns of the container bar on the corner.

I squinted against the undipped lights of the cars roaring along towards me. It was early but the Jijenga night was getting busy already.

I ran the red at the Catholic church right onto Bara Bara ya Rais, the fast dual carriageway road that ran due north over Kusini Bridge towards the city proper, before cutting across the base of the Boma peninsula and carrying traffic straight on to Front Street, which in turn ran on north around the wide curve of Jijenga bay on the other side.

So at the lights immediately after the bridge, I turned off right, onto Umoja and headed out along the spit of land leading almost directly east and out to sea, past the imposing newly opened bulk of the floodlit Hilton, with its cladding of shockingly clean orange-yellow concrete and smattering of Mercedes and Landcruisers in the car park, and on through the empty black space that was the Gymkhana Club's golf course towards the Boma headland, the capital's administrative heart.

Five hundred *shillingi npya* a beer at the Hilton, or about a fiver at the current exchange rate, I had been told. A judge here didn't earn that in a week I knew. Not in salary anyway.

And then, moments later, I was pulling into the kerb outside the whitewashed frontage of the Alhamisi, on the empty darkened main downhill drag where the only illumination was the off-blue light of the fluorescent tubes that bathed the restaurant's concrete fascia in a ghastly sheen. From out of a doorway's shadows the khaki clad figure of the restaurant's *askari* swung off the upturned newspaper stall he was using as a bench and shuffled over in his flip-flops to help me park, not that I needed any on the deserted street. There were only two other vehicles outside, a diplomatic registered Hilux and a white Landcruiser with a massive aerial, a familiar logo on the door, and the blue number plates that were reserved for the slew of NGOs with diplomatic status which meant Gerry was here. I checked my watch, finished signing the car into the proffered exercise book and slipped on my jacket, the Alhamisi was the best restaurant in Jijenga, so since being cold was a status symbol, the air conditioning would be set on arctic. Sometimes I felt I'd come all the way out to the Equator only to be in danger of freezing to death.

As I pushed open the door into the chill, sure enough, there was the solid rock-like form of Gerry of Refugee International, the off-white of his trademark scruffy half-open shirt stark against the deep tan of his thick set, bullet bald-headed features, propped up against the bar, a can of Castle in his hand. Deep in conversation with Colin from the High Commission, Gerry's back was to the wall and his elbow was resting on the counter, giving the impression that he was simultaneously looking out over the almost empty room waiting to observe anyone who came in, while making sure that he was observed talking intently. There was a sort of perpetual preening watchfulness about Gerry. As he saw me he flashed a grin and waved a thick arm cheerfully in greeting, I could almost hear the clank of the heavy gold bracelet from across the room. The Alhamisi was a natural meeting place. As I approached, I heard Gerry's opinion on the situation in his unmistakable New York accent.

'...but there isn't such a tribal thing here. At least they haven't got a bunch of killers like those *Wamwuaji* bastards from next door.'

The people who kill together were the gangs responsible for the horrors over the border in the diamond-rich and tribal-war-racked states of the interior. What's Colin talking about them for? I wondered.

'Apart from when they are in my camps,' objected Gerry.

'Well apart from then,' Colin conceded, 'But there's still the religious one! And what about Mkilwa and Bharanku? You know what the IMF are saying about staying away.'

Gerry was still expounding as I reached the bar.

'Hell, I don't know what anyone's worried about. So what if the *Wamwuaji* have their tribal brothers on this side of the fence? The Party's still got the SOU for God's sake. If there's any trouble, they'll soon sort it out.'

So it's the election, I gathered. Not quite what everyone was talking about, but increasingly so.

'But the *Wamwuaji* have guns too, don't forget.'

'Don't I know it,' said Gerry smiling broadly. 'Don't I know it.'

'Yes, I suppose you do,' Colin said thoughtfully as he turned to greet me. 'So how's our liquidator of the parish?' he asked, sticking out his hand to shake.

I was pleased to see Colin, a slight lad in his early thirties, with a suede-head haircut, a strong estuary accent, an air of professional competence and a wary friendliness. Like any diplomat, Colin could make it quite plain that he wasn't just here to look after the backs of a motley collection of adventurers, short term contractors and a passing trade of quick buck merchants and prospectors, or to bail out backpackers who'd run out of cash. But unlike most of the High Commission staff who avoided the expat riffraff like the plague, he was otherwise really quite matey with us, always keen to chat, interested in what we were up to, and keen to know what was going on in business around the country.

'Oh, fine thanks,' I said.

'Plenty of work for you out here,' said Gerry.

'Too right,' I agreed, smiling broadly. 'The whole bloody country's bust.'

Colin was ordering. So I turned to Gerry, who had something going with Clare in the office. Or had had, I corrected himself. Anyway, he seemed to be in a good mood.

'So, how are your camps?' I asked him over a beer.

Gerry smiled, 'Well, let me put it this way. I had a call on the radio today. They told me, "Gerry we have a slight problem. What's that?" I asked. "Well, they said, we have guests for dinner. Eight and a half thousand of them. Arriving on foot."' He giggled. 'Just imagine, eight and a half Godamn thousand. Just walking in.'

'Christ, no wonder you're getting a take-away,' I laughed. 'But I thought the border was closed. The army is all over it surely?' I ordered my usual, hardly looking at the menu.

'Yes, well, as far as we know officially it is. But unofficially,' Gerry shrugged and giggled again to himself. 'Eight and a half Godamn thousand. On foot. *Aya* bwana*, Castle zaidi.'*

Another round of Castles duly arrived and we rested at the bar, chatting. It was early, there was only one couple in, also *wazungu,* Europeans. The *wananchi* waiters were relaxed; the plastic swan was floating upside down in the fountain pool by the entrance where the *wahindi* management appeared locked in some whispered conversation by the front desk. The restaurant would be packed by nine and stay full until well gone eleven or twelve, but now the waiters had time for pleasantries with us while we stood at the bar. I wasn't surprised to see that Gerry seemed popular and known.

Gerry's take-away arrived in a sweet smelling carrier bag. 'See you around,' we said as he left with another Castle, and we had all known that we meant it. It was inevitable that we would, it was that sort of town.

'You're back,' observed Colin.

'Yep. Came down from Mkilwa at the beginning of April.'

'Well you must come in and update our register. We need to know where you are for our evacuation plan.'

'Oh,' I was genuinely surprised. 'Do you have one?'

'No, other than to get together at the High Commissioner's residence and wonder what to do.' He waved his hands lazily. 'But,' and he put on his bright, keen-as-mustard young civil servant voice, 'We're thinking of setting up a committee to put one together.'

'Excellent. So how soon after the forthcoming first multiparty elections for thirty years and all the instability that will come with it, do you think your evacuation plan is going to be ready?' I asked, in mock seriousness.

He laughed, 'Oooh... a couple of months at least, I would think.'

'You could always try shutting the visa section an hour earlier every day. That would give more time to work on it.'

'That's a brilliant idea. I'll suggest it to the High Commissioner.' Colin made a show of mulling over the possible advantages, 'Especially as it would make it even more difficult for people to get visas.'

'Talking about recent developments,' Colin added a few moments later in a quieter, suddenly more serious voice as the waiter turned away to fetch two more beers, 'I'm told on the grapevine that the SPU are taking an interest in your friend Chuck's

21

death. You wouldn't happen to know why, would you?'

I was startled. 'Christ no! Who told you that anyway?' I asked, half not expecting an answer.

The SPU, the State Protection Unit were the secret police, a seemingly all pervasive presence for the locals, but one that really did seem to keep itself secret as far as the ordinary run of expats went. There were no Tonton Macoute types wandering the streets in dark glasses like a bad joke out of the *Comedians* or sledgehammer-wielding executioners given free reign as in Amin's innocuous sounding State Research Bureau.

'Dave,' volunteered Colin.

'What, Dave the copper?'

'Ex-copper, I think you'll find,' observed Colin.

I snorted, 'Once a copper always a copper, whatever he's doing now.'

'Yes, well I think you're probably right there,' conceded Colin, 'But what with his bank work, he's well plugged in you know.'

'I suppose he must be. But even so, how reliable are his sources?'

Colin shrugged. 'Good enough usually I would guess. Well anyway, I thought you might like to know. But you've got to admit it was a bit of an odd accident wasn't it?'

'Was it?' I asked, puzzled. 'I don't really know. I was away when it happened. Iain just told me he'd been killed while flying up country.'

*

Leaving the Alhamisi, I tipped the *askari* the usual twenty *shillingi npya* note with its pictures of *Baba*, the stern-faced schoolmasterly 'father of the nation', and the rounder smiling visage of the current president Rais. The notes, particularly the small ones, were scraggy, filthy rags, so black with age and dirt and handling that staff at the bank wore face masks to count cash.

Driving back home over Kusini Bridge, I turned left opposite the Chinese Embassy onto Karume and the headland of Mkonge. The first house on the left was the imposing American Ambassador's residence, and I was surprised to see the bevy of girls who usually worked under the solitary street light outside were missing. Perhaps they'd been moved on, I thought with a guilty prurient interest.

At the corner of the next side road however, the girls were

definitely out, sitting on a low wall and wearing their regulation short black dresses. As I cruised past, a profile leapt out as the car's headlights caught what looked like a crocheted white gilet on top of her outfit. As I looked through the car's side window into the dark as I passed, I only ever saw their shapes by the side of the road, never their faces.

Without thinking. I ignored the turn for the last cut through to Siad Barre and the back road home, and carried on towards the coast road. Damn, that was stupid, I thought to myself too late as I rounded the bend onto Karume. It was Saturday night and the *wahindi* were out.

Every Friday, Saturday and Sunday it was the same. What seemed like the whole of the city's Asian population gathered at *Mnazi Moja*. Hundreds of cars were pulled over on the grass verges and under the palms on either side of the shore road. There were stalls selling samosas, fast food vans, hawkers and all sorts of merchants selling all sorts of *taka taka*. Families parked their cars, unpacked garden chairs for their grandmas and talked to friends while they socialised, wheeled and dealed. It was an enormous, public, impromptu roadside garden party and social club, every weekend.

It was also the oldest and most efficiently functioning dollar, dowry and daughter market in the country and it could be hell to get through when it was in full swing. Cars would be pulling on and off the road or crawling along slowly looking for parking space. There would be young *wahindi* kids showing off new and ludicrously powerful motor bikes, and doing U-turns in Gombe Road to cruise back down the main strip. In the dark hawkers were everywhere with their baskets, pushcarts and bicycles. And later at night, just down the parking strip from the grandmas and grandpas, round the back of the Coconut Grove Hotel, sitting on the walls under the spotlights or lurking at the crossroads in the dark where the cars slowed for their U-turns, there were always still the *wananchi* girls, still working, still hissing and squeaking out exaggerated kisses at the passing cars in search of trade.

Tonight though I heaved a sigh of relief as it wasn't too bad. The crowd was minimal and the traffic light, so I bombed through with my precious cargo of paneek paneer, chicken tikka masala and naan bread. The Alhamisi did a wicked garlic naan.

*

23

The Ball would have started now, I realised, back at the apartment, as I picked out the foil containers, and I guessed that Iain, my assistant manager would be revving up in his bow tie and cummerbund.

It was the Yacht Club's Annual Ball and the dress was black tie or Red Sea rig. I had long ago decided that there was something vaguely military about Iain, even if behind his round wire rimmed glasses he looked more Radar from MASH than Brigade of Guards. There was a wiry toughness and relentless determination about Iain and he had certainly inherited a confident officers' mess air from growing up on bases where his father had been some kind of RAF bigwig. He was a very bow-tie-and-cummerbund person.

Despite or perhaps because of his membership of the Hash running club, Iain was also rapidly becoming tubby from all the beers. He was more into the drinking side of the club than the running. The bar at the Little Theatre on a Friday night wasn't helping either.

Since his arrival in March just in time to take part in the annual expat inter-tribal darts match at the High Commission Club, Iain had quickly found his feet as a stalwart of the local Celtic scene. He was now a fixture of the Caledonian Society and was golfing and drinking buddies with every seconded Irish electricity supply board engineer and Scottish road builder in the country.

I shook my head once again as I wondered how Iain did it. It was a mystery to me but somehow he had managed to slip effortlessly into the local expat society from the moment he arrived, while I had to admit to myself that once again I seemed to have remained something of an outsider.

'Well, I just hope he's taken Juma,' I said to the empty apartment, as I turned on the CD player. Like many people who have lived on their own for too long, I had long since resigned myself to talking out loud.

Juma was Iain's houseboy. Iain had taught him to drive and bought him a licence, having eventually decided that despite the risks there were some occasions when he was going to get just too drunk to drive himself.

And the risks were real. These were roads dotted with potholes, where at night other vehicles either had no lights at all, or had full beam stuck on blindingly as the back end crabbed sideways, unseen, towards you. There were ditches and culverts across the unlit roads, wandering goats and cattle and men pulling wooden carts, strolling pedestrians and manic night time bus drivers chewing *qhat*, the local equivalent of speed. The roads were black, alive and dangerous, not lit, regularised and sanitised. And if you did have an accident, you weren't going to be instantly surrounded by paramedics in fluorescent jackets deciding whether or not to call the air ambulance.

Gerry's ex or not, Clare had been lucky. She had been pissed as usual and had run into the back of a broken down truck one night last year on the Bara Bara ya Rais. It had had no lights, just some branches lying in the road a few yards behind to warn oncoming traffic. Fortunately for her she had only smashed into it with the passenger side of her Suzuki, and for once she had been on her own. The whole of the car's front wing had been peeled away like a banana skin.

As it was the weekend, Nelson the houseboy wasn't about so I washed up after dinner. When I had finished, I lifted the slops bucket out from under the sink which was there to catch water from the unconnected sink overflow.

'Now will Daisy eat this?' I speculated quietly to myself, as I picked up a container with some leftover chicken, before deciding that for a dog that lived off anything it could scavenge from the scraps dumped out the front, given the number of *wahindi* in these compound's three blocks of apartments, some masala and a few spots of pepper would probably the least of her worries.

When I went down, the grille at the bottom of the stairs was open and I could hear the sound of running water. The pump was on and Mr Chavda was out in the mildly muggy heat, his singlet showing up startlingly white in the light from his caged ground floor veranda. He was watering the straggly plants that he had dug into a small bed between the low bulk of the concrete water tank and the back fence. I wondered whether he was hoping that when they grew they would screen off the wire mesh fence and the litter strewn roadside rubbish heap on the other side.

Mr Chavda was a silver haired old Indian gent, whose son worked for the firm, and had been allocated the bottom apartment out of the four in the firm's block in the compound. Of course, the whole family had moved in, according to Clare, the firm's senior consultant, who lived above me on the top floor and who seemed well in with the local *wahindi* community. Mr Chavda reminded me irresistibly of my own father in the way he naturally assumed it was up to him to organise all the practicalities of life in the apartments, be it pumping the water to the rooftop tank or making sure the security gates were locked and the empty first floor apartment was secure. For my part, if he wanted to organise these things I was happy to leave him to get on with it.

At midnight, I lay in bed listening to the sound of the African night wafting in on the night air; Zairian disco music vying for playtime with Bonny M, American rap and Bob Marley. Out at the back some returning tenant's *askari* was obviously drunk or asleep as a driver was really hanging on his horn outside a front gate waiting to be let in; and I knew the noise would set the dogs off again in a round of barking and howling.

There was little or no wind. I couldn't face the racket of the air conditioning, so, despite the window slats being fully open, I just suffered the heat and the whirr of the ceiling fan. As I lay looking up at the clattering blades I thought about what Colin had said. He was right, I decided, it was an odd accident. Even for a geologist hopping all over the place the way Chuck did and with safety as slipshod as it was here, how on earth had Chuck managed to fall out of a helicopter at 2,000 feet above the border hills?

Knowing that I would never know, my mind wandered and I noticed how the security lights outside threw the criss-crossed shadows of the window louvres and the grille of iron bars outside onto the muslin mosquito net above me. As I drifted off, it seemed as though I lay trapped under a huge spider's web enveloping the bed.

Never mind, I thought. Tomorrow I would hand in my resignation and I would be another day closer to going home for good.

Wednesday, 28 September, Jijenga

Ernest shuffled and rattled his way into my office with the tray, bringing the thermos of hot water, cups, jug of evaporated milk, ant-mined bowl of sugar and tin of instant coffee. Being office coffee boy was a very stressful occupation for Ernest and gave him the shakes. There were difficult decisions to make all the time, like where to put the tray down, which corner of the tray to put the sugar on and how many cups to provide, along with the pressure of supplying a tray to every office in the building each morning.

Once he'd delivered the coffee he always tried to establish communication and would jabber away excitedly in Kiswahili with the odd English word, on his topic of the day, be it the firm's pay rates, '*kidogo kidogo*'; the strain he was under; the President; his wife beating him; or Muslims. Ernest was RC, *Roman Katolik* he expounded, lest I for a moment think he was the Regional Commissioner. I had never met an epsilon before, but I usually got the drift.

There was a whole class of messengers, security guards and grey-haired post room boys who wore dark blue safari suits with sweat stains by midday, and hung out in a small room adjacent to the *fotokopia,* drinking cups of sickly sweet tea. To my eye they were universally small in stature. I wondered how long it had taken for the news that I was leaving to get around the floor. Not long, was my bet.

I was standing in the small anteroom to my office a few minutes later talking to my secretary Janet, a neat small bespectacled local woman under a tight wrapped blue headscarf and holder of the world all-comers record for slow typing, when I heard a knock. It was the circulating messenger whose job it was to go round the firm's main offices down on the fourth floor collecting papers, faxes, telexes, notes and letters from people's out trays and delivering them to the intended recipient including upstairs to us up in the overflow space on the eighth floor. He was grinning, '*Jambo* bwana,' he said, as he held some faxes and an envelope out towards me. But then he always grinned.

I held out my hand for the papers. The messenger took two quick steps into the room and gave them to me with the curious customary cross hands and semi-bow, almost a curtsey. I completed my part of the ceremony by taking them with an *asante* which led to the ritual circular round of *asante*s, *karibu*s and *asante sana*s. My Kiswahili was limited, so as usual I absentmindedly said thanks as well. I glanced at what I'd received briefly as the messenger backed out, closing the door behind him, his grin being the last thing to leave the room.

Janet was looking at me quizzically from behind her computer screen. She had a somewhat owl-like expression through her large thick glasses and was wearing the headphones for her ongoing struggle to master the Dictaphone.

'Is it that there is anything of interest?' she asked as I handed her the faxes, pulling open the drawer in which she kept the date stamp and pad.

'Doesn't look like it,' I said, turning my attention to a brown envelope which had been resealed with a stapler. 'Although, now hang on... what's this?' It was a large envelope addressed to Winston and I noted with a quickening excitement that it bore the logo of the People's Commercial Bank. I could feel the envelope was quite full as I swiftly tugged it open.

'I wonder what we've got here,' I said, as I half pulled the contents of the envelope out just far enough to realise what I was looking at. Quickly I cleared a space on my desk and carefully laid the papers out.

There were three bound contracts accompanied by a covering letter in duplicate signed by Mr Kiponglea, Chief Secretary to the bank.

'It's an appointment,' I said as I scanned the covering letter before picking up one of the bound documents. 'It's three copies of a contract of appointment.'

'That is good,' said Janet brightly.

My eyes skimmed across the paragraphs and clauses of the contract as I swiftly turned the pages, checking for the presence of the key clauses, analysing the proposals and mentally weighing and testing the arrangement against consideration of the background, the costs, the work involved, the likelihood of success, the risks as far as they were known and the desirability of the contract.

'Cretins,' I muttered to myself.

Janet looked up again and asked, 'What is the matter?'

'It's this New Mwanchi thing,' I said. 'Do you remember I talked with Kiponglea of the PCB about it ages ago?'

'I think so,' she said hesitantly.

'Well, now they've sent us the appointment and it's crap. Could you pull me up the letters on it?'

Janet's fingers stabbed slowly at the keyboard, then the whirring buzz and quiet clunk of the printer drawing in the paper for the first page added themselves to the hum of the air conditioning unit set into the window behind me.

*

A few moments later I was standing in Winston's office. 'They want a fee limited to ten per cent of recoveries!' I exclaimed as Winston's phone rang. 'It's a bloody nonsense. We wrote to Kiponglea in June saying there was no way. It's got to be time costs or nothing doing.'

Winston, as the partner, would have his name on the appointment ticket if we got the job, but as far as the work went it would be my show, though I would rely on Winston to manage the political flak and grasping tax authorities.

I stopped as Winston answered the phone. Discussions with Winston were continually interrupted by irrelevant calls concerning deals on detergent factories, newspapers, television stations or bottling plants.

'*Habari yako* bwana... *nzuri... ndiyo...*'

As Winston went through the ritual greetings, I thought idly about what I would be leaving in a few months to rejoin the firm at home. Winston was the junior, and therefore very much the working, partner. Yakeen was the other audit partner, a big man physically. He'd come into the firm when his old company had pulled out of the country in the seventies. He maintained an air of semi-independence and detachment, augmented by his extensive outside business interests. Most of the staff under my upstairs neighbour Clare, who in practice actually ran the auditing department as well as the consultants, thought he spent more time at his transport and hotels company than he did on any accounting work.

Then there were the management consultants. They were a group of economists of various stripes who wrote reports saying if, why, where, when, and how much, should the clapped out old nationalised parastatal sector be sold off for, and reported to the third partner, Salima, referred to by Clare as the frog prince. He was a broad bear of a man, unusual by local standards, with a wild frizz of white hair, and lips and a nose that suggested some backing for a rumour about an earlier career as a boxer. wore Kaunda suits in the office, rather than Western dress the way the other partners did, had a good sense of humour, was sharp as a knife and Clare joked he could get through a bottle of Scotch an evening if he felt like it.

'Sorry about that,' Winston said, replacing the receiver. 'It was Chairman Ossoro.'

'Of the *News*?'

'Amongst other things. He may be an industrialist client now but everybody knows that he used to be high up in the SPU.'

'So he still has influence. That reminds me,' I said. Can I ask you something?'

'Sure. What?'

'Well it's the SPU. They're political aren't they? They wouldn't be interested in an accident would they?'

Winston looked suddenly worried. 'What's this about, Paul?'

'Oh nothing really, just a geo that I knew from over at Mkilwa was killed up country while I was away and someone said that the SPU were getting involved.'

'Back in the old days the SPU were everywhere and involved in everything,' Winston replied thoughtfully.

'But not now?' I pressed.

'Well, that's difficult to say. They haven't all just vanished in a puff of smoke you know. To be honest, I think we would have had some.'

'What, here in the firm?'

'Yes, of course. It wouldn't surprise me if we still did. One at least. Possibly more.'

'That sounds as if you know.'

'No, no, I don't,' he reassured me. 'But I have my suspicions. You must understand, this would have been, probably still is, a strategically sensitive business.'

'But why? You're auditors for heaven's sake. What's so sensitive about that?'

'Well, we were the only international firm here throughout the seventies and eighties. And during that time, we did the accounts of all the major private companies, as well as all the subsidiaries of the multinationals who were working here. Now isn't that the sort of thing the Party would want to keep an eye on?'

'Economic intelligence,' I agreed, nodding.

'Yes, all the knowledge of where the money is being made, where it is going, who is thinking of investing, who is thinking of pulling out. For want of anywhere else, much of that information flowed through us. If you wanted to know what was going on in the country...'

'For whatever reason,' I prompted.

'Precisely, for whatever reason, eyes and ears in here would have been vital. With us, the Central Bank, the immigration service and the parastatal control board that ran all the nationalised industries, you have got access to just about everything that isn't completely underground.'

'And we are the only one of those that isn't state controlled.'

'Exactly.'

'So who is it?'

'Ah, well now,' Winston answered, 'as I said, I don't actually know. I only suspect.'

'So who do you suspect?'

Winston sat behind his desk, silhouetted by the light shining in through the slatted blinds behind him. He was tall and slim, unusually so for a well-off African, but William, My local number two, had told me that this was a tribal thing. His balding head was shiny, except for a fuzz of hair running around his temple and the back of his head. When he smiled, his whole face lit up, from his eyes behind their thick framed glasses, to the brilliant white of his teeth below his precise short black moustache. Sometimes he could giggle like a schoolboy. Now he suddenly grinned sheepishly, 'Now, come on, Paul,' he said. 'You know I can't tell you that.'

'But you don't have to worry about the SPU you know,' he added. 'They won't touch you. *Wazungu* can't just disappear without an explanation, it's too much trouble.'

*

Iain came in after lunch.

'Look what just blew in here today,' I said, proffering him a copy of the contract.

'Well, well, well. A live one?' he asked.

I nodded. 'I think so. It'll be big and industrial. Up for it?'

'You bet,' he said, looking excited. 'Absolutely.'

We talked it over. If we could get fees sorted so that the case was a runner, it would be the start of Iain's first serious job out here. And my legacy to him when I go, I suddenly thought with an unexpected twinge of sadness.

2 New Mwanchi

Saturday, 8 October, Jijenga

Iain and William hung around all day Wednesday waiting for the promised papers from the bank. They finally left in the ancient Land Rover on Thursday having given up waiting and deciding to collect the originals from the local branch in Mkilwa. It was a long drive. It would take them two days to do the 760 kilometres to Bharanku, with a stopover at M'gola, before catching the overnight ferry across the lake.

Iain and I decided that we would talk tactics once he had sized up the situation on the ground. He was to call me in the office on Saturday morning between eleven and twelve. If he could get through, that is.

Marilyn, the cheerful and strikingly pretty young receptionist, was on the fourth floor front desk when I arrived that Saturday morning in my big baggy navy blue cotton Bermudas. She laughed when she saw my shorts. 'It's not a school day today, you silly boy.'

I smiled back. 'Detention,' I said. 'Is Winston around?'

I thought she was in severe danger of blinding herself with the beads at the end of her plaits as she shook her head. 'I expect he'll be in later.'

Eleven came and went, but I waited, chatting to a few people in the office. Iain got through at eleven-thirty.

'How was the trip up?' I asked.

'Oh God, don't ask. The Land Rover cut out on me again, just as we came to the end of T'chame. William says that's bandit country but we got it started again. This thing is really on its last legs, nothing works on it, not even the bloody seatbelts. We're going to have to sort something out with Winston.'

Iain filled me in on what he had found. 'Well, it's absolutely typical; the bank didn't know we were coming.'

I just laughed. 'That's confidence inspiring.'

'Well quite,' Iain said grudgingly, 'Par for the course. Anyway, I have met Bwana Maedi, the local bank manager and explained who I am and what we've got to do.'

'Have they got the debenture?'

In the insolvency business, the debenture is the key. It's the piece of paper by which the company had mortgaged its assets to the bank as security for its loans.

'Yes,' came Iain's soft burr, 'and I've had a quick look and it seems to be quite straightforward.'

I knew that as receivers, what Iain and I did wasn't really all that complicated, but when a company went under there was never enough money to go round, so people fought. And if we were going to jump in to the middle of that sort of mess, I wanted to make sure of our ground so that as far as possible I could avoid us having our arses sued to kingdom come. So I ran through the basics with Iain checking that all the paperwork was in place to give us the powers that we needed.

'Good,' I said at last, satisfied with what Iain had managed to find. 'OK, so it sounds as if it's a job. Right, I'll be up on Monday and we'll get on with it.

Monday, 10 October, Jijenga/Mkilwa

I caught the morning flight.

Having spent the previous year living a kilometre or so out of town at Kharatasi on the lakeside, approaching Mkilwa across the glinting slate blue of the water was almost like coming home.

The plane thumped down heavily on to the runway and I had a fleeting glimpse of a bedraggled and sorry looking bunch of grey painted and shrouded MIG 21s standing rotting in the military compound at the far end of the runway. A real third world early seventies vintage air force. Then for a few seconds it felt as though the Boeing *saba tatu saba* was going to shake itself to pieces as the engines reversed thrust, before the crashing run slowed to a tooth-rattling judder across the bumpy tarmac strip. The runway ended right beside the lake. If the brakes ever failed, it would be time to swim.

Through the window I could see the familiar white letters of 'Mkilwa Airport' painted on the red corrugated iron roof of the dusty concrete shed which did for departures and arrivals.

It was seven hundred metres or so higher here than at Jijenga, so it was slightly cooler than by the coast, but even so I could feel a warm wind blowing in as soon as the aircraft's doors opened.

Looking out, Mkilwa itself was marked on the horizon by a high plume of white smoke tailing off into a gentle smudge in the sky over the lake. The city nestled a little way away around the shore where the lush green hills came down to the water and met the mouth of the Kakira as it emptied into the lake. I looked at the

33

plume thoughtfully.

The airport had been built out on the plain, just next to the new concrete deepwater pier which stretched out for two hundred metres or so into the lake to let the modern large roll on-roll off road and rail freight ferry from Bharanku dock. Out here in the open the sky was a huge arc of flawless blue and in the blistering intensity of the heat it was the Africa of the imagination. Mirages shimmered off the tarmac of the road at the edge of the airfield that seemed to run on south forever across the sun-blasted, burnt, parched, orange plain of whirling dust devils and meandering herds of local cattle, every rib sticking out as they disconsolately snuffled around in the dust.

I had only brought one bag so I escaped quickly; pushing out through the small crowd to do battle with the taxi touts in the car park. It was the dry season and, despite the lake and the height, once out of the aircraft I could feel the heat immediately starting to suck the moisture from my body.

The airfield road was recently graded earth and cut north-west, inland and away from the noiselessly fluttering snowstorm of lake flies, to join up with the main tarmac from the south and cross the Kakira River at the bridge amongst the first of the shanty outskirts. As soon as the road reached the river valley and hills, Mkilwa became fertile and impressive. The *Wakilwa* had long ago perfected the art of communal irrigation, and an ancient net of tiny canals and manmade streams carried the precious muddy water through the thick plantain *shamba*s and maize patches.

But it wasn't all farming up here. Mkilwa and its hinterland were potentially the country's treasure house, and geologists and prospectors crowded its hotels and bars. It was just as Chuck had said that night in Bharanku, under the hills lay huge reserves of mineral wealth - copper, gold and diamonds - that by rights should have been helping to fund development. Although the really big deposits of precious stones were out of the reach of normal commerce in the war zone over the border, there was baser stuff as well within easier reach, bauxite, manganese, pitchblende, a little iron, graphite, and commercial quantities of coal and lead ore. Hence New Mwanchi.

As the taxi's horn fought its way into town, riding along with my arm out of the window I was delighted to be back amongst the hectic bustle of the lively place I had known all the previous year. There was nothing sleepy about Mkilwa. It was a brash place, full of well stocked shops, traffic, and the buzz of people buying and selling. As we drove through the streets I saw men wheeling bicycles piled high with gunny bags of charcoal and women walking on either side of the road wrapped in vibrant flame red and yellow *kikois,* carrying improbable loads on their heads and children on their backs.

Iain was staying out of town at the Twiga Hotel, so it was off along another bumpy narrow gravel track that traced its way between the huge boulders and outcrops dotting the local landscape.

The hotel seemed pleasant and comfortable, let down by the owners' unwillingness to have paid an architect a fee to design it properly and the failure to finish off details. As I opened the door I coughed on a heavy dose of familiar overpowering lemon chemical odour and realised that they also had the unrestricted chemical warfare approach to mosquito control, obviously preferring that guests succumb to a variety of cancers and untraceable wasting diseases twenty years later, than complain to the management about biting insects and inefficient mosquito nets. They had *Doomed* the room and the spray was everywhere.

I found Iain in one of the hotel's office suites in conference with Mzee Maedi and the bank's lawyer. The banker and lawyer both looked a little glazed.

'So what have we got?' I asked after the introductions had been made.

'Well, the site is huge for a start.'

'Is it the one with the bloody great chimney that you can see from the Kakira Bridge?'

'Yes, that's the one,' said Iain.

So it was where I had suspected, a kilometre or so out from the centre of town, its tall chimney smudging the sky with its consistent white plume of smoke. It was, after all, a smelting works. A relatively small one by world standards, but still the sort of big smoke stack industrial stuff that the firm back home would never touch these days for fear of all the potential environmental costs. Here we would wing it.

'You can't really see it from the road,' Iain said, sketching as he spoke. 'Apart from the access point, it's set back behind the RI compound that fronts onto the street, but it's huge inside.'

'RI? Refugee International? Gerry's mob, the aid agency?'

'Yes, they're the ones. It's their admin base for servicing the camps up at the border.'

'OK.'

'You've got the one truck and pedestrian entrance up here, with a security hut and steel gates,' he continued, indicating the north-eastern corner.

As I listened, I realised that Iain was obviously loving every moment of this. It was at last the action he had been craving. 'I've left William camped out in front to keep an eye on it.'

I laughed, 'Poor bugger. I don't suppose that skulking around as a spy outside some factory gates is really what he thought training to be an accountant was going to be about!'

'Well, he's going to have to learn if he wants to do this sort of work won't he?'

'I guess you're right,' I conceded, thinking that otherwise there was very little else to learn.

'Well, we've checked out the paperwork and we know where we're going, so I suppose we'd better go and have a look-see,' I announced, snapping Iain's file shut and picking the papers up from the table.

I was not particularly surprised to see how quickly Mzee Maedi decided that it would be best if he volunteered to stay in town and organise some security guards to join us out at site.

*

New Mwanchi was in the big industrial zone that stretched along either side of the road out of town towards the bridge.

Off the main road's tarmac, the track down to the site was dreadful. In the rainy season Mkilwa's red tropical earth turned to tomato soup and gradually, as the roads' potholes and lakes joined together, drivers went further and further around the edges of the swelling ponds rather than risk crunching into something unseen, or getting stuck in the uncertain muddy depths of the middle. So by now in the dry season a series of metre deep craters had replaced the road, up and over the sides of which the Landie rode like a small dingy cresting an Atlantic swell.

The estate was a place of grazing goats and anonymous breezeblock compounds topped by broken glass set in cement, with *wahindi* slipping in and out through the pedestrian accesses beside sheet steel factory gates. Faceless godowns with doors welded shut against the sun were flanked by driftwood *dukas* selling cigarettes to bored *askaris* in drab overalls, floppy hats and Wellington boots.

The New Mwanchi factory compound was a classic example of its type, surrounded by a three metre high solid wall topped with barbed wire. The only entrances were a gate for lorries and a small pedestrian entrance beside it. Both were barred shut by solid steel gates. As we drew up we could see faces at a grille in the security gate, but as the car stopped, the grille snapped shut.

'Looks like they are expecting us,' I observed quietly to Iain as we climbed out of the Landie and strode up to knock on the door. 'Now I wonder who might have told them?'

*

As the gate clanged shut behind us and one of the *askaris* scurried off, Iain and I took stock of our surroundings.

Set around a small concrete yard just inside the gate were a ramshackle collection of wooden huts that obviously served as offices. Beyond them I could see that a road ran all the way around the site about twenty metres inside the walls. On either side of the road as it ran north were piled huge dumps of material, what looked like coal closest to us, with piles then of a lead grey ore and then a brownish black one further away, while I was surprised to see in the far corner what looked like the most enormous breaker's yard I had ever seen, a scrap yard, full of rusting car wrecks, the ladder chassis of trucks and the fading hues of once brightly painted bus bodies.

'Now what the hell is that all about?' I wondered, turning to Iain, 'I thought they smelted lead?

'Ah, that's what the bank down in Jijenga thought,' Iain replied, staring in the same direction. 'Turns out that they also smelt and recycle other things. They're even importing old cars and stuff from India and Pakistan to melt down for steel, so Mzee Maedi tells me.'

'Import it? How?'

'By train,' Iain said, pointing along the northern wall behind the offices where I could now see a short string of wagons sitting on a siding, with what looked like armed *askaris* on top. 'The railway comes into town through the industrial zone and then out again up to the hills. There's a spur into the site that runs close along the wall behind those dumps. The coal and the ores come down the line from the hills. The scrap comes up from Jijenga on the lake line and across on the rail deck of the Ro-Ro from Bharanku and the product goes back out the same way.'

'Hello, we're on!' I whispered hurriedly to Iain turning to face the offices as from one of the huts a middle-aged *wahindi* in a dark polo shirt, rumpled trousers and plastic flip flops headed towards us looking flustered.

*

The argument lasted about half an hour and took us from the yard to the boardroom and back out into the yard, before I decided to break it up.

'Look,' I announced stepping in between Iain and the *wahindi*, whose name we had ascertained was Mohammed Khan, the *meneja mkuu*.

'Look Mr Khan, this is not getting us anywhere. If you won't accept our appointment then can I suggest that you ask the solicitor that you say is acting for you against the bank to come up here and have a look at our papers? Maybe he will tell you what our status is.'

As Mr Khan appeared to be mulling this over, I added, 'If you'll get someone to show us around, we're happy to wait while you call him.'

Mr Khan beckoned over one of the younger *wahindi* who had appeared and stood silently on the margins of the dispute and spoke rapidly to him in a language that I did not catch. The younger man's eyes flickered between Mr Khan and me as he listened, before finally nodding to Mr Khan in agreement and turning to us.

'OK, you follow me please?' he said, leading the way into the site.

'Isn't this dangerous?' asked Iain in a low voice as we walked across the grass after their nervous looking guide. 'He could be up to all sorts.'

'Oh I don't think so,' I said calmly. 'The car, William, and hopefully our *askaris* are outside so the chances are that nothing much can go walkies and anyway, he's still convinced he can chuck us out so why should he get up to much in the way of fiddling?'

'And us?'

'Well in the meantime we have a chance to enjoy the view, check out the lay of the land and give tempers a bit of a time to cool. Sounds like a good bet to me.' Now that we had actually started, I was more relaxed as we wandered away from the offices and towards the dumps of material. 'Look, isn't that typical!' I pointed out movement on the far side of the site to Iain. 'Cattle. They've got a bloody herd of cows wandering about the site. I bet that's just so management can have milk in their tea.'

'Looks like they've just had another delivery,' Iain said, looking the other way to the rail trucks on the siding that we could now see more clearly. 'I think they must have ridden shotgun on it up from the coast.'

'You wonder why they bother if they've got that much already.' I gestured dismissively to the piles of rotting machinery.

Iain shrugged again.

One of the things I enjoyed about this type of work was that we were always operating without all the information we needed. Being able to make the right decisions with the wrong data was the secret of success. You had to trust your judgement and gamble. It gave each day, each job, an edge.

'Why the guns?' I called out to our guide. This seemed a bit strange.

'Everything has a value here, please. It is to be guarded or it is to be gone.'

I could understand that, banks were always crowded with lounging company *askaris* touting AK47s and shotguns on the petty cash run, but it seemed excessive for a load of scrap metal.

'So what is that?' I asked fifteen minutes later pointing at a single storey construction a hundred metres or so away just down from the scrap on the west wall. The building was about four metres wide by ten long, set into the corner of the site at the farthest point from the offices at the gate and I headed off towards it without waiting for an answer, at a brisk pace that took the young *wahindi* who was still looking towards the siding, completely by surprise. I was beginning to have some fun with him.

Please, it is a laboratory, a refinery,' gasped our guide, scrambling to catch up with us.

Closer up, the low concrete building was a surprisingly massive construction for something so small, with squat thick walls, a shut metal door, tiny windows and its own substation fed by overhead lines coming from the production plant at the other end of the site. It's a real bunker of a place, I thought as I peered into the darkness. At the end closest to me I could see a range of laboratory benches with stainless steel vessels, barrels of chemicals on the floor with smaller bottles stored on shelves to the side and to one end what could almost have been a kitchenette, what looked like a set of gas burners for heating up equipment and fridges presumably again for storage.

Further back behind them and beyond some kind of inner

39

dividing glass partition wall I could make out an assembly of machinery fading into the darkness. This looked larger, more industrial, two rows of lidded metre high metal vats stretching as far in as I could see and tinged as my eyes adjusted to the dimness with a light blue sheen that I assumed must be some trick of the light through the heavy glass of the tiny window slits. It meant nothing to me other than yes, it looked like a lab and some kind of refinery.

'What *is* that smell?' I heard Iain ask. It was a good question, there was an acrid stink that I could feel almost starting to make my eyes water. 'It's just like a pickling factory!'

'Please, it is shut,' said the guide, tugging at my arm. 'We should go now, see the rest of the site. You will follow me please.' I noticed that he seemed genuinely anxious.

'A lab?' It was my turn to shrug. It made sense I supposed, they would need to test samples of ore and output for quality. 'OK,' I said, turning, relieved to get away from the eye-watering stench of the vinegary fumes. 'So what else do we have here?'

'Looks like a hospital,' said Iain, wandering back from the next building along.

'Yes it is hospital,' confirmed the guide. 'For workers who are sick. Now shall we go please?'

'OK, we can go,' I announced, playing games. 'Lead on then.'

As we toured back along the first half of the southern wall we came to a series of concrete godowns, some seemed used and others seemed welded shut, obviously warehousing for stores and engineering I guessed. There was more scrap as well, but now it looked like the business's own vehicles, an abandoned staff bus riding high on its suspension minus an engine, a grader, its front axles up on bricks, the wheels nowhere to be seen, and the like.

'These are all shut up here,' said the guide. 'These are just stores, there is nothing to see,' but his words were suddenly belied by the scream of an angle grinder on metal from the godown in front of us.

But I was determined not to be so easily managed by the guide. 'But that one is open,' I said, pointing to the doorway which was ajar, and breaking off again I strode purposefully across the parched grass at the side of the road to the half open entrance and peered inside.

As my eyes adjusted to the gloom I could see that I was looking into a workshop where a pair of *wahindi* mechanics in blue overalls had an engine block mounted on a bench. At first they were oblivious to my presence, using the angle grinder to cut through the nuts holding the cylinder head down. Looking to see why, I noticed that some of the nuts appeared to have been spot welded down.

Then one of them looked up and seeing me, immediately advanced, yelling and shouting, just as the guide caught up. After a moment I allowed us to be hustled out.

'Why would they want to disassemble the engines?' I asked Iain in a low puzzled voice. This didn't seem to make any sense either if they were going to melt them down.

'To get the more valuable metals off possibly?' said Iain. 'That's my guess, copper from the starter motors, alternators and that sort of thing.'

'Perhaps,' I conceded, 'But does that mean you would have to take the head off?' Then returning to the fun in hand, I called out loudly to the guide, 'OK, so what's next?'

The actual production area was in the eastern half of the site centred around a huge ore crushing plant in the middle fed by a conveyor from the ore dumps. Another conveyor ran from it to two furnaces on the eastern side of the road and a factory connected by a covered walkway, where the casting was done. The chimney that I had seen from the airport was down at the far south-east of the site, off the furnace.

A blast of raw heat from the furnace hit me as we entered the factory, where the noise was deafening.

'So, this is what you actually make?' I shouted into the guide's ear.

The other great thing that I really enjoyed about my job was that every time we went into a new case, we took over a completely different business and had to learn how to make or do things from scratch. Since I'd been out here I, and now Iain, had made toilet paper and matches, run plantations and long haul lorries, and right now flavour of the month was textiles. Lead smelting was going to make a bit of a change.

Lying on the factory floor were two sorts of castings. The majority were large industrial size ingots that looked as though someone had simply filled a bath with molten lead and then tipped it out. I could see about fifty or so lining the far wall, each with a reference number daubed on in white paint. They were crude, but then I considered, they were presumably sold by weight, as they would just have to be melted down again for use. In between these there were some smaller pot-shaped castings and what could have been lids.

41

'What about waste?'

'Goes over the wall,' shouted Iain, pointing at another large conveyor that was carrying rubbish away from the crusher over the southern end of the site to where it would tip out onto spoil heaps spreading down the slope towards the river.

'It's a wonder they haven't poisoned everyone in town,' I shouted against the cacophony.

'Where does the lead go to? Is it for export?' I yelled at the guide, who just nodded.

'Oh yes,' he started to reply, but he didn't get much further as at that moment a furious looking Mr Khan appeared at the foundry door, accompanied by a group of armed *askaris* and a uniformed police captain.

'Hello,' I said. 'Looks like it's the end of the tour.'

*

Our ejection from the site by the *askaris* under the watchful eye of the *polisi* was brutally efficient. As we were pushed out through the door, I could see that a large crowd of locals had gathered outside the entrance. Enthralled by the site of the Landie parked across the site's main gate to prevent anything getting in or out, and William together with a dozen or so uniformed security guards strung out around the entrance and protecting a dark blue long-wheelbased Land Rover with the bank's logo and a fixed asset register number handpainted on the side, the crowd milled and seethed, stretching back down the road from just beyond the site entrance like spectators at a car crash. Rubbernecking and rumour-mongering.

'Workers?' I asked Maedi as we approached the car.

'Actually is probable,' he replied, and I noticed Mzee Maedi was staying firmly seated.

'Well then, I'd better talk to them.'

'Careful, Mr Paul,' William said, scurrying after me around the car, as I walked towards the crowd of people who were being kept back by the *askaris* with dogs.

As William and I crossed the guards' picket line, the noise of the crowd increased. A German Shepherd jumped and snarled at me, only to be yanked back firmly by the handler. Dogs were extra but worth it, I thought.

Stepping beyond the guards, I held up my hands to call for attention and swiftly the crowd grew quieter as a murmur of shushing went round.

'Workers of New Mwanchi,' I began. By my side William started to translate. 'I work for the receiver who has been appointed over New Mwanchi. My aim is to take control of the factory so that if possible I can keep it trading and sell it to a new owner with money to keep it going and save jobs.'

As William echoed my words in Kiswahili, I was able to watch reactions in the crowd. They seemed attentive, forming a respectful semi-circle in front of us as they listened.

'The management have locked us out. They are preventing us from doing our work to save jobs.'

That got a reaction.

'I will go to see the union office in town. I will see how we can work together to solve this problem and help save jobs.' I was playing politics but it was always worthwhile taking the moral high ground. Out here the unions could be quite powerful and well connected. Nine times out of ten however, *wahindi* management had traditionally relied on their connections with a *vigogo*, a big shot, to smooth the way. They had regarded the unions as nothing but a nuisance to be ignored or treated with contempt.

'Thank you. I hope we can resolve this quickly.'

I turned to go back to the car.

'You must be careful, Mr Paul,' William said as we walked back. In a rare moment of volunteering information, or even an opinion, he added, 'Some of them could have knives.'

As we returned to the car, the crowd noise rose as though a volume switch had been turned up. The crowd also turned inwards for a moment, neighbour talking to neighbour. The *askaris'* picket line in front of the gate was becoming less effective now as people began to mill about in different directions. Some of the guards were in isolated pockets, surrounded, but given the space of the dogs' leashes by the wary crowd.

I caught up with Iain beside the Landie and looked at the gate. The blank steel stared back impassively. No change there then.

'Keep the guards?' Iain asked.

What the bloody hell were the police doing? I wondered. 'Yes, I think so,' I said. Let's keep the pressure on. The Landie across the gate was a bloody good idea, Iain,' I congratulated him. 'I like that a lot!'

As we spoke, I suddenly noticed a middle-aged Asian man with a dark moustache. He was standing behind Iain, a metre or so away, and was obviously straining every nerve to listen in to what we were saying.

'Who are you?' I demanded.

'Work down the road.'

'This is a private conversation. Go away.'

The man turned so that his back was towards us, but he didn't move any further off or out of hearing range. Any more discussion about our plans could wait until we were back in the car, I decided.

Turning back to look up the road I realised that the crowd was huge; bigger than I had first thought, a couple of hundred people at least; all pushing and pulling to move past each other in the ten metre wadi of a road between the high compound and godown walls.

Passers-by were joining the throng. As I watched, I saw a man wheel his bicycle up to the edge of the crowd and ask someone what was going on. A lorry was trying to push through from further up the street. Meanwhile behind Iain and me, an ancient open-backed police Landie had chugged up and half a dozen khaki-clad louts began to get out.

At the sight of the police arriving behind us, the crowd drew back, or tried to, hemmed in as it was by the high surrounding walls and constricted by the lorry pushing its way through. A dog lunged and snarled as a woman tripped under the pressure of the crowd. A scream rang out.

And then without warning the police rushed past us, straight into the crowd, cracking sjamboks wildly in all directions. Hemmed in by high walls on either side, the crowd became a boiling mass as they scrambled to escape. I saw cowering bodies on the ground and the police beating stragglers. The bicycle went under the lorry's wheels and was crushed.

The police attack was astonishingly brutal, effective, and mercifully short.

When it was over, all that was left was emptiness, a pall of dust and dropped bags, a memory of screams, and abandoned flip-flops on the ground; while the police sauntered calmly back to their Landie without a concern in the world, and the crushed bicycle's owner had gone demented, yelling abuse and tugging at the handle of the lorry driver's door, who, not being able to see the mangled bicycle under his wheels, simply sat there in bemusement.

The nosy *wahindi* had disappeared too. I didn't see where he'd gone. Instead I caught site of a young man carrying some form of holdall, who had taken advantage of the disturbance to slip quietly out of the foot gate which was closing behind him as he disappeared into the rapidly dispersing crowd.

I turned to Iain, the grim look on his face I guess mirroring my own. 'We need to see the bastard in charge before this gets out of hand,' I said.

*

The desk sergeant seemed completely nonplussed, faced with a determined *mzungu* in reception demanding to see the Regional Police Commissioner. I only had to wait for fifteen minutes before the sergeant reappeared to lift the counter's flap and beckon me in with a motion like plucking mosquitoes out of the air. I was ushered upstairs to where the sergeant knocked on a wooden door with 'Regional Police Commissioner' hand painted across the frosted glass panel. There was a grunted command from inside and the sergeant swung the door open for me to enter.

It was a small office, the walls painted a faded institutional green with dark wood bookshelves along the wall opposite the window, empty of course. The only decoration was two framed police certificates on the wall to the left, and facing them, the standard office picture of the President hung centre space on the wall to the right behind the desk.

The wooden name block on the desk next to the swagger stick and khaki cap with gold braid announced in gold leaf letters that I was addressing RPC Temu, a grossly fat man in matching khaki uniform with gold braid epaulets and shiny Sam Browne belt who was sitting slouched in his swivel chair behind it.

'*Hujambo,* mzee.'

'*Sijambo,* bwana,' replied RPC Temu, remaining seated and without bothering to turn to face me.

'*Habari ya asabuhi?*'

'*Nzuri,* bwana. *Habari ya khazi?*'

'*Nzuri,* bwana.'

As we exchanged formal greetings, RPC Temu gestured for me to take the chair before his desk. '*Karibuni.*'

'*Asante,*' I said, reaching out for it. RPC Temu regarded me for a moment as I sat down, remaining deliberately casual, without turning his chair to face me directly.

'So,' he announced slowly, as if dragging himself to business, 'What is it that you wish to talk about with me, Mr Paul? You will

45

be familiar with how we do things here. Much of our procedure is based on English law is it not?' he said, smiling.

Not that I can recognise, I thought to myself.

'Well Mr Commissioner, we seem to have a bit of a problem that I wanted to discuss with you,' I opened.

'A problem?' Temu's eyebrows arched. 'Oh dear,' he said at last, his voice a deep base. 'I was not aware of a problem. Well, we must see what we can do. What sort of a problem do "we" have Mr Paul?'

'Why was I not allowed to file a complaint downstairs of theft over company property we have seen being removed from the site earlier today?'

'This is a civil matter; it is a dispute between you and the factory's owners.'

'That did not stop one of your men turn up to evict me and my manager from the factory.'

'But Mr Paul, is this not natural? If we receive a report of intruders on private property is it not our duty to investigate? Would you not expect the *polisi* in England to do as much Mr Paul? And to ask intruders to leave if there was a threat of a breach of the peace?'

I bristled.

'We are not here to help you enforce any rights that you claim. Our role as *polisi* is very clear, we are here simply to keep the peace,' Temu continued serenely.

'I am not asking you to help enforce rights, I am asking you to take notice of our claims when goods are removed...'

'I have told you already Mr Paul,' Temu interrupted, 'I cannot become involved in a civil matter.'

'Is a claim of the theft of the company's property just a civil matter?'

'Are you trying to tell me my job?' Temu growled, swinging round in his chair to glare fiercely at me, suddenly incensed at anyone daring to challenge his authority. He grabbed the baton from his desk and pointed it straight at my face. 'Because if you are Mr Paul, I might have to have you arrested.' His fist with the baton thumped the table. 'Right away.'

*

My expression was thunderous as I climbed into the passenger seat of the bank's Landie.

'So how did it go?' asked Iain cautiously.

'Don't ask!'

I had calmed down by the time we drew up at the hotel. Climbing out of the car I said to Iain, 'You know the funny thing is, I've got the feeling that I've seen him somewhere recently.'

'Who, Temu?'

'Yes.'

'Where?'

'That's just it,' I said slamming the door shut in frustration. 'Buggered if I know.'

3 Dinner dates

Wednesday, 12 October, Mkilwa

I nerved myself to step inside. It took a moment for my eyes to adjust to the gloom as the power was off. There was something claustrophobic about the smell, the relative darkness, the constant sound of voices flowing from the overcrowded wards.

As I looked around, a petite golden haired vision in a white coat appeared at the doorway opposite and burst into a brilliant white smile of welcome. A cheery, 'Paul, how nice to see you!' rang out.

'Hi, Sam,' I smiled back as we met and embraced warmly in the middle of the reception area.

'It is good to see you,' she said as we released one another. 'What brings you to the fetid slums? I didn't think you'd be back for a while.'

'Oh, I just couldn't stay away,' I joked. As part of the small circle of local young *wazungu*, I had seen quite a lot of Sam over the last year or so. As an expat worker with a decent rented house, rather than a researcher or student, I had tended to hold an open house policy for much of the time I was in Mkilwa; and had ended up hosting a fair few new arrivals for a while until they found their feet, including Sam. 'I've got another job on up this way, you know how it is. Thought I'd pop in to visit, see how you are. Buy you an early lunch if you like?'

'I wondered if New Mwanchi was you,' she said nodding. '*Bitings* would be great.'

'Well, yes it is. How did you know that?'

She laughed brightly up at my surprise. 'Oh Paul, this is a hospice, not the other side of the moon. We've got hundreds of *wakilwa* in here. With all their relatives here as well to look after them, do you think there's much that we don't get to hear about pretty soon? We've even got some of your workers from New Mwanchi here. Quite a lot of them actually, now I come to think about it,' she told me as we walked out into the cleansing sun of the courtyard. 'I'm almost inclined to wonder whether heavy metal poisoning from your plant is having a statistically significant impact on disease onset.'

'Not my plant,' I looked around at the beds filled with stick thin patients lined up in the shade of the veranda waiting silently to die and shook my head. I couldn't tell if she was joking or not. 'I can't even get into the place. You know I really don't know how you can face working here every day.'

'I've no choice really if I want to do my research have I?' She shrugged as we walked. 'Africa's where AIDS is and this is where the sick people are. So here I am at Mama Clem's. And even if there's not much I can do, at least I feel that I'm doing whatever good I can.'

'And how is Mama Clem?'

'Oh we don't see much of her these days. She's always off on hubby's campaign trail.'

Mama Clemantina Pesha was a local power house, a big player in regional government, aid and public works, which were after all just different sides of the same thing here. Setting up an AIDS hospice named after herself hadn't been charity, it was political business. And now her husband, the ex interior minister, Benjamin Pesha, had defected from the Party to run as opposition candidate for President.

'Oh, I'm sorry,' she said catching herself.

'No, no, it's all right,' said Paul. 'It came though while I was back home on leave.'

'What, your divorce?'

'Yes, the degree absolute. I'm a free man again now,' I said, trying and probably failing to avoid a hint of bitterness in my ironic smile. I just don't know how I feel about it yet, I thought to myself.

'Oh Paul,' she said awkwardly, 'I mean that's, that's...' she tailed off in confusion. 'I mean I'm pleased for you. That it's all over I mean. At last.'

I could see what she was going through and smiled at her to let her off the hook. 'It's OK, Sam, I'm a big boy now. It's all over and that's it.'

'So what are you going to do now?' she asked quietly.

I paused a moment before I spoke. 'Go home. Start over. It's time to stop hiding out here and go back to get on with my life.'

'Oh Paul, come on, you haven't been hiding!'

'Haven't I?' I said conversationally, almost to myself rather than her. It has felt like it over the last two years or so, I thought.

And then to my utter astonishment she reached around and embraced me wordlessly in a hug, burying her head against my chest. As my arms automatically, but cautiously responded to embrace her back, I was at a complete loss for words.

After a few seconds she released me and turning away so that we could walk on, swiftly changed the subject. 'Do you think he's got a chance of winning?' she asked.

'Who, Pesha?'

'Yes.'

I laughed and shook my head. 'Hey, how would I know? Why don't you ask your resident political correspondent?'

'Ish?' Sam looked wistful. 'I wish I could, but he's down in the big city for the duration, as well.'

I nodded. I should have thought of that. Ishmayeel had got himself a job as a reporter for the *News*, one of the new independent newspapers. 'The election?'

'Yep. It's all hands to the pumps on the rag while it's on.'

'Do you get down to see him much?' I asked gently.

'Sometimes,' her smile brightened as she looked up at me. 'I'll need to spend more time down there soon too. I'm almost finished here and I'll need to dig out some data at the Ministry of Health for my thesis. We'll have to get ourselves a place since I don't think there's space for us to shack up in the digs he's got at the moment.'

'Well, you know you guys can always stay at mine until I go if you need a room. There's plenty to spare.'

'Oh Paul, you're brilliant,' she said, reaching up to kiss me on the cheek as we walked. 'Thanks. What would we do without you?'

I wondered if I was blushing.

*

As Iain and I walked up the wide acacia-lined avenue that was the town's commercial heart, looking up towards the purple majestic mountains inland, there was something almost alpine about the brilliant blue sky and clear quality of light that was in stark contrast to the dusty road we were walking along and the grinding siege we had been landed with.

I couldn't get over how scruffy the courthouse was.

It was built from breezeblocks, plastered and once painted institutional white and light blue, since when the long and short rains had been and gone and come again; the weight of the tropical downpours battering the surrounding fragile earth and sending up splatters of mud-red water which stained the bottom metre of whitewash a shitty brown. The press of sweaty bodies in the open hall and along the corridors, and the ever-present dust blowing in through grilled glass-less windows in the long dry seasons, had turned the blue of the corridors a grubby grey.

Below the painted walls, rain had leached the earth itself away over the years so the crude lumps and bumps and hollows of the concrete foundations showed a bulging metre proud, if that was the word, of the surrounding dirt. There was a look of stained teeth, etched and eaten away underneath by gum disease, something seedy, unpleasant and unclean about the whole place.

It stood as a block of its own on the edge of town and next door to the local Gymkhana Club, with a sprawling grass yard all round.

An old transport container concreted into place in one corner of the yard, with breezeblocks around three sides and bars welded across the door space did duty as a crowded holding cell, with prisoners' faces always pressed against the bars looking out silently at the comings and goings on the Court's steps or holding whispered conspiratorial conversations with lawyers in baggy suits, frayed collars, scruffy shoes and black academic gowns.

Iain had been served personally with a dubious looking photocopy under an illegible scrawl of a signature of what was apparently a court order to move Iain's Land Rover on pain of imprisonment. So he and I were trooping back up to court again to check it out. As we reached the gate Iain waved to a figure who detached himself from the circle around the cells and sauntered over to meet us. He was tall, slim, and very erect, with his head held back and a sort of questioning look in his eyes. He held out his long, bony-fingered hand and Iain shook it as he made the introductions.

'Advocate Mabulla, this is my boss, Paul.'

Advocate Mabulla studied me for a moment as he put out his hand and then smiled. He had huge gaps between his front teeth, 'I am pleased to meet you, Mr Paul.'

'I am pleased to meet you, Advocate Mabulla,' I replied, as we shook hands.

Marvellous, I thought. They have a nasty little cowboy of a lawyer with lots of dodgy dubious cases and a big car. Ours is tall, gangly and wearing a shabby black gown.

He had, however, a firm, self-possessed Western style handshake but as he smiled in greeting, there was an off-putting quality about him which I couldn't really put my finger on.

My problem was, I just didn't know how far we could trust Advocate Mabulla, if at all. We were being tied up in knots by the other side with adjournments and setting dates for mention. But I didn't know whether the way he was playing the case was part of a strategy; incompetence; or cooperation with the other side.

'You will want to challenge this order. I do not think that this will be possible, but we have time to talk, bwana. The Court, it is running late.'

Inside, half an hour later, the whole Court stumbled and shuffled to its feet under the bored eyes of a khaki-clad policeman in the corner, as the huge bulk of the honourable fountain of justice, Judge Ngalo, squeezed into the court room from his chambers to begin his afternoon's hearings.

*

By the time we got back Iain's Land Rover had been moved, with a forklift truck, the *askaris* said, which had allowed a small lorry and a car to escape the compound in a roar of dust and to race away around the corner of the RI compound and out of sight.

When we returned again at midnight to check in as normal and deliver flasks of steaming hot coffee to the *askaris*, all was still in the chill night air. The guards had thick greatcoats on and were huddled around the charcoal *jiko* that Iain had supplied, in a *duka* that they had commandeered directly opposite the factory gates. There was a quiet conversation, a round of *asante sanas* as Iain handed round the flask and collected their notes scribbled on pages in an exercise book, of all the movements, in and out.

'It's all been quiet,' he reported back to me at the car. 'No problems.'

'Well it would be. They dragged us up to court to get us out of the way and then got whatever it was they wanted out of there while we weren't around.'

'What do you reckon it was that was so important?'

'Could have been anything,' I shrugged, 'probably cash and all their papers about offshore bank accounts, at a guess.'

I looked up at the silent walls. 'Looks to me like we are in for a long one.'

Tuesday, 18 October, Mkilwa

The hearing was in chambers, the judge's private office, a three metre square room with a desk, bars at the windows but no glass. There was no power so the light wasn't working on this dull day. It felt more like a cell than a court.

Judge Ngalo was sitting behind the wooden desk and looked up as I shuffled into the back of the room. Advocate Mabulla sat facing him at the left side of the desk with Iain behind him, penned in by the open door. An advocate I hadn't seen before was standing at the right with Mohammed Khan behind him and a policeman was standing in the corner looking bored.

The new advocate was explaining to the judge that unfortunately he understood the company's existing advocate had been unavoidably double booked as he had been called to appear at the high court in Jijenga that very day.

'In the circumstances, we request as a matter of simple natural justice, an adjournment of the hearing for two weeks to allow the company to be properly represented by the advocate of its choice.'

With the scrape of his chair, Mabulla bobbed up to address the judge. 'But New Mwanchi's advocate has known of this hearing for many days now and this is already its second adjournment, your honour,' Mabulla objected. 'My clients are seeking to drink at your noble fountain of justice, your Honour. Surely justice delayed is in danger of becoming justice denied?' Mabulla was fond of his rhetorical flourishes.

Judge Ngalo sat there, impassive as a toad on a lily pad. 'Do you suggest that he should have ignored a summons from the High Court then?' The question was sly.

'No, no, your Honour,' Mabulla hastily interjected. 'But this advocate has been involved in representing the plaintiff. Surely he is sufficiently familiar with the case to respond on the points in the brief for this mention, the facts of which are well known to all parties?'

The other advocate stood, shaking his head firmly, 'I am not sufficiently versed in the facts of the case to be able to act in this hearing. We move for an adjournment to allow proper representation. Surely, no court in the land will deny that?'

'Your Honour,' Mabulla started to address Judge Ngalo, but he was interrupted.

'Advocate Mabulla,' the judge's gravelly voice was suddenly loud as other noise seemed to stop. 'I think that we have no choice in this matter but to adjourn the case for further mention.'

'But, your Honour,' tried Mabulla.

'Sit down Advocate Mabulla!' the judge said sharply in a fierce commanding voice. 'You are not, I trust, going to suggest that I rule against a matter that is clearly a point of natural justice?' The voice was deep, strong and menacing. The judge had power and he knew

53

it.

'No. No, your Honour,' Mabulla folded, sinking onto his wooden chair.

'Adjourned for mention on… well, let me see,' Ngalo said, picking up a large desk diary and reaching for his glasses and thumbing through a distressingly large number of pages before looking up. 'Unfortunately I have a large number of cases on at the moment,' he sighed. 'Wednesday the 9th of November?' he queried.

As I looked at the judge, I suddenly started as I realised what I was seeing. Silently I nudged Iain and nodded his attention in the direction I was looking. A few moments later, a muttered 'Christ' told me that Iain had spotted it too.

The other advocate shook his head with regret over his colleague's busy court schedule and suggested that later would be better.

As the horse-trading started Iain and I exchanged looks of disbelief. Judge Ngalo was making his judicial appointments in a New Mwanchi complementary desk diary. 'We've just got no hope here at all!' I muttered under my breath to Iain as the police sergeant called us all to stand as Judge Ngalo declared the session closed.

Khan and the advocate scuttled past us and off as soon as they left the room and a few moments later I saw them sauntering down the path and through the gate, in earnest discussion.

'So what was that all about?' I asked Iain and Advocate Mabulla as they stood on the veranda outside.

'Well, Mr Paul,' said Mabulla, 'they are lying.'

'What?'

'Their advocate. I am sure he is not in Jijenga. In fact I know he is not, but I cannot prove it.'

'So why didn't you challenge them in court?'

'Because I cannot prove it. You want me to accuse a fellow advocate of having deliberately misled the court? Without proof? That is a very dangerous thing to ask, Mr Paul.'

'OK, OK, but surely we can use this against them? If we did somehow get proof from Jijenga.'

'Mr Paul, how long is that going to take? I do not want to be defeatist, Mr Paul, but you have seen the judge. Nothing but cast iron proof will do in front of him.'

'And probably not even that,' muttered Iain.

As we talked I noticed Judge Ngalo emerging from behind the corner of the court building and watched as he waddled regally along the path towards the gate to the next plot.

'And if we get proof? He will have another excuse and will apologise for innocently misleading the court. And where has that got us? More hearings, more time, no further forwards.'

'Now look where they are all off to,' I said, nodding at Judge Ngalo as he walked through the gate and out of sight behind the dark evergreen bushes on the other side of the fence, in the direction that Khan and the advocate had gone.

'Gymkhana Club,' said Iain, standing beside him. 'Ngalo and Khan are both members, so naturally they go there for lunch. Theoretically, I should be allowed reciprocal access as a member of the Jijenga club but somehow my application form hasn't yet been sorted out.'

As he spoke a beige Landcruiser drove past the court, indicating for the turn to the Gymkhana Club. It was driven by a *fundi* but I recognised the fat features of the passenger in his uniform, polished Sam Browne belt, gold collar insignia and peaked cap.

The car turned and as it disappeared next door behind the bushes we could hear it crunching up the gravelled driveway.

'Well, well,' I said. 'Now why doesn't that surprise me?'

'Who was it?' asked Iain.

'Temu,' Advocate Mabulla replied, staring at the cloud of dust hanging in the air.

'My mate, the Regional Police Commissioner,' I added bitingly, as the dust dissolved into fading wisps in the air and then away to nothingness. 'Also off to the Gymkhana Club for a spot of lunch no doubt. But there was something about his profile, and a car that rang a faint bell in the back of my mind again.

'If Mzee Temu is meeting the others, this is not good, Bwana Paul,' Mabulla almost whispered to us. He was shaking his head. 'The RPC is a powerful man in the region. He would not attend just any normal case. This has worrying indications.'

'Well there's not a lot we can do here,' I had decided. 'Come on, let's go,' I said wearily.

But as Iain and I turned away, we were caught by a whispered, 'Bwana Paul,' from Advocate Mabulla who held out a hand to touch my sleeve. As I turned, Advocate Mabulla nodded towards the Gymkhana gates as a white Hilux twincab pulled into the Gymkhana. In the back I could the strong features of a wiry small man. They were a set of hard edged, hook nosed features that were becoming increasingly familiar from billboards across the country.

'Is that not Bwana Pesha?'

'The candidate?' I asked in concern.

'That is the one,' nodded Mabulla slowly. 'I am sure of it.'

Friday, 21 October, Mkilwa

I could hardly hear Winston over the crackling line in the post office booth.

'What's going on up there?' Winston was asking.

'We're just doing our job Winston, why? Are you getting grief from the bank about progress?'

'No it's not that. This is from... higher up.'

'What? High up in the bank?'

'No, higher up than that.'

Higher up than the bank? I wondered to myself. There was a real edge in Winston's voice that I had never heard before. What could he mean?

Winston sounded hesitant. 'This is well... political,' he ventured eventually.

'Political?'

'Well, yes. From the top. From the *very* top,' Winston emphasised.

I could see Winston's problem now in talking about this over an open line.

'I see,' I said, thinking quickly. 'Well, I'd better come down to talk.'

I could hear the relief in Winston's voice. 'I think that's a very good idea.'

*

Iain was waiting for me outside in the post office hall. 'So, what was that all about?' he asked as we pushed our way outside.

'Winston's under pressure to have us called off.'

'What sort of pressure?'

'He couldn't say but I think he sounded scared. At a guess I think he's had the President's office on the line.'

'Wow. Are you going down?'

'Yes.'

*

Iain gave me a lift to catch the midnight flight.

African nights were either incredibly light with a huge moon casting a curious blue sheen over everything, or solidly black in the complete absence of any man-made light in a way that was unimaginable at home. It had been overcast all day and the night was moonless, so the world beyond the reach of the Landie's lousy headlamps was a complete void. As the shacks thinned out, we came to a battered oil drum, its alternating bands of red and white paint obscured by caked layers of dust and mud, warning of the massive hole dug in the road a year ago, in anticipation of a culvert that had yet to appear.

We pulled off the road onto the dirt track diversion, dipping down off the embankment and heading along a line of stunted trees towards a shallower place to cross the gully.

'Jesus Christ! What's that?' Iain shouted, slamming on the brakes just in time as I, unrestrained by a seat belt, threw out a hand to brace myself against the dashboard to stop myself smashing into the windscreen.

From behind the tree immediately in front, a huge truck seemed to rear up at us. Its engine roaring, it crested the rise, the full beam of its lights tearing crazily at the sky, and then raking our Landie with blinding glare as the truck lurched back onto the apartment, its cab swinging wildly on its suspension as it righted itself. It wasn't stopping for anything and it seemed incredible that anybody could be so stupid as to drive at that speed along such a narrow cart track. As the lorry thundered past, Iain somehow managed to squeeze us off the road to the left, praying aloud that there was some space before the ditch. Only a few metres behind the first truck roared another white painted forty tonner, and then another, and another, filling the night with a deafening thunder of engines, brilliant headlights waving madly and swirling shadowy curtains of dust. They all seemed brand new, monstrous and anonymous with no number plates.

'What the hell's going on?' shouted Iain above the noise.

From my vantage point I had seen the blue circular logo on the doors of some of the vehicles as they thundered past. 'RI relief lorries,' I yelled above the din, 'coming up from the Ro-Ro dock. They must be off to the camps.'

We sat and waited in silence as twenty, twenty-one… twenty-five finally went by. It was like standing too close to the railway line as a thundering express train passed.

For a moment we were too stunned to move. Then as the roar of the last truck faded away, Iain drove on, the yellow glow of the headlights reflecting madly in the billowing dust.

'Do you think they're going to Gerry's compound?' wondered Iain looking out of the back window to where the rapidly fading tail lights, blurred red in the broiling clouds of dust, were disappearing into the darkness behind us.

'That would make sense. They could spend the night there and refuel, before heading on to the camps tomorrow morning,' I said. 'I'd guess that's why Refugee International's got that there. After all, then it's only a 130 kilometre run to the border.'

'Have you been out that way?' asked Iain.

'Yes, I went last year. It's a murram road. Officially it's graded gravel, but in reality it's just rutted mud, dust and sand. You'd want to tackle it in daylight. And then once you get to the frontier, the camps are spotted across the landscape like boils, all the way south along the riverbank. I guess it'll take them all day tomorrow. And that's if they don't push on. The really big camps are next door, and that means getting past the army and some very nervous border police. And then back again.'

'Well it doesn't look like those guys were in the mood to stop for anyone,' observed Iain. 'I wouldn't like to try and pull them over to ask for passports!'

Thursday, 27 October, Jijenga

Ishmayeel matched Sam for petiteness and for the way his brilliant white grin could light up a room, but otherwise he was her exact opposite, his hair a glossy black, his skin the nut brown of his *wahindi* heritage.

I pulled open the fridge in my apartment for a round of beers as Ish laid out the pizza boxes. 'So, what's brought you back down to the big city?' Ish called over his shoulder from the living room. 'Have you been pulled off Mkilwa?'

I smiled to myself as I came back into the room with the cold cans and a couple of frostie mugs. As always with Ish, the conversation danced across politics, Sam, the election, Mkilwa, the rag, social life, food, drink; driven all the time by Ish's infectious enthusiasm and boundless energy. But you could always trust Ish to get straight to the point. 'It's funny you should ask. Is this off the record?'

Ish smiled in return as he took the proffered can and glass and shrugged. 'Of course.'

I pulled out a chair to sit down, 'Well it's odd. We thought that we were going to be. I flew down to talk to Winston, but then, we weren't.'

'Why?' Ish wrestled out from behind a huge slice of extra cheese, ham and mushrooms.

'The President's office called Winston back during the afternoon. No reason given but they told Winston that they wouldn't interfere.'

'Hmmm.' Ish chewed and contemplated this information with the attuned sense of the cultural and political nuances that seemed to be his gift from straddling the differing worlds. A local born *wahindi*, Ish had been brought up in London and was a computer programmer by profession. It was only following Sam out to Africa while she worked on her thesis which had brought him back. Now he slipped between the expat and local worlds with a natural ease and for lack of anything else to do, he had fallen into a freelance reporting job on the English language *News*. 'I don't like the sound of that,' he opined at last.

'What do you think is going on?' I asked, intrigued. 'I can't make head nor tail of it.'

'Well, it's a mix of old fashioned protection and patronage. If you can make money, the next thing you *need*,' Ish emphasised, 'is protection, to be able to keep it and spend it. And if you want the top protection you don't just go to the local cops who you're having trouble with, you go to the top politician – the President.'

'The whole place is corrupt you mean.'

'From your viewpoint yes, but here it's seen as natural,' Ish protested. 'It's just part of the centuries' old traditions of patronage and deference. It's like the way the clan system works, the President is just the ultimate elder.'

'Well then,' I said. 'Why doesn't the President step in to protect them? If what you are saying is right, they've paid their dues over the years. Why haven't they been able to collect?'

'It's got to be politics, I suppose,' reflected Ish. 'Everything is at the moment, with the election and Pesha stirring things up about corruption and the *wahindi*. Then there's the PCB nearly going bust and putting together that list of its top hundred key defaulting debtors, and don't forget, New Mwanchi was close to the top. They are known to be close to the Party, they are *wahindi* and to cap it all,

59

they are based in Mkilwa which is Pesha's home town. Do you really imagine that Rais is going to step into that minefield just now and bail them out? But actually you could go further,' he mused, almost to himself.

'You know, you really ought to ask yourself, why has PCB, the nationalised bank don't forget, appointed you as receivers of one of the country's biggest firms slap bang in the middle of the chief presidential challenger's home territory, just in the run up to the election? If there isn't a political message in there, I don't know what is.'

'What's the message, though?' I asked.

'That the President and the Party are still the big men with the power. It's saying; if you in Mkilwa don't toe the line and support us, we can make trouble for you, however big you think you are. It's New Mwanchi's problem that they are just a pawn in a bigger game.'

'And mine, too?'

'Well I suppose so,' agreed Ish. 'Elections out here are all about patronage. You don't vote for the man of the people to be chief do you? No, you want *vigogo,* the big man, the rich man, the man who is powerful, to be chief. Because the big man, the rich man, the powerful man, is the man who can then give you patronage, grant you favours, look after you.'

'It's a different pitch from the bollocks that we get at home,' I laughed.

'You bet,' Ish agreed.

'Yes, but why does Rais care then?' I asked puzzled. 'He's had his two terms and he's got his money and is off to retirement. What's the election to him?'

'But that's just the point,' Ish jumped in, 'he has to be able to live on to enjoy his money. Losing elections round here is a dangerous pastime. Who's the last African leader you can think of who stepped down or lost an election and went to live on peacefully in retirement?' he challenged.

'Well, I guess...'

'Rais can't run a nasty little exploitative one-party state for years, propped up by his East European advisors until the wall comes down, and then expect to settle into happy retirement just because the Western aid donors have said, "thou shalt have multiparty elections or thou shalt have no more cash."'

'So who's he looking to for protection once he's gone?' I asked.

'The new President, obviously. Who else is there?' countered Ish.

'Well now that's what's been puzzling me. So why then has Rais picked such a nobody as a candidate if it's that important to him that they win, for his protection?'

'Ah well, the Party's going to win anyway. They have the countryside sewn up. So Rais has picked a guy from Bharanku, which is an unpopular minority area, and that's going to make it even easier for him.'

Now I really felt lost as Ish went on.

'To keep his protection, Rais has to keep a handle on the new guy. So he's picked someone who can only win with Rais's help. And he's done that by picking a nobody from slaver city. The risk is of course that he's gone too far.'

'What do you mean?' I asked, feeling concerned.

'As a *wazungu*, you probably don't really see it, but to the locals across the country and particularly across the water in Mkilwa, Bharanku is an "Arab" city, it's the key city for the Moslem half of the country running from the lake down to the coast which is then much more mixed. The old memories and tribal rivalries run deep and bitter, let alone the religious divide. Remember slavery was only stamped out less than a hundred years ago here. Running a guy like that against Pesha from the other, mainly Christian side of the lake, could be a recipe for trouble.'

4 Helping with enquiries

Thursday, 10 November, Jijenga

That morning as I left for work, I picked up a note from under the Suzuki's windscreen wiper.

The page had been torn from a small spiral bound lined notebook leaving a ragged fringe. It was in English, or near enough: *Dear owner of this vehicle. You are required to have a person, that is the askari, who will be looking after that property of yours. If you won't do that, don't be surprised once you find your car number being at the police station. With thanks, the askaris.*

Starting the engine, I looked across at the huddled bodies, seemingly asleep on the steps at the far end of the car park. *Askaris* were such a constant presence here, such a part of the furniture, that I often almost forgot they were there.

From the apartment, the drive took half an hour along the coast of Mkonge and onto Boma if I left sufficiently late to avoid the worst of the rush. It was a drive along roads named after a parade of modern African heroes, preferably dead ones, to replace the old colonial standbys.

To my left, the big high white houses with their red tiled roofs, colonnades, balconies and separate servants' quarters, stretched back from the grassy stretches and coconut palms that fringed the road. Tucked away behind high blank whitewashed walls, broken glass glinting on their pediments, the white paint disappeared under muddy brown stains at their feet.

'Cheeky sods,' I said to myself, thinking about the *askaris*.

I smiled and looked out to my right across the brilliant blues, turquoises and aquamarines of the shallower water, cut by the giant slow moving sharks' fin sails of the simple local fishing boats, across to the Boma headland hazily visible to the other side of Kusini bay, and the winking sunlight flashing off the windows of cars on Umoja.

I could see the long strand of beach lined by its old colonial housing plots and fifties apartment blocks that formed the most expensive town dwellings in the city. I was looking at modern Jijenga, old colonial Jijenga and before that Arab and Portuguese Jijenga. When I looked at a map it was still obvious how much the city had kept its old racially divided layout.

The pleasant tree-covered hill of Boma, set far out in the shining ocean, cooled by pleasant sea breezes, was home to the presidential palace, the embassies and headquarters of the great and the good, and the old expat enclave of the Gymkhana Club and now the new Hilton.

On its northern side, the Boma headland protected the vast, near circular, natural harbour of Jijenga bay, fringed by a narrow crescent of flat land running from the south-west of the bay to the north-east. The south half of the crescent was the souk, a densely packed network of crumbling colonial roads angling inland from Front Street into a tangled semi-gridwork of narrow streets, Asian owned lock-up shops surmounted by rickety offices and ramshackle apartment blocks and open African market spaces. It was a crowded traffic-choked trading bedlam during the day but for anything anyone wanted in town, from computers to blankets, its thronging noisy streets were the place to go.

Northwards, the shops and residences petered out as the buildings gave way to industrial compounds, freight forwarders and shippers, before piers, docks, cranes and godowns of the harbour proper. Jijenga was, after all, first and foremost a port.

To the west, tumbled hills and slopes rose sharply, out towards the outer ring road and beyond where town planning disappeared into the *nyumbaya*, a maze of inner city *shambas*, piles of burning rubbish, choked river valleys that flooded every long rains and a straggling hive of bars, *dukas*, goats, sewing shops, charcoal vendors and pot holed dirt tracks with names like Soweto and Enza, down which no *mzungu* ever drove, before ten kilometres or more inland the hills relented and gave way to the African plain proper at T'chame.

South from Boma the city had sprawled across the network of marshes, swampy tidal tangles of sunken trees, straggling mangroves and evil smelling mudflats, interspersed with small hills and headlands that marked the Kusini River's exit to the sea. A tide of development had rolled down along the coast, an explosion of compounds, plots, beach houses, apartments, hotels, shops and private enterprise. All now accessible from the city by the new dual carriageway of Bara Bara ya Rais that cut inland of the swamps.

And scattered everywhere between the modern developments were *dukas* selling fruit and vegetables, organised markets, sections of shanty housing and great swathes of permanent slums creeping down to all but the most hopeless of marsh, sweeping back up into the hills and up the river valley as far as the eye could see.

All except across the reedy swamp just beyond the next promontory south, where a single concrete road spurred off seawards from the Old Bahari Road running across the marsh on a small embankment, to a quiet wooded area visible a kilometre or so down the track. Between the silent screen of trees and the road, nothing, not even the birds, stirred across the flat sodden landscape. But the ever lounging squad of paramilitary riot police, the Special Operations Unit, whose red berets could be seen in the distance by its high white gates, announced without saying that this was the government compound, the official 'town' residences for the senior Party members, ministers, Baba and the like.

Relaxed this morning, I bought the *News* and the government paper, the *Citizen*, from the street boys sauntering down between the crawling traffic as I edged towards the lights to join Bara Bara ya Rais. And then as I pulled up outside the firm's offices in the shabby nationalised tower block in the centre of town, one of the street boys waved frantically to me, beckoning the car into a space, lifting the windscreen wipers before he had stopped, with a cheerful smile and a, 'Hello fadder, wash today?'

Inside, as I waited in the lobby scrum for the lift I gave my eyes a moment to become accustomed to the gloom. Looking around I was struck again by how awful and tatty it all was, the ingrained dirt, the cracked paving stones covered in sand, the broken light fittings, the elevators that didn't work, the water dripping from the air conditioners and trickling down the walls in plumes of algae and scum, the missing tiles and ceiling panels and the hand painted notice advertising, 'Sekretorial services'.

The whole place seemed desperately in need of a World Bank whitewash loan project.

The middle elevator of the three was working, as it usually did, except when there was a complete power cut, but once the doors had closed, it was pitch black other than the glowing red of the flickering floor buttons as the lights had failed.

The start of the building's refit was now four months overdue. The water worked for half an hour or so each day which gave the messengers time to fill the buckets so we could flush the loos.

The messenger on the eighth floor reception bobbed a bow and grinned at me in welcome as I stepped through the doors.

'*Hujambo, bwana.*'

'*Sijambo, bwana.*'

'*Habari ya asabuhi?*'

64

'Nzuri, bwana. Habari yako?'
'Nzuri, bwana.'
'Safi.'
'Safi. Unatake kahawa?'
'Ndiyo. Asante sana.'

And so, as the messenger scurried off to the cubby hole with the kettle to tell Ernest to organise my coffee, I walked down the dark wood panelled corridor to my office. I couldn't help but smile as I did so at the contrast between the pushing and shoving that I had just endured to catch the lift, where any idea of consideration for others was a completely alien concept; and the punctilious verbal politeness of African society with its precise gradations of deference on grounds of hierarchy and age. Children begged to hold my feet in greeting, *shikamu*; elders were always respected *mzees* not simply *bwanas*.

I squirmed inwardly as I got out my keys, unlocked my office and sat down behind my desk, conscious as always of how incredibly rude I and other *wazungu* must seem, with our discourteous mangled greetings and crass ignorance of station and clanship.

I operated on autopilot until the coffee arrived so I took time to go through the *News*, soaking up the election coverage. After a few minutes, Janet walked in with a draft letter which her forefingers had eventually finished the night before.

'It is cold in here,' she said. That surprised me. I hadn't noticed, but now she came to mention it, the air conditioning was on and rattling away behind me. I swivelled round to look at it. It was funny how I could switch off to the fact that it was blowing a gale from over my shoulder even though sometimes I had to weigh down my papers with the big hole punch to stop them blowing off the desk. I was sure that I'd turned it off last night before I left. Oh well, I shrugged to myself. I had the only keys to the office. I must have left it on, I thought, turning back to my desk. Coffee would be arriving any moment.

Later that morning I was working in my office when my reverie was interrupted as Clare popped her broad friendly face around the door.

'Hi,' I said, looking up, 'What brings you up to my ivory tower?'
'Just wanted to know, have you been to the new Hilton yet?'
'On my salary? You must be joking.'
'I'm not going,' said Clare firmly, 'Not until I get shitface to buy me a meal there. He can afford a room too.'

Shitface was Gerry of the RI. Gerry the gimlet eyed chancer at the Alhamisi with the eternal grin. A fixer if ever I had seen one. Squat and powerful, he made a lot of his flashy jewellery, his gold bracelets and his Rolex watch. He'd been some kind of wheeler dealer, he'd been married several times, he'd been around Africa for more years than anyone could remember and now he was Refugee International's official ambassador to the country. I couldn't remember ever having seen him without a can in his hand. Although to be fair you could say that about most of us.

Clare, in contrast was a plain north country girl, rather too large for her bones and with a tendency to go too red in the sun, but even so, Gerry and Clare had a relationship. Affair would be a better word. Strange affair, a still better two words. Like most other things with Clare, it had been off, on, off, on and now it was definitely off, forever, never again. Until next time.

'So he's still here then?' I asked.

'For the moment,' snorted Clare.

'Is he likely to be going somewhere?'

Clare shrugged. 'If he doesn't have to go back for treatment then he'll just have to go when he stops fighting it basically. They want to chuck him out and make him the scapegoat. He spends most of his time in the camps or across the border at the moment, trying to negotiate on the refugees. The government wants to just send them all home, but the aid people don't want them to go because they'll all be massacred as soon as they cross the border.'

There had been articles in the press for weeks about lawlessness in the refugee camps. It was an open secret that they were out of control in all of the neighbouring countries, full of armed gangs of genocidal murderers who didn't give a damn for their fellow refugees, the aid agencies or anyone else.

'What's this about an illness?'

'He's got leukaemia,' Clare said. 'That's what I couldn't tell you before.'

I stopped and thought of Gerry the last time I'd seen him, pissed at the Alhamisi, giggling and cackling away drunkenly.

Has he bollocks! I thought to myself. I don't believe a word of it. He's bullshitting again. And I can't believe that you are still falling for it!

'Do you fancy some lunch across at the Africa?' I offered.

*

66

Service at the Africa was its usual desultory all-day breakfast self. The chef on duty with a frying pan to cook eggs or omelettes on request was a particularly blank looking woman who put slices of bread into the toaster beside her every so often. Then a round stuck. She ignored it as smoke began to rise, billowing up to hit the suspended ceiling, before starting to drift down the room while she carried on manoeuvring some fried eggs around the pan with a spatula, seemingly completely oblivious. We had had enough. We got up and left the battlefield.

We stopped to buy chocolate in Sharik's hotel lobby shop.

A large fat local man said *shikamu* and bobbed a respectful nod to Sharik as he squeezed into the overcrowded kiosk and edged past between us and the imported biscuits, black hair dye and pirated Chuck Norris videos at the back of the shop.

'*Shikamu*?' Clare hissed in dramatically exaggerated disbelief at the respectfully formal greeting, her eyebrows arched as she nodded her head at Sharik, 'him?'

Sharik was short, fat and very much the *wahindi* shopkeeper. Not the sort that any self respecting *wananchi* would regard as his superior even if he was some kind of wheeler dealer and had as a sideline some ill-defined business brokerage role in the firm.

Clare found him irritating and referred to him disparagingly as 'everybody's favourite uncle'. He was smug, liked to think he knew it all and had an opinion on everything.

Now he asked, 'How are you getting on in Mkilwa?'

'Oh we're still in court,' I said.

'See,' he said and smiled patronisingly. 'I told you so; these guys are too clever for you.'

Sod off, I thought, selecting an overpriced Kenyan Mars bar and checking how far past its sell-by date it was.

As we paid and turned to leave the cubby hole of a shop, the fat man squeezed past again. Just as he was behind me, he stooped down for a moment and standing up again, handed me a piece of paper. '*Samahene* bwana, you dropped this, I think.'

Surprised in the act of pulling open the awkward glass door, I took it with a hasty, '*asante*.'

'What was that?' asked Clare, who'd gone out in front of me.

'Oh just something I dropped,' I said as the African disappeared round the corner into the main lobby and out of the front door.

I was sure that I hadn't let anything slip. Along with the work in my folder, I was carrying the drafts of my next newsletter home, my pre-election special. Given my outrageous comments about the Party and Rais, I was paranoid about security, always keeping each draft either locked away, or as now, in my folder where I could keep an eye on it.

I paused for a moment in the hotel lobby as Clare perused a boutique window. The paper I had been handed was A4, folded in quarters. It didn't look like the firm's, it was too cheap, coarse and absorbent even for them, with the ruled lines a blurred blue fudge, trailing off short of the edge of the paper.

I opened it out. I had been right, it wasn't mine. It was a note from Dave, asking if we could meet at the Golden Shower that evening.

*

As I waited for a gap in the streaming evening traffic to be able to turn into the car park, I idly stared at the election posters on the wall opposite.

The podgy, gormless features of Ahmed, the Party's candidate, his eyes hidden behind thick rimmed glasses, smiled out inanely under his white kofte from thousands of sites everywhere I looked. He could have got a better picture from a booth at Woolworth's. The same shot appeared in his press ad with the simple message, 'Vote for Ahmed, he's the best.'

Pesha's posters by contrast were powerfully haunting, but not necessarily in the way he might have intended. His photograph was a striking image against a blue bordered white background, his head tilted slightly forwards, his eyes looking up at you direct, boring in. His smile was a strange affair, almost a smirk, as if he hadn't been able to decide whether to look stern or approachable. The whole effect was to make him look menacingly, leeringly, completely insane.

Posters were everywhere, stuck across advertising hoardings, cars, or each other, while rival supporters had ripped jagged white-fringed strips out of the faces of the opposing candidates.

For sheer numbers, Ahmed seemed to be winning the poster war but the weather was doing Pesha's work for him. Ahmed's posters were bleaching in the sunlight, the green background fading to blue, the photograph turning yellow. But even where the Party's supporters had torn off Pesha's face, a dark blue border was left edged with white with a blank space in the middle. A haunting gone but not forgotten image in my headlights as I turned across the street.

*

The Golden Shower was a mosquito-plagued snack bar-cum-brothel behind tall hedges at the busy crossroads just the Boma side of Kusini Bridge, the courtyard dominated by the eponymous Golden Shower tree. Tables were scattered around a courtyard and the thick bushes and trees screening it from the road were strung with brightly coloured fairy lights and dotted with spotlights. Somewhere off in the darkness a generator thrummed away to itself while a crowd of particularly sullen looking prostitutes lurked at the tables at the far end of the garden, eyeing up any *mzungu* or likely *vigogo* who walked in as a potential punter. I idly speculated on how often they got a taker. Often enough to make their investment in a Coke worth the rent of a seat in the bar, I concluded.

As I sat there, suddenly thrust in front of my startled view was a black *makonde* sculpture, the regional speciality. I loathed them and waved it away. '*Hapana,* no I don't want anything like that. It's too small. I like the big ones. The giraffes with spots,' I added inconsequentially to deflect the disappointed hawker.

Dave arrived a few minutes after I had sat down. With him was an African. Though I'd only seen him briefly in the shop, I was immediately certain this was the man who had handed me the note.

They sat down at the table with a handshake from Dave and a nodded *habari* from the African who immediately set about arranging some service by hissing and waving at a waiter.

'*Wewe,*' he shouted when it didn't work. One of the staff looked up from his conversation at the bar. The African held his hand up to pluck the air for service.

The waiter shambled over, idly flicking a cloth at some flies on the next table.

After the formalities, it was down to business.

'*Hapa bitings?*'

Of course they had bitings. I ordered goat and chips. Dave and the African, chicken. One of the surprises about Africa was how good the chips always were. And 'Castle *mbili na Spriti moja.*'

'Castle *baridi,*' I interjected. It was a *wazungu* oddity to like drinks *baridi* – cold, or better still *baridi sana,* very cold. The locals' continued preference for drinks *moto* suggested the village electrification programmes hadn't been too successful. But they were all mad for the sweet sodas.

The beers and the Sprite arrived with a round of *asante sanas*. We waited in respectful silence while the waiter popped the crown corks and poured out the first part of each of the drinks into the glasses.

'Cheers.'

'Cheers.'

Dave and I took first sucks at the froth on our beers.

'OK,' I opened the conversation, slowly and carefully pouring more beer into my glass, a good deal more skilfully than the waiter had managed. 'What's up? Why all the cloak and dagger?'

Dave remained silent as a boy appeared without speaking beside us with a bowl and jug. He went round the table, holding out the bowl to each in turn and we each automatically clasped our hands above it as he poured water into our cupped palms for us to rinse before our food arrived. *Wananchi* eat with their hands.

'This is Mr Mkate,' said Dave, when the washboy had gone, making the introductions. A formal African handshake this time, forearm to forearm, and a grunted, 'Good to meet you.'

'Mr Mkate is from the SPU,' Dave continued. 'He's working with me on something for the bank. And now it involves you.'

There was a sudden screaming and flurry of commotion in the corner, the girls scattering, men were rushing across and a small crowd gathering, shouting, and jostling to get a view but not too close.

'What is it?'

The back of Mr Mkate's thick bull neck was towards me as he looked round to the source of the noise. 'Is snake,' he said.

A stick had appeared, and then another. I could see blows being struck and people jumping back. Then one must have hit home. Suddenly blows were raining down, the tension and fear was released, people were relaxing, no longer scared but laughing, chatting, and then there was one big *mama* with a long thin shape dangling over the end of a branch as she tossed the lifeless form into the bushes.

'You get them here, this close to the mangroves,' said Dave, nonchalantly.

In the West the rich are often thin. Here they were almost always fat, *vigogo*, running to huge swollen paunches as evidence of ready access to too much beer and too much sugar with no exercise.

Bwana Mkate was fat, I noticed.

I had met Dave, a crop headed ex city fraud squad officer, now working as a private consultant a couple of times and now, smoking his Café Crèmes he conformed to type. He was pleasant enough in a bluff, no nonsense, and distant way.

'Has the bank told you anything about this lot in Mkilwa?' Dave asked directly in his soft London accent, taking me by surprise.

'No, not really. What's your involvement?'

'I was brought in about a year ago by the Yanks the IMF have put in to sort out the bank. My job is to investigate the frauds they are finding across the PCB,' Dave explained. 'And in April they asked me to have a look at New Mwanchi. The company had raised a bill to an Italian company for an export of about two million dollars and sold the debt to the bank.'

'So?' I asked.

'So, when the bank went to collect the cash from the Italians, they didn't pay.'

'Surprise, surprise,' I said sardonically.

'Quite,' agreed Dave. 'The Italians said they had a credit note which cancelled the outstanding bill.'

'What for?'

'For supplying machinery.'

'Did they provide any machinery?'

'No one knows, I went up to the factory in May to try and do some digging and they threw me out on my ear.'

'In May? But that's four months before we were appointed.'

'What's more the credit note and transaction is all official.'

'What do you mean?' I asked, puzzled.

'Under the forex control rules it needs Central Bank approval. I've seen the correspondence. Don't ask how.'

'I wouldn't have dreamed of doing so.' Things happened in Africa when people started asking questions. Unpleasant things.

'What's more, approval was granted within twelve hours of the application.'

'Twelve hours!' I exclaimed, shocked.

'That's right, the same day. People worked overtime at the bank to get it out.'

'That's impossible. Or rather it's not.' I rubbed my thumb against the finger of my right hand suggestively and shrugged.

'You get it,' said Dave, nodding.

Mkate was looking bored. Presumably he knew all this already if he and Dave were working together.

'So who are the Italians?' I asked, as if I couldn't guess.

'A front,' confirmed Dave. 'I had some digging done in Italy. The shareholding goes offshore to Bermuda and beyond. The director is a nominee lawyer based in Monaco but I'm pretty confident that when I get to the bottom of it, I will find it's owned by the same people.'

'So it was a fraud?' I asked rhetorically. 'We're dealing with a bunch of crooks who have the Bank in court and who have already thrown you out on your ear – and PCB passes it to us as a job without a word of warning. Thanks a bunch,' I said with feeling. 'I'll have words with Kiponglea next time I saw him – dapper little bastard.'

'That's not all,' said Dave.

'There's more?' I asked. I had been watching the interplay between Dave and Mr Mkate. Mr Mkate seemed to be sitting back surveying the scene and covertly, I was sure, the bar girls. Was he even listening? Dave was leaning forward. His voice low and insistent, discrete and intent. Did he trust Mkate? I couldn't tell.

'Oh yes. When we started digging into the background we quickly found it wasn't quite what it seemed,' Dave continued. 'I've had some friends of mine back home try and trace some of the exports. Up to last year they went strictly to England and Europe, particularly Holland, although over the last two years or so they've started to ship back to Pakistan as well, which doesn't make any sense at all to me. Each to a trading company that is either linked or untraceable. At first I thought it was just a transfer pricing scam, you know selling cheap to a captive trader overseas, who then bumps the price up to the full open market value before selling on. That way you get to keep both the profit and the hard currency out of the country.'

'Tax evasion?'

'Of course; duty evasion, sales tax frauds, transfer pricing, understating imports to avoid duty.'

'All the normal then?'

'Economic sabotage,' said Mkate fiercely, suddenly switching his attention back to the conversation. I sensed a hardness, a power that I had missed before.

Dave raised his eyebrows expressively at me. He looked long suffering. 'Possibly,' he conceded, 'but possibly not.'

'Well, what then?' I asked.

'It's the odd connections in Europe, particularly the heavy trade into Holland, which always makes my ears prick up. We all know about the tax evasion that goes on here to get money out of the country. But this is a bit different. It's too complex just to be to hide stuff from the tax guys out here. Nominee companies in Bermuda, I ask you!'

I was frankly sceptical at this stage. 'Yes, but,' he said, 'firstly a hell of a lot of international trading is done from the Netherlands. Look how many multi-nationals have their headquarters there! The Dutch have been a sea trading nation for even longer than we have; they've tax treaties with almost every country in the world. If you are into almost any type of international business it's the most tax efficient place to be. And anyway, perhaps New Mwanchi have just been going a long time and have had lots of money to conceal. Perhaps over the years they took the time to set it up properly. You don't know what it has been like to run a business here.'

Mkate was talking to the waiter, ordering more drinks. Dave leant forward towards me, shaking his head. 'No, it's not just that. I've got this funny feeling about the place,' he said quietly. 'Call it a hunch if you like, nothing more.'

'So why are you talking to me?'

'Well,' said Dave, sitting back. 'We, that is, Bwana Mkate and I, are going to try to take another look. So firstly I want to know everything you know about the place, layout, how it works, who's who, the lot. Any information I get from the bank is somewhat suspect and I don't want to be seen to be asking too many questions in case I tip them off.'

'You think they have an informer inside the bank?' I asked, nodding. It would make sense.

'It's a risk,' he conceded. 'You lads have really stirred up a hornets' nest out there. So, secondly, I want to know what you have in mind so I can make my own plans.'

'Well,' I said as Mkate turned back, 'the layout is like this,' and I began to describe the site from our short tour.

*

'OK,' I said, sitting back. 'So what happens next?'

'As far as you're concerned? Nothing. You just keep on with what you're doing. Keep grinding away through the courts. They'll have investigated you already and decided that you are what you are. Just an accountant doing a job.

'There is one last thing though that I came across while I was looking at the Central Bank forex records,' Dave added. 'It could be something or could be nothing. They've been importing some interesting chemicals for a while which is odd in itself,' he said without elaborating, 'but over the last year or so they've suddenly started importing large quantities of acid and mercury. Would you know anything about that?'

'What? Mercury, as in the metal?'

'Yes. They brought in about a hundred kilos last year.'

'Why would they want to do that?'

'Nobody seems to have any idea. They never have before, but I would be interested to find out.'

'Hey, you never know, Dave. Perhaps they just use this sort of stuff for processing their metals. Not everything's suspicious you know.'

'It is when you've been a policeman as long as I have, son. Now then,' he said leaning forwards intently, 'tell me again about this smell.'

*

After Dave and Mkate left, an hour and a couple of beers later, I stayed to finish my last Castle and decline the advances of two of the girls.

Mkate was from Mkilwa. That had been clear as we talked. So he had presumably been assigned to help Dave because he knew the area, the local language and probably some of the people.

That sort of help could be very useful, I thought. Or very dangerous. And was it my imagination or had a third girl trailed Mkate out?

Just an accountant doing a job. I shook my head. Time to go.

I looked up as a two metre tall, painted giraffe loomed over me, lit by the strings of bulbs between the trees around the bar. The old trader in his ragged shirt and floppy white hat was back again. The giraffe had reticulation, it had painted eyes, nose and mouth. The trader had an expectant hopeful gap toothed smile.

'*Twiga* bwana, *twiga kubwa... na* spots.'

I stared at it blearily, '*Ndiyo.*' It certainly was a giraffe, it certainly was a bloody big giraffe and it certainly did have spots. I toyed momentarily with the practicalities of getting it back to the apartment. It would just about fit in the Suzuki, diagonally, if its head stuck out of the passenger window. Then I shook his head and got up somewhat unsteadily to go.

'*Hapana, mzee.* No thanks, I don't want it.' I slipped the surprised old man a fifty bob note. 'Nice try, bwana. Better luck next time,' I said as I left. It made me feel better.

5 From our own correspondent

Friday, 11 November, Jijenga

'Gin and tonic?'

Life went on as usual after that odd evening.

'Oh my, yes, how civilised,' Sam trilled from across the room where she was looking at some pictures. 'Isn't it wonderful to be moving in with a Brit?'

The tourist trade was improving and there were now a couple of galleries selling quite sophisticated prints and paintings, some by Africans, some by *wazungu*.

'They're nice,' said Sam, over her shoulder, studying one of my pair of striking black and white Mutashobyas. 'How much were they?' So I told her. 'Oh that's quite reasonable isn't it? Especially if you've got a limited edition like that.'

She was broad in the beam as one of my bosses back home would have put it. I thought she had the air of a small but powerfully determined bulldozer. Watching her walk anywhere from behind, I always had a powerful mental image of clanking caterpillar tracks and shovels.

'Yes,' I said, from the sofa. 'It should make you quite a nice living. Run off a couple of thousand of your prints, mark them all up as whatever out of five hundred and start selling them off to tourists. Away you go. Who is ever going to know? Make a fortune over the years.'

Sam, intent on examining the pictures, was nodding absentmindedly and hadn't really been listening but Ish coming in from the kitchen with more drinks threw back his head and laughed. 'You cynical bastard. You get worse, not better.'

'So what was that press release all about then?' I turned back to Ish. 'There's something oddly unreassuring about the police and army issuing a joint statement that there won't be a coup after the election!'

'It's a bit of a hanging non sequitur isn't it?' Ish agreed '"of course we'll support the government". But it was in response to the letter.'

I obviously looked particularly blank at that moment. 'Didn't you hear about it?' Ish asked in surprise.

'No.'

'Someone circulated a letter to the junior officers, saying

basically, that if it looks like the election is going the wrong way, just watch your step boys.'

'Meaning what?'

Ish held up his hands. 'Whatever anyone wants it to mean, I guess.'

'Who sent it?'

'Well that's a good question,' Ish drawled. 'Some plutocrats apparently. *Habari* got hold of it and printed a copy but the police were round before the first edition hit the street and threw the editor in jail. I think there's a copy going around our newsroom on the quiet but everyone on high is running around like a headless chicken not daring to squeak but not quite knowing what to do with it.'

He took a drag on his beer, 'It's nice to know the church is finally taking a stand though. There was a wonderful headline in the *Citizen* the other day, "Now is not yet the time to arrest editors", did you see it?'

I shook my head.

'Wonderful, it just about said, "but in two weeks' time boys – round them all up".'

'It's excellent,' Sam brayed, tearing herself away from the art to rejoin the mundane world. 'What was it the paper called him recently?'

'Fat,' prompted Ish, helpfully.

'That's it,' she nodded, waving her glass vaguely in his direction in acknowledgement and warming to her performance. 'Fat, complacent and to charisma what Princess Di is to marriage.' Sam dissolved into booze-induced giggles. She had moved on, 'I mean really, what a way to talk about the President!'

She was blonde. Very blonde. Dibby really at times. I'd been hard pressed at first to decide and had thought it was all an act. But no, she really was hopeless. Lovely, fun, and a hell of a lot more organised than she let on, she had to be to run her research project in the face of local bureaucracy up in Mkilwa, but when she came down to Jijenga and could afford to be, she was hopeless.

'That'll have been one of the opposition newspapers then?' I observed rather unnecessarily. 'So how's the project?'

'Oh the usual, I've been doing some work in the national archives on the statistics, comparative mortality rates, that sort of thing. Honestly you should see it in there. There are all these old, battered, African files with little bits of paper with scribbled notes on them that go way back. You really get a feel for what it must have been like. Three white colonial administrators with responsibility for this huge area and all these issues getting dealt with by correspondence. And of course nothing ever got resolved; it all just used to drag on for years and years.'

'Ready for a top up?' I asked.

'Yes please. Anyway, what I really wanted to see were the registers of births and deaths but that's on microfiche.'

'No microfiche reader?' I enquired.

'No, no, don't be so cynical, of course they've got a microfiche reader.'

'But *mama*, there has to be a problem,' I goaded her.

'Oh yes! We have a problem.' She picked up her glass. 'The bulb has been blown since 1989.'

That's what I liked about them, they were like a breath of fresh air.

Monday, 14 November, Jijenga

'Ah, Paul, am I glad to see you,' Winston greeted me.

'Why, what's up?'

'Do you know anything about this?' Winston went over to the cupboard on the far side of his room and carefully unlocked it and handed me a big brown envelope with PCB's crest on it. Winston's and the firm's names had been blocked out painstakingly in blue ink capital letters.

'From the bank?' I lifted the flap and peered inside. 'Looks like another appointment,' I said cheerfully.

'It is,' said Winston.

I looked up at him. 'What have we got?' I said, as I started to pull the papers out.

'We haven't,' he said, 'at least I hope we haven't. That's what I want to talk to you about.'

Surprised, I let the papers slip back inside the envelope. 'What's the problem?'

'These came in when you were on safari.'

I'd had to explain to my office back home that 'on safari' simply meant away on a trip, as otherwise they thought I was away lion watching every time they got through on the phone.

'I didn't know what to do with them,' he continued, 'so I just stuck them in my cupboard. I was away myself last week when on the Wednesday I received a message by telex that by any means, I must, call Mzee Mulango, immediately.'

I was intrigued. We usually dealt with Kiponglea, the head of the bank's legal department. What was so important that the bank's managing director had to get involved personally?

'So I had to travel sixty kilometres to find a telephone to call Mulango,' Winston continued, 'who told me that whatever I did, not to do anything with the documents. So here they are. I just want to know what my position is.'

'Well,' I said, 'have you done anything? Have you formally accepted the appointment?'

'No, I've not signed anything,' he said.

'Well then, you should be in the clear,' I said. 'You have to actually agree to become a receiver. People can't just foist it on you.'

Winston gave an exaggerated brow-mopping 'phew', taking the envelope back out of my hands. He appeared to cheer up immensely as if I had just lifted a huge weight from his shoulders.

After a moment, I said, 'Oh come on Winston, you can't leave me in suspense. What's it all about?'

'Well,' said Winston slowly and carefully, looking thoughtfully at the envelope, as though ordering things in his mind, 'have you heard of Lazima?'

'Lazima?' It rang a vague bell. 'Yes, Kiponglea mentioned it at one stage. He seemed to assume I would know who he meant and that I'd understand when he said he'd like to do something about it but of course he'd never get the chance. So I let it go at the time.' Obviously this had been a mistake. 'What is it?'

'It is, or was, the Party's trading organisation,' Winston explained. 'It used to run all the regional trading stores, and the nationalised industries back in the seventies. All the Party high-ups had a hand in it and it had a hand in almost everything that went on in the economy.'

'OK, I see,' I said, nodding, 'I get the picture. But now presumably it's been looted, is as bust as a bust thing is and in hock to the bank for millions, if not billions?'

Winston grinned, 'Yes, I should think so.'

'Anyway, this…' he said, turning to lock it away again in his wall cupboard. 'This,' he shook the envelope, before throwing it into the cupboard, and shutting the door, 'is my appointment as receiver and manager of Lazima.' He turned the key and straightened up.

'Shit!' I was so shocked, I laughed out loud, who the hell had pulled that stunt? 'You can't be serious. But the election is only a couple of weeks away.' Jeez. No wonder Winston was nervous. This really was playing with the big boys.

'Someone at the bank is playing politics here aren't they?'

'Precisely,' said Winston, putting the key back in his briefcase. 'And we need to do whatever we have to in order to keep the firm out of it. Mulango was on safari over the weekend. He got back into town on Tuesday to find that in his absence all this paperwork had been raised and sent across to me. He was absolutely livid when I spoke to him on the phone.'

I was giggling by now, 'So I expect it's not all sweetness and light at the bank at the moment?'

'No. An unholy row I should think,' Winston agreed.

I shook my head sorrowfully, 'Excellent. What a way to run a railroad.'

'How's Iain getting on in Mkilwa?' he asked, changing the subject.

I shrugged, 'Ah well, not so good I'm afraid. We're still in court on a regular basis, including today, as a matter of fact, but the way the fix is we aren't really getting anywhere. In fact, unless something dramatic happens in court this morning, Iain's catching tomorrow afternoon's ferry back across the lake.'

'Why?' asked Winston.

'I'm pulling him out. We're not really achieving very much at the moment, so he might as well come back to Jijenga.'

'OK, that makes sense,' said Winston.

'He'll stay over in Bharanku Tuesday night, M'gola Wednesday, and be back here late Thursday, depending on the roads, the weather, and the car.'

Iain had said yesterday the long drought had broken early up by the lake as it always did, with the first of the short rains, fierce tropical storms, hours of ferocious winds and torrential rain. After a few days it would settle down to dull overcast and wet weather for a month or two, but those first deluges would turn the roads by the lake to mud, to be churned into thick deep brown slime by the passing cars and lorries, making driving treacherous. And depending on the severity, the lake crossing could be very uncomfortable too. The problem was that the storms blew up so fast that the ferry could be well out on the lake when they broke without warning, leaving the boat no option but to just ride it out.

The only mercy was that the truly awful storms didn't last long, usually blowing themselves out in a few hours, fading away like a nightmare on waking, leaving behind a clear blue sky, bright green vegetation, shining mud and steaming puddles, as people emerged from shelter into the temporary freshness before the sun turned the air into a steamy sauna. That reminded me.

'Winston, we have got to sort something out about the Landie. It's a complete nightmare.'

Winston grinned, 'OK, OK, yes, I know. Look, do me a favour. Take it up with Yakeen, will you? Cars are his baby.'

But Yakeen was out. Next time, I thought to myself as I walked out of Kahawa House into the dusty white sunlight.

Wednesday, 16 November, Jijenga

Yakeen was out again, so I called in on Clare. I always tried to pop in and see her whenever I was down on the fourth floor. I liked to follow her ups and downs, her daily mood reversals about men, booze, the firm, Winston, Shitface and whatever, whoever. She was looking cheerful today.

'You're on good form today. It must have been a light night at the Yacht Club,' I greeted her. 'What are you giving up? Is it men or booze this time?'

'No, nothing like that.'

'That's a pity, I was going to start a new sweepstake.'

'You bastard, I can't believe you did that.' No, it was a client she was laughing about. 'The accountant won't come out of his office. There's no books and no records, you can't verify stock – you can't even trace the fixed assets.'

'Sounds familiar.'

'It's really sad,' Clare went on. 'They're a bunch of naive South Africans who wanted to be first in the market and they didn't do any research. They thought it would be just like SA and the seller's really stitched them up. He's sold them their fifty per cent at way over price and he's sat back laughing. He'll wait until they give up and he can buy it back cheap. Or if they make a go of it, he gets to cream in the profit while they do the work.' She was shaking her head with mirth.

'The accountant's suicidal. He just sits in his office all day. He told me that every time he goes out and talks to people it just gets worse. He talked to the tax man, next thing he knew they brought in

81

this huge tax bill. He doesn't think they owe it, but who knows… He says, "If I stay in my room and don't talk to anyone, surely it can't get any worse."'

'Oh yes it can,' I laughed. 'Any news of shitface's latest camping holiday?'

'Yes he's back,' conceded Clare grudgingly.

'How did it go?'

'Oh fine,' she said. 'But there are problems up at the camp.'

'Oh, what sort?'

'Well the usual politics, guns and stuff.'

'Speaking of which, I've found you a job.' I said delving into my folder. 'You're always talking about how you fancy travel and excitement. How about that then?' and I handed here the full page advert I'd cut out to show her.

'I don't believe it!' she said, jaw agape. 'Is this for real?'

'I guess so, it's from this week's Economist. You can keep it,' I said, waving goodbye.

She gave me a distracted wave in return, while shaking her head, obviously still fascinated by the ad.

'It's coming to something when the CIA has to advertise vacancies. He'll love this,' she added almost to herself as I left.

*

Gerry had all sorts of problems. Funnily enough, I saw him that night. As usual he was pissed, unusually he was desperately trying to shake of a girl who was after him.

I had gone out with Ish to the Europa Bar, an out of the way sort of place down a dirt track off the Old Bahari Road towards Mutabendewe Beach. It was a real *wazungu* and whores hideout of three interconnecting rooms, set out in large booths where the older white guys could sit and talk and drink, while their young black professional girlfriends sat in rented silence or gossiped together in low Kiswahili. Run by Gary, a silver-haired ex-surfer from Hawaii, the place was styled after an American ski lodge, all dark wood and alpine view posters, with a bandoleer of bitters shots hanging above the optics and was as close to a Western bar as you were ever going to get out here, with reliably cold beer and great food. For the moment at least, it was the fashionable place to eat and drink and was its usual noisy self as we walked in.

Back at the table with the beers, 'How's the scribing going?' I asked Ish.

'Oh, OK, I guess.'

He had the latest on life at the *News* where he was making most of his living as a freelance paid by the word. Looking for new strings to his bow he had launched a restaurant critic's column which added entertainment to any meal. On a weekly basis I reckoned, it should keep him going for a couple of months before he started to run into problems finding somewhere to go, or food poisoning, whichever came first.

'Are you making any progress?'

'Well, it's difficult. One thing I've decided is that I really want to make a go out of this.'

'What, as in permanently?'

'Yes. I've made up my mind that I want to stick with journalism when Sam and I go back, to make a real career out of it. So I need to get into the papers at home and as far as I can see the only way to do that is that I have to pick up a really good juicy story if I'm going to stand any chance of breaking in.'

'No sign of one?'

'Nothing that is going to set the world on fire at home. At least not yet,' he said brightly. He was never one to let anything get him down.

'I am also writing for the features section. Basically anything I can get a couple of thousand words out of, they'll publish. I've really surprised myself with how quickly I have discovered a talent for blagging. If you don't mind knowing that every so often someone is going to say, "No, bugger off," it's amazing what you can get if you can just pluck up the nerve to ask for it,' he said, modestly. I'm thinking of trying a motoring column – Hello, is that International Motors? I'm a journalist from the *News*, I'd like to do a test drive on your latest Landcruiser...'

'So where did you get to last night? I didn't hear you come in.' I asked, interested in the practicalities of why Ish had stayed in town this week, rather than going with Sam who was off up the coast in Kigoyo for a few days at some health-conference.

'Well, I went to see the girls who strip...'

I nearly choked on my beer.

'...Have you been there?'

I couldn't say as I had.

'Well it's this road up towards Kaolo. It's just wall to wall bars. The road's called Gaza Street, hence Gaza strip.'

Aha, I thought. It was becoming slightly clearer now.

'I went out with the sub-editors. They work from 3pm till late, but then those boys really know how to party afterwards. I only got back home at 7am. I tell you we only just escaped with our lives. Those working girls at the bars, you know, they just dive straight in. Hope I didn't disturb you when I got back? Are you sure that you don't mind us camping out like this?'

'Hell no, as I say I didn't hear you. Treat the place as home, you know that you two are welcome to stay at my place for as long as you like.'

'Hey thanks, Paul,' he said. 'Thanks really kind of you, we really appreciate it. I don't know how we'll ever repay you.'

'Don't be daft. It's OK, no problem at all. I'm just glad to be able to help.' I stumbled, unsure myself what my real motives were and unable to meet his smiling gaze. 'I'm just being selfish really, I like the company.'

He laughed. 'Yeah sure.'

'So what's the inside story on Bharanku?' I asked, to cover my embarrassment, turning the conversation sombre.

We *wazungu* had been the last to know as the news had broken on Kiswahili radio at lunchtime, with the messengers whispering the word around the office to local staff in hushed tones that the morning ferry from Mkilwa to Bharanku had gone down.

'Well it looks like it's really bad. Rais flew back across there this afternoon. Talk is that tomorrow might be declared a day of national mourning.'

'The office messenger told us that according to the radio it turned turtle just outside the harbour at Mkilwa,' I said, 'but didn't sink immediately.'

'That sounds about right from what I've heard so far at the rag,' said Ish. 'It was the older one, the smaller passenger and car ferry, not the big Ro-Ro, thank God, or there would probably have been even more casualties.'

'There's going to have been enough as it is. Any word on numbers yet?'

'Nothing definite. But it's going to be hundreds, certainly.'

'Oh, absolutely,' I said, 'bound to be. But what I don't understand is why? That old steamer must have been nigh on fifty years old. It looked as though it probably took tanks across to Normandy. Why did it suddenly roll over just outside port and sink?'

'No one knows, but I guess they'll be trying to find out. Rumour is that they've asked SA to send up some navy divers to go down and have a look at the wreck. Thank heavens you think Iain crossed over yesterday,' he observed, shuddering. 'Oh, it's horrible. It doesn't bear thinking about.'

It was hideous and he was right. It didn't bear thinking about. We changed the subject.

'Well, visas are a bit of an issue of course. All the East African countries are getting upset at the number of their citizens being slung into jail in Europe for smuggling. Its small beer at the moment but it's starting to be a worry for the powers that be here. We had a piece on it last week, it tied up with the arrest of a gang up in Mkilwa for shipping out hash.'

'I know I saw it, something like thirty-five *wananchi* behind bars in Sweden of whom thirty-three are for drug offences, wasn't it?'

'Yes, something like that. But now the Europeans are all delighted that they can bring in visa requirements.'

'What, is that Schengen?'

'Yes. But that's just an excuse. They've all been wanting to do it for ages to try and cut down the numbers and to cut down on drugs, particularly the Brits. It used to be the Nigerians but these days they are hiring anyone they can find to act as mules. One of the problems for smugglers these days seems to be routes. Anything or anyone coming in to Europe or the States direct from Nigeria or the producing countries like Afghanistan or Pakistan, say, is automatically suspect, so the Nigerians are thought to be looking for more innocent seeming people or places through which to run stuff.

Of course most of it goes into Holland but even so the British have been well and truly stuck. It's diplomatically very sensitive, commonwealth countries and all that, and they've been very touchy about appearing racist. But now Schengen has come along with its dismantling of most of the EC's internal border controls and it's the answer to their prayers because they have all had to introduce visa requirements for non-EC citizens.'

'And 9/11?'

'And 9/11. That has made everyone more twitchy about all sorts of traffic from what are after all largely Moslem countries.'

'Look at the embassy bombings, Nairobi, Dar Es Salaam. Why not here? Or I suppose, people from here?'

'Precisely! Every reason in the world to want to tighten up.'

'So, perfect, the government back home can shrug its shoulders sorrowfully and say, ah well, we didn't want to but we have to abide by EC law. Sorry chaps.'

*

It was just about then that Gerry of the flashy jewellery had arrived at the Europa Bar trailed by a stunningly monosyllabic French girl with long blonde hair who turned heads as she walked up to the bar and leant across to order a drink. Quite how she managed to get that short a skirt to sway like that, while showing that much leg, intrigued me.

They sat down, the scowling Gerry managing to place himself next to me at the end of the table, the noise of the increasingly crowded bar neatly forcing the French girl into a separate conversation with Ish at the other end of the table. Something that Ish didn't seem to mind at all, I noticed.

'So who's this one?' I subtly enquired, with a jerk of my head in the blonde's direction.

'Oh she's some Frenchie bit, come out from the Hague,' he muttered into his Castle, 'another bloody bean counter. You should get on with her.'

So I gathered that she was an accountant. But it turned out no, it was worse than that, she was an auditor from head office. Come out to check up on the books, and yes Gerry would have another Castle. Gerry and she had already had a major run in, and surprise, surprise, he was still smarting from the encounter.

'How's it going?' I asked. Gerry steepled his hands like a defrocked priest, his muscular forearms and chunky gold identity bracelet resting on the table.

'Ah now then,' he said. 'Now there's a story for you.'

'Do tell,' I prodded.

'Well if you must know, it's a bloody nightmare and it'll be worse when that Godamn shit Tengisa makes Minister of Foreign Affairs,' Gerry finished with vengeance.

'Why, what's he to do with you?'

'He's the Godamn bastard who's jacked my hospitals.'

'How the hell do you steal a hospital?'

'It's Godamn simple,' said Gerry, warming to his theme. 'You just don't give it back.' Gerry looked shocked when I laughed out loud. 'Look, we have a supply of these fully collapsible, transportable hospitals. It's all tents, but there are operating theatres,

86

wards, the works.

So as soon as the refugee crisis started, HQ shipped three of these things out here in support of the local organisation. We're sort of a federation of individual country organisations and unless we have to get directly involved because, say, there's a civil war, HQ just acts as a sort of coordinating and supporting body for the local staff.'

'OK,' I said. 'So what happened this time?'

'Well, it was an emergency, so HQ sent these hospitals out as a loan and the Hague will want them back so that they can keep the books straight for the benefit of the top brass over in New York when it comes to seeking more dough from the donors. The only trouble is, it was all done in such a rush that my predecessor didn't bother to get the local oppos to sign the piece of paper to say those were the terms. So Tengisa, who heads it up, said thank you very much for the gift, very generous of you. He knows it wasn't a Godamn gift.' Gerry disappeared cursing into his can of Castle, coming up for breath to wave at the barman to bring another.

'Anyhow my job at the moment is to try and get the Godamn things back,' he continued. 'The problem is that Tengisa is looking to be made Foreign Minister post-election so he's going round proudly trumpeting that he has wangled a donation of three hospitals.'

'So what can we do? We can hardly repossess them.' He shook his head. 'I don't think so. No, we'll get them back eventually after we've paid whatever price he wants for them. There'll be a deal. There's always a deal to be done.'

Yes, I knew there was always a deal, about anything.

'And so the last thing I need hanging about just at the moment is an auditor.'

Well I could see that. Which is more than the barman could, who didn't seem to have noticed Gerry's frantic waving for a refill, so Gerry looked around for a waiter to order another Castle. 'Oh Christ no,' he said. 'It's Lydia. I've been trying to get rid of this sodding girl for weeks,' he hissed conspiratorially towards me as he looked up and with a big fixed grin said, 'Hi Lydia,' to the beaming guided missile purposefully homing in on him.

Lydia was a fixture of the local scene. A vaguely Mediterranean looking girl, married to some sort of a Russian who ran one of the beach hotels up towards Kigoyo. She didn't seem to spend much time up the coast and was forever to be seen around the city of an evening, accompanied by one of the floating population of South African croupiers who worked the casino or whatever visitors she could find.

I'd noticed her when we'd come in, dancing loudly in the bar with a group of drunken visiting South African cricketers. She appeared to have sized up the shortest and baldest as her companion for the night. Ish and I had kept our heads down. We didn't think she'd noticed us.

Now she fell onto the bench next to, if not on, Gerry, caught hold of his left arm and started whispering to him. Watching, I could see his body stiffen and tense, an unusual situation for Gerry. By now I was seriously pissed, again. That was one of the dangers of going to the Europa Bar. We had been waiting an hour and a half for food to arrive. The food was good, excellent even, but they only had one cooker in the kitchen. When you could seat seventy-five people for dinner and were popular, that was a serious disadvantage for the diners if not bar sales. Ish's review, one of his first, had been entitled *Patience Rewarded*.

'Have you tried being deliberately rude to her?' I said into Gerry's free ear. I sat back and observed for a few moments. This didn't seem to have had the required effect but it was potentially quite fun. Ish was deep in conversation with the French girl. I looked round the bar again with a drunken contentedness and wondered whether it was getting to the point where the ritual trip up to the staff at the end of the bar and complaint about the delay in arrival of the food was due, as was customary in these circumstances.

I glanced to my left at Gerry, whose head was still bent left towards the girl. Lydia seemed to be keeping up something of a monologue, unfazed by the uncharacteristically monosyllabic non-communicative grunts which were all she was able to extract from Gerry. Gerry's hands were on the table. He was fiddling with his lighter, turning it over and over, flicking the lid off. It would have to be a Zippo wouldn't it, I thought, part of the image. Striking it. Closing it. Fiddling with it again. Encouraged by the possibilities I leant over again and confidentially shouted in his ear, 'You could always try setting fire to her.'

There was some commotion the other side and she got up and walked outside. Gerry with a muttered, 'You bastard,' in my direction, followed her.

I sat back contented. Smugly happy I let myself drift for a

moment on the sea of noise. I was never sure afterwards whether she had just finally got the message from Gerry that he wasn't interested. Gerry had told me that he'd been trying to shake her off for weeks, or whether I'd been too loud and hadn't been quite as discreet as perhaps even in my drunken state I would have intended. I never asked Gerry and he never mentioned it again. Ah here was food, excellent. I shoved any twinge of conscience aside as I reached out for my platter full of chips.

Thursday, 17 November, Jijenga

There was a knock at the door. It was eight o'clock at night. Who on earth would this be, I wondered as I put down my book. Behind the security grille outside was Iain.

'Hi, mind if I come in?'

'Of course, of course,' I said, as I slipped the lock. 'Come in, come in. Beer?'

'Ooh, yes please. Sorry it's a wee bit late.'

'Oh that's all right, I didn't know whether to expect you. I didn't know how late you would be getting back in today, as it's such a long drive down. Castle?'

'*Ndiyo, asante.*'

I handed him a cold can from the fridge and opened another one myself to keep him company. 'So have you been home yet?'

'No, I just thought I'd pop in on my way back because I cut through the back way from the main road.'

'Do you want some food?' Sam called from the kitchen. 'I'm doing a sort of pasta bake and there'll be tons of it.'

'No, no thanks,' said Iain, 'I'll just get off home to dump the kit out of the car and get off to the Hash.'

'You're mad,' I said, 'you must be knackered, besides, won't you be too late?'

'Well I'll probably miss the run, but I'll go for the down-downs and a bite. The Irish electricity guys are out for a drink tonight. I think it's Tom's birthday. We'll probably head out to the Europa for a few beers and perhaps some food afterwards.'

'You've heard the news about the ferry, I take it?' I asked him.

'Yes. William picked it up as we drove down. I've not seen the papers yet so it's all a bit second-hand. Sounds absolutely horrific though.'

'Dreadful. Was I glad that you had called from Bharanku

yesterday morning to say you were heading off.'

Iain nodded. 'It really brings it home to you, doesn't it? A bit of bad luck, a bad connection and I could have missed the Ro-Ro and decided to take that ferry.' He shuddered.

'Yes, well you didn't. And I'm glad to see you here. Have a seat,' Iain seemed tired after the drive. It must have been quite a trip. Too tired to be off boozing at the Hash, I thought.

'Crossing OK?' I asked as we sat down.

'A bit rough. Thank God we had decided to catch the big Ro-Ro. We caught the tail end of one storm but we were close into Bharanku by that stage, so we made it OK. Unlike the other one.'

But Iain hadn't just come straight to me to say "Hi, I'm back." He had a story to tell me.

'I was just swinging left past the cathedral at the Askari Monument to go down Lake Drive towards the pier on my way to the ferry...' Every town in the country seemed to have an *askari* monument to the dead of the First World War or the last local one. It was like a national preoccupation. '...I'd slowed down as I came to the junction. We'd been in court on Monday, of course.'

'No luck?'

'No, the usual rubbish, lasted until the afternoon and then adjourned again. I've done a file note if Janet can type it up.' I took the notes from him. 'By the time I had wrapped up with Mabulla on Tuesday morning I was so pissed off that I thought I'd just collect our bags and grab lunch before hopping on the afternoon ferry. I had sent William to get the tickets and arranged to meet him at the café.'

'Anyway, I was just rolling as we came up to the Askari Monument when the police waved me over. I didn't know what was going on at first but suddenly there were cops everywhere – hundreds of them all down the street, all done up to the nines, shoving everyone off the road onto the pavement with waves of their batons.

'Even the kids in the middle of the road selling papers had disappeared. And then I heard the sirens. The police all snapped to attention.' I could see it in my mind's eye, butts and beer bellies wobbling in salute. 'There was one poor chap who was trying to get his walkie talkie back from his mate across the road. He nearly got himself run over as the convoy came steaming up the road. He had to jump back out of the way. There was a police car in the lead and then a couple of Landcruisers, followed by a Merc, all really moving, doing sixty or seventy easily as they chicaned out round

90

past the monument before they heeled over again for the bit of the left bend and straightened up to accelerate away down the main street. Huge amounts of spray up from the road as they went through the puddles.'

'Was it raining then?'

'No, we'd had the worst of the storm in the morning. Terrific downpour and winds of course, but it had passed on. That was one of the reasons I had decided to get the bigger Ro-Ro. It's always so much steadier if there's a storm on the lake.'

Events had just demonstrated that all too clearly.

'It was Rais of course. He had been to see some cadets at a passing out parade up the lakeside and was on his way back to the airport to fly down to Jijenga. I don't know if he was late but he certainly wasn't hanging round to wave and press the election flesh. I don't think he's over popular up there.'

'No – it's opposition territory. Pesha's *wakilwa*.'

'Anyway, after that of course it was chaos. There were a couple of local cop Landies tearing their guts out trying to keep up with a bunch of SOU in the back and then it was a scrabble as everyone raced to slipstream them and avoid getting caught up in the traffic as it sorted itself out. The traffic police didn't bat an eyelid, just waved everybody off and then disappeared – gone to look for a *dala dala* driver to shake down I expect. So there I was trying to get out against the flood tide of traffic while every street kid in Mkilwa was at my window trying to sell me papers, maps and peanuts. Eventually I took my life in my hands and pulled out. And just as I was heading down past the bank, who do you think I saw?' he asked triumphantly coming at last, and reluctantly, to the point.

'I don't know.'

'That chap, Dave. The English guy you met.'

I looked blank.

'You know – the detective from the Met.'

'Oh him.' I froze, 'So you haven't seen the papers today?' I asked suddenly, trying to keep my voice steady and the tone of my enquiry inconsequential, casual almost.

'No, just what William has picked up on the radio.'

'Go on.'

'Yes, well, he was crossing the road just opposite Rashid's, there was a whole group of people at the crossing point there.' I nodded, I knew Rashid's shop halfway down Lake Drive and the pedestrian crossing outside well and felt Iain was getting somewhere at last.

'He was sort of sandwiched in the middle of a group of guys, so I tooted the horn and waved.'

That surprised me. 'Which way was he going?' I asked. 'Do you mean he was heading up from the docks towards the monument?'

'Yes.'

So Dave would have been walking up hill, away from the pier, up into town, but to where I wondered? There were shops that way, a church, the bank and the police station. Was that where he was headed? And if so, why? I had filled him in on Temu and his apparent sympathy towards New Mwanchi so surely Dave would be giving the local *polisi* a wide berth?

'Was he with them?' I asked.

'Who?'

'The group of guys.'

Iain looked thoughtful as he tried to judge his memory. 'It's difficult to tell – sort of, I think. He was walking kind of slowly, he looked stiff, almost as if he was in pain. Funny thing was – as soon as he saw me he really seemed to perk up. He smiled and broke away from the group. He had to sort of rear up a bit backwards with his arms to get clear. They seemed to be crowded together as they crossed. They were all sort of bunched up, you know, how you get when you've people shuffling along slowly in front of you as you're trying to get along.'

'Were they trying to get along?'

'What Dave and the men?'

'Yes.'

'Well, aye, I suppose so. You know it's hard to tell. It seemed to me that Dave was sort of there, with them but not with them really. They weren't talking, for example,' he said, fastening on a detail.

I left it for a moment.

'I was right at the edge of the crossing. He turned and ran straight round in front of the car to the passenger side door. He looked like he needed a lift, in fact he looked just awful, so I leant over and opened it. He was in and we were off in seconds so as not to hold up traffic, before we'd even said hello.'

'What about the other guys?'

'Which?'

'The ones that were crossing the road with him.'

'Oh, I didn't really notice. I was too busy watching him hop round the car and then I was leaning over to get the door catch.'

I drew breath and stopped the conversation. I needed time to think. I took refuge in irony. 'So he's walking away, he sees you and immediately wants to hop a lift going somewhere different, he knows not where – that about the size of it so far?'

'Well… yes, if you want to put it like that.'

Iain was getting uneasy at my sudden complete concentration. What he had thought was simply an odd story was now something different, darker and burdened with a greater significance by my intense interest and thirst for obscure detail – I seemed to want to know every nuance, to judge every scrap of evidence for some private calculation of my own. He was nervous. There was something he didn't know.

'So, what happened next?'

'Well as I say, by this time I was pulling away. The crossing was clear in front of me as the knot of people had reached the traffic island. It was a good thing too, because just as he went past the front a bloody bike zoomed straight past on the outside between us and the guys. It could have run somebody over. Bloody idiots the lot of them. Anyway, there was still traffic fallout from Rais' convoy piling up the other way and behind us from the junction, and I needed to meet William and hit the ferry, so as you can imagine, I wasn't hanging about. I was booting it as he climbed in and there was a huge surge of traffic after us as we all headed off down the hill. Pandemonium it was.'

'Didn't you say anything?'

'Aye. It took a moment or two because he was sort of out of breath from dashing across and shutting the door as we took off.'

'OK, OK,' I insisted, 'so what did you say?'

'We both sort of started to talk at once, you know how you do, then you both shut up to let the other one go first and then both take the hint and start again – funny the way it works.'

He could see me bristling with another exasperated exhortation so went on hurriedly. 'We hadn't got far to go – it's only a couple of hundred metres down to the turn as you know. I, well I said hi, how are you sort of thing and he asked me which way I was heading. So I said a café just round the corner for lunch before I go to get the ferry – d'you fancy something or can I drop you somewhere?'

'He was quite pale and I sort of got the impression he was thinking fast. He didn't reply for a moment and we had to wait for a gap in the traffic so I could turn right. It seemed ages before he said thanks but no, just to drop him off on the corner thanks. He seemed to be quite ill or to have been in some kind of an accident, he had bruises on his face and was shaking. And then he did something odd.'

'What?'

'He said please could I skip lunch and get something to you. He asked me if I could please give it directly to you, you would know what it was about. And there was something else.' He trailed off a bit hesitantly.

'What?' I bit back the urge to shout, to grab his shoulders and shake the information out of him. Under pressure Iain started to stall.

'Look it was all very quick. He was talking as he got out, it was on the corner and the traffic was still roaring about so I couldn't really stop for more than a moment. I was really worried for him because as soon as the door opened he threw up into the gutter as he just about fell out of the car before he leant back in to give this to me. But before I could ask him to get back in so I could take him somewhere he was off, he disappeared into the crowd without looking back. Almost ran, he did,' Iain quickly qualified.

'What did he say?' I insisted. 'It's bloody important.'

Iain hesitated and started to speak slowly and deliberately. I felt suddenly calm, waiting to hear Dave's words as carried to me by this surprised, innocent and ad hoc messenger. Iain almost had his eyes closed. His hands were spread out in front of him as though he was measuring in his mind's eye distances and positions. He looked as if he was visualising the scene, trying to recall every detail, every scrap of emotion, every flash of colour that might make his words accurate.

'He said whatever I did, I mustn't tell anyone else about this.' Iain put his hand in his pocket. 'He was struggling to get it out of his shirt pocket. He said he'd never been so serious in his life. He said to hide it, keep it safe and take it straight to you. He said Nobody. Nobody, but you. Understand? I was so surprised I just nodded. It was then that I noticed his hands, they were red and blistered on his palms and around his finger tips. It looked as though he had burnt them quite badly and that's why he was having difficulty in getting it out. I didn't really notice what he'd left until a minute or so later when I'd pulled over to pick up William.' Iain opened his eyes and his myopic gaze turned to me, looking puzzled behind his glasses. 'Now why should he say that?'

I didn't say anything in reply.

After Iain had left, I just looked speculatively at what he had

94

handed to me. It was an anonymous Philips C30 Dictaphone tape. I turned it over in my hand. It wasn't fully rewound so it had obviously been used. I wondered what was on it and what it meant. We had a transcriber set in the office on which I had been trying and failing to get Janet to use to type up our letters and reports. I bet that there weren't a dozen other people in the country with a machine that could play this.

So I didn't just have whatever Dave had been able to tell a surprised and unknowing Iain. There was more. And there was only one way to find out how much more.

Sam was looking at me interested as she set the dish down on the table. 'So what was all that about?' she asked.

'Oh nothing,' I said as I pulled my Dictaphone out of my pilot case beside the sofa. 'Just something that Iain's brought down for me from Mkilwa.'

'He was lucky.' she said, referring to the ferry

'Yes he was,' I agreed absentmindedly.

The tape clicked into the handheld player B side up with the familiar plastic snap of the cover shutting. Holding it to my ear, I flicked play button down with my thumb and heard the familiar high pitched speedy squeakiness of fast reverse for a fraction of a second before I pushed it forward again.

I listened for a moment to the tape. It was Dave's voice all right. It had the characteristic intonations of a man using a Dictaphone, the clipped expressions, the odd explosions of breath from the microphone being held too close, the slightly dead sound of each phrase as interrupted by a minute click and a microsecond of silence each time he pressed the on button to say something new, and the way words and phrases, full stops and paragraphs were sometimes cut and disjoined, as he'd started speaking momentarily before the tape cut in or cut it off before finishing. But it was Dave. Definitely.

I listened, I pressed the fast forward and heard the same squeaky noise until it suddenly stopped, leaving the half wound tape spooling on with nothing but the whine of the motor and tape. One and a half sides then, I thought. Assuming he had started on side A.

I would have another go with Janet. I would ask her to transcribe it when I went into the office.

'Hey that smells good,' I said, turning back, the momentary spell broken as I realised that dinner was nearly ready and that I'd better organise the table.

After dinner I carried on reading my book, hearing the narrator's voice in the quiet of my apartment as he told his fictional audience about kin and kindness. That to be of a kind is to be of kin, how feelings towards your kin were the root of the word kindness, an ancient word now buried so deep in its modern Western usage that it has all but disappeared and being kind is now a general duty, not a specific responsibility that that you are born to towards just those of your kin.

And as I read, the word trail led him to the German word, *kinder*, and a poem by Goethe, a black night, a beach, fog, a father who hears the wind and a child who sees a ghost.

I had just heard a ghost. Dave. A white ghost, a *mzungu*, one of the three whose names had appeared in the paper this morning.

The poem ended in confusion, death and failure.

Amongst the other names. The long lists of names. The lists Iain wouldn't have seen yet.

But as it ended, the narrator dragged his audience back to the here and now as if awakening from a dream to the land of life, not ghosts, and confessed that he wasn't sure what it all meant, and maybe that was why he talked so much.

The names of the drowned. The *polisi* in Mkilwa had released the list yesterday in time for the black bordered front page of this morning's *Citizen*. The list with Dave's name on it.

But I was tired, so I went to bed.

6 The island

Friday, 18th November, Jijenga

We met Clare on the apartment's stairs, it was election day, a public holiday. There had been rumours of a postponement in view of the disaster but it seemed as though voting was going ahead. 'Let's go to the island,' Sam suggested.

'Good idea,' I said. I wanted the chance to get away, 'We may as well watch the city burn from there as anywhere.'

'You're awful,' said Clare

*

The island was half an hour's rolling chug out from the yacht club's pier on an ancient diesel powered dhow, a tropical speck in the deep blue gulf with a bounty bar beach of such dazzling whiteness under the electric sky and arc light sun that our eyes screwed up and felt gritty. Some palm thatched *bandas* for sun shelters, a bar and that was all.

As the boat dropped anchor a few metres off shore, Ish dived off into the brilliant clear water, striking out strongly for shore to claim a *banda*.

Meanwhile we support troops struggled down into the small dinghy, disembarking onto the hot sand a few minutes later, laden down with those essential beach supplies, the eski filled with frozen frostie glasses and the white wine properly chilled.

As well as the dhow service, the island was also a favourite destination for those few yacht club members who actually sailed. I had never been keen on boats. But today, the sight of a small catamaran leaping over the waves and tearing across the bay in bounces of spray was quite attractive.

As I looked back across the strait, blue-black towering thunder clouds loomed over the city, sombre and threatening, like the mood. It was as though it was truly a world away from the blistering heat out on the island.

By local standards this was a playground for the super rich, so much so that last year locals had sailed out and mugged everyone on the island. It lent an extra frisson to an afternoon out. Every time a sail came into view you did just wonder.

It was good to be out of the apartment. Ever since last night my mind had been going round in circles as I tried to decide what to do about Dave's tape. Should I just hand it over to the *polisi*? Would they even be interested? They probably wouldn't know what to do with it or even play it? Or if they did, how did I know they wouldn't hand it sell it straight back to whoever Dave was investigating. But then, what was that to me anyway? Perhaps out here in the clear air I'd have a chance to think about it afresh.

And anyway, this was great, a chance to wind Sam up about her thesis over more bottles of wine than were probably good for any of us, with snorkelling at the same time. Excellent.

'How's it going?' I asked her, after the first splash and rounds of drinks.

'Oh just lovely thanks. I've got just about every icky infection you can think of, and some you probably can't in the patients I'm studying, so you can imagine what it's like.'

'But I thought you were working with HIV cases in a hospice?' asked Clare

'Yes I am, but HIV doesn't kill you.'

'It doesn't?' Clare sounded genuinely surprised.

'No. Stop me when this gets too ugly but HIV gives you AIDS, which is a syndrome, a state you are in, not a disease itself. What HIV does is to knock out your immune system so that your body can't fight off infections. So the first symptoms start as skin disorders, stuff called seborrhoea dermatitis, and skin inflammations, particularly on your face.

'Then as your body tries to fight the infections you develop swollen lymph nodes and begin to lose weight. And all the time you tend to have symptoms like diarrhoea, fevers, open ulcers and thrush.

'Eventually as your immune system starts to fail completely the opportunistic infections become more serious, leaving you open to things like herpes, shingles, and tuberculosis. Your brain can have lesions which can lead to dementia. By the end full blown cancers such as Kaposi's sarcoma are common, as is lymphoma of brain, autoimmune diseases such as thrombocytopenia and infectious pneumonia. Like I said, we get the full show.'

'Jesus,' whistled Clare. 'And you work with this?'

'Yes, the question is how fast does all this progress, and what if anything, are the best things poor countries without access to expensive retroviral drugs can do to help slow it down in victims.'

'I tell you what though,' Sam said, rolling over on the sand to face me, 'my Mkilwa results are odd, to the extent that I really can't explain them. I'm going to have to do some more stats work on it at the archives and High Commission library when we get back next week.'

'What sort of odd?'

'Oh some of the Mkilwa samples are showing death very quickly, statistically it's quite significant. It's almost as if there was a predisposition. I'm wondering if there is some genetic susceptibility in the *wakilwa*.'

'Or could it be environmental factors?' I asked, 'like pollution?' I thought about a large smokestack and lead smelting.

'Could be, there are environmental issues that can affect the immune system. They're usually pretty serious and obvious though but that's the sorts of thing that I'm trying to screen now.'

She had a way of acting out conversations with dramatic effects, pauses, gestures, interrogatory fingers raised, eyes widening in mock surprise. She was truly theatrical. And yet it was Ish's family who were the thespians.

'Have I told you the story about my visual aids?' she asked.

'No.'

'I have been looking at whether diet makes a difference and I thought I'd make use of himself here to help out with my surveys,' she said, waving at Ish, 'so he got all artistic for me. My peasants out in the villages where the patients come from aren't too good with lists of words, so I had him draw a picture of a fish for *samaki,* chicken for *kuku* and leg of wildebeest for game meat and so on.'

'OK,' I said.

'So then I could ask my peasants "Which of these do you eat?" and point to a picture. I thought it would make it easier.'

'So?'

'It was a complete bloody disaster. They look at me as though I'm mad. "Why would we want to eat a picture on a piece of paper?" they say. They just really didn't get it.'

'Sam?' I asked.

'Yes,'

'These villagers of yours – are they Muslim?'

'Quite a few of them, yes.'

'Ah,' I said. 'Well that might be part of your problem.'

She looked puzzled.

'Well, Islamic traditions,' I tried gently. No, I thought, I was obviously still not getting through. I could see that. 'There's no tradition of representative art,' I continued. She still looked puzzled. 'It's forbidden by the Prophet you know.'

It was quite entertaining to watch her gulp and laugh at the same time. 'Oh Christ, you mean I've probably pissed off entire villages by trampling on their taboos?'

'Excellent,' I laughed. 'So that'll be a grade F for the cultural sensitivity and understanding part of the thesis. What was it you were doing by the way? Was it social anthropology?'

'God knows why,' said Sam, shaking her blonde curls regretfully. 'I should have stuck to straight biology. Chopping up little furry things. Or worms. Worms are great fun,' she sounded genuinely regretful. 'I've got a lot of time for worms. In fact I'm looking more and more kindly on them. For a start you can't do questionnaires on them.'

'Well you can't do questionnaires on your peasants.'

'Well, yes I know, that's part of the problem,' said Sam.

'I worry about my research assistant too. He doesn't really seem to understand what I want from him sometimes. I mean, I see one of his roles as protecting me from all these little requests for money and what have you and keeping the locals off my back. Yet he obviously doesn't see it like that. You can see them come up to him and sort of whisper in his ear. I suppose they're asking is *mama* in a good mood, and then he comes over and says "*mama* there is a problem" and gets them to talk to me. Well I appreciate that shaking down *mama* is the best paying game there's been in town for years but it does get to be a little wearing.'

'Well,' said Ish. 'I suppose you have to appreciate that he's going to have to live there long after you've gone, so he has to keep in with the locals.'

'Yes,' I said. 'And what sort of cut do you reckon he gets from all these little pieces of business?'

Sam, bless her, looked genuinely shocked. 'I hadn't thought of that. Do you think he does get something?'

I shrugged. Ish looked thoughtful. 'It's possible I suppose. It'd be a very African thing to do.'

'Oh bloody hell,' she said picking herself up in a mock strop and looking out at where the waves were starting to pick up as the tide came in. 'I'm off for a swim.' She announced. 'Do you fancy it?' she asked Clare.

*

100

'She's her own worst enemy,' he said to me. We were lolling on the hot sand in the shade of the banda. The cooler box and another Castle was in reach, Sam and Clare were out beyond the waves. 'She starts to think about it and gets herself so agitated, she just winds and winds herself up. Whereas when she's not thinking about it she just gets on and does it. You've seen her, she just bulldozes her way through.'

I knew what he meant. 'So I'm not good for her with all my teasing, am I?' I asked gently.

'No, no, you are,' he protested. 'As she says herself, she needs to talk to people. I'm very involved with what she's doing and so are all the other bods she deals with, the medics and aid workers or whoever, they're all part of the same industry, the same set up. It's a very cliquey little world and it's quite rare, quite good for her to have someone to rant to who isn't part of that. Someone who is completely separate but at the same time who actually understands some of what's going on.'

'Oh good. I wouldn't miss the next instalment of the thesis project from hell for anything.'

I changed the subject. 'How's the rag – any progress with your paperwork?'

'I saw Chairman Ossoro yesterday, he's trying to get me a work permit. He's very short, isn't he?'

'Yes,' I said.

'Sits in his big office behind his big desk.'

'Oh yes, and he's got all those low chairs in front of it so you sit looking up at him.' I had met him once. 'Very sophisticated.'

'There's this guy who works in his office just to go through every newspaper to highlight anything about the Chairman.'

'Makes sense I suppose.'

'There was a huge cartoon of the Chairman as a wonderful sort of poison dwarf figure in one of the Kiswahili papers last week. This chap was busy,' Ish stuck his tongue out between his teeth in an impression of earnest concentration, as he mimed, 'colouring in the whole bloody cartoon.'

'In that case, I'm surprised they just don't print the *News* on yellow paper. So are you still planning to stick with journalism from here on in?'

He looked thoughtful for a moment. Lying there with his hands behind his head, staring up at the woven roof of the banda, he had the effortless air of somebody who was naturally confident.

'Well I don't want to go back to writing code for widget manufacturers that's for sure. I guess the plan at the moment is to try and get some stories into the press back home to build up a bit of a portfolio, do some freelance work and try and take it from there.'

'Why the change of heart? You had a good career there, your stint in the US and all.'

'Yes, but,' he was serious now. 'In a hundred years' time I'm going to be dead and buried. But I want to live on. I want to leave something more behind than a line of code. If I can get into making a living at writing, that would be great, but almost as important is the fact that people could be reading what I write in a hundred years' time. It's a sort of bid for immortality, my name would still be alive, I want to be able to speak to the future.'

'Wow,' that took a moment to sink in. 'That's not going to be easy is it?'

'What, out here? You wouldn't believe what it's like trying to be a journalist out here. There's no investigative journalism for a start. Nobody asks any questions.'

'Now I was wondering about that,' I said. 'There was a story the other week, somebody had been arrested for planting a bomb on one of the ferries. But there was no explanation as to why or any follow up the next day. What does that mean? Why does that happen? What's going on? Particularly since then – bang, so to speak, down goes a ferry.'

'Well,' said Ish. 'It's simple, the journalists go along to the police commissioner's office every evening and scribble down faithfully what the commissioner tells them there is to report and it goes in the paper. Then they do the same thing the next day, and the day after that. They don't follow things up, they don't do any investigation, nobody asks any questions.'

'But that's it, why not?'

'What, question someone in authority, further up the hierarchy? You just don't do that here. Hey, look they're coming.'

The girls were returning up the beach, obviously deep in conversation. Even at this distance you could almost hear the text size getting larger with the wave of Sam's hand. Waves were a very Sam gesture. They could be a flourish, they could be completely dismissive, they could be despairing, all involving or everything at once.

'Before they get back, can I ask you a favour?' said Ish. 'Could you take Sam into town with you on Monday? I'm going to be out and about seeing what's happening about the election and I'd like to make sure she's looked after.'

'Of course I'll take her in but what's the problem? D'you think there'll be trouble?'

'I really don't know,' Ish was staring into the distance pensively, 'perhaps I'm being over cautious.' Then he turned to face me, suddenly a serious undertone and insistence to his voice, 'but promise me you'll look after her?'

'Of course,' I said again distracted by a movement behind him.

The butch-looking girl from the banda next door with the short cropped blonde hair and the square jaw had been asleep on the beach, curled with her arm outstretched across her boyfriend. I had automatically pigeonholed her as German from her colouring, she had particularly strawberry blonde hair and white skin which showed up red.

Now she had woken. She stretched and sat for a moment or two looking around her. Then she said something to her boyfriend, stood up and walked down to the sea. I watched languidly but sharply focused. Where she had been resting on her hip whilst asleep her flank now showed a round glowing patch of persistent blushing pink about a handsbreadth in size.

The beach sloped sharply and this late in the afternoon the waves had started to become more powerful with the incoming tide. She was only a few yards in before the waves were crashing into her at waist height. As they did so her body shuddered at each smashing impact, her generous thighs and bottom wobbling in resonance.

To get further out she lifted her arms away from her sides, arching her body forwards as if standing on tiptoe and jumping forwards and upwards to try and force her way out against the crest of a wave. Further down the beach kids were screaming in on boogie boards that made the sea look Hawaiian in scale and size and powerful greenness. But my eyes were on her. Her legs taut, braced against the shock of impact, her back slightly arched and hollowed, her arms spread wide, wrists drooping as though preparing to bend across the wave, her bottom pertly pointed out towards me. As she did so it looked to me for a fleeting moment like a most submissive sexy gesture. And then it was gone. There was a crash of falling green water into which her legs disappeared. For a moment the gaily fluorescent costume showed up a bright triangular ghost under water before fading from view hidden by the churning foam of the plunging breakers.

She wasn't by any stretch of the imagination either pretty or my type. But it was strange, I reflected, how a single movement, an oddly struck pose at an unusual moment could press some or other of those erotic buttons for an instant and make a memory.

'These two are looking very serious aren't they?' Sam announced to Clare 'What are you talking about?'

A guilty thought, I said to myself, thinking back. 'Nothing,' I said out loud.

*

'I'm sorry some people might find that a funny little story of bureaucracy and inefficiency gone mad but I don't. I've got to live it day in and day out and I just don't find it funny anymore. I have a serious sense of humour failure when it comes to their multitudinous little ways of ensuring that nothing ever gets done, everything gets screwed up and nobody gives a damn about anybody else.' Sam was good value when she ranted.

'It's a society that runs on a very strictly codified duty,' I protested, 'but it's a specific duty to your family and your clan, your tribe, which is really just your extended family.'

Clare chipped in, 'I had a long chat with Idris in the office last week about filing, of all things, and why he does it the way he does. He told me that you surname is your clan name and it's your first name that denotes you as an individual. That's why he files letters by first names, not surnames, so he could search by individual. Made perfect sense to him.'

'Even Winston has said something along the lines that he had to have children for his clan. He even made some comment that we Westerners don't seem to have the same priorities.'

'Well that's pretty daft,' protested Clare. 'He's hardly seeing a representative sample in his secondees is he? What a stupid thing to say.'

'But you can see it everywhere you look here. If you aren't part of my clan I don't owe you anything. From our culture we don't understand that and it just seems callous and inconsiderate to us. But to them it's not. Being inconsiderate implies an assumption that you should be considerate and choose not to be. Here culturally it just doesn't seem to occur to anyone that it's an option.'

Clare was looking at me. 'Do you seriously think that's why the arsehole in the next block is always playing his radio so loud? That it just never occurs to him to think of anyone else and turn it down?'

'Absolutely. Up at Kharatasi last year we had a woman, a worker, who was badly burned in an accident. She went off to hospital and for the next few months the personnel manager was drawing out cash from the company to pay for her treatment and the medicines. Only it turned out that when we caught him stealing other stuff, he hadn't been paying for anything, he'd seen a horrifically burnt woman as just a chance to make a bit more on the side and he'd been forging receipts and pocketing the cash.'

'So what happened about the woman?' asked Sam, after a moment.

'What woman?' I was at a loss for a moment.

'The woman who was burned?' she clarified.

'Oh, well,' I had to think. 'I assume she was looked after. I did mean to try and go up to see her at the hospital, but what with the court case, our warehouse fraud up country and trying to sell the business, I didn't get around to it. I did tell the new personnel guy to make sure she got the treatment she needed.'

Did I mean that to sound so defensive? I thought to myself. I opened a beer from the eski with a satisfying hiss and looked out at the sparkling blue ocean.

'You come out here and think how could people do something like that, I said reflectively. 'You just don't understand it. Then after you've been here a while, you start to. You start to see how it could happen. People here just don't identify with anyone outside of their clan or at most, tribe. And if they don't identify with other people, they just don't identify with their suffering, don't feel any responsibility for them. So you start to understand how people could do that. You actually start to understand how the Nazis could work.'

I faltered. For a moment I was lost in thought. Going vague as my wife used to call it. I knew really. I owed it to Dave. Sending me that tape was possibly the last thing he had ever done. He had given the tape to Iain to give to me for safekeeping, not to pass it over to some *polisi* as soon as the weekend was over. I had to transcribe it, to find out what was on it, and then decide what Dave had wanted me to do with it. I had to get involved. I had a duty. I owed him that much.

'You know Tippu Tip had one of his houses over on Bharanku,' Sam looked blank for a moment at my tangent. 'Tippu Tip was one of Zanzibar's most famous slavers. Infamous really. He used to come on expeditions over this way. But at the same time he used to help Livingstone out, which seems strange since Livingstone was campaigning against slavery. Stanley eventually ended up giving him part of the Belgian Congo to run, which was a bit rich seeing as it was where he used to catch his slaves.' Sam still looked blank.

I waved my hand dismissively, 'Well, it doesn't matter. Anyway what I was going to say was that there is a local story about his house on Bharanku. I have no idea whether it's true or not, but it's interesting in this context. It's said that when he built it, which would have been in the 1870s or 1880s, he followed the traditions. And that meant he buried forty or fifty people in the foundations.'

I was looking at Sam, who seemed to be thinking so what? What's the relevance?

'Alive.'

Sam blinked. She seemed shocked for a moment. Then she turned away and stared out to see where the dhow rode at anchor, a dark shadow against the sea's glare of the old Arab slaving ships of the East Coast. She shook her head. 'I don't know, I don't know,' she whispered. Then a moment later, still in a quiet sad voice, 'Yes, I do. You know, I think I can see them doing it.'

They are not kin, I said to myself. Now where had that come from?

7 Render unto Caesar

Black water was breathing silent, thick and oily in the full bright tropical moonlight. And yet there were shadows too, darker pools of blackness floating silently in the water.

As I walked along the white strand, staring out along the silver path to the low hanging, speckled, corrupted, silver ball tarnished by age in the sky, one by terrible one the humps, the hollows began to resolve themselves into sodden forms.

Closer up, the sense of unease became more palpable. There were things floating in the water. They looked like logs, but they didn't drift purposefully the way that crocodiles do. They were silent, there was no squealing or grunting or splashing the way like hippos. And up ahead one had grounded, the gentle waves sighing and murmuring a little as they caressed and washed around the body.

At the water line, I stood above the black shape, oddly distanced and detached, knowing that they must be from the boat. There was one. And another. And another. Out across the bay they littered the surface and now they were a gruesome wrack, drifting in to shore to be left bloated and bedraggled like a tragic offering by the gentle motion of the water. One by one, the lake returning sorrowfully what it had taken.

As I walked on there were more dark bodies, here a man, there a woman. And the terrible thing was I knew them. I knew them all. Here was Kiponglea. Here was the impassive face of Gerry, a scarf of weed tangled blackly around his neck.

Looking up, with the foreboding now gripping my heart, I saw there were other bodies just ahead, all dark shapes, all black in the night. But now some were definitely 'white', I don't know how I knew.

Heading forward, the feeling of dread grew as I stepped over first one and then two, the faces were closer to home now. Up ahead there was a group, I seemed drawn to them, it was as though the whole focus of the horror lay in these three bodies just ahead, a small hump of darker blackness which drew me towards it like a magnet. With a panic rising and swelling within me I could feel my heart beating faster and the black bilious taste, the gorge, in my mouth. I swallowed desperately hard against the burning pressure in my chest as I drew closer and finally stood over them.

There was Juma.

There was Iain.

Their faces were quiet, peaceful even.

In the middle, there was Dave, his eyes screwed up and his face clenched into a grimace as if he had been frozen, struck solid in the act of bracing himself against something, some death agony.

Then as I, on my knees, crouched beside him, suddenly his eyes were open. He was smiling and his arms reached out for me, the claws pulling at me, tugging at me as I struggled backwards to get away.

I screamed as I scrabbled away from him, trying desperately, desperately to kick myself free and shook and banged my back against the pillows and the headboard. My heart pounding, I saw the moonlight streaming in through the windows across the mosquito net and the empty duvet cover I slept under twisted and turned around about my ankles.

There was a tentative tap on the door, 'Paul, are you all right?' I heard Sam call, quietly from out in the hallway.

'Um, yes. Yes I'm OK. It's nothing,' I stuttered, gasping at the sudden shock of being awake.

I gulped at the warm night air, blinked and tried to untangle the bedclothes as the darker blackness receded against the brighter moonlight of the real night.

'Nothing,' I said to the sound of the empty hallway.

It took a long time to fall asleep again that night.

Monday, 21 November, Jijenga

The lift ascended upwards in darkness, clattering to a halt at every floor, doors opening onto gloom or brightness depending on whether the floor had been partitioned off into a corridor in front of the lift, or whether you could see through to the side of the building and the windows overlooking Boma and the sea.

Our floor, the eighth, was one of the darkest. As Sam and I stepped out, the wall immediately facing us was dark, mahogany-coloured wood. Across the top were proclaimed the names of all the countries in which the firm had a presence. Below, like a scroll of war dead, hung the gently tarnishing brass name plaques of client after client, Western subsidiaries, that had or had had their registered offices down the hall in our advocate's safe.

As I opened the door to our office Janet was sitting behind her desk and a static crackled charge, sudden electric whirr and beep announced that her computer was switched on again for the start of another day.

I handed her the tape as we exchanged *nzuris*. She settled down on her chair, arranging herself in front of the screen, reaching for the headphones as she took the tape. She looked at one side, then the other and slotted it into the machine on her desk.

It whizzed for a second then slowed, the transcriber controlled by the foot pedal beneath her desk. Despite the machine's speaker I could hear nothing. Janet was scanning the tape on her headphones. Finally with a tremendous whine the tape began to rewind to the start.

'I think this is the start,' she said looking down at her keyboard as though it was the first time she had noticed it was there. 'I shall begin.'

As she started to work I stood behind her and watched over her shoulder until she shooed me off with an abrupt, 'Go away.'

'So is there anything I do to help out until Ish shows up?' asked Sam as we drank a coffee.

'Well not really,' I lied, pulling my papers out of my pilot case and looking over to where Janet was obviously struggling, her eyes a blank as her glasses reflected the blue of the screen. As I watched she very slowly played the tape. Looking puzzled she replayed the section, before typing a distressingly few words. A third listen and she muttered to herself before deleting something and trying again. This was going to take forever.

'Is that going to work?' Sam asked quietly, following my glance across the room and nodding at Janet.

'Not really, no,' I conceded.

'So why don't I do it for you while I wait for Ish?'

'Well...'

'It's OK, I'll square it with Janet.'

'Well OK, and thanks, if you don't mind?'

'Of course not,' she said. 'It'll make a change from typing up patients' notes.'

*

I was working on some papers at about eleven o'clock when from way down below on the streets there was suddenly more noise than the usual cacophony of horns, and was that chanting?

I stood up from behind my desk to get a better view out of the window down Aga Khan towards the docks, the government buildings and the main Courthouse on the old quayside. Up the road was coming a crowd, singing and chanting. The mass was a solid front as it moved in knots and whirlpools and eddies of people looking on and moving away, talking, discussing, pointing. The procession came down the wide, somehow inexplicably, momentarily empty streets. The police must have blocked the roads off further up, maybe near the new post office. I couldn't see that way but there didn't seem to be any traffic coming. So for now as they reached the junction with Samora, the crowd had the road to themselves. I headed into the next door office where Sam, Janet and William were looking out of the window as well.

'What is it William? Can you hear?' I asked.

'I, I don't know. Is very difficult.'

'Is it the election petition case?' Sam asked.

'I don't know, it may be. They all say something.' He grimaced, his hands up by his head in a peculiar rocking motion as though he was trying to visualise the English word, turning this way and that to see if he could recognise it. 'Like a disgrace,' he said at last.

'So, not a result then?' I said, as I came and stood behind them and looked down once more into the stark white heat of the day.

The crowd was passing now. It had flowed left at the roundabout, the column now passing between the clock tower and the boarded up fascia of the failed housing bank beneath the blank, empty windows of the British High Commission in the tower above. The Union Jack and the Republic's flag hung limply on their masts from the front of the building in the dead morning air.

The head of the crowd was out of sight now, along Samora. It wasn't exactly Oxford Street, but it was the main shopping centre of this end of town. If I was the police I'd be nervous about an angry crowd down there. And sure enough, strolling along behind the stragglers in their familiar khaki uniforms were twenty-five? No thirty, police, walking casually, their AK47s cradled in their arms or hanging loose by their sides.

'Well there's a disciplined piece of crowd control,' I observed as William muttered something that I didn't catch. 'What was that William?'

'*Siafu*,' he repeated. 'They look like *siafu*.'

Siafu, soldier ants. The thick columns of insects which marched through the bush, devouring everything in their path. I'd never seen any but if William said that was what they looked like, I was perfectly prepared to believe him.

'Ish says that this could get ugly,' Sam said as we turned away from the windows. Shooting a glance to check that Janet and William were out of earshot, 'ugly and ethnic,' she added in an undertone. 'I've just finished your tape by the way,' She said more loudly. 'That's it just coming off the printer now.'

'That's great, thanks.' I said looking across. 'Has anyone seen Iain yet this morning?' I asked.

No one had. Perhaps he wasn't well. We had closed the office on Friday for the election. It wasn't as though you could phone in sick here. Perhaps he would send Juma in with a message later. I decided that if we didn't hear from him by tomorrow morning I would pop round to his apartment and check him out.

Sam brought the papers and tape with her as we headed back into my office.

'So what's it about?' I asked as I held the door open for her.

'Well it doesn't seem to mean very much to me to be honest. Mostly it sounds as though it's about the lab. You know it's funny, your man Dave, a tough old cop like him and it sounds as though he's scared of the dark. He gets quite romantic at one point, starts going on about a blue glow in the moonlight.'

But there was some kind of a glow I thought to myself. I had noticed something like that at the lab.

'The odd thing though, is about the chemicals,' she said, handing me the pages.

'What chemicals?'

'The ones listed on this tape. Like the acetic anhydride for example.'

'What? Acetic as in vinegar?' I asked starting to leaf through the sheets.

'Anhydride,' she nodded, 'like super concentrated acid with all the water driven off.'

'Well that explains why it smells like a chippie.'

'But then there's also the chloroform, the sodium carbonate, the activated charcoal. It probably doesn't mean much but they don't really make sense.'

Not being a chemist it didn't mean anything at all to me.

'Why? What about them?'

'They're all stuff you use in organic chemistry. Acetic anhydride's used for drawing water off compounds and manufacturing pharmaceuticals and the like. So,' she said looking at me with a puzzled expression, 'What on earth do they have to do with smelting lead?'

'Beats me!'

And I added to myself, I wonder why Dave was so interested?

*

Clare was between men again and had come out with us to Caesar's. We were there early and as I got the first round of beers in at the bar the satellite news logo came up on the big screen hanging between two palms opposite the bar. It was a local station, pirating CNN and filling it out with the fledgling local programmes in Kiswahili. Soon there was a knot of waiters watching intently and listening to the announcer. Others sidled up and joined the group.

'Anything interesting?' asked Ish as I pulled the chair out from under the round table with a clatter against the flagstones and sat down.

'Difficult to tell. Mostly, it's election news I think, but there's also something to do with the hospital, and I thought I heard *Mutabendewe* mentioned but I can't be sure.'

As if a switch had been thrown, the spell was broken and the sleepers awoke, the clump of silent waiters sagged and fell away. They drifted off, each remembering something they needed to do. Only the announcer's voice continued and one was left. He looked over his shoulder as the others went and turned back to the screen, watching for a few moments more but in a desultory, relaxed way, before he too faded away.

'I guess it's the first election results coming through. Some of the constituencies ought to be declaring by now,' Ish turned back to more domestic matters. 'It was odd that Iain didn't come in to the office today, wasn't it? Given the election and the bits and pieces of trouble over the weekend, you would think he would have got in touch just to let you know where he was and that he was all right.'

'Oh he'll be all right. He knows that if he wants a day off to recover it's not a problem at the moment. If he's not in tomorrow I'll call in on the way home to check on him.'

'Hey look, there's Colin,' announced Ish.

I squinted against the lights hanging from the thatched banda surrounding the courtyard tables. A familiar figure was striding up the path to the bar at the entrance. I waved and he headed over for a beer.

'Did you hear the news about Dave? It's dreadful,' Colin was shaking his head. 'Absolutely dreadful. Of course, I hear that they still haven't found the body.'

'But I thought they had brought ashore lots of bodies,' Sam said.

'They'll be foot passengers, the people up on deck when it went over,' he said.

'But his name was on the casualty list. If he was below decks or in a cabin, they'll only find him once they raise the boat, won't they?' asked Clare.

'Well,' Colin shrugged, 'Apparently he bought a ticket and his name was on the register. But you know what it's like, everyone just piles on. They only inspect your ticket. It's not as though they check your name against the register.'

'But if he's missing and his name's on the register, then even if they can't find his body, you've got to fear the worst haven't you? After all if he was all right, surely he would have let the High Commission know?' I said.

'That's about the size of it,' Colin agreed.

I leant back. The millions of stars above were shining brilliant white above the courtyard. It all just felt so, so insignificant.

Nodding my head towards the screen by the bar I changed the subject. 'Looks like the first election results are coming in.'

'Have you heard? The Yanks are on a Situation 1 security alert according to the embassy, cars filled with fuel at all times, week's supply of food in the house and don't go into work if you don't feel like it.'

'Wow. Can you send a copy across to Winston?' I said.

'But I don't know what the fuss is about,' opined Clare. 'Nothing serious has happened. Some of the guys in the office went to vote on Friday, sat around for eight hours and ended up being told to go home and to come back tomorrow.'

'So what did they do?' Sam asked.

'That's just the point. Their reaction was, oh well, *pole sana*. Now can you imagine that happening back home? People would go mental!'

Colin circulated off to talk to a *wananchi* at another table, and we got more beers in and ordered pizzas.

'See the guy that Colin's speaking to?' Clare said; through the firm she was becoming well plugged in to the local financial and banking bureaucracy.

'Yes.'

113

'He's director of capital markets, responsible for the stock exchange.'

'I didn't think there was a stock exchange yet?'

'Well no, there isn't. I guess it's not that demanding a job yet,' she conceded.

'Don't worry, it will be,' I rejoined. 'So he's the man who's going to supervise trading in PCB's shares when that starts is he? Wow, lucky guy!'

There were a couple of subjects guaranteed to get Clare going and the planned flotation of PCB was certainly one of those buttons, as I well knew.

'That's going to be the biggest fraud perpetrated on a gullible public that I have ever come across in my life. Everyone knows that bank is bust and they are still going ahead.'

'What's this about the President having called to see the list of the bank's hundred biggest defaulting borrowers?' asked Ish.

'Yep,' said Clare.

'That'll never get published – I can imagine who's on it – no, I know some of the company names on it,' I said, ticking them off on my fingers. 'There will be Lazima, the Shahs and my friends up in Mkilwa for a start.'

'Yes, and that's not all,' Clare agreed. 'There are be big private names too – like directors of the bank – Party people, their wives, the chairman, you name it.'

'Some of the largest defaulting debtors of the bank are its directors?' Sam asked.

She was shocked. I wasn't. I knew about the chairman, obviously, and I could have guessed most of the rest that Clare had mentioned. It was so obvious. I was just surprised that Sam was seemed so stunned.

'Of course,' I said.

'Jesus.'

*

'Anyway, so AWA. Sam concluded with the expat's motto, Africa Wins Again.

'Well, you may say that, but to be fair, it seems as though NatTelCo is really getting its act together at long last. We had an engineer pitch up the other day at the apartment to get the phone working. Didn't even hassle us for some *chai*.'

114

'That's good.'

'Yes, both home and office in contact with the rest of the world. Bit of a novelty but we'll just have to see how long it lasts.'

We schmoozed on over the beers. The conversation winding its way around life, work, politics and the banks.

'Talking of stealing, how is the banking world?' I asked Clare, coming back to our discussion of earlier in the evening.

'Ah, well now you know, it's not just a list of bad debts the President wants.'

'No?'

'No! It's a meeting.'

'What?' This was a surprise.

'The President has called a meeting of PCB's hundred biggest defaulting debtors.'

'I wonder if our friends are going to be there,' I thought aloud.

'I assume so,' Clare agreed.

Ish piped up at this, 'Boy I'd like to be a fly on the wall at that. Of course in the old days it would probably be to request that they have a whip round for another couple of million dollars for some Presidential fund or project or another. These days we're all starting to wonder whether the President is serious. The trouble is, how can you tell?'

'The IMF guys in at PCB are really are up against it,' Clare was muttering into her beer. 'They need the unqualified wholehearted support of the powers that be or everything they're trying to do in the bank will come to nothing. And at the moment they haven't a hope in hell of getting it.' She shook her head sadly.

'The guys that are in, they came out here and saw PCB as a big challenging bank job. The problem is that it wasn't. Well it is, but it's something more than that as well. It's a political job. They've come up against real political players, real political process, real political power and they've tried to play the political game on the assumption that the sponsoring institutions will back them up. And they are losing. They're on their way out.

D'you know what the head guy told me? He's got memos, copy memos on bank's notepaper, signed memos, telling the bank's junior staff, "this looks like a good loan, make it, but don't record it in the bank's books." Can you believe that?'

I shrugged. 'Yes.' Of course I could believe it. 'I'm a bit surprised that they've found something in writing, but otherwise, so what?'

Clare laughed. 'You've been out here too long. If I told that to anyone in the office back home they'd never believe me. You didn't even turn a hair.'

'And people know it,' Ish pointed out. ' I think we're seeing the slowest bank run in history. It's not panic out there in the streets but it is happening. I talk to people about business and they're scared. They're looking at their money, they're looking at the bank and they're looking at the elections, and they're taking it out.'

Clare was disgruntled. 'At least it's slow – hell, perhaps that's the plan.'

'If you're going to have a collapse, at least have it slowly?' I mused. 'Yes, perhaps.'

'Hell, the IMF keep pumping in money.' Clare was serious again. 'Did you know the donors came to see the IMF – told them they were being too strict. What you want to have all those conditions on it for? I tell you these people are queuing up to throw money in here.'

'And where's it going?'

'All the way to the top. I shouldn't tell you this but I've heard it's the Attorney General. He's on the bank's Board – what a position to have. You know everything that's going on in the bank and you're in charge of the system that the bank has to go through to get it back. Chief Justice too, I'm told. I hear rumours that one of the expat companies has blown the gaffe on the two of them on a shakedown.'

'That could explain the problems we're having,' I said.

'Damn right.'

'Any chance of a change with the new government?'

Fatboy, the new President, was making lots of noises about being tough on corruption, we were following his speeches in the *Citizen* as we drove into work these days.

'He said that nobody who is corrupt is going to have a position in his administration,' said Sam. 'It was in that long interview with the *Finance Mail*.'

It had been a sort of keynote address to the business community and it was being heavily promoted on all the front pages.

'He said that even if there wasn't sufficient information or proof against somebody,' Sam continued, 'if there were sufficient allegations that confidence in them and thus the administration was undermined, he would remove people.'

'Yes,' I said. 'But he's got to say that. He's got to come on tough as he comes into power. All the donor agencies and countries cut off aid a year ago because of corruption. And it's not just aid to

116

particular projects, this is balance of payment support aid.'

'What's that?' Sam asked.

'This country relies on aid,' Ish explained to her. 'Every year they do the budget and less than half of government expenditure comes from the tax payers or from borrowings. The rest of it comes from aid donated from Western Europe, that's you and me as taxpayers at home.'

'Now, as of last year that's stopped coming,' Clare joined in, 'Only it hasn't stopped them running the feather bedded parastatals and paying their millions of bureaucrats.'

'But,' I concluded, 'the fact is, the country's broke, and unless Fatboy gets the aid flowing again the whole thing is going to come to a grinding halt. And the only way to do that is to convince the West that he's going to be tough on corruption and tough on tax collection. I doubt it'll really mean anything.'

'Well now, that's right,' announced Ish. 'And the Dutch have already given way, they've announced fifty million dollars is going to be released to help support the refugee camps on the border.'

'And the rest. The other odd bits and pieces,' Clare spat. 'How about the twelve million dollars to allow the army to buy new vehicles? As if every third vehicle on the streets isn't already a new army Landcruiser, Nissan Patrol or Merc.'

'Now that's what I call vital development expenditure,' I said, cynically. 'Then of course there's a new Landcruiser for each new member of parliament to help them with their official business.'

'But there's still the daily coverage of corruption going on in the *Citizen*,' insisted Sam. There were people caught today.'

'It's chickenfeed,' said Ish sadly, 'clerks and small fry.'

Sam nodded.

'And "redeployed", not even sacked, if you read the detail.' I pointed out. 'And yet it's a front page story. It's cheap PR. What it doesn't tell you is whether Fatboy is actually going to do anything about the *vigogo*.'

'That's the first question I asked at the Central Bank.' Through her work with Salima Clare was becoming very, very well connected I decided.

'And?'

'What I hear is, the Attorney General will be the first, the very first mind you, to be reconfirmed in office as a carryover from the old regime by the new President once he's sworn in.'

'I see,' I mused. 'Well that just about settles it. All we do in our job is try and apply the law to sort out each party's rights to a cake that's too small. If the law won't operate to allow us to do that there's not much point our being here.'

*

As we left Sam stopped to scan the boutique windows surrounding the café tables for anything new, while Ish and I chatted. As I glanced back into the restaurant I noticed that one of the waiters who had been studying the television earlier in the evening was now clearing our table. As I watched I noticed as he quickly looked round the rest of the restaurant to ensure that all the other diners were engrossed in talking to each other. Having checked to see he was unobserved he picked up Sam's Tusker bottle which she had left half finished and choosing the cleanest looking glass he carefully poured the beer into it and placed it to one side for later before clearing away.

*

As I walked into the bedroom back at the apartment, there was a sudden burst of sharp reports outside. They sounded like shots.

'What on earth was that?' exclaimed Sam from the hallway.

'I don't know, backfires maybe?' I looked out through the bars over the pitch blackness of the road behind the apartments but didn't see anything. There had been five or six cracks close together and close to home. In silence, we listened for a while. The disco started up again and there was nothing. Just the normal night sounds.

Tuesday, 22 November, Jijenga

Sam was planning a day researching her statistics in the High Commission library so she hitched a ride into Boma again with me. We scanned the papers as we waited for the lights on my drive in. No news and nothing about hospitals. As ever the *Citizen* provided some unintentional humour.

'Someone's died. It says here that she'll be buried in her home region anytime after her body arrives back there.' She looked up and continued in mock earnestness, 'Good, that should make it much easier.'

I laughed.

Iain still wasn't in by the time we arrived which was unusual. He

118

lived closer and somehow during the week he always managed to get up early enough to beat me, God alone knew how, given the Hashing, the Little Theatre and the rest of his social life.

Where is he? I thought as I walked out into the corridor and unlocked my room next door. Perhaps Ish was right, I would wait until lunchtime and then take a trip over to his apartment and see how he was. It was unlike him not to be here, or at least to have sent Juma.

The day's task was going to be to write a very dull report to the lenders on why there were still tax problems on Kharatasi and what, apart from paying bribes or sacking the firm's tax manager, we ought to do about it. I wasn't looking forward to it. Dave's tape would at least be a distraction.

I glanced at the transcript. Sam had put question marks where things were unclear, but there didn't seem to be too many of those. The tape was obviously notes that Dave had made as he walked around the factory. Bloody hell, what d'you know, I thought. He really had managed to get inside.

Sam was right though, I thought, as I read through the double spaced A4 pages she had transcribed. It didn't seem to mean very much.

From the snatch I had listened to back at the apartment the other night Dave had sounded tense, working quickly and speaking quietly; but not unbearably anxious or rushed and I hadn't noticed any background noise.

It must have been the middle of the night, I concluded. Then there would have been no one around other than the guards at the gate. I wondered how they had got in. Security would be tight because of the receivership and our *askaris* sitting outside the gates, but I supposed it had probably been easy with Mkate along. Clare had been right, no local was going to argue with a *vigogo* like a member of the SPU. Dave would have needed keys to get into the various buildings and only the chief security officer was likely to have had the keys, the *wahindi* wouldn't trust anyone else with them. That would be who Mkate would have leant on. That would also explain why they seemed to have no trouble with the *askaris* and seemed confident that they would have time to look around without interruption.

Dave had obviously taken quite a walk around the site that night. Leafing through the pages the early part looked like a pretty uneventful tour of the sheds and offices. He had been through the offices and the godowns at the bottom of the site, making notes about production records and despatches, shipments in of containers of scrap engines from Pakistan, descriptions of some small machined containers, and names off a shift rota of *wahindi* engineers who seemed to work there. But he had spent a lot of time at the end in the lab. It seemed to have been recently cleared out and that's where he had made his list of the chemicals that had intrigued Sam.

I really couldn't see what was of interest, given that he was supposed to be looking for some evidence to do with a fraud and fresh air invoicing.

Then there was the sudden ending. Was that someone coming back, had they, or he, been discovered? The transcript just stopped, dead with a, 'They're coming, no time for any more. Will complete later.'

I scanned through it again and shrugged. 'Well,' I said, feeling puzzled. 'I can't see what he was making a fuss about.' All the same, as I put the pages and tape in an envelope, I had an odd feeling. Perhaps there was something here. There was certainly something niggling at the back of my mind. But just right at that moment I didn't have a clue what it was.

Oh well, I thought, can't be that important.

I didn't get much further as I was surprised to hear through the wall the phone ringing in Janet's outer room. It occurred to me that the phones had been working for a while now. As I sat down, Janet put the call through to me. It was Clare. She was obviously in some distress, she sounded close to tears. 'Paul, can you come down?'

'Yeah sure, what's it about?' There was a moment's silence and then.

'It's about Iain. There's been an accident.'

'I'll be right there.' I said, throwing the papers and the tape into my pilot case.

*

The Land Rover was on its side in the roadside drainage ditch. It was a shocking sight, a blackened burnt-out shell. A crowd was gawping along the edge of the road overlooking the wreck. I stared down at the carcass blindly. There was none of the scrum of looters I had semi-expected. There wasn't anything left worth stripping from it.

It had happened late on Thursday night or early Friday morning.

'As far as anyone can tell he was pissed.'

Well that made sense. He was always pissed when he was driving late at night. We all were.

'They think he just went into the ditch.'

Well that was plausible too. Hadn't we all done it or almost done it enough times on a bad bump or been blinded by some idiot coming the other way?

It all felt that remote, almost abstract. I think I must have been in shock.

'But why would it catch fire?' I asked, distractedly. 'I've seen loads of cars go into ditches here and none of them have ever caught fire.'

Clare shrugged, 'Who knows? Bad connections? Bad luck.'

'Yes,' I said, 'he was talking about bad connections last time I saw him.' Suddenly I felt sick, the sun, the brightness, the light, the happy chatting crowd surrounding the car, the vibrant colours, were all too much. I needed to get away for a moment, to have some space.

Quickly I turned around and started to walk away, up the road. It was particularly rough and rutted, the tarmac disintegrating, subsiding where the road went over the swamp so that huge vertical ridges stood out along the road like spines amongst the pockmarked moonscape of the remaining cracking, crumbling tarmac and potholes.

I walked back blindly along the embankment, away from the wreck, towards the distant band of trees and houses a kilometre or so away on the higher ground at the other side of the marsh, rising like the shore seen by a drowning man, distant, unattainable. The land was open here, empty, and in the rains it became a swamp where not even local developers would build a house. So at night there was a stretch of two kilometres or so in the pitch black, interrupted only by the black and white painted curb stones that marked the turn across the reeds to the government compound, before the rise back up the other side where the generators threw pools of light amongst the first *dukas* and the taxi patch and the soccer field towards which Iain had been heading and beyond which was his apartment.

But why would he have crashed? I kept asking myself. The road was rutted, sure, but that meant you didn't go that fast. It was straight and yet, half way along, he'd gone off.

The other half of me knew he would have been hammered. He'd had a long trip down. After the Hash and a Europa Bar bash he wouldn't have finished until two or three in the morning. Perhaps he'd just fallen asleep at the wheel or perhaps he'd swerved to avoid something coming the other way, a pickup truck without lights on the wrong side of the road because it seemed smoother. Iain might have zigged when he should have zagged and that would have been that. The other driver would have disappeared into the night as fast as his wheels could carry him.

It was going round and round in my head: Bad connections, bad luck.

I was a couple of hundred metres away from the wreck now and there was something tugging at my attention. I stopped and looked around despairingly. The trees were closer now, somehow darker in their greenness, more foreboding. The ochre road to the government compound curved round, away to the right out towards the ocean, neatly delineating the edge of the trees and away up to the left. It was a couple of kilometres to the higher ground of the houses of Kaolo Beach.

I turned and looked back. The crowd around the ditch was almost slap bang in the middle of what would probably be the most isolated spot you could find in Jijenga, certainly that you could find on Iain's way home, with acres of salty marsh spreading out on either side.

Then I looked down. Down at the road. Down at the glinting road. Down at the broken glass on the road. From where I'd been looking back at the trees from the car there had been flashes of light from the road. Now I was closer, I could see what they were. Tiny fragments of broken glass scattered across the road. As I watched, a lorry painted Chinese light blue, belching black smoke, growled and clattered its way past me, crushing and grinding the shards further into the dust, while the crowd swaying around in the back of the truck looked down blankly at me from their three-metre high rusty blue skip.

I was squatting down now as I reached out on the buckled tarmac and picked up a sliver of something shiny. That was what I had noticed from back at the crash and had drawn me here. I held the sharpness between my fingers. Close up the glass appeared greenish in colour, but not the green nuggets of broken windscreen or side window glass, because it was silvered. It was a broken wing mirror, smashed up and down the road. Straightening up I looked further along, towards the trees. I couldn't see anything. I looked down at

122

the piece of wing mirror again. It was definitely green tinted glass. The Landie had had green tinted glass in its wing mirrors, hadn't it? I thought. But so what? So did lots of other cars. My eyes wandered along the edge of the wood to the big white gates of the compound, and as I carried on turning, to the line of scrub and palms a kilometre or so away across the marsh that marked the dunes, beyond which lay the sea. Bad connections, bad luck. 'What a God forsaken, bloody spot,' I muttered to myself.

'Are you all right?' Clare asked, as I rose.

She had come up to join me and I hadn't noticed.

'Yes, yes, I'm fine. I'm just a bit, you know…' I struggled for a word. 'Depressed,' I eventually concluded, lamely.

'We all are,' she sighed. 'Come on,' she said quickly, after a moment, 'Let's get out of here. At least it was quick for them.'

At first I didn't catch what she'd said, or at least the meaning didn't really sink in. I was lost in thought. I stood looking at the glittering glass I held between my thumb and forefinger, catching the light with it as I twisted it this way and that. It seemed an age before I held out my arm at full length and let it drop away down the road's embankment. Looking back from here, past the crash, to the start of the *dukas* on the horizon at the other side of the marsh, the road surface ran on an embankment, about three metres above the muddy bottom of the four or five metre wide ditch. The Landie had gone over the edge just before a culvert, where the road crossed the meandering river which slowly drained the marsh towards the sea. There the drop was more like four metres.

'Come on,' said Clare gently. 'Let's get back.'

'What did you say just now?' I asked, as I started to follow her.

'I said at least it was quick.'

'No, after that.'

'I didn't saying anything.' She seemed puzzled.

'No, no, you said they or them.'

'Yes, well the police said they both had broken necks.'

I stopped in my tracks. I was afraid. There was more.

'But who is "they"?'

She had stopped as well and stood looking back at me. 'Sorry, didn't you know?'

I shook my head. 'No, all I knew was what you told me about Iain. Who else was there?'

'Juma, his houseboy.'

'What?'

123

Clare shrugged her shoulders helplessly.

'Yes. I'm sorry, didn't you know?'

'No.' Oh my God, I thought. What a place. What a bloody awful place.

We started to walk back to the car, I was shaking my head. I just didn't understand it. I knew that Iain had taught Juma to drive, had bought him a licence and used him as a driver every so often, but I wouldn't have thought he would have used him that night. It didn't seem to make much sense.

Iain didn't get to us until seven-thirty or so and didn't leave until half an hour later. When he left us, he was in a hurry to get across to the Hash. It was just possible that Juma had been at Iain's apartment that evening, I thought. Juma often used to look after the place while he was away. It was useful for security. But unless Iain had specifically arranged for him to stay on, Juma would have probably gone home by that time. Iain wouldn't have asked him to stay when he would have been so uncertain about what time he was going to get back.

Of course Iain knew where Juma lived because he had been round to pick him up a few times, but would he really have unloaded his car at the apartment that evening and then taken time out to drive into the *nyumbaya* to pick up Juma? He wouldn't have known Juma was definitely going to be there for a start. He might have been out at his *shamba* or pissed. And what was Juma going to do while Iain was at the Hash and getting tanked up at the Europa Bar? Sit around outside all night?

We stopped at my white Suzuki which I'd abandoned, teetering on the edge of the embankment. I looked down at the ruin in the ditch.

Clare rested her arms on the roof on the other side of the Suzuki with her chin on her arms.

'Seen enough?' she asked.

'Yes, almost,' I sighed, as I fished for my keys. I unlocked the driver's door and slid in behind the wheel. I reached over and unlocked hers. And then I was seized with a need. A need to look, to see for myself. For Iain. I felt I owed him that. I had to confront it. But I didn't know what it was. It was a nameless formless horror, all too real in the stinking skeleton of a pyre out of sight in the ditch beside me. 'No, I haven't. I just want a last look at it,' I said, as she was getting in. 'Do you want to wait here for a moment? I won't be long.'

'OK,' she said.

The small crowd on the embankment above the crash parted to let me through, like a curious red sea.

The blackened wreck lay fully on its passenger side in the fetid mud at the bottom of the ditch. The stench of burnt rubber still hung in the air. Looking down from the road, facing me, were the metal bones of the chassis, the wheels on the driver's side reaching up towards heaven as if in some sort of mute appeal. I slithered down the embankment, catching myself against the rear wheel and feeling my boots sink into the ooze and slimy mud of the bottom. As it had fallen, the cab on the passenger's side had become crushed and tilted so that the shell sprawled away sideways as though in its death it had almost fully rolled over, its underbelly exposed to the uncaring sky.

I scrambled up the lower bank on the other side of the ditch which had caught the car and now I was looking at the passenger side as it sloped down towards me away from the road, framed above by its chattering and chirping halo of red-robed African bystanders.

What did I expect to see? I didn't really know.

What did I see? I don't really know that either.

The fire had burnt fiercely, the tyres, the paint off the body and the plastic wheel arches were all gone completely. Leaning forwards I put my hands onto the side of the roof and peered more closely down the side. The rear quarter panel looked badly dented, had that been there before? Probably, I thought. I seemed to remember that the Landie had a big bash on the back somewhere. The plastic wheel arches used to stand out a couple of inches from the car. What was left of the one at the back looked cracked and scratched but that didn't actually mean very much. It had been in enough bumps and scrapes around the country. As my eyes wandered forward I couldn't see any obvious signs of damage on the driver's side except for the mirror, the wing mirror. The driver's side wing mirror. It was missing.

I stepped sideways along the length of the car, towards the front and looked more closely. It was difficult to tell. Of course the wing mirrors were made of plastic, all I could see where they had been was a congealed lump of something. Presumably the rest had burnt and the glass had shattered.

Steeling myself, I looked inside the cab. The bonnet had fallen open and obscured the windscreen so it took a few moments of peering into the gloom out of the bright sunshine before the blackness started to resolve itself. The fire had completely gutted the interior leaving the wire skeletons of the seats, all coiled springs and retaining wires, and the charred metal stumps of the steering wheel and gear stick. My eyes wandered over the familiar, yet awfully transformed and blackened, clutter. The big bar of the jack behind the seats was there, so was the blade of the *panga* which Iain always used to keep in the back. Amongst the ash, lying against the side window and in the well between the seats, charred, but still recognisable, were some of the coils of rope he used to carry around.

There were melted, mutated, disturbingly organic blobs of this and that which took a while to resolve into plastic shapes; the seatbelt fasteners twisted into tortured shapes, hung like limp faded black lilies from their anchor points on the floor, still clasping the buckles with their charred fragments of seatbelt fabric like the wings of some ghastly black feeding insect, as they drooped down in the darkness towards the well of the passenger side, into the ditch.

I had seen enough. I returned to the Suzuki. Oh God. Next of kin. Someone is going to have to tell his parents. Someone is going to have to pick up the telephone to get the unreliable line home, to pray that the phone is answered, that it doesn't get cut off, to greet the voice on the other end, to say the words.

My stomach was in knots. I was going to be sick. There was only one person it could be.

'Where do you want to go now?' Clare asked.

What a question, I thought. I was taking deep breaths, fighting my gorge.

'Office,' I croaked. Suddenly in slow motion I was out of the car again, bolting for the ditch. I made it, just.

I was shaking with nerves as I sat in the car again. Clare was looking at me but I was keeping my eyes firmly on the tumbled hovels that crenulated the horizon around the poisonous green of the swamp ahead.

'We need to go to the office. I am going to have to make a telephone call. Someone has to tell his parents.'

*

Sam was in her room crying. Ish had brought her home at the news.

I lay in mine staring up at the ceiling.

I got up around six or so in the evening and pottered around the

126

apartment, not really doing anything, not really thinking anything. I lay on the sofa for the sake of somewhere different to lie and watched as the blue faded to darker and darker and darker turquoise while the first brilliant white sterile stars came out and then the black tropical night was on us.

I closed the balcony doors against the insects and switched on the living room lights, a bright yellow glow banishing the darkness and the shadows. I could hear noises from their room so I went into the kitchen to make Sam and Ish a cup of *chai* for when they got up.

The power went off as I finished, so I lit some candles for the living room. We sat on the sofas in the dark, not saying anything, occasionally sipping our tea. We didn't need to say anything.

By about eight I stood on the apartment's rear balcony thinking quietly.

Inside Sam was having a candlelit shower, I could hear the water gurgling through the drain in the cement floored room. Somewhere outside a child was wailing, while drifting across from one of the compounds towards the coast came Western music. First rock and then Country and Western. It sounded like someone was holding a barbie or pool party.

Something else was drifting on the air as well. The smell of burning rubbish wafted up to the black sky from the three-sided breezeblock pen across the road.

The apartments reminded me of all I'd ever imagined about council estates, the blaring radios, the screaming kids, the litter, the broken down and rusting cars awaiting restoration surgery or to be towed away.

There was a Corolla that I'd started to notice around every so often. It was back in the car park again. I recognised it for the 'I love Islam' sticker in the rear window.

The hiss of the shower stopped. 'Bloody ants,' I heard from somewhere inside. She would have the Doom out any second. The ants were everywhere, not helped by the houseboy Nelson's new habit of bringing multicoloured bunches of bougainvillaea for *mama* every few days, particularly when he wanted a loan.

I smiled, the bougainvillaea petals started to blow off after a day or so, especially when we had the front balcony doors open. Three petalled flowers of purple or white began to drift round the apartment, fluttering and rustling past doors in any breeze. There was something spooky about starting up suddenly having caught some movement out of the corner of my eye, only to find myself being watched by a dried parchment flower that had scurried round a corner and stopped, looking at me as if aware of my presence.

The apartment had two small balconies. The one at the front overlooked the scrappy piece of grass between the three blocks and the concrete rectangle of the car park with its broken down fence, beyond which a line of jerry built *dukas* lined the road. Between the fence and the *dukas* there was a huge area, covered with litter and tin cans where all the local inhabitants dumped their rubbish into and around a breezeblock built, three-sided semi-skip affair. Occasionally someone would set fire to the accumulated pile to clear it which was how I eventually realised that it was supposed to be the incinerator.

The balcony at the back was off the kitchen. It was a sort of outdoor scullery, a washing area with taps and a basin. I had strung rope between three of the down pipes so Nelson could hang up the washing. It was usually more peaceful as it faced away from the other apartment blocks and their blaring radios and overlooked Mr Chavda's putative garden and the track behind, beyond which was a scattering of private houses, some occupied, some half built and some still empty plots and in the late afternoon it caught the sun as it sank beyond the building sites casting a particular golden glow over the grotesque architectural fantasies of the country's rich *wahindi* and corpulent politicians. It felt enclosed, hidden, and private.

I gazed out, looking down onto the neighbouring compounds surrounded by their blank whitewashed walls topped with broken glass and bolted double gates. It was an insidious thing. Once I had decided I hated the place because of the constant noise, every moment I was at home I was listening. In the quiet, every fibre of my being was in a state of screaming anticipation, on edge, waiting for the music to start, or someone outside to start shouting up for access to one of the apartments, or for a driver at one of the fortified compounds to sound his horn impatiently to summon an *askari* to come scurrying out to unlock the gate for the bwana arriving home to his rambling corrugated iron roofed bungalow or quasi Moorish castle. No time of day or night was safe from the demanding blare.

I stood leaning on the balustrade staring out blankly, not really looking at anything but thinking quietly. It was almost completely dark now and there was still no power. The sky had clouded over. Daisy the dog came snuffling round the back of the water tank and along the fence. It was a while since I had seen her as she seemed to have made herself some kind of a den amongst a pile of rusty old water tanks in the corner of the site. Even from up here I could see how she had swollen, she was very pregnant and it wouldn't be long now, I guessed. I could smell the rain coming up the headland and felt the sudden coolness in the air. The generator of the house across the way burst gutturally into life, drowning out for a moment the cawing of the crows as they fought noisily amongst the rubbish or hopped along the telephone wires running just at the height of the balcony. It was a squalid, dirty view at its dismal worst and my mood matched it.

The rain broke suddenly with a hissing crash and blast of cold air and the frogs roared out a sawing, burping, croaking chorus in welcome. Perhaps they were croaking in memory of Iain. And perhaps of Herbert Simon Temu.

I had seen his photograph on the front page of the paper that morning. While Judge Ngalo looked just like a huge bloated toad sitting behind the bench of the court in Mkilwa with his fat body tapering triangularly to a domed rounded head and thick rubbery lips, Temu in his photograph had the added disadvantage of huge round glasses through which he had been peering myopically. The picture was of him in dress uniform with Sam Browne belt, peaked hat and braid and ribbons as befitting the Regional Police Commissioner of Mkilwa District. As it was a head and shoulders shot the resemblance to Ngalo who I had mostly seen behind the bench was accentuated.

RPC COMMITS SUICIDE, this morning's headline had screamed.

According to the papers, he had left his wife and two grown-up children in Mkilwa and travelled to Jijenga for a family celebration with his other wife and children, which presumably made him a Moslem. But the fact that the celebration was a christening seemed to militate against this. There were some mixed marriages here but not that many. Apparently all had gone well with no sign of problems until at some point in the evening the RPC had left the party and said he'd rejoin them later. Then, according to the report, in his full dress regalia, as befitted an RPC on an important formal occasion, he had walked to a semi developed building plot four blocks away from the party, had sat down inside the unfinished building, put his service revolver to his head and blown his brains out.

Only I didn't believe a word of it.

The *Citizen's* journalist had obviously done his best to explore the causes of the tragedy by quoting as fully as possible from the police briefing. Was it money? 'Oh no,' the relatives had all said, 'the RPC was a wealthy man.' No fewer than three family members were willing to be quoted to say that he was rich.

Was he really down over the election aftermath? Mkilwa was the opposition's home town where most of Pesha's hard core tribal support was based. Surely at this time, if no other, the RPC should be there? The question didn't seem to have occurred to the *Citizen*.

So, if you're a wealthy man, a well connected regional police commissioner, with two wives, grown-up children, presumably with a house (or two), *shamba*, Landcruiser, what could possibly drive you to suicide? *Chai*, housegirl, *askaris*, *fundis*, everything the average *wananchi* aspires to or could ever hope to get. What would make you throw it all away and blow your brains out? Was that what we had heard last night? It just didn't make sense.

I shook my head as if coming out of a dream, took one last look at the half built house surrounded by weeds and bramble that was rapidly disappearing into the gloom. The police, their Land Rover, the ambulance and the usual shoaling pattern of brightly chattering, cheerful, noisy ring of bright colour around the death plot were all long gone. That was now hours ago.

I felt surrounded by death. Dave, Iain, Juma. Now Temu in the plot right out at the back of my apartment. What was going on? We had heard shots last night I was sure. Not one shot. Shots.

The noise of the neighbours' generator had died away indicating that the power had returned and when I opened the kitchen door to go in, the light came on when I pressed the switch. A watcher from below would have seen the harsh bright blue white of the kitchen fluorescent bulb bathe the balcony with a brief glow before the door was quickly shut to keep the mosquitoes out, returning the balcony to the dark and my lingering questions: Why then? Why now? And why there?

My pilot case was in the living room. For a moment I thought about picking up the transcript on my way to bed. But I didn't.

8 Debts and revelations

Thursday, 24 November, Jijenga

The next week was a nightmare. But at least it kept me so busy that I didn't have time to sit around and think too much. Sam was away off up country that week but Ish was around, thank God. I saw a lot of him. We were mutual therapy. We needed it.

Colin of the High Commission arranged the paperwork to ship Iain home. All things considered, it was surprisingly quick and smooth. An accidental death certificate issued, his body in coffin and down to the airport for the Thursday morning flight out.

Colin mentioned something about a coroner's inquest in the UK but that the death certificate should satisfy them.

And all the time I wondered to myself, what about an autopsy?

Meanwhile Juma's body had disappeared. We *wazungu* weren't involved with that at all. We knew he had family, a *shamba* somewhere in Kaolo but no more than that. Someone somewhere must have claimed him, I suppose. The firm probably sorted out a death benefit grant of a hundred quid or so to ship him home.

As we stood in the early morning light at the airport, watching the coffin being unloaded from the van, Colin said quietly, 'You realise of course, that the police will want to see you.'

It was an odd comment. 'Why?' I asked. Colin seemed evasive or hinting at something.

'Just a word to the wise,' he said. 'You were after all one of the last people to see him alive.'

'Well when I saw him, he was stone cold sober. What about the Hash crowd? They must have been with him all evening, at the run and the down downs and the pub? Why would they want to see me?'

The *fundis* had the coffin by the handles now and started to carry it through into the gloom of the Customs shed. We walked behind.

'Oh, I think they might just want to establish his movements. He did come to see you specifically I understand.'

Now where had Colin got that? I wondered. 'I was surprised that you didn't need anyone to come and identify the body,' I said.

'Identify what?' Colin snapped. 'Listen, I saw the body. That car crashed and then burnt. I'm sorry, but there wasn't much to identify. His own mother wouldn't have recognised him.' Colin was back in control. 'No. Formal identification will have to wait until the body gets back home.'

I must have looked blank.

'Dental records,' he said gently. 'It'll be the only way.'

One odd thing that I had come across in the last few days was that no one in the Hash crowd I had spoken to remembered having seeing Juma with Iain that evening at the run. But well, if he was waiting in the car they wouldn't have. I hadn't yet managed to find anyone he had been with at the bar afterwards either.

It wasn't until later that afternoon that Clare and I went to Iain's apartment to start sorting through his things.

The shippers were arriving on Monday to do the real packing, but I thought we had better just go in to and check through his stuff, do a bit of an inventory and look after any valuables.

Clare, bless her, had volunteered. I had wanted to turn her down. It seemed right that I did it, he was working for me and we had been closest. But she had insisted and now I was glad.

We parked out at the front and walked slowly and reluctantly into the gloom of the ground floor lobby. It was cool and dark out of the sun and felt achingly hollow, our footsteps echoing on the concrete floor, the rattle of the spare keys from the safe in Salima's office as I picked through them for the two outer locks, the unoiled creak as the security grille swung open, the snaps of the deadbolts as with two clicks we were in, all seemed to breach a watchful silence. I couldn't keep *quiet as a grave* out of my mind. Get a grip on yourself, I thought.

Before us stretched the same old living room, his collection of Scottish prints and African pictures hanging on the far bright blue wall above his bookcase with his stereo and tapes.

Everything was there, just as I had seen it only last month when I had been round for dinner, the model MG on the coffee table, the single malts in the alcove, the family photographs on the windowsills.

It was all there but somehow, indefinably, not there, somehow silent, empty, and lifeless. Was it just the lack of Iain's presence? I felt ill at ease, as though I was trespassing, about to be caught. It was as though I kept expecting him to pop through from the bedroom and say, 'Hello, what are you doing here?'

I sat down on the sofa and looked around. I stared for a while at the neatly arranged bookshelves, *Trainspotting*, *A Guide to Jijenga*, *Birds of East Africa*, something else by Irving Walsh, *Lonely Planet*, *Photography*, *Halliwells*, books on climbing the Munroes and corporate turnaround. My eyes ran over the familiar titles. The books were a mix of sizes and types reflecting Iain's interests. What was it that was bothering me about them? I pulled out the Irving Walsh book and looked at the cover, *Marabou Stork Nightmare*, with an appropriate picture on the front. Well that was fair enough. The great scavenger storks with their butcher's beaks and red scaly crop were enough to give anyone nightmares. I flicked it open idly at random. Looked like short stories. I snapped it shut again and looked at the cover for a while.

Then I put it back. The gap on the shelf was waiting for it. I slid it back in neatly next to the hardback reference book *Birds of East Africa*.

Clare was calling me now. She was in the kitchen asking me if I could see any of Iain's bags anywhere. I felt disconnected from the world, from reality. Why did nothing seem to make sense anymore?

Perhaps it's delayed shock, I thought. I seemed struck dumb and still.

It didn't make sense. And it was the not making sense that mattered. There was something on my mind, something else I had seen, something trying to get out, something that I had noticed somewhere and see but not seen, something that was trying to come to the surface.

'Paul!' Clare was shouting now. 'Paul!'

I shook my head. I had almost been there but now it was gone.

I looked around the room. In the alcove the bottles of Scotch seemed strangely disturbed. Iain had been proud of his collection, bottles turned so the labels were clearly on show. Now however, they were facing any which way. I shook my head to dispel the thoughts. You are getting spooked, I thought to myself.

'Coming,' I said, getting up, and went into the kitchen to help her.

As I did so, I looked out of the dining room window through the mosquito netting, and across into the walled muddy patch of wasteland behind the apartments. To the right was the opening with its two metre high sheet metal gates, the access from the back alleyway to the theoretically more secure parking here out of sight of the road. Beside the gateway was the small two metre square breezeblock *askari* hut, with its rust red corrugated iron roof.

A thought suddenly struck me.

'Be back in a minute,' I shouted to Clare and walked out of the front door.

Coming out of the gloom of the building's passageway into the bright sunlight beating down into the courtyard, I couldn't at first see into the hut for the glare. But as I reached its corner, I stopped and turned to look back at the apartment. Because the apartment had windows on both sides there was more light inside it than the *askari* hut and I could quite clearly see Clare in the kitchen. A bit blurred and dull perhaps through the green mozzie netting, but definitely there. I turned and walked across the front of the hut, it had simple large gaps between the breezeblocks for windows and a door and a slatted wooden bench running along the back wall. In the dim shade of the interior an *askari* in khaki fatigues and floppy hat was slouched along a bench in the corner with a copy of the *Citizen*.

'*Hodi. Habari* bwana*?*'

'*Nzuri*,' he replied. '*Nzuri*, bwana,' starting up as though caught.

The five hundred *shillingi npya* note helped to calm the situation and get his attention.

'Bwana Iain's apartment?' I said, pointing.

'*Ndiyo*.'

'Visitors, Swahili?'

'Bwana?'

'Visit?'

The *askari* obviously didn't understand. This was going to be more difficult than I had thought.

'Apartment Bwana Iain,' I said, pointing at his apartment.

'*Ndiyo*,' nodded the security guard. 'Bwana Iain *kiafu*.'

'*Ndiyo*,' I said. 'Yes, he's dead. Swahili visit?'

The *askari* shook his head. I needed to think of away to describe this. I looked around, trying to think how to do it.

'Ah,' I said, pointing my index fingers upwards to show I had grasped a point. The *askari* looked at me intently, concentrating on my actions. 'Apartment Bwana Iain,' I said pointing.

He nodded.

'Swahili,' I said, pointing at him. '*Wananchi*.' Citizens, the Africans' term for themselves as opposed to *wazungu* or *wahindi*.

'*Ndiyo, wananchi*,' he was nodding again.

Good, Swahili people. 'Visit,' I said, and with this I mimed with my hands a door handle being depressed and a door opening and then I said. 'Go in,' sliding my right hand forwards through the imaginary door. 'Come out,' I said, sliding my hand out again, my left hand coming back as the door closed.

I was through.

'*Kabisa. Kabisa. Ndiyo, ndiyo*,' he was nodding vigorously.

A second five hundred note.

'*Jumatatu na jumaunne.*'

'Monday and Tuesday, *asante, asante sana. Na, wananchi,*' I was hunting again for the words.

'*Bei gani?*' How much, was all I could think of. I continued holding up my fingers as I did so. '*Moja? Mbili? Tatu? Nne?*'

He held one finger up. '*Jumatatu, moja.*' So, on Monday there was one.

'Bwana *kubwa*,' he sat, puffing himself out and arcing his arms away from his body to indicate a big man.

We were both nodding at each other now in encouragement, as was the next note in my hand. He was smiling.

Yes. Now then, how about Tuesday. '*Na, jumaunne?*' I asked.

The smile and the money vanished instantaneously, it was as though he had forgotten until this moment and suddenly became scared.

'*Jumaunne,*' he hesitated for a moment. '*Jumaunne, tatu,*' he said quietly. '*Polisi,*' was almost hissed.

He seemed to be shrinking before my eyes. I reached into my back pocket and fished out two more notes. His eyes fastened on them.

There was one last thing I wanted to know.

'Bwana *kubwa, jumatatu,*' he nodded warily at me. 'Bwana *kubwa Polisi?*'

He looked confused for a moment and then shrugged.

'*Bwana kubwa hamna* uniform,' as he pinched the sleeve of his khaki fatigues to show me. No uniform. I nodded.

'*Bwana kubwa happa,*' and he waved his hand down the length of his body. 'Kaunda suit.'

'Ah *ndiyo, ndiyo*, I understand,' I said, proffering the notes. '*Asante sana.*'

'*Asante sana* bwana,' we chanted together as he gave a little bow, taking the notes with the tips of his steepled hands and started to scuttle backwards around the side of the block away from me and the car park.

Clare was still in the apartment when I returned.

'What the hell was all that about?'

'We're not the first to be here,' I said. 'The police were here on Tuesday at least. Three of them.'

'Oh,' she didn't sound surprised. 'I suppose it makes sense.'

But on Monday, before them, there was bwana *kubwa*, a big man.

135

Wananchi, an African. Now who would he have been, I wondered, in his anonymous Kaunda suit?

We were just locking up to go as Sharik arrived. He had the apartment upstairs from Iain's, the firm tended to get a few in a block rather than just one or two, it made them easier to look after.

'Are you tidying up?' he asked, shaking his head. 'Sorry business that. Did the police make much of a mess? I hope there weren't too many valuables out when they came, still it's a bit late to start checking now. They'll be long gone. Thieves the lot of them. Still when you've got our sorts of politicians in charge, it's not really surprising.'

'No, no, not really,' I said. 'I think someone has had a go at his booze, but nothing valuable seems to be missing. Even his passport is still there. So I really don't know what the police or this other chap were doing here.'

'What other chap?'

I turned the key in the lock and nodded towards the open back door of the apartments. 'The *askari* out the back. He told me that people, the police, had been round on Tuesday, but that someone else had been around on Monday. You didn't see anyone, did you?'

Sharik shook his head emphatically. 'No. I knew the police had come round but I know nothing about anyone else. I was upstairs on Monday afternoon and I didn't hear anything. This *askari* must be mistaken. Did you give him anything?'

'Yes.'

'Well, he will have been making it up. You do not know these people like I do. He will have made up what he thinks you want to hear in the hope that you will pay him some more. That is just what it is like here. They tell you want they think you want to hear. They always have done and they always will do. Nothing ever changes here.'

'So you don't think that Ahmed's election will make any difference then?' I said, sorting through the keys on the bench for the security grille's deadlock.

Sharik gave me his smug patronising smile. 'No, I do not believe so. Ahmed has been a man of the Party all his life, a cog in the bureaucracy for years. He is not going to change his spots now.'

'You don't think it will be any cleaner then?'

'Of course not,' he shrugged as though it was self evident. 'Ahmed has now got to start paying his dues to the people who got him elected. Of course he must now make the right noises for external consumption but mark my words, nothing will come of it.'

'Won't it be better for business? You can't deny that things are getting more liberal.'

'Only because they have had to because of the aid. These people are socialists. They've been socialists for the last thirty years and they still are. They are anti-business, both philosophically and practically. They do not like business and they do not like the fact that they cannot control it.' He waved his hands in disgust. 'Things will go on just the same as before. You will see.'

I turned the key in the lock with a clang and shook the grille to make sure it was secure.

'So would you have preferred Pesha to win?' I asked, turning to him.

Sharik's face had fallen. He looked upset at just the thought. 'Oh dear me no,' he hissed. 'Oh no, that would have been worse, much worse. That man would have been a disaster. He is vicious, vicious, I tell you. He would have been the end.'

'So you reckon we're better off with the Party?' Better the devil you know?'

Sharik shrugged and turned to go up the stairs. 'I have lived with them all my life. You get to know your way around it all.'

'Best of a bad bunch, I suppose.'

Clare and I walked out into the sunlight at the front of the apartments.

'Yeuch,' she whispered, as we got into the car. 'He is such a creep.'

As I undid the T-lock and started the engine, I had to resist the urge to look back. I could swear that I could feel Sharik's eyes on the back of my neck from behind the matt green mosquito netted blankness of his apartment's windows.

*

Back at the office, I returned the keys to Salima.

'How did it go?' he asked.

Salima was always very courteous, interested in what was going on. Very human somehow, someone who you wanted to talk to. For all his broken-nosed brutal, stocky looks, quiet good nature and refusal to wear Western dress, underneath it all he was as sharp as a pin and absorbed all that went on.

'Fine, fine,' I said. Then without thinking I asked. 'Did the police get the keys from here to go round on Tuesday?'

'I think so,' he said. I think it was Tuesday lunchtime that they came for them.'

'Are you sure?'

'Yes, I think so,' he replied, surprised. 'Why?' he asked, shutting the safe.

'Oh nothing, I think I just got the wrong end of the stick from an *askari* about someone on Monday. Either that or he got it wrong.

'Well, I'm sure it was Tuesday.'

'OK. By the way, did the police mention anything about finding Iain's keys in the car? He must have had a set with him when he crashed, after all. Presumably in the same bunch as the car keys.'

'No, they haven't said anything to me. Perhaps they would have been lost in the fire.'

'Just wondering,' I said. Oh, the airfreight people are going to need those back to go in and pack on Monday. I'll pitch up and supervise.'

'They'll be here,' he said. 'Why don't you go home? Have some rest. Things must be very difficult for you.'

Salima was right. I ought to go home. I wasn't thinking straight. A rest would do me good. Why did some of these things matter? Why were inconsequential thoughts chasing themselves around my head? Of course the door keys would have been in the fire, but they would still have been usable, wouldn't they? Salima certainly didn't seem to be concerned about whether they had been found or not. He was right, though, I thought. There were more important things to be thinking about at the moment.

But still it wouldn't let me go. If Salima hadn't released the keys to the *Polisi* until Tuesday then who was it that the *askari* had seen visiting on Monday?

Had he seen anyone at all, was the first question. I thought back to my talk with him. He had been happy to talk, eager to please, he wouldn't have known what answers I wanted or expected, would he? Except that he might have calculated that if he told me he had seen people then I might give him more money for their details. So Sharik could be right, but the *askari* would have to have been quick to have worked that out. He had certainly seen the police on Tuesday. I was certain of that. The fear when he remembered had been real enough.

So there was only one thing to do. I needed to talk to the *askari* again. I would see him on Monday, during the packing. I would have another word.

But if he was right that left another mystery: who was it that he had seen? And how did they get in? As far as I knew there were three sets of keys to the apartment. The spares were in Salima's safe for whenever a *fundi* needed them. Iain's and Juma's would both have been in the car at the time of the accident with them.

The police can't have found any usable keys in the car after the fire I concluded, otherwise why turn up at the office to borrow a set? But that was a mystery in itself. Why had they gone to the apartment? What had they been looking for? There didn't seem to be anything obviously missing. Even his passport, which I would have expected them to want for some bureaucratic process of shipping the body back, was still there.

And there was another thing. The accident happened on Thursday night. The police must have identified the vehicle as belonging to the firm straight away from the plates. Given that there were two dead, how come it wasn't until Tuesday morning that they got round to notifying the office?

What had they been doing in the interim?

Was it deliberate delay or just the usual inefficiency?

Questions, questions, questions. Something and nothing. All weekend I swung between resignation and agitation.

Monday, 28 November, Jijenga

We were at Iain's apartment again at nine o'clock. We were a bit superfluous to tell the truth but we thought we ought to be there.

As workmen scurried around, opening up cardboard boxes and piling in belongings, Clare and I floated, trying not to get in the way.

It was about half past ten when the foreman said, 'Bwana, please look.'

I went over to the bookcase at the end of the room. The picture had been taken down, the books were stacked in a carton, the CDs ranked beside them and a *fundi* was indicating a pile of cassettes.

'What is it?' I asked.

The workman chattered away to the foreman.

'Is not there bwana,' he said. 'Do you know where is?'

'What's not there?' I asked puzzled. What on earth was he talking about?

In answer to my question the worker picked up one of the cassette boxes from the shelf and opened it. Instead of Runrig, there

139

was… well, nothing. He opened another and the same, a third, a fourth, a fifth and a sixth. All empty. All the cassettes were missing.

'All,' the foreman said, waving his arm at the pile of thirty or so boxes.

The packer and the foreman looked at me for a moment as if expecting some kind of guidance.

I sighed. 'I don't know,' I said. 'Perhaps he had them in the car. It doesn't matter, just put the cases in.'

The foreman nodded and issued instructions in Kiswahili.

Deep in thought I seemed drawn to the back windows. I had lied. The Landie had no stereo. So where on earth had his music cassettes gone? Who would possibly have wanted to take all Iain's collection, and why?

Outside the sun was roasting the growing pile of sealed cartons stacked by the back of the truck.

I looked across to the breezeblock *askari* hut, against the bright light of the yard its interior was impenetrable blackness.

Moments later I was outside. A few short strides took me to the entrance of the hut. The sense of déjà vu was overwhelming as inside I saw a khaki fatigued figure sprawled on a bench, head covered by a copy of the *Citizen*.

'Bwana.' I shook him, 'bwana.'

My heart sank. It was a different *askari*.

Thankfully he had better English. Another few hundred *shillingi npya* later however, it seemed I was no further forward. This was the afternoon and evening *askari*. The *askari* I had spoken to was the night-time and morning *askari*. But this was the morning so where was he? Unfortunately the morning *askari* had now disappeared and no one knew where he had gone. Even the *Polisi* had been looking for him, but had not been able to find him.

So that, it seemed, was that.

What was it Dave had said back that night at the Golden Shower? A funny feeling. Now I had it too. Only I suspected that in Dave's case it hadn't been a hunch or anything mystical, it was just his policeman's experience, intuition, call it what you will. The ability to read all sorts of small clues and start to feel that there was a pattern there, that only later, once grosser signs emerged, could others start to see. His gut feel for when something was wrong. Meanwhile all I had was still Dave's damn transcript which was dullness itself. What had he thought so important?

At lunchtime I dropped Sam off at my apartment and drove round

140

the bay to the freight forwarders' offices in the harbour district. Having signed off the paperwork so that they could begin the process of clearing Iain's effects through Customs, I headed back out through the familiar network of alleys, godowns and compounds on my way to the High Commission to drop off Iain's passport and to ask Colin what else needed to be done. As I reached the main road, I was halted by stationary traffic. A white-suited traffic policeman was holding us all back and looking sideways. From somewhere close by there came the mournful hoot and the unmistakably slow approaching clatter of a goods train heading down the line.

A few moments later a battered yellow and black diesel engine trundled slowly into view. Behind it, the freight wagons clanked and rumbled along the track across the road and into the docks. I could see the train quite clearly. And then, after the containers, as if to taunt me, the first of the flat bed trucks and their unmistakable loads rolled past in front of my eyes.

The ingots were on a series of open wagons. And on the first and last, there lounged two armed *askaris*, AK47s dangling casually as they jolted by.

Why? I asked myself. This is *wahindi* paranoia gone mad. What casual thief do they think is going to want to steal two-metre long lead ingots, or even be able to? It just doesn't make sense.

*

At the High Commission Colin was sympathetic but matter of fact.

'You shouldn't have any problems with the freight. The forwarders will handle it, they're reliable.'

'Yes, fine. Listen, I wanted to say thanks.'

Colin looked embarrassed. 'What for?'

'Well you know, helping out with everything.'

'Oh that. Don't think anything of it. It's part of what we're here for. How are you bearing up?'

'Oh, I'm OK, I suppose. Still in a bit of shock really.'

'No problems I can help with?' he asked. 'No police hassle I trust? Or anyone else?'

'No, no. I'm just a bit confused about a few things at the moment, but...'

'Confused? What about? What things?' he interrupted pleasantly, but firmly.

'Oh, there's just some odd things that are bugging me. Bits and pieces that don't seem to make any sense.'

'Such as?'

'Well,' I hesitated. These weren't things I had really thought through until this moment. Certainly I hadn't tried to put them into words. No wonder they came out sounding particularly weak.

'Well, I went to look at the car on Tuesday...'

Colin was nodding, 'It's OK, just tell me. You probably need to let it out. So you went to the car. It must have been upsetting for you.'

'Yes. Yes, it was. But the thing I haven't been able to figure out was the seatbelts.'

'Seatbelts?'

'Yes.'

'What about the seatbelts?' He looked puzzled.

'Well, they didn't work. It was one of Iain's ongoing complaints about the Landie, that the seatbelts didn't work. He complained about it all the time.'

'And you think this might have contributed to the seriousness of the accident? Is that it?'

'Well, yes, partly.'

'You mustn't blame yourself for the fact that they didn't work. That wasn't your fault surely?'

'But it was, to an extent at least. Perhaps I hadn't pushed it hard enough in the firm, perhaps...'

'Come on,' said Colin firmly, 'that's enough. I'm sure you did what you could.'

I was shaking my head. 'Perhaps if I'd done something about it, he'd be alive today.'

'It's no good thinking like that,' said Colin. 'You mustn't blame yourself.'

I was quiet for a moment.

'But I do think about it,' I muttered.

Colin put his hands on my shoulders. 'Why?' he asked.

I looked up at him. 'Because when I looked in the cab, they were done up.' Colin looked surprised. 'The seatbelts were done up. The buckles were still in the fasteners.'

I was looking at Colin intently now. Looking at him but not seeing him, looking back, looking down into the blackened stinking shell in the ditch. And thinking. Why? Why were they done up? Was that it? Was that what had been niggling at the back of my

142

mind all week? One stupid simple observation that I should have thought about straight away. Dimly I was aware that Colin was speaking to me.

'But it's no good thinking that if they had worked he would still be alive.'

'I wouldn't bet on it,' I murmured to myself.

There was a moment's silence.

'What did you just say?' asked Colin, sharply.

'I said, I wouldn't bet on it.'

'Look mate, you're upset, we all are. Iain was a great bloke, but hey, take it easy. It was a terrible accident...'

'Was it?' It was my turn to interrupt, angry now. A raging certainty was growing inside me. Things were starting to drop into place.

'Yes it was,' said Colin firmly.

'How do you know?' I demanded.

'Well, that's what the police said. This is a dangerous country, accidents happen here, we all know that.'

'Don't they just,' I said with venom.

'Now, hey,' said Colin, sharply. 'Hey look, calm down. You need to take it easy. What's got into you all of a sudden?'

'I'll tell you what's got into me. What's got into me is seatbelts.'

'So what about seatbelts?' Colin asked, sounding exasperated for a moment.

'Seatbelts that were fastened.'

Colin was staring at me impassively.

'Iain had been complaining about the seatbelts not working ever since he got the Landie,' I said, my voice rising. 'So why were they done up when the car went into the ditch?'

Colin was silent, it was as though he was backing away from me.

'Why would he have fastened a seatbelt that he knew didn't work? It just doesn't make sense,' I went on.

'Look, none of us know for sure what happ—'

I overrode him. 'So you don't know it was an accident. It doesn't make sense, I tell you. Iain would never have fastened that seatbelt, he would never have been wearing it while driving the car, he would never have put it on, alive.' There, I had said it. I had put my worst fears into words, given them voice, recognised and made them real. They were out now, born into the world for good or ill.

'You're cracking up,' he said. 'You need some rest. You've got to be careful with that sort of wild talk.'

I wasn't listening to him. My mind was racing ahead. Two broken necks that seemed awfully coincidental for one car crash. Both bodies burnt in a car fire. Now they would be difficult to post mortem properly, I bet.

And then there were the missing keys, that delay in notifying us. The visit, the visits, I corrected myself, to the apartment, the missing *askari*, the out of place books. Of course, the apartment must have been searched.

And the only thing… I was cold now, the only things missing were Iain's cassettes. His tapes.

No one out here was going to kill Iain for his Runrig collection, that was for sure. But perhaps there might, just might, be something on another tape that was worth killing for. A tape that Iain had no longer had. A tape that was smaller than normal tapes. A Dictaphone tape made by a recently deceased, presumed drowned, ex-fraud squad detective on his final investigation, into a known bunch of crooks.

And were was that tape now? With me, us, Sam, Ish and I. Back at my apartment.

I ran out of the High Commission with Colin shouting after me.

9 Shotgun Blues

Tuesday, 29 November, Jijenga

I rested my head in my hands. It was gone midnight and across the table from me Sam was packing away her notes and her laptop.

There was something about this tape. There had to be, or at least if I was right, someone somewhere thought there was.

But what? The answer was eluding me. I had read through the transcript time after time this evening, making notes as I went.

Rubbing my eyes, I looked across at the sheets of A4 paper strewn across the table top, covered in jottings, lists, bullet points, arrows and most of all, question marks.

The tape was all about New Mwanchi. That was clear.

I sat back and closed my eyes. So what did it all mean?

I had places: Pakistan, Mkilwa, Jijenga, Europe.

I had processes: shipping in, crushing and smelting or importing, dismantling and smelting, casting and exporting.

I had people: the *wahindi* management, engineers and chemists; the *wananchi* workers, and *askaris*.

I had chemicals: acetic anhydride, chloroform, activated charcoal, sodium carbonate, mercury, acid, hydrogen gas.

I had lab facilities, specialist refinery equipment, a smelter.

It was all so straightforward, so normal, so above board.

And yet Dave had obviously thought it important. I only had to look at what he said to Iain to confirm that.

And if I was right, others thought it equally important, or might be. Important enough to kill for.

All the time, running through my mind was the horrible thought, what if there isn't anything? What if there isn't anything on the tape that the killers want, or fear? I might be searching for a clue to what was going on that simply wasn't there to be found.

I scratched my head. The whine of a mosquito was irritatingly close.

But it is here. I know it's here, I thought to myself.

I had tried to summarise the tape.

Dave and someone, Mkate presumably, had got into the site. My hypothesis was that it was late at night. Someone had supplied them with keys and kept the site *askaris* on duty at the main gate, so I guessed that Mkate and the SPU had their hooks into the chief *askari*. That would make sense. They seemed to have known, or been shown, their way around, so perhaps it was a guided tour. The chief *askari* again at a guess.

They had been round the foundry. Dave had made notes about the ingots lying around and details of shipping arrangements to Rotterdam and Southampton. A short spur from the siding led right into the main shed and some of the blocks had already been stacked onto flat bed railway trucks.

The furnaces were still being fed by an automatic hopper system. They would need to run hot for twenty-four hours a day to remain usable.

From there they had inspected the ore piles and coal dumps before reaching the scrap yard. They had toured the heaps inspecting the scrap metal of every description piled high all around.

From Dave's notes it seemed to be a mixture; local general scrap, girders, off-cuts, containers, railway wagons and crashed motors, anchors, and hull sections from lakeside shipwrecks. And then there was the imported stuff; largely lorry, car and coach bodies, chassis and engine blocks from Pakistan, some of the wrecks still gaudily painted with Kabul Express or Islamabad Trading Co.

Most of the scrap had come in on open wagons and was piled in huge heaps. In amongst it however, were some old battered and locked containers in which Dave noted the scrap engines arrived in, kept locked away until they were stripped down in the godowns apparently because there were salvageable bits on them.

Then he had been through the godowns, the engineering shops at the bottom of the site. He made notes of names and rotas. Recorded that engines had been dismantled in one room where only *wahindi* seemed to work. One engine was sat on blocks on the floor, obviously waiting to be dismantled but Dave noted that its cylinder head nuts had been spot welded down so that no one was taking it apart again without a cutter or an angle grinder. There were piles of blocks, heads, radiators and alternators scattered in heaps in the adjoining godown. He seemed to think that this was significant.

He checked out the lab which had seemed deserted. Drained and scrubbed, was one of Dave's comments. It was much as I remembered having seen it from having peered in through the window six weeks or so before. At the closer end a range of benches with supplies of laboratory glasswear, a number of stainless steel pressure cookers, gas heaters and fridges. Now the chemical stores seemed to have been emptied and there was a skip just inside the door into which all the old containers had been dumped, apparently in preparation for disposal.

The far end seemed much more mysterious and Dave had obviously spent a while looking around puzzling over what, if anything, it might mean. I had no idea what you might expect in the way of kit an assay office, but from Dave's tape this had had a lot of surprisingly heavy equipment. A row of large metal vats two metres in length by a metre deep lined each wall, each with internal paddles that were obviously designed to stir the contents, a heavy lid that could be sealed shut, connections to pump in gas and a thick power lead which Dave traced to a dedicated electricity substation just outside. Scattered right at the far end were six or seven heavy squat, thirty-centimetre deep, thick walled, cast metal tubular containers with screw tops and thick cast lids. Dave thought they might tie up with some moulds he had spotted in the main foundry. By the end however Dave sounded just as in the dark as when he started despite the vague blue phosphorescence he commented on when he started to investigate the vats.

And that was it really. But then for some reason, Dave seemed to be on his own.

A hurried, 'They are coming back,' and no more.

Well it just beat me. Foundry, scrap, lab, workshop.

Dave came back to scrap again. Foundry, scrap. Why import scrap? Lab. Workshop. Wasn't there enough in this country already? There were wrecked lorries every couple of kilometres along the Jijenga–Bharanku road.

Scrap.

There were tonnes of it on site, literally tonnes. Unused. Enough to keep them going for years by the sound of it.

Why keep importing it?

It seemed a long route: Pakistan, Africa, Europe. Was it just an excuse to get Forex out? It was certainly a possibility.

'So how's it going?' asked Sam

'Oh I don't know, I can't make any sense of it.'

'You and me both,' she said shutting her file.

'Why do you say that?' I asked, looking I suppose for something to distract me.

'I've been doing my stats on mortality rates and do you know what? It's not Mkilwa that's odd, well it is, but it's more specific than that. It's your New Mwanchi site that's the anomaly. The increasing death rates from opportunistic infections amongst the workers over the last year or two and the fast rates of progression are what's throwing the Mkilwa population statistics out. It's a clear cluster but I just don't understand it. And I've found something else too, there's also an associated cluster of acute leukaemia.'

'So what causes that?'

'Well it's a cancer so it's a runaway mutation of a white blood cell.'

'But caused by?'

She considered. 'It's difficult to pin down, there are various theories at the moment. Some think it could be viral – a bit like AIDS in a way. There's a lot of evidence that it's environmental, anything from exposure to chemicals like benzene, or some anticancer drugs, through to radiation. But there's also a school of thought that looks at inherited factors, some genetic abnormalities or other blood diseases that can predispose you to suffering.

'You would really need a separate epidemiological study of this population to screen for each of these factors to find out which might be relevant which is just beyond my scope. It's an interesting fact that someone else will need to follow up, if they ever do.'

She told me not to stay up too late and I assured her that I wouldn't as we said goodnight and I went back to my problem. Workshop. Lab. Foundry. Casting.

Perhaps I should ask Salima, I thought. What was it Clare had said? 'Salima knows everyone. I'm convinced he actually runs the place. Not just the office, the country.'

It was two in the morning before, exhausted, I eventually flopped into bed and fell asleep.

Wednesday, 30 November, Jijenga

The firm had organised a memorial service. Despite the rumblings of trouble in the *nyumbaya* and up country in Mkilwa and Bharanku which had led to Ish disappearing up country on behalf of the rag, much to Sam's distress, there was an impressive turnout. I think every single member of staff and their families must have been there, all in their finest. The Muslim men easily identifiable by their embroidered white *koftes*. The expat crowd was mixed. Iain's Celtic tiger drinking buddies, Jay and Ned, and of course Colin, representing the High Commission. In Ish's absence I escorted Sam to the service.

I had managed to avoid Sharik on the way in and Sam and I squeezed in to a pew next to Clare and Gerry. For want of something else to do, I sat talking to Gerry for a while as we waited for the service to start.

'Any progress?' I asked.

'On what?' he replied, looking a little puzzled.

'The hospitals, Tengisa, your problem.'

'Oh,' he sighed. 'That. Well now, no, no, I must say, not really. D'you know what the really irritating thing about it all is?'

I shook my head.

'Well...' he coughed. 'The thing is that the little shit doesn't actually care a toss about the hospitals, all he wants is the publicity.'

'Then why don't you give it to him?' I asked.

'What do you mean?' he asked warily.

'I mean, why not just give them to him?'

'What, the hospitals?' he demanded incredulously. 'Are you out of your mind? I'm trying to get the bloody things back, not give them away for Christ's sakes.'

'Shh,' hissed Clare at him. 'You're in a bloody cathedral for God's sake.'

'But that's just my point,' I said. 'You haven't got them any more have you? He has. And even if you did get them back theoretically, you wouldn't be looking to take them anywhere else quickly, would you? You've still got, what is it, half a million refugees in camps at the border?'

'More like three-quarters.'

'Well, there you go, then. So perhaps the way forward is to go along with reality for the moment.'

'Go along with reality? Just recognise that he's stolen them and give up? Is that what you're saying?'

'No, no, of course not. It's just that you might offer him more publicity as part of a deal.'

'I don't follow. What do you mean?' but Gerry seemed intrigued by this as a possibility.

'Look, he's stolen the hospitals, but you can't kick up a fuss, it wouldn't do you or the Agency any good, might even get you kicked out of the country, and he might still get good PR out of it locally for standing up to *wazungu* bullying, right?

'Alternatively, you could go along to see him and say, "How about we here at the agency would like to give you the opportunity for some extra good PR. For a start, we won't challenge the story that you are putting out that these hospitals have been presented to the country as a gift, because of your superior diplomatic and

149

negotiating skills, but—"'

'But?'

'That's on one condition, an understanding, an opportunity for both sides to profit out of the situation.'

'Which is?' He sounded incredulous.

'That as and when the next crisis comes along when the hospitals are needed, I don't know when you might want them, a year's time maybe, two, perhaps?'

Gerry was nodding.

'Anyway, whenever that is, Tengisa then has the opportunity to call a press conference and announce that the country is now successful and so vital a member of the world, that to play its part in the community of nations, it is going to donate—'

Gerry was smiling now.

'Yes, you've guessed it, three fully working portable hospitals as a gift from the people here to the poor suffering refugees in the Balkans or wherever.' I stopped. 'Will he go for that do you think?'

Gerry was grinning broadly.

'Oh yes. Oh yes. I can just see the slimy creep loving the idea.'

'What's he got to lose?' I asked. 'It's effectively two bites of the cherry versus an all-out street brawl with one of the world's most respected aid agencies. It's a no-brainer I would have thought.'

Winston read the sermon in a quiet stumbling voice. It didn't matter as the dark cool of the cathedral behind its thick walls of absorbing stone was a silent respectful hush, other than an occasional sob. Marilyn the receptionist had black beads in her hair, I noticed.

As we filed out afterwards into the blast of bright sunshine, Salima, intercepting purposefully, caught me on the top steps.

'How are you?' he asked.

'I'm fine,' I said. I seemed to be telling people that a lot these days.

As I looked across the road amongst the milling crowds at the market between the trees across the road from the cathedral, a figure caught my eye. A big man. Dressed like Salima in a dark grey Kaunda suit.

There were many things that drew my eyes to him even though he was standing slightly back from the edge of the road, at the side of the container bar that backed on to a patch of waste ground that did for a car park-cum-roadside taxi rank.

The first was that he was standing still. Around him people were moving along the road or in to and out of *dukas* and bars. Those that didn't want to move were sat in the shade of the awnings outside the bars, sipping on a *Spriti* or a *bia* or just passing the time with friends, acquaintances and perfect strangers.

Not this man, he was standing, leaning against the side of the bar, his arms folded across his chest. He seemed relaxed, almost deliberately casual, but watchful. I stared at him for a moment, screwing up my eyes against the glare but I was certain that I was right.

It was Mr Mkate, and he was watching us.

'Bloody hell,' I whispered under my breath.

'What was that?' asked Sam from beside me on the steps, surprised. 'What did you say?'

'Look, I'm sorry about this, can you excuse me for a minute, I need to catch someone before they disappear.' I dashed down the steps leaving Sam and Salima together.

The crowd from the service had spilled out down the cathedral steps and was milling about on the pavement at the bottom as people saluted each other with high forearm African handshakes and full Swahili greetings. A funeral was an important social occasion.

'*Habari. Nzuri.* Sorry. I have to catch someone. *Habari.* Sorry, I'll be back. Sorry, excuse me.'

As I pushed my way through the crowd looking over their heads across the road. I saw him start to move, sidling backwards. By the time I reached the thinning edges of the crowd, the traffic lights at the corner turned green, releasing a surge of traffic in both directions, catching me up short at the side of the road. Through the gaps between the roaring traffic I could see Mkate disappearing between the cars parked on the waste ground. Then over the roar of the traffic I heard an engine starting.

All I could do was watch as in a cloud of dust a battered white Corolla bounced and spun across the sand at the back of the patch and out amongst a blare of horns, onto the tarmac of the road diagonally opposite, running away from the lights to my right.

'Shit. Shit. Shit.'

'You all right, mate?' said a familiar voice from just behind me.

It was Colin. 'Saw you heading this way and thought I would follow you over. Thought we might have a quiet word or two.'

For a moment I wasn't sure whether I believed him.

'It would be better to talk down here anyway,' he said, looking back up towards the throng at the top of the steps. 'Best not air some of this stuff in front of people like Salima, don't you think? Oh, and Paul?'

'Yes?'

'A friendly word of warning. In view of the er, present situation, I wouldn't go wandering off like that. It's not safe, not with what's going on.'

'I can manage,' I said striding off angrily. Other than Ish's digging for the paper, a bit of unrest over the elections didn't mean anything to worry about for us that I could see.

When I returned there was no sign of Salima. Instead, Winston was with Sam, he wanted to apologise for not having told me first. 'I'm sorry for that. I know he worked for you and you were close but Clare was in the room when I got the news from Salima.'

'It doesn't matter,' I said. 'I understand.' I was puzzled however. 'Why did Salima tell you? Why was he the first to know?'

'Salima is very well connected,' said Winston. He does work for all the ministries. I think it was just that he was the name they called when they found out it was one of our *wazungu.*'

*

'What was all that about?' Sam asked pointedly, as we walked back to my Suzuki together. 'You shouldn't have done that to Salima. He seems very concerned and to want to be very supportive.'

'Yes, I know, I'm sorry.' I was looking across the road. 'I'll go and see him in the office.'

'Well you should, he's very…' Sam searched for the right words, '…very human, he seems to be the most aware one in your firm, the one who's most tuned into your lives and what's going on.'

Traffic was backed up trying to get out of the car park. We sat in silence for a while as I gave it a chance to clear.

She was right of course. Salima was concerned and interested. I would see him tomorrow.

'It was strange to have a memorial service,' I said, after a few minutes. 'Like a funeral without a body, having had Iain shipped home in a box like that. It must be a nightmare for Customs at the other end though.'

'Why?' asked Sam.

'I mean they'll have to check it like anything else coming into the country.'

'But Colin will have sorted out all the paperwork, so they'll know all about it.'

'All the same, if you think about it in that way, Colin didn't pack the box. There's always the possibility that smugglers could use anything to ship drugs or stuff in.'

'You don't really think they'd open it do you?' Sam seemed horrified at the idea.

'No, probably not, it's such a one off I would have thought. There'll be so much freight going through the airport. I should think unless they've got specific intelligence, they'll only inspect a very few things at random or anything that the sniffer dogs pick up.'

'Perhaps they'll just X-ray it.'

'No, I wouldn't have thought they would even bother to do that.'

'Would the X-rays go through the coffin anyway?'

'I don't see any reason why not. It really was only a box made out of thin aluminium sheeting after all. Not like a lead lined coffin or anything.' I shuddered. 'Ugh, this is morbid. Can we change the subject?'

'Yes please,' Sam said, nodding.

Across from the cathedral two finned old Peugeot taxis, 504s, sagged together for mutual support, like two old fat indolent sharks, too lazy to chase the minnow-like schools of people that swarmed past them, just preferring to bask and watch with an evil air of menace. This place is getting to me, I thought, and shuddered as I stared out of the window.

What had caught my eye was Colin. I had assumed that he had gone, that his was one of the gaggle of Landies that had driven off as the car park emptied. But I could see his white long-wheelbase was still parked across the other side of the cathedral steps. So what, I asked myself, is he now doing across the road at the far side of the taxi rank?

At that moment, he turned and looking around him, started to make his way towards the curb, heading back to the road and the cathedral car park, and away from the spot behind him, beside the bar where Mkate had been standing.

'What's the matter?' asked Sam, concerned.

'Nothing,' I shook my head.

'Is it Iain?' she asked gently. 'You mustn't blame yourself. We're all upset still. If only he hadn't had that tape.'

It was a non sequitur, I was puzzled for a moment.

'Why?' I asked. Had she been thinking what I was thinking? 'What has Dave's tape got do to with it?'

'Well if he hadn't got it and this cloak and dagger mission to give it to you, he might have driven straight home. Think about it, he had to come past his own apartment to get to us and then on to the Hash and the Europa Bar. If he hadn't had to come out to the apartment, perhaps he would have just stopped at home and still be here today.'

No, she hadn't made the connection.

'Oh, come on,' I said. 'You can't blame Dave's tape for all this.' I started the engine.

'Well what are you blaming?' she asked. 'If it was an accident, then it was an accident and that's all there is to it.'

We must have been half way down Karume when with an awful jolt to the pit of my stomach, the bolt struck. I had an answer to my questions. Just one that I didn't want to be true.

It was all on and about the tape.

What I hadn't been able to figure out until now was the why, the why the tape was so important. What it was that mattered about the tiny details Dave had noticed, the names, the processes, the locations. Now I thought I knew

I didn't realise that I had pulled the car off the road and come to a halt on the verge at *Mnazi Moja* just before the hotel until I gradually became aware of Sam's voice beside me.

It must just have been a few seconds. She was asking, 'Why have you pulled over? We don't need anything from the shops here, do we?'

My mind racing I wondered what I could do to try to check the horrible thought that had just sprung fully formed into my head.

'Sam, you do research at the High Commission library don't you?'

'Yes.'

'Has it got a good reference section?'

'Probably the best in the country.'

'Do you mind me dropping you off at the apartment and heading in? I want to look some stuff up.'

'Why don't I help?' She volunteered. 'After all, I know my way around.'

I was uneasy at the idea, but as I tried to convince myself I was barking up the wrong tree I couldn't really think of a good reason why not other than that my idea was completely daft. And someone with a knowledge of chemistry who would be able to look up what these chemicals are used for would be useful.

'Well, OK thanks. If it's not any trouble?'

154

'Oh Paul, after all you've done for Ish and me? Besides which, I could do with something to take my mind off poor Iain.'

*

It took us about an hour to find what I had known we would, even as I had hoped to God that we wouldn't.

'Paul!'

I looked up from the report I was reading.

'Paul!' she said insistently, beginning to read in a whisper and not looking up for a moment as though transfixed by the paper in front of her, '*Acetic anhydride in particular is a key chemical with the easily identified very pungent odour of pickles.*' She was scanning through the text, '*Conversion is a relatively simple and inexpensive two stage procedure.*'

I was by her side and reading over her shoulder now.

'It's all on your tape,' she whispered, 'Don't you see?' She said, pointing to items in the description that we both knew matched items in the transcript's description of the lab equipment and chemicals.

It was all there, the stainless steel pots for pulverising the blocks, the stoves for cooking the mix, the purifying chemicals and filtering equipment. It was all there.

'I don't believe it, it can't be true,' she said in horror.

I shushed her to keep her voice down. 'Can't it?' I asked pointing to the relevant section in the analysis I had found so that Sam could read, '*While South East Asia is the largest producer, 75% of Western Europe's supply comes from South West Asia and in particular Afghanistan, smuggled out through Turkey and Pakistan.*'

'Come on,' I said nodding to the exit, 'let's go to the beach.' Still looking stunned, Sam glanced up in surprise. 'We need to talk.' I murmured, 'but not here, somewhere nice and open.' Sam got it, where we wouldn't be overheard.

*

My mind was racing as I pulled the little Suzuki onto the fringe of brilliant white sand at the edge of the beach. Because I just knew.

Someone knew.

Someone, somehow, whoever it was in Mkilwa, must have discovered Dave was making notes on tape. That had to be what this

155

is all about.

And they could only have found out from someone who knew that this was what he did, someone like Mkate; from searching his belongings and finding other tapes; or from Dave himself.

If it was from Mkate, they would know that he had been making a tape at the factory that night. But they wouldn't know everything that was on it.

If it was from searching his things, they would suspect, but would not know for sure.

If it was by beating it out of Dave, they might know everything, something, or nothing. It would depend on what Dave had let out, before they killed him.

And they had killed him; I was convinced of that now. Whoever they might be, the gang of big *wananchi* in civilian clothes who Iain had seen, I was convinced it had to be them, having picked Dave up from the hotel.

They had probably abducted Dave from his hotel at the point of a gun. Why else would he have gone quietly? '*For a quiet word bwana.*' Perhaps they had taken him in the foyer or breakfast room. Dave might have had the tape on him for security. He wouldn't have wanted to leave it in his room. Too easy to come back and find it had been ransacked. So there he was, in custody with the tape until, as Iain came along, he had seen his chance.

Would they have already beaten him when Iain saw him? Iain had said that he seemed stiff. But they wouldn't have given him a going over at the hotel, surely? No, they would have been taking him somewhere, somewhere to begin the interrogation. But they could never have expected to get caught up in the crowds and tumult of Rais's motorcade and the mêlée of cars and people in its wake.

It was as if thoughts were tumbling through my mind faster than I could register them.

Then Dave had reared up in the street and made his dash for it, to be picked up by Iain in the Landie of all people, a rolling rescue that roared off down the street. It must have looked planned, organised, arranged. Of course, a conspiracy! It would be the only explanation.

On foot, after having been dropped off by Iain that lunchtime, how long would it have been before they picked him up again? It could only have been a few hours if not minutes. Mkilwa was too much of a company town for that, there would have been eyes everywhere. And then it was a question of how long before he started to talk or before he was dealt with.

They would have been able to identify Iain's car reasonably quickly, I thought. He and the Landie had been in the management's face for long enough. That would just have been more evidence of the conspiracy for them. They must have thought Iain and Dave had been working together.

A cold certainty was gripping my heart now. The logic rolled on remorselessly, inevitable, clear, bright and chilling. I felt sick. They would have known that Iain would need to take a ferry to get back to Jijenga. They just wouldn't have known which one.

The men with Dave would have watched Iain pick Dave up and drive away, heading down into town, towards the docks, towards the old ferry ticket office, the boat which sailed out every morning and back every evening.

Oh my God, what if the ferry going down hadn't been an accident? What if it had been a desperate attempt to get Iain? One that had failed, a futile waste of life, because Iain wasn't catching that boat? He was only driving in to town to pick up William to head out of town again, past New Mwanchi and down to the pier by the airport for the early afternoon Ro-Ro sailing that day. He had already checked out of his hotel.

The roar of overwhelming certainty descending was deafening.

Hundreds dead. Drowned. For nothing.

But then there would have been the message to Jijenga as well. The backup.

So the message to Jijenga must have been: Find Iain if he returns. Find him and find the tape. Then tidy up the loose ends.

Finding Iain must have been easy, I thought. These were people with connections. One call to someone, one call to the SPU's agent in the firm say, and Iain's apartment would be identified. And then it would just be a matter of lying in wait. They could have picked Iain up as he came back from the Europa Bar. Perhaps Juma had been in the apartment, getting it ready for his return.

Damn. Damn. That was what I should have asked the *askari*, when he was around to talk. Were the people there before Bwana Iain got back, on the Wednesday and Thursday? Were there people waiting for him?

But of course when they picked him up, he no longer had the tape. And unless the message was well informed and specific, the Jijenga end wouldn't have known what sort of tape they were looking for.

So when they didn't find it in the car, what happened? They must

157

have searched the apartment looking for tapes. My mind went back to the *askari*. The *askari* who had now so conveniently disappeared, who no one could trace, and to all the cassettes from Iain's apartment that were now nowhere to be seen.

Well bwana *Kubwa*. Well *Polisi*. Was that it? Was that what you were after?

If you have stolen those tapes, what do you think you have? Do you now think that you have got what you were looking for? Do you think you had proved that there wasn't anything else to find? Or do you still think you are missing something?

Iain would have seen lots of people at the Hash and Europa Bar. What are you thinking? Are you wondering if he had passed it on before you got to him? And if so, to whom? Iain knew so many people.

How much time did you take to ask questions before you killed him, you stupid shits? I was screaming at them inside now. You stupid, stupid, bastards.

You didn't think it through did you, you bastards? You didn't think. You just killed him and then you searched the car. You didn't find anything there so then you thought, perhaps he went to the apartment and you had missed him. So you searched there too. What did you do? Did you sit there in his apartment; did you drink his whisky while you looked? I hope you bloody choked on it. And because you didn't really know what you were looking for, you took all the tapes you could find. All his cassettes. All his music tapes. You bloody idiots. Much good may they do you, you bastards.

The question is, how long was it or will it be before someone looks at the tapes that you stole? How long before someone realises that these aren't the tapes they want, aren't even the type of tape they want? Or have they already realised? I hope you pay the price for cocking it up. I really do.

*

We were both in shock I suppose. We sat down on the warm sand beside a palm tree and gazed out over water that was so dazzling that it hurt the eyes to look at it. Neither of us wanted to speak.

Sam was shaking her head. 'It just can't be true,' she said eventually, staring straight ahead to where Boma's green headland was visible across the bay.

'Can't it?'

'There's got to be some other explanation.'

'You're the one who knows the chemistry,' I said. 'You tell me, what else could they be doing?'

'You're building an awfully big case out of some chemicals and the sort of lab equipment that you'd find anywhere in the world aren't you?'

'Am I?' I wondered. I didn't think so. But I did think they were making smack.

'But why?'

Why was the easy part. According to the report I'd found, refined morphine blocks sold for £150 a kilogram in the tribal lands of Pakistan. Converted into heroin, the end product sold for £80,000 a kilogram in the UK.

'No', she said. 'Why here? Why New Mwanchi?'

I wasn't sure how much I ought to tell her.

'I think I've figured it out,' I started.

'Figured what out?'

'All of this, what's happening. New Mwanchi, smack, H, drugs. Dave, this tape. It's all linked.'

She was looking at me in open-mouthed horror. 'What?' she mouthed. I was surprised, stupid of me I suppose. She was furious – with me – it was so unfair.

'What are you talking about?'

'I think New Mwanchi are smuggling smack into Europe.'

I got as far as telling her that I thought Iain and Dave had been killed because of the tape before she erupted.

'You really are out of your mind,' she screamed.

*

Am I getting paranoid? I wondered. After all what has actually happened? Nothing.

'What are you doing?' asked Sam, as I opened the cupboard in the hallway and started to rummage around. I had been dreading this question ever since I had made up my mind what I had to do, rehearsing what I was going to say over and over.

'I'm getting out my shotgun.'

Sam didn't like guns. 'Why, what's the matter with you?'

'I think we're in danger.'

'What, over New Mwanchi? No we're not! We can't just be made to disappear?'

It was frightening how quickly we were each taking refuge in anger.

'Oh no? Can't they? Bullshit, that's just wishful thinking. Seen Dave recently have you? Everybody who touches this tape dies, or has a way of just disappearing and now like it or not, we think we know why. Think about it. Dave. Iain. Juma. The roads here are dangerous but at the moment they're looking distinctly fatal. Why not us next?'

'Well I don't want anything to do with it,' Sam said, as I walked down the hallway. 'What are you going to do with the gun?'

'Put it on the table in the living room.'

'Well I don't want to know.'

From behind me I heard the slam of her bedroom door.

The apartment was too small to fight in. After an argument, there was nowhere to go that wasn't in sight or sound of each other, but out. And if I was right, out could be fatal.

So there was no choice but to stay in. A silence, the atmosphere hanging heavy like smoke, the fight unresolved, dangerous, a loose thread that might unravel us.

In silence I walked down the corridor and into the living room.

There had been a spate of carjackings last year towards M'gola. The gangs were after the big four by fours, it wasn't as bad as Kenya yet but there was an uneasy feeling this was a start.

So I had arranged for Kharatasi's chief *askari* to buy me a short barrelled pump action shotgun and a box of cartridges. I had never held a gun in my life before but this was something naturally I didn't trouble the local *Polisi* with.

I'd kept it after we'd sold Kharatasi. Strictly it had been bought with the business's funds so I should have handed it over to the new owners. But it didn't appear on any fixed asset register and having gone to all the trouble of acquiring it, I was now strangely reluctant to let it go, even though I'd never fired it and had no intention of doing so. With its dull black gunmetal sheen it was a very military, fashionable looking thing with a big boxy central section and a folding metal stock. Like something out of *Terminator 2*, I thought. All I needed were a pair of Arnie shades.

For want of anywhere better to keep it I had stuck it in the bag with a half set of golf clubs I'd brought out from home with a vague and so far completely vain, intention of learning to play. I had bought a book to teach myself how to swing a club. I didn't have one on how to operate a shotgun.

*

I pulled the heavy weight out of the golf bag and cradled it respectfully and gingerly in my arms as I shut the living room door. It was slightly warm to the touch. The wardrobe in the bedroom was next to the immersion heater. I guess now's the time I had better work out how to use it, I thought, putting it and the box of cartridges down on the dining room table.

I took two cartridges out of the box and picked up the shotgun to examine it. It couldn't be that difficult a thing to work out, I thought to myself, turning the shotgun around to try and see which bit you twisted, pushed or pulled to make an opening for the shells to go in.

A click, and a slot had opened. I looked at the opening and then at the shells. Now if it pumps like this, I calculated, surely they must go in like that. The first one was a snug fit, so I pushed another in behind it. A few moments later and I had four shells in. They slotted in one after the other like batteries into a torch.

Now I pumped the handle under the barrel experimentally. Had that loaded one in the breech? I didn't know. I was suddenly struck with a thought. Did it have a safety catch? And did the pumping cock it? I didn't know. Bloody typical, I thought. I should have tried doing that without any shells in it. Now of course I didn't know how to get a shell out of the breech.

Great, well done, Paul, I thought bitterly. You may or may not have a loaded shotgun which may or may not have a safety catch on and which may or may not be cocked, and you don't know how to clear it.

Worried now, I picked it up and carried it to my bedroom, with the minimum of jogging. I didn't even know how sensitive it was. Then I laid it on the floor and pushed it carefully under the bed. I just hope it doesn't go off one night when I'm going for a leak, I thought. It'd be embarrassing to blow your own feet off.

The door to Sam's room was still closed. I stopped outside. I felt awful, an agony of impotence. Tentatively I knocked.

'Sam, can I come in?' There was an indecipherable noise from inside, so quietly I opened the door and stood awkwardly in the doorway.

She was sitting at her desk with her back to the door, fiercely concentrating on staring at the blank screen of her open laptop. Despite the swiftly falling turquoise dusk she had left the light off. I could see she had been crying, but there was nothing I could do.

*

We were sat beside each other on her bed in the early evening darkness, our backs against the headboard; she had her legs drawn up under her chin. The air conditioning clattered away noisily above us. We were rowing. Again.

'You are out of your mind. You don't know anything. Iain and Juma had an accident. Nothing more. An accident, you understand? Everyone says so. Iain had been drinking. They were drunk and driving. It's tragic but it was waiting to happen. We've thought so often enough, haven't we? Even Colin at the High Commission said as much.'

'No he didn't.'

'It was an accident. Dave had an accident as well. For heaven's sake, hundreds of locals did as well. What are you suggesting? That someone sunk a whole ferry with God knows how many people on it?'

'Seven hundred is the official figure.'

'Yes, but you and I both know that no one really knows do they? And I don't really care if it was a thousand. The point is, do you think it was sunk just to get him?'

'No.' I didn't tell her what I really thought.

'Well then.'

'No, I hadn't really thought that. Not even here. I just don't think he was ever on it.'

'It was an accident. The boat sank, he drowned, just like everyone else on board.'

'But what would he have been doing on that boat?'

'How the hell should I know? You don't! You don't know anything about what he was doing here really. He could have been doing anything on it. It's a big country and the bank is everywhere. He could have been investigating anything.'

'But he wasn't investigating just anything was he? He was investigating New Mwanchi. And I think he was doing so because he suspected what I now think.'

'Which is?'

I shrugged, somebody had to come out and say. 'Like I said, I still think it's drugs.'

There was a moment's silence.

'This is nonsense,' she said. 'That place is a smelting works. What could that possibly have to do with drugs? What about all the

162

other equipment in that lab? The mercury? That's got nothing to do with drugs.'

'No, listen. Please,' I begged her. 'I don't know about that other kit, perhaps it means something, perhaps it doesn't. But the drugs thing makes perfect sense. Please let me tell you.' I was pleading with her. 'And if I'm right it's a completely brilliant scheme.'

She looked at me. She had fallen silent. She seemed to swallow hard. 'OK,' she said, after what seemed an age. 'So tell me.'

I was talking quietly. 'Look, what is it that these people do?'

'They smelt lead.'

'And scrap.'

'And scrap. So what?'

'And they export what they produce. Nice big two-metre long lead ingots that weigh tonnes each and yet they need an armed guard to be shipped down from Mkilwa to Jijenga. The same way that the trainloads of scrap coming in from Pakistan need armed guards when it comes up from the port, particularly the containers of engines. Now why is that?

'I bet they even time the imports and exports so that the guards get used for trips both ways. That would be smart and cost effective wouldn't it? So what do they do? They import scrap. Now doesn't that seem odd to you? They've got tonnes of rusting metal sitting in the yard already, but what do they do? They spend hard currency importing yet more on a regular basis. Dave sent Mkate off to find out shipping details, didn't he?'

Sam's silhouette nodded.

'So why import? There is plenty lying about locally that you could get cheap, for *shillingi npya*, not dollars, and that you wouldn't have to pay duty on? Why not use that first? Why buy in the scrap at all? There's no evidence anywhere that they smelt it, or export it, or actually do anything with it at all! And as for this story that they strip off bits like alternators and so on, where's the resale business for that here? No, all that seems to come out of the place, as far as anyone outside is concerned, are lead ingots. And they go back down to the coast under armed guard and away. So what's the deal?'

'It doesn't make sense,' Sam said.

'It doesn't. Not unless the scrap is covering up something else. Now, all those engines from the containers that come in, for example. What happens to them?'

'They get dismantled.'

163

'They get dismantled. So why bother if you are going to smelt them down? Why do they go to a separate godown, kept locked up, where only a few specific *wahindi* work, taking off the cylinder heads and sumps? Why would they want to, why not just melt down the whole lot? I can understand taking off the alternator or starter motor if you wanted to recover the copper, say, but sumps and engine heads? That doesn't make sense. And why pay *wahindi* to do the work? Why not some *wananchi* grease monkeys? All they are doing is getting a few nuts and bolts undone and prising them apart. And why did Dave find a cylinder head that had been spot welded down?'

'Well there are ordinary *wahindi* here too, you know. They're not all merchant princes.'

She was right of course. While this was a country where whatever people said or thought, race in practice still defined and determined so much, the social and racial stratification between *wananchi* and *wahindi* was fuzzy at the margins.

'True, but only specific *wahindi* are allowed access to these engines in secure conditions. Now that doesn't make sense unless there is something in there that no one else is allowed to see. There are some big engines going in there, big diesels from buses and the like. I bet there's plenty of room in the sump and cylinders of one of those to transport anything you want. These are going to be big consignments and the local Customs officers are fat, lazy and greedy. And anyway, they're not looking for drugs coming in here, where's the local market rich enough to afford them? No, the locals are more concerned about arms for the interior or conflict diamonds.

'So if it is drugs, then at least getting the stuff from Pakistan to here is no problem, which puts the drugs one step away from a known source and East Africa isn't yet regarded as a major transhipment point. Africans in general get a good shakedown when they get to Europe because they are often used as mules, but what we are talking about here is different. This is industrial in scale.

'And then there's the lab. The right chemicals, the right equipment. Good God, no wonder Dave got interested when I mentioned the smell. And what did he find when he went in and had a look around? He thought they were preparing to shut down operations. The laboratory had been cleaned, everything had been shut down, drained off, scrubbed clean, equipment removed. Perhaps that was what went out in the lorry the first day we were there.'

'Whatever, this is still nonsense,' she said.

'No, no it's not. One of the major problems facing any drug smuggler is getting the product into the end market, Europe or the States, from a known producing area. So you need a way to disguise both the drugs and where they are coming from. You can bet your bottom dollar that anything exported from Columbia or Pakistan direct to the UK gets a pretty thorough going over on its way through Customs.

'But here? These guys are sending off two-metre long ingots from Africa. It's beautiful really. How the hell is a sniffer dog going to find anything buried in tonnes of lead? How are Customs going to X-ray it for God's sake? It is absolutely brilliant.'

'But how do they put it into the ingots?'

'They're making little carrying containers. Do you remember the thirty-centimetre containers Dave found in the lab? Small squat containers with thick walls and screw-on lids. They cast those out of some of the scrap, with good thick walls, probably line them inside as well with something insulating, and put in kilos of the stuff. Then they screw on the lid, probably weld it down so it's sealed up good and tight.'

'After that it's simple, they make two slightly undersized half ingots in moulds that put a storage space in the centre. Then they put the two together with the container in the middle, set the whole thing into a full size mould, pour more lead in around it to complete the ingot and cover the join, and hey presto, perfect cover. That's why the containers need good thick walls to protect the stuff inside from the heat of that last bit of lead.'

'They're exporting to related companies remember, as well. Everyone here thinks that it's just to evade taxes and keep Forex offshore. What if really they number up the ingots, let their guys the other end know which numbers to look for and away they go?'

'Assuming for a moment that any of this is true, what if it goes astray?'

'No problem. It just gets lowered into a furnace to be melted down by the recipient. Who's going to notice a relatively small bit of stuff getting burnt off inside? If they did, they wouldn't be able to get at it in time to find out what it was. Who is ever going to know?

'Neither the African staff here nor the European staff at the other end need know anything about it. The *wahindi* can cast an ingot on a later shift using *wahindi* labour, and at the other end, I bet they just take ingots "at random" to a lab for testing by a *wahindi* chemist. It would just be normal quality control procedures as far as anyone looking on is concerned.'

'But isn't there any way that someone could spot it?'

I had thought about that. 'The only give away is likely to be the density. If you accurately measured the ingots and compared their weights, those with some form of inclusion are likely to have a slightly different density. But given the size and the roughness of the casting, that sort of variation is going to be too small to get picked up by Customs. And what if someone the receiving end does spot that? Well, his *wahindi* boss is just going to say, "Well done, segregate that ingot and send it to the lab for testing." No problem whatsoever.'

'So what we are going to do?' whispered Sam in the darkness.

'What can we do? We sit tight for now. Presumably no one knows we have the tape at the moment, otherwise they would have come looking for it, or worse.'

'Can't we tell someone?'

'Tell who?'

'Colin? Get the High Commission to protect us.'

'No.' I shook my head. 'Colin thinks I'm cracking up as it is. And what can the High Commission do? This is all still, as you keep reminding me, pure speculation. After all the tape doesn't actually say anything specific.'

In the darkness I could tell that all the stress of the day seemed to have got to Sam now. She was starting to cry.

'Sam?'

I pulled her gently to me and held her to try and give her some comfort. 'Sam it's all right.'

'Surely we should tell someone. In case anything happens… happens to us.' Sam sobbed in a muffled voice.

I shook my head. 'We can't tell anyone.' And then by mistake I thought out loud, 'Oh Christ, what about Ish?'

Sam jerked up, distraught at the thought, 'You mustn't, promise me you won't tell him.' She was panic stricken and grabbed at the front of my shirt. 'He'll want to use it, he's so desperate for a big story. He'll go looking for it and he'll get himself killed. You mustn't tell him, you mustn't. Promise me you won't.' She was sobbing freely now but there was a fierce determination and desperation in her voice.

'It's OK,' I said holding her to me and stoking her hair. 'It's OK, I won't tell him. I promise.' Sam was right though. If Ish had this, he'd be dead before it hit the newsstand.

'So what do we do?'

'I don't know. Yet.' I hugged her to me. 'I'll think of something.'

Should we go to the police? I wondered. But I knew the answer already, the police had issued the ferry casualty lists which included Dave. Besides, would this sort of scam really be operating without high up *Polisi* protection? No wonder Temu had been so pissed off with us when we started hassling New Mwanchi. Poor bastard, I thought. That was probably the explanation. He really got it at payback time.

She was right in another way too. We were going to have to do something. But at the moment, I just couldn't figure out what.

10 Pantomime

Saturday, 10 December, Jijenga

The rest of the week passed. Then the next week. Nothing happened. No more deaths. No threats. No one came calling, not even the *Polisi*. Iain's things had gone, there seemed nothing left. Even out in the city and the country things seemed to have quietened down although you could still feel a tension in the streets, and the army and *Polisi* presence on the streets of Jijenga was noticeably heavier than in the days before the election. We sat tight and waited as the days ticked past towards my departure date and Sam even felt comfortable enough to venture to one of the hotels up the coast at Kigoyo for ten days or so to run one of her aid training courses.

I woke up to the weekend. This early in the morning it was cool for the time of year.

I slipped out through my mosquito net and padded quietly down the hall to the kitchen to make coffee.

As I sat back on the sofa, outside for once there was silence other than the gentle lowing of a cow on the grass below the balcony. And then as I watched, a taxi rattled its dusty way up the rutted road outside the apartments and swung into the car park. With a bang of the doors out got Ish.

Sunday, 18 December, Jijenga

It was the Sunday before Christmas, the last night of the run and Ish was clowning around. 'I'm a pantomime virgin,' he confessed cheerfully.

'So am I,' I admitted.

He opened another beer. 'It's the adult night I hear, last bash of the season, so it's going to be a bit more risqué than usual. A bit more "babes".' He snitched his fingers in the air in front of him to indicate the quotation marks for emphasis... 'in the woods.'

So we both went, we had to, it was as simple as that. Even a miserable old sourpuss like me who wouldn't join the Yacht Club ghetto knew too many people who would be in it to stay away.

But tonight I needed it. I had a desperate reckless gaiety and need for company. Ish and I sat at the back, in the hot sweaty darkness under a black-purple sky. Out front, down from us, the bright stage seemed distanced, unreally lit, a frantic nursery-coloured dream.

Each of us had our store of three, gently warming ice blue cans of cheap imported beer for the first half, stacked under our plastic school chairs.

'I'm not getting any younger,' squeaked the dame's falsetto, his/her folded arms shuffling from side to side for the umpteenth time to jiggle his/her sagging pillows.

'You're not getting any!' heckled someone.

Being December, the theatre, more a breeze block compound without a roof than a building, was swelteringly hot in the darkness. By the end of the show at half ten I could feel the sweat dripping from my face and the rivulets rolling down my back under my sodden T-shirt. I felt as though when I stood up to decamp to the bar there would be a warm damp patch on the seat.

And I was getting drunk, a deliberate sort of drunk. And that was dangerous.

By midnight the bar had turned into an impromptu leaving party for the dame and principal boy. It would go on until the wee small hours. It was time to collect up Ish and go. I finished my can of beer.

I fought my way on through the hubbub, the crowd was ten deep at the bar and blocking my way out. As I squeezed past the crowd, I overheard snatches of conversations amongst the throng.

'...which of our friends at home do you think is attractive?'

'Well, the girl I'd most fancy buying in a slave market would be...'

'I don't know what Baba taught, but it certainly wasn't economics...'

'...It was wonderful. We brought Mary, our cook. It wasn't until half way through that she suddenly twigged that Mike was a bloke, not a *mama*. Cracked her up it did...'

'Never let the skin grow back across their backs, that's my rule...'

'...eight hundred, nine hundred? Who knows, they're all just guesses. You know what it's like here, it's a scrum to get on board, some people would have bought tickets in advance, some people just getting the standing passenger chit at the gate for a few *shillingi npya*. Nobody will ever know how many foot passengers there were on board.'

'...The Funbar is a good career for a local girl. Almost one of the best available...'

'Never trust a fat African, that's what I say...'

'...I can't afford to become friends. It has happened to us too

169

often. You can't invest in being close to people you know will be going again in two years' time.'

The local permanent expats mixed with the blow-in temporary contractors, but it was a different sort of life.

Just by the exit I saw Clare, she was swaying in the still night air.

'What's the latest on shitface?' I enquired. Asking her about Gerry was often akin to lighting the blue touch paper and then stepping smartly back to observe the show. Clare seldom failed to disappoint and this time the squeak definitely went up an octave or so.

'Oh he's back in the country. Did I tell you about his card?'

I shook my head.

'He sent me a bloody postcard from the Seychelles.'

'Mm, nice,' I encouraged her.

'Nice? I'll say it's nice. Do you know what he wrote? Hi, remember me? Of course I bloody remember him. He's the one who's pissed off out of the country without a word and then it turns out he was off to see another woman.'

'I was at Rooftops on Wednesday night and there he was, pissed as a fart, almost too drunk to stand. I tried to have it out with him but I couldn't get any sense out of him other than that the shit's going to hit the fan.'

'What about?'

'It's his last wife. She was Somali, something to do with Siad Barre apparently. But she's got the dirt on him and she's threatening to blow it in the newspapers. Just keep watching the *News*. As if you didn't know.'

*

By the exit Ish had caught hold of Colin who was expounding on British diplomatic corps duties. Presumably on an off-the-record basis.

'What really pisses me off are those bloody travellers. They come breezing in here and they forget that this isn't home. I had one in the office the other day, he had lost his passport and his dosh, the stupid sod. Expected me to arrange to have him flown home.'

Ish was nodding and making appropriate keep talking sort of noises. A key journalistic skill presumably.

'It's the hippies who are the worst though,' Colin continued. This isn't England or Europe or even the States and they just don't realise it. In theory you still need a licence here to have your hair in dreadlocks. You get caught with dope on you and they'll bang you away for twenty years. Just like that prat they caught up at Mkilwa just before the election, trying to smuggle hash out to SA. He'll be lucky if he ever sees the light of day again. Nothing we can do about it however much they bleat. This isn't our country, it's the locals' and they make the rules.

'But what's worse, if they get put in jail, the one thing I do have to do is visit them. African jails are smelly. I don't like African jails, and I don't like having to visit them to see stupid sods who get themselves locked up in them. So I don't like people who do.'

Good, I thought drunkenly. I pushed my way towards them. I wanted a word with Colin – several, actually, and I was now in the mood for it.

I wanted to ask him some decidedly undiplomatic questions.

It had proved a bit more difficult to catch up with Colin than I had thought. Colin seemed to have gone to ground, become more like a typical diplomat and keeping away from the expat hoi polloi.

Ish was asking as though for confirmation, 'So he had broken his neck?'

Colin nodded.

'They both had!' I barged in. It was more a statement or an aggressive accusation than a question.

Colin hadn't noticed me lurching up. I had taken him by surprise. He looked down at his beer can or at his feet and nodded. 'I don't know much about the other one.' He looked up and caught my expression. 'Not a British subject.' He shrugged by way of explanation.

This was exactly what I had wanted to ask. I hammered on, shaking my empty beer can to emphasise each word. 'But don't you think that's unusual?'

He shrugged again. 'Maybe,' he said, looking around. He sounded tenser. Looking for someone. Looking to see who was watching. 'Maybe not in the circumstances.'

'Well it strikes me as unusual that they should both have broken necks.'

He shrugged again. 'Well, perhaps it is unusual.'

My head was spinning. We were in a pool of silence in a surrounding whirlpool, a maelstrom of conversation, a roar of noise. 'Well,' I said, and then stopped. Colin had stiffened. His moment of indecision, if that's what it was, had passed. He stood solidly,

171

suddenly soberly, staring into my eyes. He waited out the silence a while. Ish waited as well, watching me.

'Well what?' Colin asked eventually.

I shrugged helplessly. Colin saw his advantage and pressed it home ruthlessly. 'Are you trying to make a point? What point are you trying to make?' he demanded, louder each time.

It was no use. 'Just, it seems unusual,' I tailed off weakly.

'Accidents happen,' he said definitively, almost jabbing his finger at me. 'It's a dangerous country. Just don't you forget that.'

In my drunken state I felt detached and angry. His shrugs, his impassivity, were starting to have a power. If he just stonewalled me solidly, it might have meant something, it might have communicated a, 'Yes, you know something but I can't tell you.' But then we would have known that, so to deny diplomatically and convincingly for his country he would shrug. So could I believe his shoulders, any more than his words? Probably not, but they were having an effect.

The moment of silence stretched, a bubble of tense stillness between the tables with their pink check covers and plastic patio chairs scattered among the simmering heat-sodden throng at the bar.

'You're pissed,' Colin said eventually, sounding disgusted. 'Go home and watch out you don't end up like that yourself.'

As I slumped out of the porch's yellow pool of light into the blackness, I looked round but couldn't see anything except the looming shapes of the cars parked between the inky bulk of the trees and the ghostlike figures of the *askaris* in their dusty khakis, emerging silently from the shadows, waiting for their *shillingi npya*.

*

As I drove my squiffy way home I kept an eye out for any cars I recognised. I didn't see any. But that, I thought drunkenly to myself, didn't prove anything at all.

'Makings of an interview there?' I asked Ish as we bumped off the tarmac onto the dirt road.

'Possibly, possibly,' he said distractedly.

'So what were you talking about before I busted in?'

'He was telling me about how we back in the UK can't afford to upset the government here.'

'What do you mean we can't afford to? We pay their bloody bills? We've got so much bloody aid coming in here you would think we could say what we like!'

172

'But that's just the point. We have to keep the aid flowing and we're in competition with everyone else to get it in here.'

'Sorry, I just don't get that. Why would our government compete with the Dutch or the Japanese to spend our tax payers money here?'

'Because it doesn't really all get spent here does it? The Japanese government donates money for road building; so who got to build Bara Bara ya Rais? A Japanese contractor. The Japanese government donates money to support local democracy; what gets bought? Landcruisers for MPs. Who do you think supplied Tanzania's air traffic control system that the UK funded?'

'It's all just hidden subsidies to domestic industry?'

'Not all of it, but enough.'

'And it doesn't get caught as a subsidy by things like the EC and World Trade rules?'

'No, that's the beauty of it. As aid it's completely outside those sort of rules so governments in the West can really use it to channel money to where they want it to go at home in a way that they can't do any longer with straight subsidies.'

'And that's why they need to keep Jijenga onside? So as to keep the channel open for themselves.' I considered this for a moment. 'So is this your new breakthrough story?'

'Don't know,' he said thoughtfully, 'it might be. Colin really had it on tonight didn't he? But I doubt he'll want to go on the record if I call him tomorrow.' He laughed, 'Damn, another scoop slips through your ace reporter's hands.'

'Is that what you're after these days? Features section not enough anymore?'

'Well, you know how it is.'

'Yeah. I know,' I agreed. And then after a moment I asked, 'D'you know anything about Temu?'

Ish was looking out of the window as we passed the endless walled residential compounds. 'Temu, Temu, I've heard that name just recently. What's the context?'

'Regional police commissioner,' I said.

Ish had it now, 'Yes, yes, of course. He was the RPC for Mkilwa wasn't he? The guy who committed suicide just after the election.'

'Yep, that's right. Found shot,' I said.

'Yes, that was a little too close to home, wasn't it?' Ish added.

In all senses of the phrases. 'Too right. Did you know I met him?'

'No?' said Ish.

'Yeah, I had a couple of run-ins with him up in Mkilwa on New Mwanchi. For some reason I couldn't get him and his boys to do anything about anything that was going on up there.'

'Well,' said Ish. 'That sure must have come as a surprise.'

There was a pause as I slowed down to skirt a particularly bad pothole. 'Could you do me a favour, Ish?' I asked quietly.

'Yes, sure, whatever,' he agreed.

'Could you find out if there was ever any more news about his death? What the rumours were, whether anybody knew anything? You know what the papers are like here, front page story one day and then just disappears completely.'

'Yes, sure, I'll ask around. But apart from the obvious, why the interest?'

'Just curiosity really' I shrugged. 'But keep it quiet would you please? I don't really want anyone to know I'm asking questions given what happened, and we'd crossed swords.'

'Yeah, sure,' Ish nodded. 'Sure, I understand. Funnily enough I'm off back up to Mkilwa tomorrow for the rag. That's where I'd heard the name, they want me to do some digging into the ferry and the Chairman definitely mentioned Temu as well.'

It was a measure of how disturbed I was that I didn't really take in the import of what Ish was saying.'

I was nodding too, 'Thanks, mate.'

Actually he didn't. But that was deliberate on my part.

Saturday, 24 December, Ras Bahari

The Christmas trip to chimp country inland from Mkilwa was definitely off. There was fighting near the border so tourists were being 'discouraged'.

Instead we drove up along the coast to Ras Bahari.

We sat on the steep sand that evening and watched as the huge waves crashed in and rolled foaming and boiling up the beach before they were sucked down, the backwash from the falling water taking the legs away from the following lesser sets as they pushed forwards in their turn, so they seethed and writhed impotently, unable to stride up the strand.

The pantomime dame's predecessor at the Parastatal Privatisation Commission had cracked up here and just refused to return to Jijenga one day. I could understand that. It was so isolated here, so peaceful, with the rhythmic boom of the surf, the

174

susurration of the backwash along the shore, the buffeting bouncing wind. It would be a lovely, lonely place to commit suicide, I thought.

It was one of my favourite places in Africa. It was the golden light time of day. Later, as the sun set and the sky grew a shining turquoise, I walked behind Sam and Ish as we made our way up through the coconut palms back from the beach to our bandas. They were holding hands as they went.

'How are you doing?' Ish called across.

Not good, I thought guiltily to myself, thinking back over the last few months and then over the last few years back in England. Especially about the few years. What was my fault? And what would have just happened anyway? Although as I thought about it, I didn't see what else I, or even we, could have done.

'I'm fine,' I lied out loud.

At dinner, Ish had an announcement to make, some really big news, he had found a tumble down seaside house to rent a bit further down the coast out of town for a couple of hundred dollars a month. Ish had moved in on Monday and it came complete with a houseboy called Martin who had fallen upon his washing with manic gusto.

'And plenty of bleach?'

'Oh absolutely. I've not quite got used to having razor sharp creases pressed into my boxer shorts,' he said, as a waiter appeared with another round of drinks

'Well congratulations!' I said brightly raising my can 'Here's to your first home together.'

'And thanks to you,' said Sam reaching out to gently squeeze my hand.

'Still I think it's a while before we can really move in,' added Ish.

'Why?' Even as I said it I noticed a look of surprise on Sam's face.

'Well I'm going to be needing to spend a lot more time up in Mkilwa, have you heard what's going on up there? Probably not I guess. The new RPC has set up special units to round up opposition activists. He's complaining that the local courts are taking too long to jail them which is stretching the police's patience.'

'Poor things.'

'So Boma's shipping him out some magistrates to help speed up the trials.'

'So why haven't I heard about this?'

'Because it's being hushed up. They've introduced a special permit that reporters need to have to cover the region.'

'Have you got one?'

'No.'

'Ish! You didn't tell me that!' Sam was now clearly worried.

'It's all right, I'll be safe, I've got my contacts, I know what I'm doing up there. But while I'm away it would be best if you stayed on at Paul's place, if you don't mind that is Paul?'

'Of course. As long as you guys want, you know that.'

'But what about you?' Sam insisted, 'and why would I need to stay with Paul?

'Listen love, I know what I'm doing. It's probably nothing but as far as some people here are concerned, I'm just a *wahindi*, and what's more a reporter on the rag. People will know where I live, so it's not safe for you to be there at home on your own.'

'But then you're saying that you're not safe!' Sam protested.

'I'll be all right. The Chairman will back me up, he's very well-connected with the SPU you know.'

I stayed out of it, this was their relationship, their fight. I would be there for them, whichever way they wanted to go, but they had to make their own decisions. But I was concerned about what Ish was saying. Relying on Chairman Ossoro was all very well, but Ish had to know that he could only rely on him for as long as Ish was useful to him and his friends, and as long as they stayed on top. If Ish outlived his usefulness, or if his contacts' grip on power slipped, what price the Chairman's protection then?

*

We were alone and Sam was crying. I felt awkward, unsure as to how to comfort her, unsure of my own emotions.

'Can I give you a word of advice?' I ventured quietly at last.

'Uhhuh,' she mumbled into her hands.

'If you love him, let him do what he wants to do. He's young, he's keen, he thinks this is what he wants to do, that this is his best chance. Whatever you do, don't be someone he could ever blame if it doesn't work out.'

'But he's putting himself in danger,' she sobbed.

'You think he doesn't know that? He may be being reckless but the truth is that we both know that he knows far better than we do what risks he's running.'

She sat still for a while. Then eventually broke the silence.

'Listen to you.'

'Yeah, what do I know, I'm just a sad old divorced git of an accountant.'

'That's not what I meant.'

'So what did you mean?'

'You're right, and you're not a sad old git.' She turned and smiled at me. 'You're, you're a lovely man, you're really nice.'

'Oh Christ, don't tell people that, I'll never live it down.'

'No I mean it. You're really sweet, you'll get through this, you'll find someone again, you'll see.'

As she stood to go back to their room she bent forward and kissed my forehead.

'And thanks Paul,' she murmured as she turned to go.

For what I wondered? For not telling him? I looked at the empties on the table and waved to the waiter. I felt the need for another beer.

Thursday, 19 January, Jijenga

I had had my formal leaving dinner from the firm at Coconut Grove. Tonight, with a week or so left before I planned to go, was to be shorts, T-shirts, food, and serious beers with friends at the Europa Bar.

As we bumped down the last bit of track off the main road we passed a white Landcruiser charging the other way, heading back into town.

'Wasn't that Gerry?' I asked.

'Was it? I didn't see,' said Sam from the back. 'I thought Clare said he had left.'

'Was leaving, I thought she said. And not till next week.'

'Oh. Perhaps it was then.'

*

Clare was installed in the bar when we arrived. She had already staked out a table. In fact it looked as though she had been there some time.

'So has he gone then?' I asked Clare.

'Who?' she sneered, 'shitface?'

'Yeah.'

She looked like someone trying to give the impression that this was a matter of supreme indifference to her but was failing miserably. Gerry was still obviously a very raw nerve.

'I must say he was looking well the last time I saw him,' I added. 'Very bonny for somebody who is terminally ill.'

'Christ you know what he just said to me?'

'No what was that?'

'He was there at the bar, pissed as a fart when I came in. He gave a big smile when he saw me come in and shouted out so the whole bar could hear, "Oh god, you're looking thin. Lost a lot of weight, haven't you? Have you got AIDS?"' she spat. 'Bastard. Bastard. Bastard!'

I was impressed. Even by Gerry's standards this was out of order. 'Absolutely charming.'

'Do you know what he said then?'

'No.'

'He asked how would I like to go back to his place and have great sex?' She picked up her can of Castle. 'So I just looked at him and said why should we have great sex now? We never did in the past.' Clare chortled. 'He was just sooo pissed off! Do you know what else he tried to tell me? He said he'd never been married. I think he's so pissed all the time now that he doesn't know what he's told people and what he hasn't. At least I've got a fairly good memory. I can remember when somebody's told me how many times they've been married. So he legged it outside and pissed off. You've only just missed him.' She shrugged.

'I'm disappointed,' I said.

'Why?' enquired Clare, thrown by the swift change.

'Well I've kept taking the *News* and you promised he'd been in there but he hasn't been, other than for the usual for the camps and stuff.'

'Why, what did I say?'

'You said, "Keep taking the papers, it'll hit." So what is it?'

'Oh I thought you knew.'

'No. All I know is that you were saying that there's something that one of his wives was going to give to the press, but you never told me what.'

'Oh well, do you remember you gave me that CIA recruitment ad?'

'Oh yes?'

'Well, that's what made me think you knew. His last ex has been telling the press that he has been working for them. Which obviously didn't go down a bundle back in the Netherlands with head office.'

That creased me up. Gerry a spook. I couldn't think of anyone less reliable, or less likely.

'Christ no, I can see it wouldn't. They must have gone ape shit.'

'Yes, well he'd told me a week or so before you gave me the ad, so I thought you knew.'

'Oh God no,' I said. 'You were just whinging on about wanting a job involving lots of travel and excitement.' What a prat Gerry was. A spy. He'd love that.

'Well,' she said, 'you sure picked a bad time to leave. The shit is going to hit the fan tomorrow, or if not tomorrow, the day after.'

'Why, what's up?'

'The Governor.'

'What as in the central bank?'

'Yep, conflict of interest.'

'What sort of conflict of interest?'

'Just the usual, the bank lending to him via companies under his control, kickbacks from contracts.'

'Shit, I thought he was on the side of the angels.'

'God no.'

'So where is all this coming from?'

'Well I don't know, but just look who is out of town.'

'What! You don't mean the Yanks?' I said, meaning the IMF contractors at PCB.

'Yep, now that's a very African way of doing things dont'cha think? Uncontactable for two weeks.'

Clare disappeared to the other end of the bar. She had her parents over. We would all be going home changed people. We wanted our families to know why. And the only way to show them was to have them over for a visit.

As the beers flowed, I turned to face the roar of noise in the bar.

*

Sam had finished her fieldwork and had come down to live in Jijenga full time to start writing up her findings and try and complete her research in the central library. I looked over to where she was chatting excitedly to Clare about their new beach home, but Ish was talking to me.

179

'Hey thanks for that money laundering video by the way. Useful background, this place is wide open for it. If you've got the hard currency, nobody gives a damn where it comes from.'

'That's right. I sold a factory to a Nigerian investor for a couple of million dollars last year and I certainly didn't ask too many questions.'

Ish looked at me. I waved my hands at him defensively, 'Hey, off the record and don't start on me bwana. Business is business.'

'Sure is,' he agreed.

'So no good stories to pin the career on?' I asked, changing the subject. 'There must be something coming out of the election and Bharanku surely?'

'Well, the only thing so far with any promise seems to be Temu. But that's strictly local interest.'

'Temu?' I asked, not too intently, I hoped.

'You know, you mentioned him to me the other day. You wanted me to find out what I could, so I had a bit of a dig. Discreetly of course.'

'So what did you find out?'

'Well for a start, he came down from Mkilwa the day after the ferry disaster.'

'That's a bit odd, isn't it?'

'You're telling me. The greatest disaster in the country's history happens in your harbour just days before the first multiparty general election where the main opposition candidate comes from your town, and are you on station? No! The very next day you go off on some jaunt to Jijenga.'

'To do what?'

'That's the very strange bit. The story in the papers was about a wedding, but no one, but no one, really seems to know.'

'Given all that was going on, perhaps he needed to consult with the politicians.'

'Perhaps, but no one seems to think he did and even if he'd wanted to, why not use the phone for Christ's sake?' Ish shook his head firmly. 'No. Think back, there was talk of cancelling the elections because Rais was going to be travelling to the scene. I mean he and Temu would even be passing each other going in opposite bloody directions! No, as far as Temu is concerned, at the time of the biggest local crisis there is just this great black hole, shrouded in mystery of where he was and what he was doing from the Thursday before the election to the Tuesday when he was

180

found.'

So, I thought, he could have been in town the day Iain died.

'Dead,' I said.

'Shot dead, absolutely. Suicide.'

'Really?'

Ish shrugged. 'That's what is being said, but really? No one seems to know.'

'What do you think?'

'I don't know. It is funny though how things always happen at once isn't it? The same day that you ask me about Temu, I'd just got a brief from the rag, from the Chairman himself in fact, to go have a look at the same thing, to go on safari to Mkilwa and see what I can dig up, to do some real investigation work!'

'Why?'

'To find dirt, and to see what sticks to Pesha I guess.'

Is that for the rag? Or is it for the Chairman? Or is it for his 'friends'? I wondered.

'Why you?'

'D'you know I think it's because I'm the only one who can do it?' Ish seemed to be really delighted at the thought. 'I'm the only one of his staff to ask questions. You know I think I'm the only real journalist on the whole rag.'

And Temu died himself a few days after Iain, I followed the thought through. Just enough time for someone to have found out that they had the wrong tapes perhaps, someone who might not be happy that Dave had been allowed to get inside the factory up at Mkilwa on Temu's patch, and then away in the first place. Oh God, I hope so, I thought, with a grim satisfaction. I wondered how many shots this suicide had actually taken but knew I could never ask Ish that question.

Was this what it had all been about up to now? Had it been Temu trying to stuff the genie back into the bottle? And had he then paid the price for failure?

'Well *Safari njema*, and Ish.'

'Yes?'

'Be careful.'

*

Even Winston made it later on. I told him my list of office SPU suspects in confidence at the top of my voice, but got no change out of him.

The evening disappeared in a roar of noise that filled my ears and head like a boiling beery deluge, into which I sank, and sank, and drowned.

*

It was well past midnight before Sam and I bounced away into the blackness in the Suzuki, she would be staying at the apartment rather than alone at the beach house while Ish was away. Behind us the bar was still going strong and Ish was off out somewhere into the *nyumbaya* on some mission of his own.

'So, if Gerry's not a spy, who do you think is the SPU mole in your office?' Sam asked.

'It has to be Sharik.'

'Why?'

'Well, Mkate's SPU, and he passed me the message in Sharik's shop for the first thing.'

'That's just coincidence. You could have been given it anywhere.'

'Yes, I could. But I wasn't. How would Mkate know I was in there regularly?'

'But it's where everyone in your office goes for bits and pieces isn't it? It's so convenient being just next door.'

'OK, so why is he still on the firm's books? What does he do when he's there? No one seems to know. Why have a part-time wheeler dealer on the payroll?'

Sam shrugged. 'Sure, so that makes him a secret policeman.'

'Yes, but remember the *askari*?'

'Which *askari*?'

'The one at Iain's apartment, the one who seems to have disappeared.'

'Yes.'

'Well the only person who knew I had spoken to him was Sharik. It came up in conversation as I left the apartment.'

'OK, but…'

'Who else could have known and arranged for the *askari* to disappear?'

'But you don't know that anyone did arrange for the *askari* to disappear, as you put it.'

'So what else happened?'

'Oh come on, Paul. You know what they're like here. You handed over, what, a couple of thousand?'

'Yes.' It was more actually, but I wasn't going to tell her.

'That's probably several months wages for the poor sod.'

'Yes, but...'

'And you said yourself, he seemed frightened stupid once he remembered the *Polisi*.'

'Yes.'

'So he has probably just taken the cash and done a runner hasn't he?'

'Possibly.'

11 A quiet night in

Friday, 20 January, Jijenga

I struggled through Friday, my last official day in the office. Beery-eyed and bleary, shutting the door on the nauseating heat, my head throbbing to the icy rattle of the air conditioner.

I had had Janet and William bring the filing up to date after their own fashion, so luckily there wasn't too much to do, even if I could have focused on it, other than to shuffle out quietly at noon for a toasted cheese sandwich in the soporific warm shade of the terrace bar at the Africa Hotel.

By about two-thirty, the battered tin tray with its pot of instant coffee, navy blue thermos of hot water and bowl with its remarkable content of sugar and ants was the nearest thing to dealing with my in-tray that I had touched all day. At least I had managed to stop the messengers bringing me a jug of evaporated milk.

Instead, I made desultory notes, some odds and sods for my valedictory newsletter, and then it was time to go back to the apartment.

My plan was to have a quiet night in.

But at about eight, just as we were settling down to read after supper, there was a knock at the door. Sam looked at me in surprise as I got up to answer it. We weren't expecting anyone.

I opened the door. Outside on the concrete landing, behind the security grille, Mr Mkate loomed, silhouetted by the harsh brightness of the security lights shining down into the stairwell through the gaps in the breezeblock tower. He seemed huge and powerful and all around him the bright white air was alive with dancing flickering floating moths.

'*Habari yako* Bwana Paul?'

'*Habari yako* Bwana Mkate?'

We stood either side of the bars while we went through the greeting ritual while I held the inner door ajar, closed off as far as possible against the mad, light-battering moths.

'*Hujambo* Bwana.'

'*Sijambo* Bwana.'

Silence. Flickery, thunderous silence. But I made no move to open the cage door between us.

Mr Mkate stood there, still and impassive. As a policeman perhaps he didn't notice the cell-like bars between us. Perhaps he saw them as normal, who knows?

Greetings concluded, the silence stretched on. It must only have been seconds but in the suddenly heavy atmosphere it felt eternal, damming, inevitable.

He had his head cocked to one side politely listening, waiting. All of a sudden it seemed to me that he might be able to wait forever. An elemental force, an unmovable object, solidly standing, blocking our only exit from the apartment, from the country, forever and ever. Watching. Not bored, not resentful, not emotional, just waiting and watching with an alien quiet.

'Well,' I asked, after what seemed an age. 'What can I do for you this evening, Mr Mkate?'

He smiled. This was his opening.

'It's terrible about Bwana David,' he shook his head sorrowfully, 'terrible news.'

'Yes,' I nodded, although it was hardly news. 'Has the body been found?' I asked.

'No. It is still missing.'

'Well that's awful. What do you think happened?'

Mr Mkate seemed to just shrug. I got the impression he wasn't really looking at me, his attention was elsewhere.

'Who knows? Perhaps he is food for the crocodiles.'

'That's horrible.'

Mr Mkate was suddenly serious, almost solicitous, perhaps concerned, even conspiratorial. 'This is Africa Mr Paul... Horrible things... happen here.'

His voice was slow, was he searching for words in English? Or were the pauses deliberate?

'Like your friend, Bwana David. Things can be very dangerous here. Even the very ground can be dangerous. Many dangerous things come out of the ground.'

There was something wrong with Mr Mkate, as I watched he was starting to become enraged, almost without reason, almost without knowing it, he was having some kind of fit. 'Dangerous things bwana, more dangerous than lead. Yes, more dangerous even than uranium. I know this now. I have discovered this.'

And in a moment he was ranting uncontrollably, meaninglessly, but always about danger, dangerous things from out of the ground, more dangerous than lead, more dangerous than uranium, things more dangerous still, his voice rising higher and higher. What on earth was he talking about? Then as suddenly and as inexplicably as his fit had started, he began to calm down, his voice dropping as the seizure or whatever it was seemed to pass and he gathered his thoughts. 'You must be very careful,' he concluded, more quietly now.

What was he saying?

'Especially as you are going home soon.'

I started. Now how the hell did he know that? But then he was a secret policeman and he was plugged into the expat financial network. I drew a deep breath. It was time to face up to the situation. I looked him in the eyes, through the bars.

'What can I do for you Bwana Mkate?'

'I have been told that you are departing. I have arranged to visit you to enquire whether there are any properties you are to leave behind.'

'Where did you hear that?' I asked, as I worked my way through his sentence.

'Oh, from numerous people. Many people know about your movements. You would be surprised Mr Paul.'

Would I? I thought. Possibly not 'And what sort of thing would you be after?' I asked, as casually as possible.

'Oh many things. Many expatriates are disposing of their personal effects before they return. I am however particularly interested in any tape cassettes you may have.'

'I see,' I said. A moment of silence elapsed, grew, invaded every nook and cranny, every pore in my body, every flickering moth and hanging spider's web.

This time Mkate took the initiative. 'Can I come in Mr Paul?' he asked politely.

The corridor behind him looked empty. I hesitated a moment. It felt churlish to refuse. What reason could I give to turn him away? A thousand questions rushed through my mind at once. Options, alternatives, but in the end they all boiled down to one thing. Was it safer to keep him out or let him in?

And what if I did keep him out? I had almost a week to go before I flew home. I wouldn't be able to hide from him and the authorities he represented forever.

So I bowed to what seemed like the inevitable, slipped the latch on the security grille and pushed it as he stepped back to let it open.

'Sure, *karibu* Bwana Mkate.' I gestured to him to enter.

'*Asante sana*, Bwana Paul.'

'Oh, bloody hell!' I cursed as I went to pull the grille shut behind him.

Outside the telephone wires had been pulled out of the wall socket. It could only have happened this evening. I would have noticed if they had been dangling like that when we arrived home.

Mkate remained expressionless as he squeezed his bulk past me. 'What is the matter, Mr Paul?'

'The telephone wires,' I said, pointing, at a loss for words.

Mkate shrugged in his impassive way.

'It is dreadful bwana, what can happen to wires outside in this country. Your telephone, it had only recently begun working?'

'Yes,' I said, 'but how did you know?'

Mkate gave a slight nod. 'I did not. I was only suspecting.'

Mkate had done it. I was suddenly sure of it. He had pulled out the wires before he had knocked on the door. But why? So that I could not ring out?

'That is unfortunate,' he continued. 'But you know I always think that in this country, being without a telephone is not such a bad thing. People can talk to each other much more freely when there is no telephone between them. Do you not agree?'

All I could think was, what on earth was he talking about? Surely he wasn't worried about us being interrupted by a telephone call?

*

Mkate greeted Sam, who remained on the sofa with her book. Business, or at least most types of business was obviously in his view man's work. As he turned back to me I noticed that she was staring at him in something like horror. Now that I could see him more clearly in the light I could see that his skin was looking grey and blotchy. And while he was still huge, his suit was hanging off his enormous frame. He had obviously lost a good stone or so in weight since I had seen him last.

'Tape cassettes, what sort of tapes?' I asked him.

'Oh,' he said, with a smile. 'English ones. They are the best. I wish to learn things. Many things. Do you follow?' He turned again to the bookcase. 'You have many such tape cassettes,' he said, gesturing vaguely across the room.

On the bookshelves, there were indeed many cassettes. There were video tapes that we had used to sit in the dark to watch at Kharatasi, with our two little oil lanterns for illumination and the generator chugging away in its little outhouse just down the back

187

steps. Then there was the music: an indie rock and roll call of my youth, Psychedelic Furs, Neil Young, Nirvana, the Pistols, the Sisters of Mercy.

But no smaller cassettes, no Dictaphone tapes. They were mostly in my pilot case in the spare bedroom.

The thought was at the front of my mind, 'they', whoever 'they' were, assuming there was a 'they', had to know what sort of tape Dave had sent. Mkate must know.

'Have a look,' I said, perhaps a bit loudly. 'I hadn't really thought of selling those. They're well, a bit personal. Too many memories.'

'All of them?'

'Some more than others.'

Mkate was looking slowly and lugubriously along the shelves. His massive head was cocked to one side, a bulging black roll of fat swelling out over his collar. A fat policeman I reflected. A very fat one. Always a very, very bad sign. Especially in Africa. What was it I had overheard someone say at the Little Theatre? '*Never trust a fat African.*'

Glancing sideways my eyes met Sam's who seemed fixated by Mkate, unable to keep her eyes off him. She nodded urgently at his back and downwards and mouthed the words at me 'Look at his hands,' I turned back to Mkate and focused on his hand which was hanging free. The palm was badly blistered, with what looked like weeping sores. I racked my brain, hadn't Iain said something about Dave having burns on his hands? Was there a connection?

Mkate was still looking, working his way along the line of cassettes. I couldn't see but I wondered whether he was moving his lips as he read the titles. With every second, every infinitesimal shuffle by him along the bookshelves towards the door to the little hallway which led down the centre of the apartment to the bedrooms, the tension grew.

'You were with Dave at New Mwanchi, weren't you Bwana Mkate?' I asked.

'Yes.'

I was surprised. I hadn't really expected him to answer.

'So what happened that night?'

Mkate shrugged nonchalantly. 'We gained access to the factory on the Monday evening. It was a very dark night. The sky was black with the clouds of the rains. I spoke to the chief of *askaris,* a very patriotic man, and explained how it was his duty to his country to provide me with the required assistance.'

I bet you did, I thought.

'We toured the factory,' he continued, 'and Bwana David made notes with his tape machine. Then we looked at the supplies and Bwana David made more notes.'

'What about?' I played the innocent.

'Oh, concerning the scrap. Notes about its origination. He seemed particularly interested in that, actually. In fact once we had gained access to the laboratory he asked me to go with the security officer to the main offices and see if we could find records of shipments in while he remained behind to investigate. A brave man Bwana David.'

I let that go for the moment. 'And did you?'

'Yes, exactly. There were shipments that were going back for many years.'

'What did Dave want to know?'

'The origination. Where they were from, who had sent them?'

'And what was the answer?'

'There were many. But many were from companies in Pakistan. I noted the names because I believed Bwana David would wish to investigate them further.'

'So what happened?'

'The chief of security and I were returning to rendezvous with Bwana David by the godowns when there was a huge commotion.'

'What sort of commotion?'

'At the gates bwana, cars and lorries arriving. It was the *Polisi*,' he said, as if it was the most natural thing in the world. 'Then all of a sudden the chief *askari* disappeared. I could see the *Polisi* coming onto the site; they had switched on the lighting around the offices and factory. There were about a dozen of them, with the officer of course.'

'Officer, what officer?'

'The man in charge of the *Polisi*. And Mr Paul, this was obviously serious.'

'Why?'

He turned to look at me. 'Because I recognised the policeman. It was the Regional Police Commissioner himself.'

'Temu?'

'Yes Mr Paul,' he nodded, and returned to the shelves. 'Mzee Temu.'

This was bringing things home again. Temu, the police

commander for the whole region, had turned out in person to lead a dozen policemen, scrambled to investigate suspected intruders at New Mwanchi.

'But by that time I was close to the godowns and met Bwana David coming out.'

'How did you escape?'

'We traversed the wall. As you had said to us at the Golden Shower, there was a construction where a belt carried waste over for its disposal. We climbed a ladder onto the structure, and ran along it. At last we were clear of the wall and we jumped off onto the piles of waste and got away.'

'It must have been quite a fall?'

'How far we fell was difficult to tell in the dark, and we slid down the pile of the earth and rocks for many metres. God was on our side, of course. The structure had been designed to prevent intrusion by robbers climbing up and onto the rails to obtain access to the site. The construction was not designed to prevent people getting out.'

'Were you hurt?'

'We were both bruised, I believe, but nothing serious. We parted as we had arranged, to stay at our different hotels for security reasons. We made our ways back separately. For security, you understand.'

'So what did Dave tell you when you met up again?'

Mkate shook his head slowly. 'I did not meet him again, he did not come to our rendezvous. I waited for twenty-four hours as was our agreed procedure and then I checked his hotel. He had left that very morning exactly, with other men, who I believe were local *Polisi*. I went to stay with relations. Then I heard that he was dead, drowned on the ferry. It is very sad.'

I really couldn't tell with Mkate. He was so unemotional, so matter of fact in his delivery, I just couldn't begin to tell how he felt about what he was saying. I couldn't even begin to guess why he was choosing to tell me, never mind whether it was the truth or not.

'And the chief security officer?' I asked.

'He has disappeared.' It was said somewhat offhandedly.

'You are the SPU, can't you trace him? Surely your organisation can trace anyone in this country?'

The flash of steel in his answer was chilling.

'How can I trace smoke, Mr Paul? The furnaces at New Mwanchi burn all day and all night to melt metal.'

190

'You mean you think…' I was lost for words.

'*Ndiyo* bwana. I think. In Mkilwa exactly, it is easy for *wananchi* to disappear. All the elements conspire to make it so. There is water, the lake; there is earth, the many tonnes of rock being disposed of every day on the conveyor belt from the crusher; and then there is fire, that can allow things to be hidden in the thin air. How do you expect me to search air, Mr Paul, for your proof?'

Now he was down to it.

'No, for proof, we have to look elsewhere. Here, for example.' He looked at me again as if making some judgement of his own.

'I need to speak to you about Mr David.'

Whose side was Mkate on. It was a question I could ignore no longer. How could I tell? How could I be sure? I could play dumb, just hand the tape over to him and trust to getting the hell out. We'd done nothing. Except for the tape of course, I thought. Even if we denied listening to it, he and they, if he worked for them, would assume we had.

If I didn't hand it over we would be in danger if they suspected that we had it.

But if I did hand it over they would know what was on it and then I really would be in danger. That's just great Dave, I thought bitterly. Thanks a lot. I stalled.

'Why is New Mwanchi so important Bwana Mkate? What is it about the place?'

'I think it is politics,' he said. 'It was all politics at that time. You will know we had our first multiparty elections to happen in the next few days.' He shrugged. 'Bwana Pesha, he is important for the politics.'

'But what's that got to do with New Mwanchi?' I asked.

'He is *wakilwa*,' said Mkate, as though it was obvious. 'New Mwanchi is his *shari*.'

I already knew that Pesha was from Mkilwa, but Mkate had also said that New Mwanchi was Pesha's *shari*. That was a difficult term to interpret. On the one hand it could mean his affair, his concern; on the other, it could mean his problem.

'Bwana Mkate, do you know how Bwana Iain died?'

His back was to me as he scanned the shelves slowly. He didn't seem to move a muscle or show any surprise at all.

'Bwana Iain? Who is Bwana Iain please?' He turned ponderously to face me, an eyebrow lifted up in query. 'I do not think I know a Bwana Iain,' he said.

Was he lying? I couldn't tell.

'Don't give me that. You were at his memorial service, Mr Mkate, don't you remember? At the cathedral, at the end of November. You were standing across the road watching us all come out.' Watching us. Watching me.

'Ah yes,' he said. 'I remember that occasion. I did not know the details of this. I had just arranged to be there to see persons. But this name Iain is still unclear to me. Can you enlighten please?'

'Iain was my assistant,' I said sadly. The one who was working on New Mwanchi. The one we talked about at the Golden Shower. He died in a car crash a few weeks ago. Just after Dave did,' I added for emphasis. 'At least that is what I have been told.'

Mkate nodded. 'Yes, I know of him now. But as for the story of his death, you do not believe this? You are wise Mr Paul to question things. One must always question things that one hears, to test them for the truth.'

'Do you know?' I asked quietly.

Was that a smile playing around Mkate's lips? I wondered. I could feel the anger welling up inside me, the frustration, the fear, needing a release. 'Do you know?' I insisted.

He shook his fat head slowly and turned back to face the bookshelves.

'I am sorry Mr Paul, but no, I do not know how your Bwana Iain died. I might suspect as you do, I think, but no, I do not know.' He paused.

'Oh, come off it Mr Mkate,' I said, frustrated. 'What do you expect me to believe?'

'You may believe whatever you wish bwana,' he said, without the slightest hint of having taken any offence at my tone. 'The fact remains, I was not there to spy on you or to meet you. I had other affairs in hand. Other persons with whom to deal.'

So who could he have been watching? I wondered. I was on the steps talking with Salima as we came out when I first saw him. I had seen him watching us and pushed down to confront him only to be held up by traffic and joined by Colin. And meanwhile, just about everyone in the firm from Patrick and Marilyn to Sharik and Clare, had come filing out of the front doors.

If it wasn't us, it could have been anyone, I thought. I knew that it was impossible to really tell from so many metres away. But deep down, I was sure he had been watching our little group at the top of the stairs. I knew it, I felt it in my bones and nothing would shake me from my conviction. And then when he had seen me coming. Me and I suppose, Colin, I thought, coming towards him, he had cut and run.

'And you are wrong Mr Paul, I was not there to watch you.' He turned his back to me again and looked at the shelves.

'Now you *wazungu*. You are different,' he said, reverting back. 'Generally, you cannot just disappear the way that *wananchi* may.'

'Oh no? Seen Dave recently have you?' I said. Or Iain, I thought.

'Not without an explanation being provided by the relevant authorities.'

'Like an accident.'

'Exactly sure. Like an accident. That is acceptable to your authorities.'

'Our authorities?' He had thrown me completely. Our government? 'What has it got to do with our government?' I asked.

'Well no one wishes for there to be trouble, Mr Paul. This was a time of great sensitivities in all side of course,' he said. It was as though he expected me to know, to understand.

'There was the election.'

'Precisely,' he nodded. 'There was the election. Rais was retiring.'

'But what has that got to do with anyone outside the country?'

'With Rais gone, so go his connections. But who was to succeed him? That was a grave concern to all,' he stated, as though it was self-evident.

'But what does anyone care outside whether it was Pesha or Ahmed?' I insisted.

'For many reasons Mr Paul. What if your government knew things about Pesha that made him unacceptable to them as a president of a commonwealth country?'

Like he was up to his neck in drug smuggling, for instance, I thought.

'The President has pledged to purge the Party and country of corruption. Did Bwana Pesha ever make such a pledge?'

'No.'

'Did the President threaten to expel all the *wahindi* if he was elected?'

'No, but…'

'We are a divided country Mr Paul,' Mkate insisted. 'Rich and poor. *Wananchi* and *wahindi*. Jijenga, Bharanku and Mkilwa. Christian and Moslem. It is the Party that has helped to create this country,' he said, with sudden emphasis and conviction, almost passion in his voice. 'It has been all of these things and none of them. It has forged a unity. There are forces here that would tear this country apart. No one, inside or outside of the country should not be aware of the seriousness of this.'

'And Bwana Pesha?'

'Bwana Pesha is one of those forces.' He stopped as if to consider for a moment and there was the merest hit of a shake of his head. 'But I was surprised that Bwana David was so interested in what was coming in to the factory. I myself was more interested in what was coming out.'

I waited.

'I had suspicions about this plant that is exporting to Europe, yes exactly to Rotterdam. I had to ask myself, what else could this factory be exporting? And you Mr Paul have to ask yourself, for what is Rotterdam famed as a world centre of trade?'

Drugs and oil I thought; so I was taken by surprise by the obviousness of Mr Mkate's answer.

'Diamonds, Mr Paul, Holland is world renowned is it not as the centre of the world diamond industry? And we here in African are world renowned as the centre of the trade in illegal diamonds are we not? In fact just across the border.'

'Conflict diamonds?'

'Yes exactly. To fund the wars. And do we not have a war just across our border? Do we not have camps full of thousands of people? Do we not have armed militias trading across the border? And what do you think they are trading, Mr Paul?

And then I had to ask myself, if there are diamonds going out, what could New Mwanchi be bringing in from Pakistan and Afghanistan amongst its scrap?'

Again my thought of drugs was surpassed by Mkate's.

'Arms, Mr Paul. Arms for the wars over the border. Guns. Or perhaps even guns for a different purpose. Not guns for an existing war, but guns for a new war, a war that is being planned. Where there is a war or a thirst for war there is a desire for arms. And where better to obtain these requirements than from places such as Afghanistan and Pakistan. Places from where New Mwanchi is purchasing its supplies of scrap metal. Now please, Mr Paul. Does this not strain credibility?'

Could it be true? I asked myself. Was Pesha such a threat to the delicately balanced conflicting interests that made up the country?

Would his election have destabilised the country to such an extent. Could it even have plunged into civil war? What would our government's position be on that? Or even on being faced with an expulsion of *wahindi*? Another Ugandan Asian situation? Another partly Moslem failed state, another Somalia or at least a Sudan? Another potential al-Qa'eda safe haven? I shuddered and nodded. It was something that they would take extremely seriously.

And how would instability here affect the coastal states? Could trouble spill over, the anarchy and violence of the interior extending out across the lake over the plains to the heavily populated racially and religiously mixed coastal region? Would the High Commission take that seriously enough to connive in covering up the death of two nationals? I was starting to think that it might, it just might.

So what would the role of a vice consul be in that sort of situation? I wondered. How great would the cooperation be between the local authorities and the High Commission in getting one of the bodies away home and clear, with minimal fuss? Pretty high, I guessed. No wonder it had all gone so bloody smoothly. Jesus Christ, how could I have been so blind? Now at last I started to understand how Colin had been acting.

Mkate was at the end of the bookcase by now. To his left through the open door was the corridor which led down past the toilet and the walk-in shower room on the right, and the entrances to the little bedroom that I used as a study and the guest bedroom on the left, towards my bedroom. The light in my bedroom was on as I had been sitting on the bed dictating myself some notes for a newsletter while Sam had been preparing dinner. Through the open door you could see the bedside table and sitting on it was my Dictaphone with some tapes.

Mkate looked down the corridor. 'Aha,' he said. 'Some more tapes.'

Before I could register a protest or make a move, his bulk filled the corridor and he was striding towards the room. Startled I sped after him but I wasn't quick enough. It was only a few paces down the corridor and into the bedroom.

'Do you mind?' I called in ineffectual protest. How very English of me. He was already in the room. Standing by the little brown bedside table holding the Dictaphone in his big podgy hand.

Turning to me as I came in. 'They are very small bwana, aren't they?' gesturing with his hand to the tapes on the bed.

'Yes,' I snapped, 'and they are not music cassettes, they are

Dictaphone tapes.'

'I know Mr Paul, exactly. Mr David had one,' he was talking almost to himself, rather than to me. 'The first time that I saw, I thought he was using a *mobili* phone.' He was holding the machine to him now, weighing it in his hand. He had his thumb on the controls, he was shuffling it in his palm as though getting it comfortable and seeing how to put his index finger over the record button.

'Mr Mkate, please,' I began.

He looked up at me and as he did so he idly slipped the control back. He jumped as if startled at the short squeak as the tape went into rewind. As he did so his thumb came off the main control and the button slipped back into neutral. He looked down at the machine again as if puzzled by what he had done and then he pushed the control button forwards again.

For a moment you could hear me speaking, the words I had been composing an hour or so before, the news about our leaving. But then what I had just done ran out. Because he had only rewound a second or so.

But instead of hearing blank tape, a silent hiss, a quiet carrier wave, there was still my voice. And here, now, here in our bedroom, my heart stood still. Because Mr Mkate, an officer with the SPU, was holding in his hands my Dictaphone, and listening to my words, as I had dictated my November newsletter.

We could both hear me clearly: *When you've had a one party state so long, you've had no practice of doing this sort of thing. New paragraph. A general view might be irritation that the party has been so stupid as to mismanage stealing of the election in such an unnecessarily cackhanded way. Full stop.*

Mkate was starting at the Dictaphone in his hand as if transfixed. The tape rolled on relentlessly.

As a ruling party, if you're going to fix elections, you might at least have the decency to put the effort in to do so properly and not have this sort of shambles. Full stop. With their rural majority, brackets, of a population of fourteen million, only about one or two million live in Jijenga. Close brackets. The party was always bound to win hands down out in the boondocks where minor but widespread fiddling could have gone on quite easily.

'This is sedition,' Mkate was shaking his head. He turned back to look down at the tape recorder and all I could see was his huge head swaying from side to side. 'This is espionage,' he said, his voice starting to rise dangerously the way it had outside the door.

The tape spooled on: *Mkilwa was different. The Party had to win against a well organised and powerful challenge or be faced with an opposition secessionist party.*

In a panic, I lunged for the Dictaphone, knocking over the bedside table and sending other tapes flying to the floor. He pulled his hand away and I slammed into him as he twisted.

The next few moments were a blur to a surreal soundtrack of the oblong plastic lump of the Dictaphone expounding on the sorry state of the nation in a static-charged crackly, tinny voice as Mkate and I wrestled.

Suddenly we were both down on our knees scrabbling for the tapes with one hand, while grappling each other with the other.

A blatant and serious threat to the stability of the country. They had to cheat to do so but it was so mismanaged it defeated part of the purpose of the election.

As we flailed and fought we crashed from the wall and into the bed. It lurched sideways as we both went down onto the floor. He was huge, a monster. His weight, his strength was enormous. I had had the element of surprise for the first instant, but now he was starting to react. I needed a weapon, a club, anything. If he got the upper hand he would crush me to death. Dimly I could hear Sam screaming at us from the living room.

It's a republic and they grow a lot of bananas.

My scrabbling hand flung out under the bed and touched cold metal that clanked against the concrete floor. Blindly I grabbed at the object and pulled it towards me. Mkate was getting the upper hand now. I saw him start, his eyes widening as he caught sight of what I was pulling out from beneath the bed.

Letting go of my throat he lunged for the gun. My grip was round the breech and barrel. Mkate had got hold of the shoulder stock and was reaching for the trigger guard. In desperation I tried to let go of him completely, I grabbed the gun with both hands, yanking away from him and pointing the gun away, while kicking him hard.

There was a huge roar of noise and my arm felt like it was being wrenched out of its socket, as a sheet of flame leapt from under the bed. There was an explosion of plaster and concrete shrapnel from under the headboard and I was lying there stunned, heart pounding, eyes blinded, the acrid smell of cordite stinging my nostrils and then there was silence. Blessed, blessed, silence.

'Is, is he dead?' asked Sam, in a quiet nervous voice.

I was stunned. 'Jesus Christ!' I said, pawing at my eyes. I had caught part of the blast with my face to the wall in the struggle, and had God knows what peppering my face by the way the blood was oozing down it. My mouth seemed to be moving and I reckoned I must be moaning. Apart from the ringing in my ears I could hear almost nothing. I felt as if I were floating, a dreamlike sensation of being completely disengaged from what was happening around me. I was in a state of shock or deaf or both. It took me a moment to realise that she wasn't talking about me, but about Mkate.

Shaking my head to try and clear the ringing in my ears and stars in my eyes, I sat up, or tried to. Mkate's body lay across my legs and pinned me down at the waist. It was like being trapped under a dead whale.

'I don't know. Give me a hand to get up.' Sam advanced on tiptoe into the room. Her trembling hands came down to me, then started to help me roll him off my body.

I was still dazed. I couldn't work out what had happened, but there was a huge hole blasted in the bedroom wall just under the bedhead.

Kicking backwards, I got my knees free and enough room to get some purchase and push Mkate from my lower legs.

He moaned.

'No, he's alive. But what the bloody hell happened? I thought he was going to kill me.'

There was blood on Mkate's temples. He was groaning a bit but essentially seemed to be out of it.

Pulling myself up with Sam's help and the aid of the upturned bedside table, I slumped onto the edge of the bed.

'Jesus!' I said, looking around.

The shotgun had gone off. That much was obvious. Neither of us had been shot, thank God, that seemed clear. My illegally held shotgun had gone off, I thought. During my fight with an SPU officer. The mental tape was running appallingly now. As I had tried to snatch back the evidence of sedition out of his hands and got into a fight with him. And the gun. I had tugged the barrel just as he was grabbing for the trigger guard. The gun had gone off less than a metre from the wall, without either of us having a proper grip. It must have been the recoil, I thought. It had slammed the stock back straight into the side of his head and taken him out.

The gun had gone skidding and smoking across the floor. It had fetched up with an unheard clatter against the opposite wall.

My side was bruised and bloody, my shoulder and upper arm burnt and pitted with fragments of masonry.

Oh, bloody hell, I thought, rubbing my eyes as if waking from a ferocious dream. There was no doubt about it now, Sam was involved whether she, or I, liked it or not. But what on earth do we do now?

12 No Whitewash at the Whitehouse

'How long has he had AIDS?' Sam asked with concern as she cleaned me up.

'Ow!' I protested, starting as strong disinfectant stung my skin 'What do you mean?'

'Oh come on Paul, he's got all the signs,' she said pointing out his symptoms, 'the weight loss, the skin lesions, the ulcers on his hands that aren't healing, all the opportunistic infections that are starting to run riot because his immune system is shot to hell. I bet he's starting to get attacks of thrush. And then there's the outbursts of course.'

I must have looked uncomprehending

'Brain lesions, they can bring on sudden outbursts of dementia and rage. I would say that your Mr Mkate is fairly late term.'

'I don't know. He looked perfectly OK when I saw him six weeks ago.'

Sam looked shocked. 'But that's impossible, it doesn't come on that quickly.'

'Are you sure?' I asked thinking about my cuts and bruises and cross infection.

'Of course I'm sure! What do you think I've been working on for the last two years? What else could it be?'

*

I had thrown on a clean T-shirt and half an hour later we were standing either side of the Suzuki nervously scanning the car park as I unlocked the driver's door. But there was no apparent movement from the dark huddled shapes of the sleeping *askaris* at the far end of the yard.

Mkate lay imprisoned and unconscious behind us in the apartment. We had wrapped a roll of parcel tape round his hands to immobilise his fingers before using some thin sisal rope to bind his wrists and feet. He was gagged by tape wound around his head and across his mouth, and blindfolded by yet more tape across his eyes.

With Sam's help I had dragged him into the small shower room just off the corridor and dumped him onto an old foam mattress from the spare single bed that I had squeezed and folded into the shower space. There was one small barred window high up in the outside wall. After we had finished with the tape and rope, I was pretty sure that when he came to he wasn't going to be able to stand up and reach the window or call out, but it seemed stupid to take any chances.

I searched his pockets for any sharp items and it was the work of a few minutes with a screwdriver to take the handles off the door and remove the bar that operated the latch so that when I pulled the door shut there was no way of opening it from the inside.

'This tape is the problem,' I said.

'Then get rid of it,' Sam suggested, opening her door.

'But we can't, it's not as easy as that. Look, if we get rid of it then they don't know what was actually on it. Dave might have said everything. If that's the case then they still have to get rid of us. So long as we keep the tape out of their hands they just don't know what is on it, so someone may decide that the fact that we simply had it is dangerous enough.'

'So give it to them then.'

'But we can't do that either,' I said as I slipped the T-lock off. 'You've seen the transcript. Dave didn't say a lot, but he said enough. We've managed to put two and two together and make four from it. Once they've heard it, they'll know more or less what we know, which will be enough. Besides, giving up the tape won't be enough. They'll know we could have made a transcript, which we could have other copies of.'

'So what are we going to do?'

'We're going to give it to them,' the engine caught.

'But you just said we couldn't.'

'Ah but we're going to give them the tape in such a way that it clears us.'

'What? How are you going to persuade them that we haven't listened to it?' Sam seemed sceptical.

'No we're not going to do that. We're going to make it so that when they listen to it, it seems completely harmless.'

'But you can't just wipe it,' she protested as we swung out of the gates, past the grass verge and the apartments' noxious rubbish dump and out on to the road. 'That would be suspicious in itself.'

'No. I've got a plan. We just need to get to my office and pray for power,' I said as we rattled and bumped out into the night.

I wasn't thinking as I drove and headed straight out on autopilot to the coast road and my normal route in to work.

That would have been fine except this was a Friday night and as I turned onto Karume towards Mnazi Moja, the place was heaving.

Shit. Despite the trouble in town, or perhaps because of it, the *wahindi* were out in force tonight.

I had been an idiot. I should have cut down the inland route along the centre of the headland. Should I turn round and go back?

But it was too late, already we were hemmed in by traffic, the bulk of smart Japanese four by fours, the clattering reliability of generations of Peugeot 504s and Toyota Corollas and the practicalities of space carriers and minivans.

Now the crowds and noise were everywhere as horns hooted all around us as cars jostled and pushed, children ran and played, and hawkers touted their wares to the chattering crowds in the light of headlights, hurricane lamps and even the odd fringed lampshade of a standard lamp, plugged into a small portable generator, sat on the back of a Hilux twin cab.

We were stuck, crawling, exposed, and feeling vulnerable.

Inching forwards, up ahead I could see the turn inland beside Papa's as we crept ever closer. A motorbike whizzed past my ear like a demented mosquito, cutting through the lines of crawling jostling traffic.

'Let's cut off,' I said to Sam.

'Good idea.'

We edged onwards. Traffic was nose to tail with even more cars trying to get on to Karume from the Papa's turn. No one was taking any prisoners.

'You're just going to have to shove your way across,' Sam said.

'Yes, yes, I know,' I snapped, but we were stuck. All I could see were the high headlights of the oncoming Landcruiser boring straight into my eyes. Oh, what the hell, I thought. It's the firm's car, and I turned the car's nose into a gap behind an old pickup. The Landcruiser I was blocking blared his horn. I shouted back.

'Let me through then, you sod.' As I pushed through a magical gap in the traffic, behind me roared a Patrol, headlights on full beam.

Jesus Christ, he's going to come straight into the back of us, I thought.

'Look out,' I shouted to Sam, as instantaneously I braced myself for the impact that didn't come, as the Patrol's driver stood on the brakes at the last moment and screeched to a stop inches behind us.

It was enough. The charging car had obviously shocked the driver of the Landcruiser for a moment and as the pickup moved forwards, I grabbed my chance, gunning the engine and squeezing across the road, through the gap.

Behind us I heard a cacophony of horns. Glancing in the mirror I just couldn't believe it. The Patrol had bulldozed its way through, its aggression intimidating the Landcruiser driver to a halt, and now the Patrol was charging up the narrow road behind us.

'Bloody hell,' I shouted to Sam. 'This bloke is a maniac.'

But he was right on our back bumper now. The roads were a bit clearer and with the charging chrome bull bars filling the back windscreen we were doing upwards of seventy-five Ks. I translated mentally. That was nuts on these roads, fifty miles an hour.

The cab was filled with the blue white light of his headlamps and boiling clouds of dust as the engine roared. I could hear the spray of gravel and stones as we took the corners.

He was rushing from side to side, jockeying for position behind us now.

'Shit, he's going to run us off the road in a minute.'

'Why don't you let him past?' screamed Sam.

'I can't,' I shouted back. Partly it was that I just couldn't, I didn't have the space to slow down to let him past, and partly I didn't want to let him past. What if it was us he was after? What if that was what he wanted?

The red of the rear lights was reflecting back at me in the mirror off the massive stainless steel bull bars across the front of the Patrol.

Jesus, we have got to slow down. We were screaming up to the junction with Siad Barre. The plots fell away beside the junction of the track we were on and the verges on either side widened out as he reached the tarmac.

Traffic was light.

'Hold on!' I screamed, as with a bone-jarring thump, we took the tarmac, barely slowing. The tyres screamed and squealed as I wrenched the wheel hard over right and heeled over in my seat, willing my weight into the corner.

The car was lifting sideways, inching higher into the air as we powered through the turn. I held onto the wheel for grim death.

Had I overcooked it? Would it roll? For an eternal moment it seemed to hang. And then with a bang, the wheels slammed down again and we careered back across the road, straight into the path of an oncoming lorry.

Sam screamed as I fought the wheel, dragging us back onto the right side of the road, as the lights, big wheels and horn grazed past us at a crazy speed of almost a hundred and fifty Ks.

For a moment I held my breath. 'Jesus!' And then my eyes frantically flicked to the mirror to see... nothing. Blackness, tail lights disappearing off in to the darkness.

'They went the other way,' Sam said.

My heart was racing. 'Bloody *wahindi* kids, I bet,' I said, swearing seriously under my breath. 'Out joyriding and decided to bomb it round the block to get back to the other end of *Mnazi Moja*.'

I was shaking my head with the emotional overload as I pulled to a halt on the verge in the darkness. I needed a moment to get my breath back. I really hadn't needed that just at that moment.

'Are you all right?' we asked each other at the same moment.

'Yes, I think so. That really gave me a fright,' Sam said.

'Me too. The inconsiderate bastards.'

Hand in hand, the moment in the darkness stretched to an age. Outside cars whizzed, roared and whined past every few moments.

Eventually I broke the stillness. 'Shall we go?'

'Yes.' She nodded.

We drove on in silence. The window was open and the warm night air rushed by.

'One of the key connections to the Party was through Pesha,' I was musing out loud as we reached the streetlights on Bara Bara ya Rais. 'That makes sense. He's *wakilwa* and he's well off. It explains something else as well. All the way through the election he was able to beat the government up over scandals like the coffee estates but seemed to be fireproof himself. To get where he did in government, in the Party, there must be some dirt that someone knows somewhere, but it just wasn't used in the election.'

'He'd obviously got a hold, he'd got something,' Sam agreed. 'But if he was the conduit and therefore quite powerful in the Party, why did he quit and go independent?'

'Well, suppose that Rais didn't want him?' That had to be have been it, I thought. 'Pesha would have had his own power base which would have made him independent and therefore too threatening for Rais to have as a successor. So Rais picked Ahmed.'

'Ahmed, who no one had ever heard of.'

'Quite,' I said. 'How's this?' I asked, laying out the scenario. 'Pesha was the conduit and distributor of the largesse coming out of a major smuggling ring. He was made interior minister.'

'With responsibility for law and order,' Sam pointed out.

'That's right, and the ports. It just gets better and better doesn't it? So there he was in power, a high flier, seeing himself as the natural successor.'

'And then Rais blocked him.'

'Precisely. And what's more there's the Mkilwa–Bharanku rivalry that goes back centuries between him and Rais. There's the religious issue as well, Christian versus Islam. But I think the Mkilwa–Bharanku thing is deeper. Look at the riots that have gone on since the election, but it goes further back than that, look at the ethnic massacres that happened around the time of independence, the "Africans" of across the lake against the "Arabs" of Bharanku. There's a deep, deep, deep split right there under that front of national unity, and it's there within the Party, as much as anywhere else in the country.

'So there's a real political dimension but it's probably the personal issue that tipped it. Pesha learnt he was going to be passed over, missed out. Perhaps the Party though they could buy him off. Who knows? But as it happened he was much too rich and powerful for that. His pride had been hurt. He had lost face, and that would have really wounded him. And perhaps, even, he really meant some of what he was saying during the elections. That he saw himself as an African leader, representing the Africans of Mkilwa and the countryside against the "Arabs" of Bharanku, the traders and the towns and the *wahindi* and the bureaucrats that the Africans out in the country see as running the place and getting rich.'

'They can't really see people from Bharanku as Arabs just because of their religion can they? Surely not.'

'Oh no? Look at how they dress in the djellaba. Bharanku is different. Different dress, different religion, different ways of making a living. And how different do people have to be before one starts killing the other? Germans and German Jews? Rwandan Hutus and Tutsis? Ulster Catholics and Protestants? Bosnian Serbs and Croats? Just because you or I might not be able to tell the difference, doesn't mean to say that they can't when it comes to identifying the other. And clan and tribal identity are deeply embedded. Look at Idris in the office and his filing system, people here are clan first, tribe second, nation somewhere far behind.'

'So why didn't the Party use the dirt to stop him?'

'Well it couldn't, could it? The Party couldn't go in hard and dirty because Pesha was the guardian of its dirtiest little secret of all, that drugs money had been financing it for years to act as a route to the West, to the very countries whose aid is what balances the books. I bet Pesha's got all the names, numbers, dates and amounts squirreled away somewhere and made sure the Party knew all about it, just in case something unfortunate happens. It's the sort of insurance policy that would be well advised.

'What a situation. I mean, what was the Party to do? It was a stand-off. Pesha couldn't shout about it either or he would have compromised himself and lost his leverage of having this threat in reserve. But he could put plenty of pressure on about corruption and *wahindi* links.'

'All this stuff about the coffee estate scandals.'

'Exactly. It's all good stuff for public consumption, but to those in the know there would have been a subtext. All the time that he was stirring up public anger about the issue, the Party can't possibly have missed the real point that he was making for their benefit.'

'Be careful.'

'Exactly. Be careful, and I have the power to destroy you. And how threatening to Rais and the powers that be did that feel I wonder? What would they do about it? If they couldn't touch Pesha, what about his allies, witting or unwitting? What might they do to stop this getting out?'

'Kill people?'

I shrugged. 'Why not? Think of the stakes involved here. It's a dangerous place. People have accidents. Sometimes, some more convenient than others.'

'But I don't understand,' said Sam. 'Why did Dave pursue it? Why was he allowed to?'

That had been puzzling me as well. 'I'm not sure. Perhaps it was some kind of a message, or perhaps someone in the Party was looking for some other dirt that could be thrown just at Pesha and hoped Dave might turn up something. Perhaps he and Mkate just stumbled into it unwittingly. Perhaps he was being allowed to follow his nose on the fraud and Mkate was supposed to guide him away from the problem and blew it. Perhaps Mkate had some game of his own going on.'

'Or was working for someone else?'

'Could be anything couldn't it? We just don't know.'

'But how come if you are right, Pesha who is coming out against the *wahindi* and is saying he represents the *wakilwa* Christian half of the country, working so closely with the *wahindi* at New Mwanchi?'

It was a good question and I had been wondering that as well. But in the end I felt the answer was quite simple. 'Business is business. They've been working together so long I guess they are both in it up to their necks with the other and they'll either swim together or sink together…'

I was driving wide. Rather than heading straight in to our goal, the office, at first I had turned inland away from Boma, on and along Mandela, the old Bharanku road, before cutting back north along D'Souza, round the back of Gaza and Kaoli and Sinja. These were both long unimpeded runs along the new tarmac dual carriageways the Japanese had built in return for a vote the right way on whaling and I gunned the engine, one hundred, one hundred and ten, one hundred and twenty Ks. Eighty miles an hour or near enough. The Suzuki's engine was good for it, just the brakes and steering weren't.

Out here, stretches of blackness alternated with the bright pools of the streetlights that illuminated small knots of lounging soldiers and parked olive green Landies that gave some semblance of security to the night. The lights were the reason I had chosen this route, whilst off on the sandy banks to either side the twinkle of hurricane lamps and splashes of glare from genny powered fluorescents stretched into the *nyumbaya* as *dukas* and bars plied their trade. The hustle and bustle of an African town at night, its businesses, dance halls and deals fled past like scenes in a film. As we passed each working streetlight, the inside of the Suzuki lit up, showing Sam's face set as she stared out of the side window, but I was intent on watching the mirror, looking to see if we were being followed.

And then as D'Souza descended the hillside on to the level ground, heading towards the docks at the north end of the bay, it formed the ring road, around the inland edge of the commercial centre, the boundary between it and the surrounding shanty town hills. We crossed, the lights were with us for a change as we cut over to plunge headlong into the maze, immediately gaining the cover of the souk, its criss-cross network of deserted streets, the shops locked, barred and bolted with great steel plates welded over the windows and doors. Here the streets were empty, the soldiers obviously posted to the populous *nyumbaya* leaving these streets to the *askaris* sleeping in their doorways until daytime, the occasional hissing prostitute around the corner from the hotel entrances, and odd knots of street kids bedding down for the night.

We headed left and right, bumping over the potholes of the old road around the back of the old bus terminal, left again onto the street where in the daytime you couldn't move for vegetable sellers, right again. By now I had the headlights off, we were just another knackered white Suzuki, cruising around the streets at night with sidelights. There were other cars around, a few, I wasn't exactly flitting silently from shadow to shadow but I could relax. I pulled in, crawled down a sandy alleyway and there I stopped in the blackest, furthest corner I could find and turned the engine off.

'Quick, let's go back down that way,' I said, keeping an eye on the alleyway down which we'd come. 'If anybody was following us we'll see them as they'll be turning down it as well.'

As we slipped into the darkness towards the office, we came out of the alley without seeing anyone and swiftly crossed the road heading for the shadows of the new post office. There had been no cars, no people. So far, so good, I thought.

'You didn't wipe the tape after you transcribed it?' I asked, horrified by the idea that suddenly struck me.

'No, of course not.'

'Thank God for that.'

We climbed the stairs to the eighth floor. We were gasping by the time we got to the firm's security grille and we listened in the darkness for any echo of following footsteps climbing the stairs. But there was nothing, the building was dark and silent as only sleeping *askaris* could be. This was a moment of truth. When we arrived for work in the morning, the *askaris* were always here before us, I had never had to open up the office before. My keys fitted the locks in the security grilles and then the main door's lock turning with a click, I had been terrified that we might get all the way here and be unable to get in. I gently pushed against the door. It didn't move. It was stuck. My heart in my mouth I shoved it hard and with a bang it swung open.

Prayer worked.

'Don't put the lights on,' I hissed as Sam flicked on the UPS. The green light glowed friendly as the computer beeped and stirred itself in a crackle of static. 'Kill the computer,' I called.

'But I can't, it's booting.'

'Bugger that,' I yelled and pulled the screen's power lead out of the back. 'We can't have the screen light showing either.'

I was immediately sorry that I had sounded so cross. I hadn't meant to but I had after all got her into this mess and I felt responsible. I took a deep breath and said, 'Look, I'm sorry but this is serious. It's a matter of life and death.'

'It's OK,' she said, 'I understand.'

We had the complete system of course. A Dictaphone was no good without a player with which to transcribe tapes. The beauty of the player for us now was that as well as the headphones Janet normally used, it also had a speaker so the operator could play anything that wasn't clear on the headphones.

We had never tried anything like this before. We had never needed to.

We were taking the risk that this room was not bugged, even in our whispered conversations, but I thought that it was unlikely. The phones had ceased to work again days ago, and if any room would be bugged, surely it would have been mine next door?

We had discussed what we needed to do in the car, so there wasn't much need to talk. We worked silently and quickly. Apart from anything else, we certainly didn't want any extraneous noise that might act as a giveaway.

The plan was simplicity itself. Sam put Dave's tape into the player and set it going. In the darkness it was eerie to hear Dave's voice coming through so clearly, and straight into the microphone of my Dictaphone which I was holding across the speaker set on record, and inside which was a blank Phillips C30 tape, identical to the tape Dave had used.

Dave spoke on. The by now familiar description of the factory and foundry rolled by. Then the scrap yard. I was waiting now.

Now. The moment I heard again that Mkate was off to the office to check details of the shipments, I stopped the tape.

I stopped recording and reset the new tape to the right position.

We fast forwarded.

I nodded to Sam and she set Dave rolling again. I was poised. He was coming to the end of the description of the godown. I was tracking his voice against the transcript, my index finger held on the record button, my thumb tight against the play.

I nodded a silent countdown to Sam as click, at exactly the right moment, I silently rolled my Dictaphone on to record again. The tiny red light winked on and glowed reassuringly in my hand as I captured Dave saying, 'They're coming, no time for any more, will complete later. End of tape.'

I snapped my machine off and in the darkness, static hissed from Janet's desk as Dave's tape rolled on, empty, into the darkness until Sam took her foot off the control pedal and the player fell silent with a clunk.

There was the demon whine and screech as I rewound the last bit of tape and then with baited breath, I pressed play.

And in the darkness we sat close to the Dictaphone, our hands clasped together, and listened to what felt like the most beautiful sound in the world. Dave talking, with a click and a hiss, describing scrap, noting Mkate's departure and then without any noticeable difference to the hundreds of other stops and starts on the tape, announcing his return.

'Bingo!' I said. 'We've got it.'

'Shush,' Sam waved at me to be quiet. 'Play it again. We need to make sure it's right.'

We listened to the denouement of the new tape three more times just to be sure.

'Right,' said Sam, snapping the tape out of the player. 'Now you want to keep this. Why not just tape the new version over the old? Doesn't it need to have Dave and Iain's fingerprints on it?'

'But it won't have. These things are so small and we have already handled it so much we have smeared ours over it, no one would be able to see theirs anyway. Besides which, they'll expect to see our fingerprints. After all we'll be saying we've had it all along. Remember, forensics is not likely to be their strong point.

'Anyway we need to keep this. We need the full original. It's the only real evidence that we have got, such as it is.' I took the original tape out of the machine and put it into my wallet.

Now the problem was Mkate.

*

'How is he?' Asked Sam as I pushed the shower room door shut.

'Still unconscious.'

Which was good. If we could assume that he'd been out all the time, then he wouldn't know that we had left the apartment. But where did that actually get us, I wondered? He might have had friends watching outside. Despite our best efforts they might even have been able to follow us to the office and back. And anyway, what did it really matter? We could have done what we had just done at any time over the last few weeks.

'Do you really think he has AIDS? I asked, worried now as I thought about my cuts and bruises.

'I don't know. I was pretty certain because he's got all the

210

symptoms of an immune deficiency syndrome, but then you've talked about how quickly all these symptoms have come on which just doesn't sound right.'

'So what else could cause a major immune deficiency problem but come on quickly?'

'Well, I don't know. The only thing I can think of just wouldn't make any sense at all.'

'All I want to know is whether it's infectious?'

'Well that's the good news, no it isn't.'

'So I can relax then?'

'Until I come up with an idea which isn't quite so crazy.'

Feeling that we wanted to make sure we weren't overheard we went in to my bedroom at the far end of the apartment and slumped onto the bed, lying side by side. For a while we wrestled with the question of what we should do now, arguing it this way and that in hushed voices in an increasingly desultory manner until at last we just, I suppose, gave up in despair. And so, with an African secret policeman who I had knocked unconscious, lying trussed up in the shower room, we drifted off to sleep.

Saturday, 21 January, Jijenga

I woke with a shock, jolting bolt upright. Christ, Nelson will be in, I thought. My heart pounded at the thought of him starting to clean and coming upon Mkate. I grabbed the alarm clock. It was eight o'clock, Nelson wouldn't be here for another half an hour or so and then I relaxed, falling back on to the bed with a sigh of relief. What was I worrying about? It was Saturday, Nelson wouldn't be in until Monday.

As the shower room was occupied, I used the en-suite. I turned the water on full, the jet hot and stinging on my flesh. I was still there when Sam knocked on the door and asked if she could come in? Stepping into the room wrapped in a towel she found me sitting on the shallow step which formed the lip of the square well set in to the concrete floor that acted as a shower tray. I was leaning with my back against the half wall that divided the shower stall from the rest of the room, the falling water enveloping me, seeming cooler for its fall. I sat staring at the drain, the ever-changing rivulets and runnels of water washing around my body and feet or streaming from my head before swirling noisily down the outlet.

I looked up at her over the wall. 'I've been thinking,' I said. 'I know what we've got to do about Mkate.'

The answer was self-evident. After breakfast I went downstairs and checked the water tank. Daisy came padding over to say hello and see if I had any food, so I made a bit of a fuss of her as I unlocked the steel trap to peer inside the tank. It was dark and smelt deliciously cool, but the water was so still inside in the blackness that it was very difficult to tell how full it was. We need a dipstick, I thought. My head inside the tank, I was startled to be addressed.

'Is it short?'

I looked up. It was Clare emerging from the stairwell. She was obviously on her way out to the beach from the towel and straw hat and the shoulder bag.

'Seems to be a bit. I think I'll get a tanker organised to be on the safe side.'

If there was one thing I didn't want this weekend, it was to run out of water. But first things had to be first. Many of the shops shut at lunchtime on Saturdays so we had to get a move on. Sam could call by the depot and organise a tanker on the way back.

Sam went shopping. I stayed behind, well one of us had to and it couldn't really be Sam.

I sat there throughout the morning, just hoping she would make it.

It was an extensive list. Cement, paint, paint brush, bin bags, blankets, and a small trowel. Then there was the protective gear: a boiler suit, good thick long rubber gloves, Wellington boots, a dust mask and some plastic goggles. And then the consumables: two five-litre cans of cooking oil, a jerry can of diesel, newspapers, a stack of cheap single bed sized blankets, fifteen kilos of butter, caustic soda, a whole bunch of overripe bananas and some ordinary household bleach.

She was back by one o'clock.

'How did it go?' I asked as I scurried out to the car to pick up the stuff, Daisy sniffing hopefully at our heels as we came round the back of the apartments.

'It's a nightmare out there.' she said looking shaken. 'The mobs are out of hand even in the centre of town. God knows what it must be like out in the *nyumbaya*. Ish says that the word on the streets is that the Party's loyalists have been given carte blanche to take on the opposition.

Jesus man, those mobs, they don't mess about,' Sam was shaking her head in grim disbelief. 'I was just coming up Samora when all of

212

a sudden there was a big commotion and a gang running towards the road screaming and shouting. They caught this guy they were chasing and all just really laid into him. They were kicking him and beating him until finally they picked him up and bodily threw him in front of a car that was coming the other way. It was just unbelievable.'

'I shouldn't have let you go by yourself, the town's getting too dangerous,' I said, helping her pull the jerry can out of the Suzuki.

'And leave him here on his own? Don't be soft!

I managed to get the stuff though,' she said. 'I went to that *wahindi* tool store halfway down Maktaba Street. I got just about all of it, all the hardware at least, in one hit. Oh, and I managed to find this.' Opening the back door of the Suzuki she started to pull out a shape I recognised instantly. 'Do you think this'll do?' she asked.

'It looks fine,' I nodded to her as I pushed it back into the car. 'But I think we had better wrap this lot in a blanket to carry them up to the apartment.' I didn't want anyone wondering to themselves why the departing *wazungu* in the firm's apartment had taken it into their heads in their last week here to buy a small felling axe, a sledgehammer and an electric chainsaw.

The decision on what to do about Mkate had taken a while to work through, mainly because we'd been starting from the wrong question. At first I had been focusing on was he on our side or not, or even more generally, whose side was he on? But of course that wasn't really the issue.

What really mattered was what risks did we run from doing what? So I had had to begin with the facts. And there was one fact that was all too solid – well blubbery – and self-evident. Last night I'd had a fight with a secret policeman. During that fight an illegally held gun had gone off, he'd been knocked unconscious and spent the rest of the night and this morning bound, gagged and blindfolded in a makeshift prison. Whoever's side he had been on to start with, the betting now was that he was feeling pretty sore and pretty pissed off. Whoever you might tell the story of how and why this had come about, using parcel tape and rope on an unconscious, injured man, was going to seem pretty serious, however you looked at it.

So one choice was to go into the shower room, cut Mkate free, say, 'Awfully sorry Bwana Mkate, terrible accident last night with the gun going off, you being a policeman and all, we panicked a bit, didn't know what to do, so we made the mistake of tying you up and leaving you here overnight. Dreadfully sorry. Here you are, have a cup of tea, a headache tablet and we'll help you down the stairs.'

It didn't sound like much of a runner to me, that one. Let's say he was absolutely straight, just what he said he was, a policeman working with Dave, who had come round quite innocently to see if he could buy something from departing *wazungu*. Instead he discovered sedition, was knocked unconscious and wrongfully imprisoned. With a member of the security police that should be good for what? Twenty-five years?

And if he was working for 'them', the same story would give him an ideal opportunity and excuse to move against us.

If he had been on Dave's side, did that necessarily mean that he was also on ours? What was in it for him to protect us?

Even if he had originally been really working to help Dave, how could we know that he still was? Last night, or anything else we might not know about, might mean that he had changed sides.

What's more, he could say anything to us, promise us anything to get out of the apartment. But once he was gone we just wouldn't know, we would have no leverage over him, no control, no way of doing a deal that we could make stick.

All the time I was wondering how he had got here. Had he come alone or had he been dropped off? Was the car or a colleague lurking nearby? Who else knew he was here?

Of course we could ask him. But we would have no way of knowing whether he would be telling the truth or not.

I took comfort from the fact that by the time Sam had got back from shopping, it had been well over twelve hours and nobody had turned up looking for him. Well we had some time left, we could still see whether anyone did.

So when you got right down to it, there really was no choice.

I had always thought that one of the virtues of my line of work was that it taught you to make decisions. Often you had to do so on the basis of useless or non-existent information. There are some times, like last night, where the decision is that you don't have to make a decision yet; and then there are other times when you do. Being good at the job was mastering the art of making the right choice at the right time on the basis of the wrong information.

Well I'd made a decision and Sam had done the necessary shopping. It was now just a question of waiting until dark and implementing it.

Sam was jittery all afternoon after I had helped her bring the stuff up from the car. It had taken several trips. The shut shower room door was like a magnet for our eyes. Neither of us really discussed it, but neither of us could get it off our minds. I felt I couldn't leave the apartment and toyed with the idea of suggesting that she went to the beach, but I didn't think she wanted to be alone.

The tanker arrived and I went down and unlocked the trapdoor. Inside the thick concrete walls the air was refreshingly dank, I could feel the hollowness of the big empty space and its gloomy stygian darkness, it was like opening up a great dark vaulted tomb.

With the reservoir filled, I reached through the bars of the cage at the bottom of the stairs with the stick and flicked the switch to pump water to the header tank at the top of the block. After half an hour or so the sound of the stream of running water arcing out from the roof and splattering the four storeys to the pavement below told me that it was full so I went downstairs again to turn the pump off.

Later that afternoon I took the *Citizens* that Sam had bought out onto the balcony to start my preparations.

While I worked, the window of Mkate's cell was a couple of metres above my head. If he was still where we had left him we were probably sitting back to back.

As I carried the first two bags into the apartment to go downstairs, I could see that the door to Sam's room was still shut. I wondered if I ought to say something but decided against it. She had stayed in there all afternoon since returning with the supplies so I thought I had better let her be.

Sam emerged from her room at about six and we sat together in the gathering darkness, staring out through the blank windows, silent and unseeing. Then her hand found mine and squeezed hard.

'Are you sure there's no other way?'

I just looked at her and shook my head.

'I guess you're right.' she whispered, looking away.

At about seven, Clare returned.

We heard her chatting to Mr Chavda as she came through the security gate at the bottom of the stairs. Then she knocked at our door.

Flicking on the light, Sam got up and answered.

'Hi, just thought I'd knock. I'm going out to eat tonight as I can't be bothered to cook. Do you fancy a bite and a few beers?'

From my perch slumped on the sofa I answered before Sam had a chance to speak.

'Sorry, I can't because I'm not feeling too good, but why don't you go Sam?'

215

She looked at me with wide eyes.

Sam didn't want to go I knew but I persuaded her. We hadn't discussed what we were, or rather I was, going to do. I just told her I had made a decision. She knew what it was without asking and didn't want to know any more

'There's no rush,' said Clare, 'I'm just going upstairs to get changed and showered. Do you want to pop up in say an hour or so and we'll head off? You too misery guts, if you're up to it,' she said to me.

It was just after eight when Sam left.

'Good luck,' she whispered uncertainly.

Well what did you say? 'It'll be OK. I know what to do. Now go.'

'Right then, see you later, I won't be too late.'

'That's fine, take your time. Enjoy yourself.'

She smiled a grimace and then there was the snap of the door shutting behind her.

Listening at the door I heard her knock at Clare's apartment and the door opening. I could hear her telling Clare how I would be staying in as I still wasn't feeling too good. They laughed and joked. It sounded a bit brittle but then perhaps that was me. My nerves weren't too good at that stage either.

And then, standing there in the dark, I heard Sam and Clare's voices as they floated down the stairs and away.

And I knew, this was it.

It was the big empty building plot where the late Commissioner Temu had come to his end that had given me the idea.

I knew now that I had heard the shots that had killed him, but that at the time I had thought nothing about them.

So could that now, together with the blessed God given racket of the night time disco, work for me?

*

I have tried to blank most of it out to be honest.

I have tried, and failed.

I remember moving as though I was in a dream.

I remember the racking dry heaves as I gagged and my guts knotting up when I picked up the shotgun.

I remember the rising sense of panic as I approached the door.

I remember the deafening noise of the shots and the ringing in my ears.

I remember the stench of the cordite in the air.

I remember the flickering of the ceiling strip light as it came on.

I remember the...

I remember the...

God I remember the blood, the blood, the feel of the hot blood on my hands, the way it pooled thickly on the floor and ran slowly down the drain, shocked at how thick and dark and oily it looked in the harsh blue white glow of the fluorescent tube.

I remember the terror of meeting faces in the dark.

I remember the fear soaked sweat of heaving the bags over the wall of the pen.

I remember the cold fear clutching at my heart as my hand felt slimy blood and the tear in that final bag.

I remember my hands trembling as I tried to strike a match.

I remember everything.

Everything.

None of it will ever leave me.

And then it was over.

And I was back in my apartment.

And I was a killer.

*

How can I trace a wisp of smoke? You said it, Mr Mkate.

*

Clare and Sam arrived back about twenty minutes later.

'Hope you're feeling better,' Clare said, as I opened the door to them. 'You missed a good night.'

'Yes, we went to Rooftops, did the barbecue,' said Sam, looking pained.

'Looks like somebody is putting on a show here,' said Clare, nodding at the raging fire which could now be seen blazing in the pen as we turned and looked through the sitting room and out of the front windows. 'They don't usually burn it at night; it's a bit spectacular though, isn't it?'

I turned and we all looked out at it for a moment. It really had caught, it was roaring now, all furnace oranges, reds and bright yellows, as flames licked up into the sky while puffs of exploding sparks crackled and snapped as a stream of hot red embers and sparks rushed up in to the night air with the hot billowing smoke.

It was self defence really I thought. I couldn't let him live.

'Yes,' I said. 'It is spectacular. I've been standing here watching it.'

Sunday, 22 January, Jijenga

I got up early on Sunday and took a quiet stroll to buy some eggs from the *dukas*. I walked quite carefully around the side of the block and crossed the square, through the car park, eyes glancing down at the ground for any strange trails. There were none. Light smoke was still drifting from the pen as I came up to it and there seemed to be a half a metre or so of ashes in the bottom.

'*Jambo mama, habari?*'

'*Habari* bwana?' said one of the *duka* ladies reaching the pen at almost the same moment I did. She smiled at me as I passed and then slung the bag of rubbish she was carrying over the wall puffing up a little cloud of ashes.

I met Clare as I came back again across the car park. 'Morning.' We walked around the back of the apartments to the entrance together. As we did so, Daisy scampered along the back of the fence.

I called 'Daisy' and Clare whistled. Daisy stopped and looked up at us but then trotted on regardless.

'Oh well, she's not going to come to us now,' said Clare. 'She must think it's Christmas. Look, somebody's given her a bone.'

I couldn't help but look. All she had left was some kind of knuckle-shaped white knob of clean bone stripped of flesh and marrow on which she was gnawing contentedly.

At that rate the rest would soon be gone, I decided.

I shuddered, but summoned up the presence of mind to say, 'Hmm, that's nice,' as we screeched open the grille at the foot of the stairwell and entered the blessed cool sheltering darkness.

*

During the day I did some makeshift plastering and painting. In the evening we took a short drive down to the little headland at the end of *Mnazi Moja*. A place on some low cliffs where a well thrown bloodstained chainsaw, sledgehammer and axe, after I had used it to

218

carefully chop a couple of AA batteries to exactly the right length, would sink into a good ten feet or so of deep green water. Never to be seen again, we hoped.

On Sunday afternoon Sam had gone shopping again for more local newspapers, soft fruit, bananas mainly for bulk, and kilos of butter. That evening, I lugged four black bin bags of rubbish, each filled with chopped up bananas and two pounds of butter, down to the rubbish tip.

The ash was grey, gritty and still slightly warm to the touch and I was relieved to see nothing obviously strange amongst the blackened cans and mess under the already accumulating pile of trash as I lifted the bags in one at a time over the edge of the wall.

The butter would melt in the sun in the plastic bags tomorrow during the day. That, together with the bananas, would quickly go rancid, giving the rubbish the right sort of pungent air that would put anybody off looking too closely. I had put a good layer of three or four copies of the *Citizen* at the bottom of each bag. The fat from the butter would soak into the papers which would help make sure that as and when the pile was burned again, it would burn well.

I was also hoping that when they burnt, they would give a good solid layer of ash which would help to keep buried what ought to be buried. It only needed to be for another week.

Then it would just be a matter of getting us, and the tape, out.

13 The Wake

Monday, 23 January, Jijenga

The streets were increasingly dangerous but we had no choice, we needed to go in. I dropped Sam off at the High Commission. She would be safe there until I got back and she could speak to Colin as backup if there seemed to be anything wrong. She also seemed to have some mission of her own but when I asked her about it she clammed up and refused to talk, saying she would tell me when she knew.

Next stop was the office.

As I told William with no hint of a lie, I was in just to tidy up a few loose ends.

It was the work of moments to erase the obliterated portion of Dave's transcript from the version on Janet's PC. It was the work of a few more to cover my tracks on the shotgun as well.

The mechanics of forgery were in practice very simple.

We still had the file copy of the contract that we had used to sell Kharatasi, each page initialled by the receiver for the company and by the buyer; including listings of plant and equipment and fixtures and fittings on a site by site, location by location basis.

Janet had typed it all out six months before.

Taking the file through to the privacy of my office I flicked through the contract schedules to find the easiest place. Each of the sites had a guardroom with a listing of tables and chairs. Obscurity was the best defence, so in the end I chose the salt farm, ninety acres of swamp situated three hours drive up a muddy track to no more than twelve sagging palm frond godowns filed with grey pink unsaleable salt, a concrete office block, two trucks with no wheels and a small herd of donkeys, enlivened only by the fact that a stray zebra had somehow found its way in and joined the herd.

I pulled up the relevant page on the screen of Janet's PC. It was the work of a moment to type in a new line at the bottom of the list, showing the shotgun and its serial number. That put it in the right position, then it was just a question of deleting all the items above it on the page and making sure I kept the same number of carriage returns so it would still be below the last item on the real list.

I printed out a trial copy and slid the newly printed page over the existing page in the contract to check that the addition was going to be in the right place, holding the superimposed pages up to the light to check it was.

'Well, here goes,' I thought, taking the original copy of the page out of the file and sliding it into the manual feed.

The printer whirred into life and soon back on the file, safely in the storeroom, there was a signed sales contract identifying the list of assets that the purchaser had bought; only now it included a shotgun, property of the company, identified by its serial number and quite clearly located at the company's salt farm.

And the only other copy languished somewhere in the buyer's office in Lagos, so the local police's chances of getting hold of a copy to challenge this version with, if they ever wanted to, looked slim.

I kissed Janet and shook hands in a formal final farewell to William as I left the office. Stepping out of the gloom of the lobby beside the *Sekretorial Services* office and into the sucking dry white heat of the late morning, I headed on down the hill past the *Polisi* stationed on every street corner towards the seafront.

Hanging over the front door of a particularly scruffy white building was a four-sided lamp, where only two of the blue glass panels with the white painted words 'Police' remained intact. This was Boma's main police post.

I walked in and up to the motley crowd of khaki-clad individuals, lounging behind the counter. '*Habari* bwana?' I greeted the first officer.

'*Nzuri, habari ya wewe?*' he replied.

'*Hujambo* bwana.'

'*Sijambo* bwana.'

And so to business.

Mentally I took a deep breath. 'I would like to see Mzee Mkate,' I said.

*

It was lunchtime before I met an anxious looking Sam back at the High Commission's entrance.

'How did it go?' she shouted over the roar of an army lorry grinding past, a dozen AK47 armed soldiers slouching in the back. 'I was getting worried.'

'Getting worried?' I gave her a smile. 'It was fine, fine. No problems. It took a while to find the right person, as you might expect, but no problem. Do you want some lunch?'

'Sounds like a good idea. I've got some news for you as well.' She looked out across the street. 'D'you think it's safe to go to the Africa? Ish said he'd try and meet me there.'

I scanned the junction. I could see two groups of *Polisi* and soldiers within a hundred metres, otherwise the streets were unusually quiet with even the newspaper vendor's *dukas* deserted.

'I think so, let's go,' I said talking her arm as we left the compound. 'So what's your news then?'

'No, you go first, I'm still trying to get it straight in my head.'

We made it across to the hotel and up the ramp past the *Polisi* without incident and sat at the outdoor bar, a spur of paving off the first floor main terrace which had room for a few tables overlooking the mezzanine car park. We chose the furthest spot from the bar, the table next to us was empty and it would take so long for a waiter to come for our order that there was plenty of time to talk.

'It was pretty much as I had expected. The sergeant on the front desk didn't know what I was talking about so he called the captain. The captain took down two pages of laboriously handwritten notes and then went off to find the inspector, who came and took down the same two pages of handwritten notes and asked me, very politely, to wait in the interview room. I explained how I had met Dave and Mr Mkate who had been introduced to me as a plain-clothes policeman; that Iain had come and delivered a package to me at home the other day; and that Iain had said he'd been given it by Dave and asked to deliver to me so that I could deliver it to Mr Mkate. Then Iain had had his accident and been killed and in all the upset it had gone clean out of my mind until this weekend when I had come across it again as I was packing. So here I was on Monday morning at the central police station trying to find Mr Mkate to deliver it to him.

'I explained that no, I hadn't seen Mr Mkate's warrant card. He had just been introduced to me as a plain-clothes policeman. I didn't know which station he was attached to. Basically I just played completely innocent.'

The waiter and the water arrived. The sandwiches would be a little longer, bwana.

'And then I saw a very different individual. A chief inspector came in to see me. Very civilised, very educated. He did not take copious notes. He had obviously read what I had said already. He asked me some casual questions about whether I had ever met Mr Mkate before and how well I knew Dave, which I was able to answer quite innocently. And then he explained that unfortunately

Mr Mkate didn't seem to be around at the moment, he actually worked for a different branch, but that the chief inspector had contacted his office and apologised for the delay, unfortunately telecommunications aren't all they might be here in Jijenga, particularly in the light of the present unfortunate circumstances. To which I graciously agreed. And that Mr Mkate's office would be sending someone across to collect the tape and I could either leave it with the chief inspector, or I could wait and give it to the representative myself.'

'Did he say tape?' Sam asked.

'Yes he did, I wondered whether you'd pick up on that. I had called it a package all the way through, but he definitely said someone would be across to pick up the tape.

'Anyway, I asked whether the representative was going to be long, and the chief inspector said he didn't think so, so I said I might as well wait and give it to him directly and apologised to the chief inspector, told him it was not that I didn't trust him it was just something I felt I had to, seeing as it was the last thing Iain had ever asked me to do.

'The chief inspector said he quite understood and offered me some coffee. Then half an hour later he reappeared to introduce me to *Ndugu* Khamisi.'

'Comrade Khamisi eh? So what was he like?'

'Short, thick set, dressed in plain green, olive drab, sort of Kaunda suit. Looked a real bruiser actually. Sort of big,' I said, hunching my shoulders and doing a knuckle-dragging boxer impersonation. 'A real thug, but very softly spoken.'

The waiter appeared from the terrace area behind me with our water. Sam smiled at him, then watched as he walked away, nodding for me to go on when he seemed to be at a safe distance.

'Anyway,' I continued. 'We shook hands, he introduced himself as a colleague of Mr Mkate, who was unfortunately not available today, so I handed him the package. God, he had big hands.' I held my hands out in front of me fingers and thumbs outstretched, to emphasise the point.

'He took it while I told him how Iain had delivered it to me and asked me to make sure it got to Mr Mkate. He didn't seem to be listening to me, just turning it over in his hands while I spoke, almost as though he was weighing it.'

The sandwiches had arrived.

'And as I finished he seemed to snap back to me and where we

223

were, shook my hand and said thank you very much. Thanked me for being of assistance to the country. Assured me it would all be dealt with properly. He would see that Mr Mkate got the package and the two of them walked me to the front desk and shook hands again. Damn near asked me to sign the visitors book, and here I am.' I shrugged. 'Bugger, I forgot to ask them to leave the tomato out of it,' I said, as I prised my sandwich open to remove the soft red tomato with distaste.

'So is that it, do you think?'

I sighed and shook my head. 'I don't know, but I hope so. You know what the police are like here. Once they actually notice he's missing and someone starts to dare to ask questions about an SPU man, what are they going to do? You can forget forensics for a start.'

'But we'll be safe?'

'I would think so. The police won't know where to start. No,' I shook my head. 'They'll head out and put pressure on all their usual informants in the *nyumbaya* until eventually someone, somewhere, for revenge, or just for a quieter life, shops someone else. The suspect'll be picked up, dragged back to the cells and have the crap beaten out of him until he signs a confession. Then he'll be up before a judge and banged away for twenty years to a prison farm somewhere out at M'gola if he's lucky. That's how it works out here.'

Sam said, 'So what now?'

I squashed the top back down on the first half of my sandwich and repeated the operation with the second. 'Now, nothing. We're leaving anyway, we'll just carry on as normal. They've got the tape. Full stop.' I took a mouthful of mush and plastic cheese. 'We've had it, I brought it in to them, I've handed it over. I didn't say anything about listening to it and even if I did, what's on it?' I shrugged again. 'There's no reason to bother us. If there's nothing incriminating on the tape – which there isn't – then whether or not we've listened to it or have had it doesn't matter, does it? They'll be wondering what the bloody hell has happened to Mkate, but then a guy like him is probably involved in lots of things, has lots of enemies, and nobody would know too much about his movements. So they may not even become seriously worried for quite some time. There didn't seem to be any suggestion that they knew that he had come to the apartment.'

I had finished my sandwich and refilled my water glass. I sat back. 'So, we just play it cool.'

Sam nodded slowly, 'Just play it cool. Is that all there is?' She paused, and then said, 'I let Colin at the High Commission know you were going.'

'Good. He'll be next on the list. So, what's your news?'

'Well there's two things really. You know I couldn't work out Mkate's symptoms, the confusion, the lesions and so on, it was as though had gone to full blown AIDS in six weeks or so from appearing completely healthy.'

'Yes.'

'Well, you just don't develop AIDS that quickly.'

'So?'

'So I was wondering what else could give you the same symptoms but in a much quicker timescale. So I took a trick out of your book and raided the High Commission library this morning to check on a crazy idea I'd had and well, listen to this,' she said, pulling out a scrap of paper with some hastily scribbled notes and started to read to me in a hushed voice.

The sickness depends on how serious the exposure has been. The standard unit of exposure is the Sievert. From 1 to 10 Sieverts, transient nausea and vomiting disappear within a 2 to 3 week period leading to a period of relative well being. But then, and listen to this, *damage to the bone marrow and immune system start to appear in repeated opportunistic infections and petechiae, pinpoint spots of bleeding under the skin. Skin in direct contact may show blistering and typical signs of burns.*

Is this sounding familiar to you at all?' She said, looking up.

Did it ever? Only the very real fear that we might be being watched kept me from jumping up in astonishment. I had to keep looking and sounding calm so as not to attract attention. 'Well yes, now you come to mention it. According to Iain, Dave had vomiting and burnt hands. So what are these the symptoms of?'

She didn't answer.

'At exposure of 10 to 30 Sieverts, patients suffer early nausea and vomiting 2 hours after exposure. This disappears after a few hours and death follows 4 to 14 days later, usually from gastrointestinal tract failure, the patient suffering severe frequent bloody diarrhoea and overwhelming infections due to damage to the immune system.

At exposure of over 30 Sieverts victims suffer nausea, vomiting, anxiety, disorientation and loss of consciousness with death occurring within hours from oedema, that's fluid on the brain to you,' she added, looking up.

Any exposure of over 6 Sieverts is fatal,' she concluded.

I was shocked and insistent. 'So what on earth is this?'

She carefully put the paper face down on the table between us and leant across. 'The Sievert' she said speaking quietly, 'is the standard unit of absorbed radiation.

These,' she said tapping the piece of paper, 'are a summary of the symptoms of radiation sickness.'

'Radiation sickness?' I could barely control my voice.

'It was the only thing I could think of. I told you it was crazy, but the point is that some of the symptoms of radiation sickness are basically those of a collapse of the immune system.'

'A sort of fast forward AIDS?'

'You could say that.'

'Wow.' I sat back; this needed some time to sink in. But then a thought struck me, Sam had been here before.

'You know your control sample in town, the one with the anomaly.'

'Yes.'

'The anomaly was the New Mwanchi workers wasn't it? That they had an unusually high and quick AIDS death rate?'

'Yes, I've been wondering about that,' she nodded.

'Did you screen for radiation?'

'As an environmental factor or a cause of death? No, I didn't think of it at the time.'

'Is it possible?'

'Theoretically yes, I suppose so. Exposure could either give radiation sickness which could be mistaken for AIDS or weaken the immune system leading to faster onset of the disease when caught.'

'What could be the source?'

'Well it could be a natural cause like radon gas, it's a volcanic area. Or there are uranium deposits that are mined in the hills. But I can't think of a reason that would affect a specific area of Mkilwa or New Mwanchi.'

'But if you're right, radon gas exposure is never going to be serious enough to give Dave and Mkate radiation sickness is it?'

'Assuming they got it at New Mwanchi?'

'Where else are they going to have got it from? It's starting to be a bit of a coincidence though isn't it? Do you remember what Mkate was ranting about when he arrived at the apartment that night?'

'Not really, he wasn't making much sense.'

'That's what I thought at the time but now I'm not so sure. Many dangerous things he said, many dangerous things come out of the ground, more dangerous than lead, well that's what New Mwanchi smelt, so was there a connection there? But then he said, more dangerous than uranium. Why uranium? He said something about checking it up, he kept coming back to something being more dangerous than uranium.'

'Ish! Ish! Over here,' Sam shouted, scrunching the piece of paper and stuffing it into her pocket as she jumped up to greet him. 'Jesus Ish, am I glad to see you. You wouldn't believe what's been going on here in town.'

'Oh no? Hi Paul,' he said over her shoulder as she hugged him. 'You guys looked in serious conversation. Were you talking about uranium?'

'Oh nothing, just something stupid someone said on a case the other day, "What's more dangerous than uranium?"'

'Lots of things,' Ish said with cheerful grimness, 'Ebola, plague, botulinus toxin, radium, and as you can see, African elections.'

I was surprised. 'Radium?'

'It's true,' said Sam distractedly as she pulled a chair across for Ish to sit down next to her, 'it was in what I was just reading. It's really nasty stuff, a million times more radioactive than uranium and has a half life of over a thousand years. Marie Curie found it a century ago, working in a draughty barn just outside Paris You can extract it from a uranium ore called pitchblende by electrolysis. She spent years mixing it up in a bathtub apparently and died of cancer.'

'Anyway,' Ish interrupted her, 'I'm glad I found you here. Have you heard?'

'Yes, I was just about to tell Paul.'

'Tell me what?'

'Looks like we're all out of here.'

'Why?'

'I spoke to Colin this morning,' said Sam. 'The High Commission is ordering an evacuation, all non essential personnel are to assemble at the airport tomorrow. Ish and I need to get back to the beach to pick up our stuff.'

'Do you want me to take you?'

'No it's OK thanks, I've borrowed a car from the rag.'

*

There was a thunderous banging at the door and muffled voices shouting open up.

I unlocked the inner door to find Ish and Sam, and a chaperoning Mr Chavda in the flittering light of the stairwell. 'I hope you don't mind Mr Paul, I let them in, I knew that they were your friends and it is dangerous to be out there.'

'Sure yeah, thanks Mr Chavda,' I said, rattling open the cage door as fast as I could. Sam looked really shaken.

'What are you guys doing out on the roads at this time of night?' I asked, ushering them inside as Mr Chavda, duty done, scurried back downstairs to the safety of his own apartment. The army's curfew had started at six.

'Seeking sanctuary,' was Ish's enigmatic response.

'What happened?' I asked, ushering them in and bolting the cage door behind them.

Sam was obviously very distressed. Even Ish looked shocked.

'It's started,' he said.

'Oh Paul, we only just got out alive.'

Sam was looking down unseeing at the floor as she spoke, her face in shadow. She took a breath. 'You could hear the killing coming towards the house,' she said. 'There were shouts, then screams and then silence. Then they'd reach the next house and it would start all over again. Shouts, screams, silence. They were working their way methodically down the beach in our direction.'

'There had been shooting as well. We couldn't work out what the safest thing to do was,' Ish added.

'Ish made me get into the bath.'

'It was the safest place I could think as it only had the one small window up high. I was lying face down in the hallway trying to work out what was going on and what we could do. Then there was a knock at the door. I thought this is it; they've come to kill us.'

Sam looked up. Ish was sitting beside her on the sofa, holding her hand in reassurance. It felt as though she was forcing herself to go on. 'And then we thought, wait a minute, what is this? They're not going to come and knock on the door. What are they going to say, "Excuse me chaps is it convenient if we come in and kill you?" So I opened the door. They were a mixed group, some *wahindis* and Muslims from Bharanku and they were looking for refuge. What could I do? I let them in.'

'What have you done?'

'We've left them there,' Ish said. 'What else could we do?' They seemed genuinely agonised. 'We didn't have room for them in the car and there was no guarantee that we would actually be able to get them through safely anyway.'

'People know it's a *wazungu* rented house, perhaps they'll ignore it,' Sam said.

'And as far as locals are concerned a *wahindi*...' I trailed off and a silence fell.

'Well we did what we could,' Sam said.

'Yes you did, and there's nothing more you can do so you need to try to put it out of your minds. It's all right though now. You've made it here so you're OK. No one's going to come looking at this block, everyone knows that we're *wazungu*.'

'Other than the Chavdas,' Ish said.

'Other than the Chavdas,' I agreed.

'Anyway, we thought we'd be safer here. And it's a better point to head out to the airport from,' Ish said.

'Of course.'

*

'What happened to your phone?' Ish asked. 'I was worried when I saw the wires.'

'Oh, who knows,' I said. 'Perhaps it was kids.'

'Absolutely typical. You've only just had it fixed as well, after how long? Six months?' he commiserated.

'More like eight or nine,' I said. 'But anyway, what does it matter now? We are after all, out of here tomorrow.'

I had a reasonable stock of supplies so Sam volunteered to cook. It was an evening for purposefully getting quietly, decently and seriously stewed. We set to it sitting out on the front balcony as the turquoise darkness faded to a soft enveloping black. Below us, while we waited for dinner we could see the peacefully grazing cows, the *askaris*, no longer sleeping at the far side of the car park but huddled in a knot at the entrance in their scarlet robes, their spear points glinting in the light of a brazier.

'You see that's the sort of stuff that you just can't explain to people back home,' Ish was saying, about the mobs. 'They just wouldn't understand.'

I shook my head. 'It can't make it easy for you then,' I said to him.

'In what way?'

229

'In writing, of course. In trying to find a story to tell.

'Well now,' Ish said. 'I want to talk to you about that…'

Sam shouted in from the kitchen. 'I think it's nearly ready, so can you guys set the table?'

Ish and I talked quietly as Sam clattered away in the kitchen.

'I've got some information on Temu,' he said.

'Oh?' I enquired, arching my eyebrows. 'So what's the news?'

'Well,' he started, but I held my finger to my lips.

'Let's keep it quiet.'

He looked at me across the table as I clattered a handful of cutlery.

'What's this all about Paul? Why the cloak and dagger?'

'I can't tell you.'

'Can't or won't?'

'A bit of both to be honest. But please trust me.'

'Paul, Paul. You know I need a story. You've got one. A dead policeman, a mystery. And I think you know something. In fact I know you do, don't you?'

'A suicide,' I said. 'So what?'

He leant across to me. 'But it wasn't, was it?' he mouthed. 'The word on the rag is that Temu was murdered. It wasn't suicide,' he said, definitively.

'No?'

'No. Suicides for one thing don't usually shoot themselves in the back of the neck.'

'I suppose not.' I hadn't really got that much detail on the story from the papers.

'No, they don't. They usually shoot themselves through the temple or through the roof of their mouth. I mean think about it, Paul. You couldn't even reach round to hold the pistol in the right place could you?'

'I suppose not.'

'And,' this was his killer point. He leant forward over the table and hissed to me, 'they certainly don't go on to shoot themselves another four times in the body.'

'What?'

'You heard me. Five shots.'

'And what's more you heard those shots as well didn't you? You were here. You asked me to find things out but you know something.'

'Here we are,' announced Sam. 'Now who's sitting where?'

230

As we sat down to dinner, Ish and I exchanged glances, we both knew we needed to resume this conversation, but later, alone.

As we ate, conversation ran over the things we had shared together, the trips, the experiences, the safaris, the stories.

Strangely, it was Sam who brought up the ferry business. I was surprised. It was something that normally she wouldn't want to talk about, but she had been speaking to one of her contacts at the clinic up at Mkilwa.

The wreck had eventually been raised a few weeks after it had sunk. The lake really was so shallow there that it hadn't been too difficult once the right gear was available.

'They will only have found the bodies of those people who were below decks when it went down,' she was saying. 'It turned turtle so quickly that they don't think any of them could have made it out. But those who did and the foot passengers out on deck would have been straight over into the water without any life rafts. They doubt that many of their bodies will ever be found. Or that the real numbers will ever be known.'

'It was over a thousand apparently,' Ish murmured.

'Oh God,' she said, 'that many?'

He just nodded.

We drank in silence for a moment. To Dave, I thought. Whatever it was that happened to you.

Nobody seemed to be able to say anything to follow that.

Ish was quiet, staring down into his glass.

Sam was looking at him silently. She could tell there was something wrong.

'What is it Ish?'

'What you won't have seen in the papers,' he said with a sigh, after an age. 'Is what really happened. When I was up there last I talked to the people who actually saw it.

'It was overcrowded, of course, and it had just got out onto the lake when it flipped over. It was an old ferry, it didn't have stabilisers and it always used to roll a lot. They think perhaps the wind just caught it wrong as it swung out of the harbour and over it went. Anyway, hundreds of people were thrown off into the water straight away. The rest were trapped inside but crucially, the internal watertight doors closed. A chap with a tug scrambled and got out there, followed eventually by the harbour authorities. The police couldn't reach it at first of course, because they didn't have any diesel for their boat, a *wahindi* had to buy it for them.

231

'By the time the police had arrived, the chap with the tug had sized up the situation and had a plan. You see, it was still floating at this stage, even though it was upside down. So the tug master said he would tow it back into the shallows by the harbour so it grounded and then worry about getting people out.

'But the police told him to bugger off. They said he was a stupid *wazungu* and that they were in charge, they knew what they were doing. Do you know what they did then?'

We both shrugged in silence, looking at him.

He shook his head. 'Someone had obviously seen the *Poseidon Adventure*,' he said, sarcastically. 'They cut a hole in it. It was a giant air bubble that was keeping it afloat, and they cut a sodding great hole in the top.' There were tears in his eyes. 'Out came the air; in went the water; down went the boat. I've got photographs of the hole. I snuck down to the lakeshore where they eventually towed her in to beach her.

'I met up with some of the South African divers who went down to help get the bodies out the week afterwards one night in the Just Imagine.' He took another pull on his beer. 'In the third class accommodation they'd all linked arms in solidarity. People had had time to write their names and addresses and put them in their pockets. In one cabin they found people had written a note saying that they were in there for their third day. All they needed was air. Absolutely hideous.'

I broke the horror-struck silence that followed. 'Do you think you can print that here?'

'Not a chance in hell.'

'But at home?' I asked.

'Who cares at home?' he said. 'It's a third world ferry disaster. It happens every week. There's probably one going down in the Philippines as we speak.'

*

'No, for a story, I need something else,' he said, looking directly at me. 'Something more, some human interest, some new angle. You have just what I need, don't you?'

Sam had called it a night, leaving Ish and me alone on the balcony.

'You know something about our dead policeman.'

I felt chilled.

'I don't *know*,' I said. I did, all too much, about all too many, but not about the particular dead policeman he was talking about. 'I can't tell you anything about that.'

'Can't or won't?'

I just shook my head firmly.

'Oh, so you can't tell me,' said Ish slumping back in his seat, but never taking his eyes off me for a minute.

'So how about if I just guess?'

'But…'

'There's nothing to stop me speculating is there?' he said. 'Who knows, perhaps I might just get lucky.'

'You just don't understand,' I protested.

'Don't I? Look, here we have you, mixed up in all sorts of stuff, you have to be because of what you guys do for a living, and you've been up Mkilwa way. You even told me that you had had a run in with this guy.'

'Oh hey, I met him once to complain about how lousy the local *Polisi* were,' I protested. 'But that doesn't make me some kind of expert on the subject. Or a murderer,' I added, emphatically.

He started, surprised at my sudden vehemence. 'Hey look, I never suggested anything like that,' Ish said, with his hands up defensively. 'Hey, you know that.'

'Well of course I do,' I smiled. 'But what do you want me to say?'

'Come on, you know that I have got to wonder. I mean he was shot in the plot just round the back of here and the only reason I find out it was murder was because you asked me to do some digging. Now I've got to ask myself, why did you do that? It wasn't just idle curiosity was it?'

'Of course it wasn't just idle, but it was pretty simple.' I shrugged. 'I crossed swords with him in Mkilwa. I thought he was a bent cop and the next think I know, he ended up getting wacked fifty metres down the street from the apartment. Wouldn't you be interested in knowing just a bit more?'

'Of course. But haven't you got any idea about a motive?'

I shook my head. 'Out here? Who can tell?'

'Well, I have.'

I started. That took me by surprise. Deliberately, I didn't say anything.

'Want to hear then?' he asked.

I nodded.

233

'Well, there are a few possibilities,' he said, counting them off on his fingers. 'Firstly, there's revenge. Pure and simple. Someone somewhere has a grudge. Someone he has put away and they catch up with him here in Jijenga and take him out.' He looked at me. 'Buy that?'

I shook my head.

'No, neither do I,' he said. It's too far-fetched and doesn't explain what he was doing in Jijenga in the first place, unless he was deliberately lured here. And that execution, the bullets in the back of the head. That's an execution, organised crime stuff to me, not some revenge-crazy bandit gangster. So number two is revenge specific.'

I was puzzled. 'What do you mean?'

'I mean that it was Temu that ordered the ferry cut open. As RPC he was the policeman in charge.'

'Jeez,' I whistled. 'Temu sank it?'

Ish nodded firmly. 'Now you start to think that maybe that was why he left town so quickly.'

'Yes, I can see that.'

'You might think that he wouldn't want to stick around in Mkilwa once word of what he had done got out. I mean that's a whole load of clans and families with relatives he's just drowned. But did word get out? It never hit the papers?'

'It never hit the papers because it was sat on hard. From on high. How the hell do you think the Party would think that incompetence in sinking a ferry like that was going to play in the papers on election day? It was suppressed. Full stop.'

'But up in Mkilwa?'

'Everyone knows. The bloody hull was visible from the harbour wall. You know what it's like up there. There'll have been thousands rubbernecking all around the shore. They'll have seen it floating, the *Polisi* arrive and then it sinks.' He shook his head again. 'Oh no, anyone in Mkilwa would have known, and I wouldn't have given too much for Temu's chances.'

'So what's your theory? Temu flees down here only to run into… who precisely?'

'Now that's interesting. A relation perhaps?'

'No. It doesn't work. If Temu was fleeing, how is some relative going to lure him out to this plot to kill him off?'

'No, I don't see that either. I keep coming back to the execution. Perhaps someone high up decided that as the key witness to the disaster he would need to be silenced. But that doesn't really tie in

234

with whatever it is that you know, does it?' Ish asked shrewdly.

'Look, Ish…'

'Because option three is drugs,' he said.

I was stunned.

'Drugs, what do you mean drugs?'

My mind was racing. What did Ish know, how much did he guess, what connection had he made?

'Nigerians,' he said.

'What?' I was lost. He had completely thrown me.

'Nigerians. You've seen them here, you've even sold factories to them.'

'Yes, but…' I nodded. I didn't see what he was getting at. 'The Nigerians I've been dealing with have all been completely straight.'

'But they are still here. And the more Nigerians there are, the more some Nigerians might become concerned.'

I was shaking my head now. 'Ish, Ish, what on earth are you talking about?'

'Look, we talked about the drugs issue before. Back at the Europa Bar one night. The Nigerian smugglers are after mules to carry stuff into Europe. The locals here are even more poor and desperate than they are back home in Nigeria, so they are easy meat. The trouble is that the more Nigerians there are in the country, the more trade from this country to Europe will be put under the microscope at the end.'

Christ, I thought. No wonder Nigerians aren't popular locally. Perhaps Ish had put his finger on it.

'But I still don't get the connection with Temu,' I said. 'He isn't bringing Nigerians into the country for Christ's sake.'

'No, of course not.'

'So what's the connection. And why kill him even if there is a connection?'

'Funnily enough I think it's to crack down on smuggling.'

'Now come again, Ish. You are going to have to go slowly for me. I don't think I get that one. His link to the smugglers is that they want him to crack down on smuggling?'

He nodded. 'I know it sounds crazy but think about it. The Mr Bigs aren't going to take too kindly if they've invested in getting a big operation going, only to find small timers and amateurs screwing it up, doing smaller scale stuff and queering their pitch by making this a priority target area for Customs. Which if they're in with the *Polisi*, means they've got an incentive to try and get small fry

235

stamped on as quick as possible, and as quietly as possible.'

'But hey now, Ish, just hold on a moment,' I protested. 'Temu had just done that hadn't he? His boys up at the airport pulled over a guy carrying a suitcase full of hash bound for SA didn't they, the month before the election? It was quite a coup wasn't it?'

'Yeah, sure it was. One small smuggler pulled. But against that you've just got Mkilwa as a departure point smeared across the inside columns of the world's press for a day, which is exactly what you wouldn't want if you were a Mr Big looking for a nice quiet outlet.'

'And,' he said, finishing the last of his beer, 'just what do you think you would think of that sort of performance if you were some kind of smuggling mastermind? Eh, answer me that?'

I shrugged. There wasn't anything I could really say.

'Anyway,' I said. 'That's all speculation. And pretty tenuous speculation too,' I added.

'I know,' he confessed. 'That's why I want to try and get hold of some hard evidence. If I can't get someone to tell me what is going on, I need to try and get something that does.'

'So what are you going to do?'

'Well, I don't know. He was rich, I suppose. I could, in the immortal words of Ben Bradley, try and follow the money. That's what you guys do sometimes isn't it?'

Wasn't it *Deep Throat*? I wondered. 'Sometimes,' I said. 'But forget it, Ish, you'd never do it. Not here.'

'Why not?' he demanded.

'Because even if you, with your finely honed journalistic skills, haven't noticed that the entire country is rapidly descending into total shit, there'd be no trail. Everything is cash here. There'll be no records, no cheque numbers to follow, no bank transaction to trace. No you'd never find anything, even if you had access,' I said, emphatically. 'Which you don't,' I pointed out.

He nodded sadly. 'You're right, I suppose.'

'I'm afraid so,' I said, sympathetically. 'Look, I would help you if I could, but on this one, I just can't.'

He had been counting off on the fingers of his left hand. Thumb, index, middle. These three were still held up, outstretched.

'And four?' I asked gently. 'Is there a fourth explanation?'

He shook his head slowly in answer, his eyes never leaving mine.

'No,' he admitted at last. 'No, I don't have a fourth one.' He gazed at me across the small balcony. 'Not unless you can give me one.'

'I know what you want and believe me, if I could do so I would help. But I can't, not now, not this, not here. Trust me.'

Ish stared at me. 'You're serious aren't you? There is something here. I can tell. Why won't you tell me? You put a hell of a strain on a friendship.'

'I know and I'm sorry, and I shouldn't have asked you for information if I wasn't going to be able to reciprocate, but take it from me, I can't.'

Ish took a long time to take this in and judge it.

'OK, OK,' he sighed, eventually. 'I trust you. But why?'

'I wouldn't do it to Sam.'

'Do what?'

'Tell you.'

'Why?'

'Because if I did, you would try and use it as a story. You would take it to your paper.'

'So?'

'And then you would be dead,' I said matter of factly. Like Dave. Like Iain. Like Juma, I thought. 'And I'd rather have you as an alive friend. I wouldn't do that to you, or Sam.'

'Jesus,' he whistled under his breath. 'You really are serious aren't you?'

'I have never been more serious in my life. But I promise you this, I will tell you. Once I can. Once it's safe.'

'OK, and promise me something else then.'

'Of course, but what?'

'Promise me that you'll look after Sam. And my photographs,' he added as an afterthought.

'What about you?'

'I've got to stay on.'

'Are you out of your mind?'

'Look it's only going to be for a few days. I just need to finish what I'm doing and I'll catch the next plane out.'

'Christ Ish, have you told Sam yet?'

Tuesday, 24 January, Jijenga

Something had come over me, I couldn't rest, so I folded back the mosquito net and shrugged on a T-shirt and a pair of baggies. The moon touched everything a steely blue as I wandered into the living

237

room and sat down to think.

It was the word bathtub that had finally made the connection for me. To the mysterious equipment in the lab, to Dave's questions back at the Golden Shower about strange chemicals, and everything else had fallen into place after I had pumped Sam for a few more details. Production of radium from pitchblende, a brownish black uranium ore involved its electrolysis from an acid solution, using a mercury cathode in a hydrogen atmosphere. The huge vessels lining both the walls in the lab, the ones with the electrical connections, the gas inlet pipes, the heavy lids and the faint blue glow in the dark. These were retorts for radium production. Dave and Mkate must have just got too close and touched too much, Dave had been being poisoned even as he whispered into his Dictaphone and sent Mkate off to check shipment records. No wonder his body had had to be made to disappear in a convenient accident, who could risk what an autopsy back home might show up?

From smuggling Afghan drugs into the West to smuggling radium for Afghan terrorists? It wasn't a huge leap. And after all, the lead casing mechanism they had developed for the drugs would work just as well for disguising radioactive shipments.

They were making the material for a dirty bomb. It wouldn't be nuclear but would be designed to spread high levels of highly active and long lasting radioactive contamination across whichever city it was set off in.

And Dave had been interested in the shipping details. The next shipment, the ingots I had seen down by the docks, was bound for Southampton. And the customer's factory, North London.

Jesus, I needed to speak to Colin. And fast. But with the curfew in place I was only going to get an opportunity tomorrow at one place I knew he would be. The airport for the evacuation.

*

I had given Mr Chavda the keys to the apartment. They would be safer up on the second floor in a '*wazungu*' occupied apartment than they would be in their ground floor one. They were welcome to what food we had left as well.

I abandoned the Suzuki at the apartments and Ish drove us in. The streets were quiet and the army was everywhere with patrols on every corner. The city seemed sullen and hung-over. Out towards the *nyumbaya* palls of smoke hung in the sky over the slums as

238

evidence of the overnight trouble.

Sam was silent throughout the trip. I guessed that they must have been rowing during the night about Ish's decision, but his mind seemed to be made up. The High Commission had arranged for the expats to assemble in the Africa Hotel car park late that afternoon where they were arranging a small convoy of taxis, the lead one bearing the Union Jack spread across the bonnet as some kind of talisman. While Sam and Ish organised the loading of our few travelling bags into a rusty Toyota Corolla, I walked across the dusty white car park past the handful of broken down buses and jacked up hotel vans bleaching in the sunlight.

The power must have been off because the fountain outside the office was dry again. A handful of *askaris* in baggy green fatigues were sat on white plastic patio chairs playing checkers with bottle tops on a hand drawn board perched on an upside down metal rubbish bin in the shade of the overhanging canopy outside the entrance. Inside the building it was blessedly cool in the gloom, the grey walls and metal shutters of the computer shop contrasting with the brilliant strips of vertical light which came staggering down the stairs to lie sprawled across the hallway from the slits which marched upwards with you in the stairwell.

There had been the usual jumble of cars in the slots in the courtyard out the back of the building but I hadn't noticed any of the partners' Landcruisers, as for the last time I took the concrete steps up towards the office.

When I got to the fourth floor, the sliding security grille like the gates of an old fashioned elevator, were cranked ajar and I pushed them aside. I walked in through the unlocked wooden frosted glass door into reception and past the *askari*.

'*Habari yako* bwana.'

'*Nzuri, habari ya wewe?*'

'*Nzuri.*'

'*Safi.*'

'*Sawa.*'

Marilyn was on duty alone behind the main reception desk, although almost all the professional staff were missing. 'Are you looking for Winston?' she asked.

'No, I just wanted to drop these off,' holding up the Suzuki keys. 'Can I leave them with you in an envelope for him?'

'Yes sure,' she said. 'Don't you need them?' she asked as she popped back up from behind the counter with an envelope.

'No I'm afraid not. I'm about to get off to the airport.

'*Safari njema,*' Marilyn called as I turned away. 'When will we see you again?'

'You won't,' I said. 'I'm off. This is it.'

'Off?' she said, with eyebrows arched in surprise. 'Off, you mean you are going home?'

'Yes, I'm done. Back to England.'

'You mean we won't see you again?'

'I'm sorry, no, I'm going back home to England to live.'

'Oh, that's too bad,' said Marilyn, with one of her big, pretty girl pouts. 'You lucky thing.' Marilyn was struggling with a fax that wouldn't go. 'Man, I tell you – if I ever get out of this country I am never coming back! *Safari njema.*'

'*Asante sana,* I will, look after yourself. *Kwaheri.*' I waved as I stepped over the threshold to the door.

'*Kwaheri* bwana,' I said to the *askari*.

As I walked out of the building for the last time, I could feel the heavy army presence on the streets in the quietness and stillness. Parked on the mud that passed for pavement around the junction there was the usual gaggle of ancient Peugeots and clapped out Corollas, their drivers sitting on benches under the canopy of the hotel opposite or squatting, reading newspapers spread out on the cut out cardboard boxes of the vendors, as if still waiting patiently for nonexistent passengers to tout to. Or perhaps I wondered, it was just a good position from which to observe the city's comings and goings. But otherwise as I left the building's courtyard to round the corner into the hotel, everywhere I looked the downtown streets were eerily empty, even the street boys seemed to have disappeared.

Back at the convoy, Sam was sitting in the taxi's back seat, which was propped up by strategically placed bricks.

'OK?' I asked as I opened the front door of the waiting taxi.

'Yep, fine, no problem,' she said in a flat toneless voice.

'No Ish?'

'No Ish. He wouldn't change his mind. He gave me this though for safekeeping,' she said pulling out his old battered 35mm camera. 'It's got his film with the photos of the ferry on it. For his big story.'

'Then you know that he's planning to come back then don't you?'

'He seemed excited when he spoke to me about it last night. Said he thought he was onto something big, really big that would make his name back home, said that the ferry was only part of it. That he just needed the last few pieces of the jigsaw and then he could get out. Paul,' she said fixing me with a direct stare, 'You haven't told him have you? You promised that you wouldn't?'

'No I haven't,' I reassured her. 'Funnily enough I almost did last night, I thought for a moment that it would be enough to persuade him to get out.'

'So why didn't you?'

'Because I had promised you; because I didn't think it would work; because I thought it might make him more eager to stay to gather evidence.' I trailed off. But were there other reasons as well? Was I really so trapped by a promise to Sam? Was I thinking about where telling Ish might lead? To Mkate? To us? To Sam and me?

She seemed to accept that though, content in the thought that I had kept part of her promise to her, even if not the part about trying to keep Ish from doing anything foolish. 'So what do you think we should do with it then?' she said looking at the camera.

'Here, give it to me. I'll stuff it into my camera bag with mine. If anyone wants to steal something they'll go for my flash number in preference to his. He can collect it at home.' I hadn't really thought of this before. 'Have you anywhere to stay when you get back?'

No, not really, I, I...' she seemed lost for words.'

'Well I've got space at my apartment in London. You're welcome to the spare room if you want until Ish gets back and you can get sorted out.'

With a set of cries the convoy started to form up to move out and our taxi clattered to life.

I looked over at Sam in the back and smiled, 'We're out of here.' At last she smiled a brave thank you and we squeezed each other's hands.

I wound the window down and stuck my elbow out. The grinning Mzee driver leant across and tapped my watch, indicating it might be a target for thieves, so for the sake of a quiet life rather than any real feeling of threat, I slipped it off my wrist and into my pocket.

Today they could have had my watch. That was the least of my worries. All I cared about now was getting us and the tape, now carefully stored away in the luggage, through Customs and out of the country.

'OK,' said the driver. 'We are going,' he nodded as he looked in the mirror and pulled away from the curb.

At the car park exit the lead driver hesitated for a moment. The most direct route was right, up into Boma and then down Samora or

City Drive to join Haile Selassie on the southern side of the headland, just as it became Umoja.

The convoy turned left, towards the corner at the junction with Haile Selassie and the normally bustling waterfront and brilliant reflected light of the blue bowl of the bay.

It made sense, along the flat of the waterfront and cutting across to Umoja at Kenyatta or after Nyerere would be the quickest and probably safest run cutting across the smallest part of the *nyumbaya* that lay between Boma and the airport. As we swung around the corner by the office onto the coast road, haunted by its empty *dukas*, I took my last look at a scene which had become so familiar, the huge modern bulk of Kahawa House and the South African bank, the tattered peeling paint of the hotel-cum-brothel across the junction opposite, the faded withered vegetation behind the railings of the Zambian Embassy next around the corner. How did the old joke go… One people, one nation; one railway, one station.

I looked out across the shining bay flickering through the line of palms that fringed the sandy margins of the road. Across the bay the town appeared calm and peaceful in the oppressive enervating heat of the afternoon. Above the jumble of dirty whitewashed colonial buildings, corrugated roofs of every conceivable shade of rust red and pitch black and brutalist Romanian-donated tower blocks rose the surrounding hills, a patchwork of shanty towns, sandy patches and palm trees. And away to the north, the docks with the piers and ships and oil tanks and power station tower chimneys.

The airport was out along what was officially now known as Mandela. A long wide stretch of dual carriageway branching off Bara Bara ya Rais, just before Kusini Bridge and heading inland along the side of the river valley at first but quickly climbing the side of the hills up onto the coastal plain as it crossed the main north-south coastal highway that acted as Jijenga's outer ring road.

Everyone local still knew the road by its old name, Bharanku. It was the old slave road, heading up from the coast onto the plain and out along the length of the country to the lake.

For good or ill we were on our way. Our own long chauffeured drive to freedom.

And now, as we headed out along Mandela, née Bharanku, holding hands across the back of the front seat, I had my elbow out of the window, open for the rush of hot air, while I gazed out through my cheapo sunglasses for the last time at the oh so familiar strip of road. It was a two and three lane highway in either direction with a wide scruffy grass divider and verge on either side which fell away to another great three metre wide drainage ditch and then to a sporadically tarmaced and rutted white sand service road, leading up past the ragged breezeblock surrounds of each of the industrial yards, some right up to the road, some set back. At its narrowest the whole thing must have been a hundred metres across, at its widest where the units were set back and open containers sat filled with sacks of cement for sale or broken down trucks stood outside yards, it must have been two hundred and fifty metres. And overhead pylons and wires stretched across the road and down the street. Every so often a never used set of rusty railway tracks crossed it and the two or three sets of ignored traffic lights were American style, strung from wires overhead.

This was shabby American strip belt style development, placed where land was cheap to buy and held little value and was uncared for. Where you enclosed a lot and then ignored most of it. Where if you had a pile of rubbish it didn't matter, there was plenty of space for more. The difference from America was that it was just so run down, it was so threadbare, so dirty, so full of things that didn't work and that people didn't have the skill to fix and didn't care about. This was poor, dirt poor.

But here outside the downtown district suddenly there were people everywhere again, people walking, people selling, people buying, people setting up stalls. There was a vibrancy, a life, people talking. The violence and horrors of last night seemed an eternity away. There was an energy here devoted to living, just being. This was the Africa I had come to know and love.

I shook my head to myself.

This was a country, a culture, that often conspired to infuriate *mzungu* expats, me included, rendered fulminatingly impotent by its bureaucracy and own their underlying ill defined sense of entitlement. And it was all too easy to lash out mentally, to blame the locals, to slip into a 'white mischief settler' mentality that everyone around you was just lazy or stupid or ignorant.

But it wasn't them. I thought. It was us.

They were themselves, they were living with their own values.

We were the ones who were out of place, stressed by our sense that things were out of our control and reacting by becoming insecure and aggressive.

We were the messed up ones, I thought. We needed to get out of here. I think I must have spoken out loud.

'What was that?' Sam called from the back seat, over the rush of hot air.

'Nothing,' I shouted back, 'just we're out of here.'

She smiled determinedly and squeezed my hand even tighter. 'We are.' I turned in my seat to look at her.

'He'll be all right. He loves you and he'll make it OK.'

'Oh God I hope so. Her grip on my hand was like a vice.

*

'Samora Machel' said the sign over the entrance. The bureaucracy would be the last to go I decided as the convoy of taxis queued up so that each could pay the one hundred *shillingi npya* required to enter the airport car park.

14 African Customs

The airport was the usual chaos, the normal bureaucracy overlaid with an edge of panic and extra security measures for the evacuation flight.

As the taxi drew up at the drop-off point, it became a magnet for the swarm of porters and their pimps eager to grab our luggage for the thirty metre trip to the doors of the departure lounge; where a bored looking policewoman in white shirt, pleated grey skirt and thick black knee-high socks sat at an incongruously civil service standard desk complete with fixed asset register number painted in white down one leg, and demanded to inspect our tickets before allowing us inside.

Flashing our tickets to her khaki-clad Kalashnikov-toting backup we pushed through the swing doors into the relative quiet of the tired concrete departure hall with its intermittent airline signs and factory tourism posters, where Colin was standing ticking names off a list on a clipboard as people went in.

'Colin, I need to talk to you.'

'What now? Can't it wait?'

'Yes now, it's urgent.'

'Well OK, I'll talk to you inside but you're going to have to wait until I've got everybody in.'

'OK,' said Sam hauling me past him before I had a chance to argue.

'Hey, where's Ish?' Colin called as we pushed open the doors. 'Isn't he with you?'

'He's not coming,' Sam answered him, dry eyed.

Colin had turned to face us in surprise and a mix of concern and anger. 'What do you mean he's not coming? Where is he?'

'He's not coming back yet. He's staying on for a few days, he wants to get his story.'

'Getting his bloody story is going to get him...' Colin caught himself, seeing the look on Sam's face. 'There's another flight organised for Saturday,' he said, turning away from us to check the next taxi load of arrivals, 'for the High Commission staff and people coming in from upcountry. There'll be space for him on that.'

Check-in was a block of wooden tables at the far end of the hall in front of which was a relatively orderly scrum-cum-queue.

Putting down our bags we joined one of the snaking lines and settled down for what we knew would be a slow shuffle forwards. I surreptitiously scanned the hall and was relieved to see that no one seemed to be taking any particular notice of us.

A gaggle of *wahindi* joined the queue behind us, mounds of suitcases piled on trolleys pushed by small silent blue Kaunda-suited porters who stood waiting patiently and silently as the family chatted and the kids ran about.

The line shuffled forwards.

Eventually it was our turn.

We handed over our tickets and passports. Our limited luggage was passed through to be placed on a trolley behind the counter by a porter and wheeled along behind the counter to the three Customs officers in their sky blue shirts.

The girl behind the counter smiled as she handed us back our tickets, boarding cards and passports. 'Customs please to check your bags, airport tax and immigration,' she said, indicating the desks we needed.

We knew the drill intimately anyway, but we were grateful to receive such pleasant service.

'*Safari njema.*'

'*Asante sana mama.*'

We made our way along the Customs desk to meet a large smiling man leaning forwards and standing with one foot up on the low counter. We greeted him formally.

'*Hujambo* bwana.'

'*Sijambo* bwana.'

'*Habari ya kazi?*'

'*Nzuri.*'

'*Habari ya wewe?*'

'*Nzuri.*'

'*Safi.*'

'*Sawa.*'

The formalities concluded, 'Bags please?' he enquired.

'Those two there,' I said, pointing.

'The green one?'

'Yes,' I said as he put his hand on it, 'and the rucksack beside it.'

'*Safi,*' and with a quick white chalk cross on each they were free to be trundled through the doors behind him by the porters and out of sight.

'*Asante sana* bwana.'

'*Kwaheri* bwana,' he said with a pleasant smile as he turned to greet the next travellers.

'Well, so far, so good,' I whispered to Sam, as carrying only our hand baggage; Sam's vanity case and handbag, my little backpack and camera bag, we strolled across to the airport tax booth.

Departure tax had to be paid in hard currency at a booth at the side of the check-in hall, it was also illegal to take *shillingi npya* out of the country and if found it would be confiscated. So this was the last chance to convert before hitting the airport security check giving the bureau de change two chances to prey on those who had failed to organise their dollars in advance.

We joined the short queue to pay our tax where behind the glass at the counter our dollars bought stamps which were stuck onto the face of our tickets.

The doorway out of the check-in lounge was just around the corner from the booth. There sat another police *mama* and assistant who accepted our proffered tickets with a muted *habari* and *asante*, scrawled an initial in blue biro on each of the airport tax stamps and returned them to us with a further muted set of *asantes*.

Through the doorway we joined another short line, this time for immigration.

Patiently we waited as the queue jerked forwards until it was our turn to stand at the yellow line painted on the floor.

The immigration officer waved the person he was dealing with through, and then beckoned to me. I approached the tall desk, handing my passport and boarding card up to him.

'*Habari?*' he said, perfunctorily, without smiling.

'*Nzuri. Habari ya wewe?*' I said.

He flicked through my passport, glancing at the resident permit stamps and the income tax clearance stamp before, with a bang, adding an exit clearance stamp. As he was handing me back my documents and acknowledging my '*asante*' with a '*safari njema*' he was already beckoning to Sam to come forward. He seemed bored.

Sam's passport got equally cursory attention and in a moment we were both done and ready to go through the final stage on this floor, airport security.

We were used to the procedures by then and Sam and I joined the separate queue waiting behind passport control.

There were two teams of police at the desk behind the two metal detectors, one for women and one for men.

The metal detectors weren't working of course, so the police were calling passengers through one at a time to be frisked.

The X-ray machines weren't working either so all hand baggage had to be opened for inspection.

It was a familiar routine but as we joined the queue there was a commotion up ahead.

Oh God, I thought, what is it now?

In front of us a man was being searched and the police had discovered a Walkman in his luggage. This, together with three or four tapes in his bag, seemed to have created a lot of excitement. The man sounded American, a middle-aged commercial traveller type. He obviously didn't speak any Kiswahili, however corrupted. The police were interested in the tapes he was carrying for some reason and within a few seconds a bigger, fatter man in plain clothes waddled out of a side room. The commotion and dispute quickly grew in intensity as the American became first irritated then angry. Soon we could see that the rude *mzungu* act wasn't going down at all well.

We kept very quiet, very still and very much just the innocent next couple of people in the line.

As the American was led away, the remaining police returned to their tables and beckoned us forwards.

This was it.

I saw Sam greeting the *mama* on her side with a big smile and a *habari* as she plonked her vanity case down on the table and plopped the two locks with a loud double report.

It really was worth the effort and time, I thought, as I shrugged off the backpack to join the camera bag on the table and stretched out my arms to be frisked.

The policeman ran his hands along each of my arms and down my body and legs with an expertise born of long repetition.

Back at the tables, as I heard Sam trying to explain what a pumice stone was, the backpack got a swift check-over before the policeman gestured to my camera bag.

I undid the snap releases and pulled open the top. The policeman reached in and lifted out my Dictaphone, which I had wedged in on top of the other equipment. There was no tape in it.

The more senior policeman only glanced at it, saying '*mobili*' to himself and put it down on the table beside the bag. Mobile phones were just starting to become popular in Jijenga as an alternative to the appalling land line service so it was an easy mistake to make.

Still inside as he reached in again, were the cameras, my automatic SLR held in its padded section, with the telephoto lens along the length of the bag, the flash stuck into a separate compartment in the back corner, while Ish's older manual lay across the top. In the pouch at the front were the spare films. I had thrown out the spare batteries last night.

The cameras were a big hit, particularly my automatic. My new-found *Polisi* friends wanted to know how much it had cost, where I had bought it, why I needed two cameras anyway, and surprise surprise, how they might obtain one just like it, because they did not think that such things were available in Jijenga.

It was a nice try but I knew the game. So I helpfully and courteously filled them in on the joys of mail order and how they might find photography magazines at the British High Commission's public library which would doubtless give them addresses from which they could obtain such a camera, thanked them for their interest and with their permission and no hard feelings on either side, swiftly gathered my belongings back into the case. I would sort the things out again properly upstairs.

We parted smiling with *asantes* and *safari njemas* about the same time as Sam closed her vanity case with a click-clack. 'OK?' I asked brightly, as she turned to join me at the foot of the non-functioning escalator to the first floor international flight departure lounge.

'Oh, shush,' she said, as we took the stairs hand in hand for mutual reassurance.

It felt like we were there already.

The departure lounge filled most of the upper floor of the terminal building, segregated from the boarding gates on the west and north of the building by a wide glass-walled corridor that ran all the way along both those sides of the building, broken at the north-west corner by a set of double doors and with stairs up from domestic departures at the far south-western end and stairs down at the far north-eastern to arrivals and baggage reclaim. Generally the western gates were for domestic and the northern ones for international flights.

Ranged around the southern third of the international lounge was a parade of relatively impressive duty free shops selling a range of imported electrical goods as well as the pricier end of the local souvenir market.

From arrival at the airport it had now taken us the best part of an hour and a half and about a lifetime's worth of *habaris, jambos,* and *nzuris.* The experience of going through check-in, Customs, immigration and security had been just about all I could stand, but now that we were through and into the inner sanctum of departures,

I could feel myself start to shake as the tension that had been holding me in tight, floating separate from the roaring world all around me, suddenly started to deflate in the few steps from the top of the escalator out onto the concourse by the shops.

By now it was fully dark outside and the high ceilinged hall was lit with sodium yellow bulbs while just under the building's eves tiny starlings were darting in and out through the open windows, the bolder ones flitting down to between the seats amongst the passengers, scavenging for crumbs and scraps of food, and chittering aggressively amongst themselves.

In the glass corridor between us and the airfield, staff were idling nonchalantly in front of one of the gates. The whole scene was given an eerie effect by the strobing yellow lights and roaring noise that I had suddenly become aware of as the white nose of a taxiing jumbo rolled inexorably and even more enormous towards the outer glass wall.

The huge noise of the jets filled the room, my ears and my head as the turbine whine climbed. For a moment it seemed that nothing could stop the plane now, that it must plough straight into the building, crashing through the glass walls, crushing everything in its path with its enormous bulk, but no, with a sudden jerking dipping curtsey, the advancing wall of steel came to a complete halt just short of the windows as at that exact moment the thunderous turbines quickened and died.

'The plane's here then,' Sam said.

'Shall we go and sit down?' I said. 'I could take some of the weight off my legs. They feel like rubber at the moment.'

'OK,' she said.

We walked over to the seating area that filled the north-west corner of the upper floor on the inside of the glass dividing wall.

We could see the airport staff opening the gate doors through which any arriving passengers would shortly come, to file past us along the northern corridor and down the stairs at the western end to baggage reclaim and their first taste of local immigration and Customs.

As we reached the seating area, there was a small desk blocking the only entrance way, manned by two local *wahindi* airline staff this time, who demanded to see our boarding cards.

There was a third man sitting off to one side of the desk, unsmiling, unspeaking, dressed in an anonymous grey Kaunda suit. He wasn't taking part in any of the inspections, he wasn't taking part in any of the discussions, he was just sitting. Sitting and looking. Watching. Subtle, I thought.

This was a new arrangement on us. We hadn't come across this before as final ticket and boarding card checks were usually done at the little desks on either side of the doors out of departures into the glass-walled corridor.

As I glanced around the room while we waited for our turn to go through, I could see at least two, no three, pairs of lounging security police in their khakis. Security really is tight tonight, I thought.

With our proffered boarding cards and passports getting no more than a passing glance from the airline staff we were waved through.

As we headed towards some seats facing out into the night and the glowing runway lights, I felt the hairs on the back of my neck prickling. I knew, I just knew that the SPU man was staring after us. I shuddered as we sat down. Don't look back, I thought, not yet. Put the bags down and then casually, oh so casually, just have a slow look around, ever so naturally, just to see what's going on where, just like you would do at home, to see where the announcements would come up.

I scanned the room, my eyes drifting past the seated passengers, before swivelling round to the others milling around the shops and the airline staff at the little check-in table and the SPU man's back.

I almost let out a sigh. His back was to us. He was watching people coming up the stairs. He wasn't looking at us at all.

Relax, I said to myself, as I lifted the bags up onto the seat beside me to sort them out, they aren't looking for you. No one is. Not for you and not for a tape.

There was a commotion at the desks. The American tourist had appeared. Or more precisely was being dumped there by the uniformed security police. Angry, flushed and threatening the intervention of the American ambassador if not the marines, all over the seizure of his tapes, which even at this distance we could gather had been retained, together with his Walkman for 'review'.

'If that idiot's not careful he's going to get himself arrested,' I said to Sam sotto voce.

'Is that a problem from our point of view?' she asked quietly.

I was surprised. 'No, I don't suppose it is,' I reflected.

'Well then,' she said, sitting back and popping open her vanity case to sort through the rifled contents. 'Then it's his problem, not ours.'

You are just being paranoid, I told myself. He and his tapes are just a coincidence. After all, we'd handed in the tape. Who would be looking for something that was already with the authorities? They would know I was the person who had had it, and they'd had a couple of days since then to do something about it if they thought there was anything to do.

So who would be looking for something when the authorities already thought they had it? The answer of course was no one. Unless, that was, the authorities or someone, knew that what they had, wasn't the full story. Or unless the authorities hadn't bothered to tell the police and Customs to call off the search.

We were now indelibly linked to the tape, having handed it in in its abridged format. If the full length version was to appear now, questions would be asked. That would be bad enough. But what if some bright spark tried to tie the tape and Mkate's disappearance together? That would be a real problem.

I had pulled out the cameras onto the seat next to us to repack them properly when the announcers wandered through the security area to inform us all that please be aware that boarding is to be delayed by one half hour.

'Oh shit,' I said. Sitting around here waiting to board was the last thing I wanted to do. Especially given how long it had been since we had last had anything to drink.

'Fancy a Coke or something?' I asked Sam.

'Now that's a good idea,' she said, firmly. 'A *Spriti*, I think.'

'OK,' I said, getting up. 'I'll just pop over to the stand and get one. Mind the stuff will you?'

'Of course,' she said.

Getting up, I walked back up to the desk blocking the entrance way and went to walk out, only to be stopped by the *wahindi* airline agent.

'I am sorry, sir, but you cannot come past.'

'What?' I said.

'I am sorry but you cannot come past. You must stay here now until it is time to be aboard the aeroplane.'

'But that's ridiculous,' I protested. What is the point of keeping people here? We have all gone through immigration and Customs.'

'I am sorry, sir,' he was insistent, 'it is the rules.'

Now I was starting to get angry, 'Then why don't you tell people that those are the rules before you let people through into the seats?' I demanded. 'It's crazy, you have just announced that the plane is going to be delayed for half an hour and there is nowhere in there,' I said, gesturing back at the seating area, 'to get a drink or even to go to the *choo.*'

I don't know what on earth had got into me, what had possessed me to start this. All we needed to do was to keep our heads down, keep quiet and hold tight for another three-quarters of an hour or so and we would be on the plane and out of sight of local security.

And yet here I was, building up to a full scale slanging match with the last local *wahindi* petty jobsworth it would ever be my displeasure to deal with in Jijenga, about whether I could go and get a *Spriti* to pass the time.

The frustration, the strain, the idiocy of the situation, the feelings of contempt and disgust I had been locking away for the last two years, were all boiling up, overwhelming me, a pent up anger bursting for release. I could see the *wahindi* was bridling, I was questioning his authority. Out of the corner of my eye I could see the SPU man's attention focused on us. A couple of khaki-clad *Polisi* had started up from leaning against the wall in the corner of the hall by the top of the escalator and had begun to amble slowly towards us.

The rational part of my mind was telling me I needed to cool down. I was thinking this is getting dangerous, they have had enough of stroppy *wazungu* already this evening with the Yank and his bloody tapes. I can't risk this.

But I just couldn't help it. I was genuinely incensed and that old arrogant I'm a *wazungu,* get out of my way attitude was bubbling dangerously close to the surface. I could feel the other passengers' eyes across the seating area start to take an interest and I felt I could not now give way. The loss of face would be horrendous.

His back was up too. I could see him bristling, summing up all his authority, he knew he had the backing of the full weight of the State's security apparatus turning out to back him up. This was his chance to crush a *mzungu* who had dared, dared, to question his authority, in this, his little empire of the desks.

The idea that I, as a passenger, was actually paying his salary never entered his head.

'I mean it's hardly an unreasonable request, to be allowed to get a couple of drinks, while we wait is it?' I insisted.

'So why don't I get them for you,' drawled a familiar Brooklyn accent to my right, before the man on the desk could answer. We both looked around, surprised.

What the hell was Gerry doing here?

'You sit down,' he said to me from the other side of the desk, 'and I'll bring the drinks through to you in a minute when I come.' He smiled pleasantly. '*Spriti*, wasn't it?'

'Yes, please,' I said, feeling instantaneously cold, the confrontation suddenly diminishing, the adrenaline pouring away, draining out of my pumped up head and mind, the red rage cloud dissipating, to be replaced by a cool logic.

'Thanks,' I said, walking away from the table and the fight.

'What the bloody hell did you think you were doing?' Sam hissed at me furiously as I sat down.

'I know, I know,' I said. 'I couldn't help it.'

'Well bloody well pull yourself together,' she demanded. 'We've got less than an hour until we are out of here.' She took my hand in hers. 'Don't throw it all away now, please,' she entreated.

I looked at her and nodded silently.

We embraced.

A few moments later Gerry joined us, juggling a couple of beers for himself, a lit cigarette, his Zippo, passport, ticket and two *Spritis*.

'Diplomatic,' he said, nodding at the passport in his hands. 'All of us aid guys have them. Works wonders at times.'

'Cheers,' he said, as he opened the first of his beers, standing in front of us.

'Thanks for that, Gerry,' I said. 'I'm afraid that I was about to make a bit of an idiot of myself back there.'

'Ah now,' he said. 'I owed you one, but that wouldn't have been too clever, would it now?'

'No,' I said.

'I mean now, look at the problem that the tapes have caused,' he continued, looking at me.

What on earth was he talking about? I wondered, suddenly on guard. What did this pisshead know about anything? And what was he doing here anyway, come to that?

'Tapes? What tapes?' I asked. 'I don't know what you mean.'

'Oh, of course you do,' he said. 'The tapes the police have got.'

I shook my head. I was still acting dumb, 'I'm not with you.'

That idiot, he said, gesturing to the American, who was still to be seen sitting further down the departure lounge, grumbling to himself and any *wazungu* or *wahindi* he could get to listen to his tale of outrage and woe.

'Fat lot of good his whining is going to do him,' observed Gerry,

254

to no one in particular. 'He would be better off just concentrating on getting the hell out of here.' He was nodding to himself as he spoke, 'And so would you, he wagged an admonishing cigarette and Castle can at me. And so would you.'

'Yeah, yeah, I know,' I said. 'I'm sorry. I'm tired and I was just losing it a little. But thanks again, and I'll try and keep my nose out of trouble for the next hour or so at least until we can get on to the plane.'

'So are you flying out on this one as well?' asked Sam.

'Yeah,' he said. 'I'm off back to head office for a bit of a conference and then it's back to the US on furlough to see the family. And I've got you to thank, by the way,' he said.

'Thank me? But what for?'

'Tengisa,' he said quietly, as though keen to make sure he wasn't overheard. 'We've done a deal. There's nothing in writing of course, but I think he sees the advantages of what you suggested, so I'm pretty sure that he's going to deliver his end.'

'Oh well. That's great. I hope it all works out.'

'So do I,' he said ruefully. 'It's one of the things that's on the agenda for my meeting in The Hague.'

'Are we going to see you on the plane?' Sam asked.

'You might do, I'm upstairs in first.'

Life was obviously tough on the charity circuit, I thought.

'Anyway,' he continued. 'I'll see you in a while, I just want to catch up with someone before I get on board. Keep out of trouble,' was his parting shot.

'Thanks, I will, and thanks again,' I said, as he wandered off, the empty Castle can-cum-ashtray sat on the chair next to us amongst my camera stuff.

'Oh well,' I sighed, as I reached out to repack the gear. For some reason I had bundled the Dictaphone into the backpack which was now at Sam's feet as I had scooped up my stuff at the security check. It didn't matter, I thought, it could stay in there now. I would just stow away the cameras and their bits and pieces back away properly into their compartments in the bag and that would have to do.

We sat in the lounge, looking into the blackness, an inky blackness, apart from the pools of brilliant sodium yellow light washing over the giant bulbous aircraft bodies.

'What are you thinking?' Sam asked me, gently. 'I can see it, it's going tick, tick, whirr.'

'Oh, nothing, nothing really,' I said. 'Just about darkness and light.'

She waited, looking at me a bit expectantly. 'This isn't going to be another rant?' she asked, 'Is it?'

I laughed, 'No, no, rants are off.'

We were relaxed. Our sense of humour was back. We were nearly, nearly, nearly out of here.

'No, it's just that sometimes I feel that there are two different worlds. There is this African world. This black, African world and I don't mean all the Conrad *Heart of Darkness* stuff. Look around you, it's dark and yet everything is happening, it's hustle, it's bustle but during the day everything in the open is completely baked and sun-blasted, things are sleepy and quiet. It's private time, holed up behind walls inside houses, away from the sun.

And then we've got the European world, which is sort of bright, and light, and white, and where everything happens in the day time; night time it's private and quiet and sleepy.

And sometimes I think that if we can't even agree on whether we ought to be doing things during the day or night, what hope have we got about agreeing on much else?' I asked.

'And it's like…'

It was difficult to put some of these feelings into words. 'It's like each of us… like we sleepwalk through the other's world. We are sort of disconnected and dreamlike, lucid, aware, but not really involved.'

'More like a bloody nightmare,' Sam spat quietly under her breath, suddenly vehement and vitriolic.

But at least we were nearly free now.

I wanted to put my arm around her shoulders and hug her to me. But of course I didn't. Instead we sat silently looking out through our double reflection in the dark glass of the corridor and outer window, out at the runway, the tarmac, the bustling lights, the fat-bellied plane. 'It's all right,' I whispered. 'We'll be out of here in just a moment.'

There was a movement in the reflection in the glass. People were coming up behind us.

'*Samahene* bwana,' said a voice as we turned to see who was coming. It was the fatter plain clothes man from downstairs who had pulled the American in, together with the SPU man from the airline check-in desk and two khaki-clad policemen.

'I am the head of our airport security here at Jijenga,' he said

256

pleasantly.

Seeing him close up I realised that he was older than I had first supposed, his dark hair was flecked with grey and was receding at the temples. He was meatier too than his weight belied, his moustache was a short cut military affair. His watch though was heavy and gold, as was the thick ring on one of his fingers. He seemed a quietly powerful man close up, his calmness and total control making his pleasant exterior somehow all the more frightening.

'And I would like it very much if you would come with me please.'

There didn't seem to be any choice in the matter really, I thought. There were four of them, and the two policemen at least were armed.

'Well, of course,' seemed to be the only possible answer, as I stood up to face them. There was no prospect of running. There was nowhere to go.

'Will this take long?' I asked calmly. 'I've got a plane to catch.'

'I am sure that it will not, bwana,' the leader said pleasantly. 'I hope that we will not inconvenience you for more time than is necessary.'

'If you just look after the bags, I'll be back in a moment,' I said to Sam, who was staring back at me.

'Of course,' she said, her voice level.

'Ah,' said the man in plain clothes. 'If you would be good enough to bring your bag of cameras, please.'

I looked at him in surprise.

'My camera bag?' I shrugged my shoulders. 'Of course, if you want me to, but I don't understand why.' I stooped down to shut it, all the bits of the SLR were in their correct slots, the body with its small lens, the telephoto lens, the flash, with Ish's old manual loaded in on top. I snapped the plastic fastening shut and slipped the strap over my shoulder.

'Well then, Mzee,' I said. 'Where to?'

Sandwiched between the two policemen, I followed the plainclothes men out of the seating area and through the concourse of shops to a nondescript office door.

The SPU man had obviously gone back to his watching brief at the desk, the *wahindi* airline representative had an oily smirk on his face that made my blood boil just seeing it.

If there was one thing that I took comfort from it was the very

257

public nature of my being paraded out of departures. I could feel the buzz of tension and conversation going around the room as I was led away.

Wazungu cannot just disappear, I kept thinking to myself. Not without a proper explanation from the authorities and I was very publicly alive and well and walking as I left the departure lounge through the shopping area and into a side office, where the door was pulled closed behind me by the two khaki-clad policemen. I was surprised that they stayed outside. I could see the shadowy shape of one of them through the frosted glass panel in the upper half of the thin plywood door.

That wouldn't stop much sound, I thought desperately, draining succour and reassurance from everything that I could find.

The room was sparsely furnished. Another standard civil service style desk, a few wooden chairs, a battered grey metal filing cabinet in one corner. Nothing more, not even a telephone.

'Please bwana,' he said, pulling up a chair to his side of the table, 'take a chair and be seated.'

'*Asante sana, mzee,*' I replied automatically, as I casually went to drop the camera bag on the floor in front of the desk.

'But if we could have the bag upon the table, bwana, please,' he caught me.

I looked at him quizzically but calmly for a moment as I was in the act of pulling the nearest chair towards me from against the wall. 'Why, yes. But I do not understand what this is all about.'

'Please sit down,' he said, 'and I will explain.'

I plonked myself down on the chair and put my bag down on the table.

'I mean what is happening here?' I insisted. 'Am I being arrested for something? Who are you?'

'Oh but bwana,' he said, holding his arms out in denial, 'I do hope that that will not be necessary. However, I am as I said, the head of security for here at the airport.'

He brought his hands together in front of him as he leant forward across the table towards me. He was professional, avuncular, he had almost the air of an old fashioned priest about him, a human man, confident that he was representing a force bigger than himself.

'So what can I do for you, Mzee?' I asked. 'What do you want to talk to me about?'

'Well,' he said, looking at me directly with a calm air of authority over his steepled hands, 'I am afraid to say bwana, that I must speak to you on a matter of the gravest seriousness.'

I remained silent.

'I must talk to you about a matter of national security.'

I felt my stomach do flip-flops but I hoped I kept my face expressionless.

Sitting there across the desk from him, I could feel a cold certainty settling on my heart. I was here alone, completely at his mercy. He sat there in silence waiting for my response. It seemed that he could wait for ever. He was toying with me for a reason and he could do almost whatever he wanted.

We *wazungu* weren't fireproof. We were alone, staying in an alien world, skating like insects in the light on the thin surface film above unimaginable depths of darkness within which lurked huge terrifying forces of powerful predation, given new scales and teeth by the trappings of authority that we had left behind in our retreat from empire. And beneath us as we cruised in the cloudy murk, watching ever upwards for the signs of struggles on which to pounce was the sunken ooze and slime and mulch of thousands upon thousands of years of relentless life and death struggles and soot and silt and shit forever falling, year upon year, century upon century to collect rotting in the decaying blackened ooze of the floor, home to bottom feeders of this world.

And we thought we were the big fish in the small ponds.

I could see a confession.

I could see the prison container outside the court.

I could see a trial.

I could see a judge.

I could see a verdict.

I could see a local jail cell.

I could see a noose.

All in a moment of certainty.

I swallowed. Hard.

'National security?' I answered at last. 'But what has that go to do with me?'

The truth was of course that it had all sorts of reasons to do with me.

By way of reply he glanced down at my canvas bag. 'Would you please open up this bag for me, bwana?' he said.

I acted surprised.

'But why? Do I have to? What has my bag got to do with anything?'

'But bwana, this is a security matter,' he said.

Oh God, I thought, this is it. I was surprised that he had come out with it so boldly, however. I thought that I had got away with the Dictaphone.

'If you could open the bag for me, please,' he said, indicating the grey and blue padded rectangular bag on the table.

Reluctantly, I pulled the bag towards me.

'Mzee, please, what is this all about? I have been through security already.'

'Taking pictures within the airport is forbidden, bwana,' he said, seriously.

'I know,' I said, surprised. What on earth was he talking about?

'But I am head of airport security. Our *piga pitcha* signs are very clear, are they not?'

'Well, yes!' I exclaimed. 'But *ndiyo mzee*,' I quickly added, nodding furiously. 'They are. But I think there's been some kind of mistake. I haven't been taking any pictures in the airport.'

He had taken both the cameras out of the bag and was looking at them, turning Ish's old manual over in his hands, then absentmindedly it seemed, picking up and judging the weight of my automatic.

'This is a heavy camera, bwana.' He lifted it to his eye. 'But I cannot see anything through it,' he said, in a note of puzzlement.

'Lens cap,' I said, reaching forward and snapping off the black plastic cover.

'Aha.' He smiled at me, putting his eye to the back of the camera again and pointing it at me. 'And to focus?'

'You have to switch it on,' I said, leaning forward again and flicking the switch as I spoke, 'and then press down lightly on the shutter button on top.'

'That's it,' I said, in an encouraging tone as the camera whirred briefly to itself for a moment. 'It is on automatic, so it will not permit you to take a photograph that is out of focus.'

'But why does there appear a red light in the viewfinder?' he asked, inquisitively.

'That is because there is not enough light in here to take a picture,' I said. 'It is too dark.'

'There is no flash?' he asked, peering at the front of the camera.

'It's separate,' I said, pointing at the corner of the bag and praying.

He pulled it out and I showed him how it attached to the

horseshoe mount above the eyepiece.

'It has to be switched on with the red button on the back. But I don't think it will work.'

'Oh?' He cocked an eye at me.

'I think the batteries are flat,' I said. 'It takes a lot of power. Can you hear a whine coming from it?'

He shook his head.

'No then, it's like I said, the batteries are flat. So you see, Mzee,' I said. 'I couldn't have been using this one.'

'So where are the batteries?' he asked, looking at the flash curiously.

He didn't seem to be listening.

'Here,' I said, taking the camera from him and sliding the cover of the flash's battery compartment to one side with my thumb as the top of the first of the AA batteries, freed from the grip of the terminals on the inside of the cover, sprung slightly proud of the lip for a moment. As he nodded in understanding, I pressed the batteries down and slid the cover back in place.

'They need replacing,' I shrugged. 'I'll do it at home, they're cheaper there.'

I pulled the flash off the top of the camera and pushed it back into the bag as the policeman took the body of the camera back from me.

This one is empty is it not?' he asked.

'I think so,' I said helpfully. 'If there is no yellow sign in the little window at the back, it should be.'

His podgy fingers pressed the button and slides at the back of the camera for a moment until with a click the lid sprang open and upward for a fraction of a centimetre.

'Aha!' he exclaimed, opening the back and peering inside. 'Yes, it is empty. And it closes like so?' he said, pressing the back panel home with a snap.

He turned it over in his hands and swiftly he held the camera to his eye, pointing it at me, and said, 'And now, smile please.'

His smile vanished as he pulled back from the camera and looked at it.

'But I'm afraid you still won't be able to take a picture, bwana,' I said.

'Oh?' He looked genuinely disappointed.

'It is an automatic camera, bwana,' I said. 'It knows to wind on the film and it knows when there is no film inside. And when there is no film, it will not allow the shutter to be pressed.'

He was trying it as I spoke.

'So you see, I wasn't taking photographs with it,' I said, 'I was just rearranging my bag after the search at security.'

He put the camera down, looking disappointed. 'This is a very complicated machine bwana, too complicated for here in Africa I think?

Ah but, bwana,' he said. 'How about this camera?' he said, picking Ish's battered old thing. This looks more easy. And how is it opened?' he asked, inspecting the back.

'No, no,' I yelped, raising my hand up hastily from where I had been slipping the flash into the bag. 'Please Mzee, do not do that. Don't open the camera!'

He looked up at my sudden agitation in surprise. 'And why should I not open the camera, bwana? And what is it that is of such great concern to you?'

'Please Mzee. If you look through the small window on the back, you'll see the film inside. If you open the camera, my film will be destroyed.'

He looked at me for a moment as if considering the reasonableness of my request, and then at the camera.

'But I am afraid I must, bwana. This is a matter of national security.'

'Then at least let me wind the film on before you do,' I pleaded. Don't wreck my film and my last photographs. You can see that I can't have taken photographs here in the airport because I have no flash, so please let me keep the rest of my photographs.'

He handed the camera to me. 'So wind on the film, bwana. For I must open this.'

I pressed the rewind button. Ish would just have to lose the rest of the film. Oh, well, cheap at the price, I thought.

The film whizzed back into its canister with a final click as I popped the back of the camera open and proffered it to him.

'You see, Mzee,' I said, as he took it and glanced into the opening. 'There is nothing there.'

He nodded and clicked the door shut.

He put the camera down on the table next to mine. He quietly searched the bag itself, opening the zipped pocket at the front and rattling the films in their canisters, even patting the padded sides of the bag to feel for anything hidden inside.

'So, bwana, why do you need two cameras? Is this not suspicious of itself?' he asked, almost conversationally.

'Oh, come on, Mzee. You must see us *mzungu* here all the time. I only want to make sure that I go home with good photographs of your wonderful animals. The big camera is good, with its big lens, but you saw yourself it is slow, it has to focus. The small camera isn't so good, but it is light and quick and easy to use. With it I can take pictures that I would miss with the big one. That is why I needed both for while I was here.'

'You needed both while you were here, you say.' He smiled beatifically. Aha, I thought, here it comes. And I wasn't disappointed. 'So does that mean that you will no longer be needing both when you go home?'

The question hung open in the air for a moment. It was a decision I had to make. I was just opening my mouth to speak, when I heard the sound of voices outside and the rattle as the door handle was turned.

The door behind me opened. I looked around to find to my utter relief a face I knew. It was Colin.

'Hello,' I said. 'Am I glad to see you. How did you get in here past security and immigration and so on?'

'Hey, it's normal,' he said disarmingly, as the head of security grinned. 'I'm diplomatic, remember?'

'Yes indeed,' agreed my interrogator. 'Bwana Colin is often here and is a very welcome man.'

Oh really, I thought. Well it's nice to know that you're so chummy together.

'Now, Gerry said that he thought you were having a bit of bother so I thought I would pop in and see if I could help out. So what seems to be the problem?'

Of course the answer was that there was no problem. No, we were just discussing cameras and the need to be vigilant for the sake of national security in these dangerous times.

Colin was pleased to hear that this was the case. I had the good sense to keep quiet from here on in and leave it to Colin.

'Apparently,' Colin said, 'the flight is now nearly ready. That's why Gerry asked me to find you and let you know so that you wouldn't miss the plane.'

'Well of course, in that case,' the head of security responded. 'Bwana Paul will certainly be able to go and join the flight in a moment, now that everything has nearly been resolved. There will be no need for us to detain him any longer. It's just that I am a very keen photographer and had been looking forward so much to talking to Bwana Paul about this while he waited for his plane, now that this problem has almost been resolved. But sadly, as a keen photographer, Bwana Paul will appreciate how difficult it is for an honest working man to get a camera here.'

'Oh!' Colin exclaimed. 'Well what a pleasant coincidence, because Paul has two cameras. Of course, now that Paul is going back to the UK, he doesn't need the older camera any more. I'm sure he would be delighted for you to have it.'

'But bwana, that is too kind. I couldn't possibly...'

I took Colin's lead. 'But I insist, I insist,' I said, hastily gathering up Ish's film and my camera and putting them back into my bag.

*

'What the hell has got into them?' I asked Colin as we walked back to the departure area. 'I've never had anything like that happen to me or seen it happen to anyone else on an international flight before. What's it all about? That wasn't just an ordinary shakedown for a spare camera was it?'

Colin was shaking his head.

'And they weren't really interested in that Yank's tapes or Walkman either, were they?'

'No. No, you're right, there is something else. But it gives them an excuse.'

'So what is it?' I pleaded.

'OK, OK,' he said at last, quietly. 'They've got information. They think something's going on, something serious, something destabilising. Something that could tip the whole situation over the edge.'

'What?' I whispered, in a shocked tone of voice. 'Here at the airport?' What did Colin know?

'I can't tell you,' he said, looking straight ahead. 'You know I can't.'

I stopped dead in my tracks. Beside me his footsteps halted as well. As he turned towards me, I noticed for the first time that his head hung low, it was the first crack or sign of weakness I had ever seen in his brilliantly maintained diplomatic façade. Of course, before the crash he had always been human, always been pleasant, friendly even, but he had always remained in control.

'Look, I owe you one,' I said. 'In fact I think I probably owe you a whole lot more.'

He was looking away from me now, not catching my eye as I faced him.

'An apology for a start,' I said. 'And I know that I've made a complete arsehole of myself over the last few months but you've got to realise how badly Iain's death has hit us.'

'It hit all of us,' he said, his voice low and unexpectedly full of emotion.

It was easy to forget, but Colin was an expat out here too. A young man away from home. Someone with friends in the expat community. Friends like Iain.

And at last I realised what a terrible, terrible mistake I had made about Colin, about his attitude, about how he had taken this. About how he had coped with it all, with the body, with the arrangements, with the other expats' anger and bitterness and frustration.

'Oh Christ,' I said, 'I'm sorry, Colin. I'm really sorry. I thought... well...'

He was looking at me now.

'I thought that...'

'Well,' he shook his head. 'What you thought doesn't matter now does it? Not here, not now.'

I hung my head. 'No, I don't suppose it does. But I just want to you know that I'm sorry.'

He put his arm around my shoulders as we turned to walk between the airport shops.

'I know,' he said. 'I know.'

'So, for Iain's sake, tell me?' I asked quietly. 'I need to know. I need to know why.'

'Someone is carrying stuff out tonight,' he said, slowly and deliberately. 'They think it's a *wazungu*, but they are not sure.'

'What if I told you that I thought I knew what it was about?'

'What?'

'What would you say if I told you that al-Qa'eda had a radiation weapon programme going up in Mkilwa targeted at London? What if I told you that that's why people have died?'

Colin had drawn away from me again. 'I'd say you were out of your mind.' Colin sounded so weary by this time that I felt sorry for him, even as he began to get angry and demolish my theory.

'For a start what do you mean al-Qa'eda? What do you imagine it is? Some international coordinated network directed from a hole in the ground somewhere in the Tora Bora? Grow up man, there is no al-Qa'eda, not in the sense you mean.

'Osama Bin Laden had to hire in gunmen for his videos. If it does exist these days, al-Qa'eda is an ethos, not an organisation. Bin Laden sponsors individual zealots and nutcases and acts as inspiration, not controller. And these people are as splittist as any other tiny groups of fanatics, one group in Algeria ended up sentencing all other Islamicists to death as insufficiently pure.

'Al-Qa'eda only exists in some ways now because the US has given it so much prominence. The Yanks have created this mythical enemy to fight and they have made it real by talking about it so much.

'There is no coordinated controlling mind that could plan the sort of international operation you are suggesting.'

'So it could just be people inspired by...'

'Look, don't be soft. The Americans set up the Manhattan project to get the bomb. It took them years and billions of dollars at the height of wartime in setting up whole industries to crack the problem of enriching uranium and designing the bomb. You need to be a country, look how long it took Pakistan to get the bomb, look how Iraq never made it. Christ if you could do it in your bathtub in a shed up at Mkilwa every slum on earth would have the bomb by now.'

'No, but I'm not talking about a full atomic bomb, just a dirty weapon, just radium.'

'So what?'

'What do you mean, so what? A radiation bomb would be a disaster wouldn't it?'

'How many people live in Hiroshima today? How many people live in Nagasaki?'

'Thousands I suppose...'

'No, millions. And what happened to them in 1945?'

'Well...'

'The Yanks bloody well did drop full blown A-bombs on them didn't they? That's what.

Dirty bombs?' he snorted. 'They're a myth. How far will an ordinary explosion spread debris? A few hundred yards if you are lucky? And how much radioactive material could you realistically hope to spread? The US military studied the idea of dirty bombs in the sixties and seventies. They concluded they were a complete waste of time and were hardly likely to kill anyone.'

'But what about the radiation?'

'What about it? Know many thousands of Western European Chernobyl victims do you? You clean it up. Most of your radium would be blown into lumps by the explosion. You'd collect them up, and wash down the area to clear away the dust. A few months of aggressive decontamination and it would all be over.'

There was no way he was going to believe me and as he spoke I even began to doubt myself.

'So what are they carrying then?' I hung on the edge of an abyss, waiting, knowing, a terror of absolute certainty hanging over me as the split second before Colin's reply would damn me for eternity.

I couldn't believe his answer. I had to get him to repeat it twice.

'Diamonds? What do you mean diamonds?'

'Smuggled diamonds. The *Wamwuaji* are bringing them out of the interior and into Mkilwa.'

I was shaking my head, my mouth must have been working like a fish out of water. I was at a complete loss. Was Colin agreeing with Mkate? Had he been right after all?

'And of course it's linked to Iain,' he said.

My eyes were bulging. 'Iain?' I was incredulous. 'What did Iain have to do with it?'

'We think he got too close. Like we think Dave might have.'

'But what had diamond smuggling got to do with anything? It must be going on all the time for God's sake. Why should Iain or even Dave get too close mean anything to anyone? And where did they get too close anyway?'

'Mkilwa,' whispered Colin, as a stewardess walked past announcing that boarding was about to commence.

'Of course it's going on all the time, but mostly it's small scale stuff,' he said. 'I'm going to have to make this short and I'm going to have to go, so you get this once and once only and you didn't hear it from me. Do you understand?'

I nodded dumbly.

'Diamonds are flooding in from the interior. The refugees brought them in at first but now it's an established trade. The *Wamwuaji* are running their own mines across the border—'

'But why?'

'Haven't you been following what's going on in the interior? The *Wamwuaji* are literally a tribe of murderers. They lost the last round despite the massacres, and now that they've been driven out of most of the country except the hills beyond Mkilwa, guess where they have ended up?

'Here?'

'Right, here, up country in Mkilwa and the camps, where they are using the refugees as organised cover for bringing diamonds in.' Colin was looking around as he spoke, to make sure we weren't being overheard.

'They have linked up here with some of the local politicians,' he continued. 'Not everyone was happy with the election results, we all know that.'

'Some less than others?' I guessed.

'You've got it. So they have teamed up with those murdering bastards next door. The *Wamwuaji* want guns and a base protected by local politicians from which to wage their dirty little war back across the border and with the diamonds, they've got the money to pay for both of them.'

I was nodding.

'But it means that the local politicians have gone from wanting just a slice of the smuggling action to wanting the whole of their own pie.'

'A coup?' I was aghast.

'Something's coming. I don't know what and I don't know when and I don't know whether we can stop it, but something is building. Guns are coming in—'

'Where from?'

'Asia mainly, a whole load from Afghanistan and Pakistan we think, but we're not sure how they are getting in or up to the border.'

'And the diamonds are going out to pay for them. Big time. And tonight a whole load are expected to leave to hit the diamond trade in Amsterdam somehow, somewhere.'

'And you came here to try and spot how?'

'Something like that.'

'So what's the Iain connection?'

'There's an end in Mkilwa. We know that. Temu was in it up to his neck until someone decided to sort him out. And Temu was down here looking for Iain.'

'Looking for Iain? When did you get that?'

'We have, or rather had, our local sources. Some of them even in the... well never mind. We had one of our best getting close up at Mkilwa but he seems to have just disappeared recently, but that's the way with agents.'

I felt a chill run down my spine.

'So what's the UK government's position on all of this?'

268

'Position? We don't have a position. Only interests.'

'So what's our interest then?'

'Peace, stability, the status quo. The interior is chaotic enough; we don't want it spreading out to the coast. We don't want a crisis; and we don't want a war; we don't want another failed East African state for jihadis to hide out in; and we don't want plane loads of refugees turning up at Heathrow Airport. Britain has a lot of business interests out here too, don't forget. A whole hell of a lot of investment over the years. We don't want it all going up in smoke.' He shook his head, 'I mean the Party isn't perfect, but you've only got to look over the border to see what it could be like here.'

I shuddered at the thought. 'So do the Yanks feel the same way?'

'Difficult to say.' He shrugged. 'There used to be a school of Yank thought that saw the Party as a bunch of red stooges and would have been pleased to see them go. But that was back in the bad old days.'

'The sixties.'

'Oh and right up into the eighties, at least,' he said, nonchalantly. 'So now I think that's all behind us, but you never really can tell. A bit of a law unto themselves in some ways, the Yanks.'

We were at the table into departures now. At the sight of Colin, the *wahindi* airline official was all oleaginous smiles and I was waved through.

Once on the departure side of the desk I turned and stretched out my hand. Colin took it firmly and in absolute silence we shook hands firmly in farewell.

'Thank you,' I said, and turned away to find Sam flinging her arms around my neck.

'Thank God you're back,' she said.

The crowd was nearly through the doorway to the gate and out into the screaming black, yellow and blue-white glare of the night.

'I've got to go now,' Gerry said, as we collected our bags ready to join the scrum.

'Gerry here called Colin to come and get you,' said Sam.

'Well thanks,' I started, but Gerry cut me off, he was obviously in a hurry.

'Oh, it was nothing now. Colin had only just dropped me off and I thought he would still be around the place and able to help, so I just gave him a call on the mobile.'

'Well, I don't care,' Sam said, 'I think he's been a real gem.'

'Yes, whatever,' I said. 'Listen, Gerry, thanks. I really thought that—'

'It's OK, it's OK. So like I said to you two before, look after yourselves and keep out of trouble.'

And with that he was gone and we were jostling through the gate and out down the steps onto the tarmac for the short walk out to the Western plastic safety of the plane.

Other than a distant view of his jaunty stride walking up ahead across the tarmac, his shock of white hair, his black leather holdall carried under his tanned arm and standing out against the white of his shirt, and the last glimpse of his smile as his charm swept across the stewardess at the door like the passing beam of a lighthouse, as she directed him forwards along the aircraft towards first class, we never saw Gerry again.

Storing our bags and their deadly contents into the overhead lockers and settling down into the width, height and depth of the dark blue clean enveloping business class seat, I almost felt like crying, it was as though the African world outside was melting away as I sank into the reassuring unreal reality of the airline seat that overnight would transport me to a new dawn, a new life, to be reborn emerging from the belly of the plane at the incongruous delivery room of the arrivals hall at Heathrow.

Older than when I had left, but more fundamentally changed than just a couple of years away could tell.

And as I sat looking around the cabin and started to believe, daring to hope, that we were a crack in time, an inch, a few moments away from the end of the whole nightmare, I saw him.

I knew the face.

Khan.

Walking up the aisle towards us.

Mohammed Khan.

Was I dreaming? He was walking forwards through business class.

Mohammed Khan, the general manager of New Mwanchi.

He was on board the plane.

I think it must have been because I was staring at him that our eyes met.

He must have recognised me. I was sure of it, I still am. His stride checked for just an instant, as a look of puzzlement and, was it even fear, registered momentarily on his face. His eyes darted across the rows of seats. Was he looking to see if I had anyone with me before he wrenched his eyes away, and with his gaze averted, in two swift strides he had reached the bulkhead beyond which was first class? Then he was gone.

For a moment, for a very long moment, I held my breath and stared at the gap through which he had disappeared.

Gerry's got a diplomatic passport, I thought. He's just told us so. All key aid agency representatives would have. It must make life so much easier for them as they constantly travel in and out of the country and up to the camps on the border. The refugee camps.

Import a lot of stuff, too, I thought. Food, blankets, collapsible hospitals, tents, even heavy equipment, bulldozers, graders, tractors. A whole load of people, papers, bags, goods, sacks, containers, going in and out, in and out, and up to the border, all under an international aid agency flag.

And a whole load of other containers coming in as well. Containers from the subcontinent, full of metal and scrap from Pakistan and Afghanistan. Right into the New Mwanchi compound next door to Gerry's RI overnight truck stop in Mkilwa.

And Gerry, travelling out to the Netherlands regularly on his diplomatic passport.

'Bloody hell,' I whispered. 'Do you know who that was?'

Sam hadn't seen him walk past because she was looking at the armrest controls to work out where the reading light switch was. 'Who?' she said, glancing up.

'Doesn't matter.'

And for a moment, a very brief moment, I badly, badly wanted to know where Mr Mohammed Khan and Gerry were each sitting in the privacy of first class, up ahead through the darkness of the night flight ahead.

And then as the cabin doors clunked shut, I decided that if there was one thing I did not want to know, it was that. Not now. Not ever.

It was the complete transport loop.

Had Colin got it wrong or had I? I thought to myself, as we buckled ourselves into our seats. But if you wanted to start to smuggle guns and diamonds, wouldn't it make sense to tie up with an organisation with an established network, trading on the routes you would want to take anyway? The subcontinent to Africa, Africa to the centre of both trades? Amsterdam. Home to heroin and diamonds.

A few minutes later the jet was rolling down the runway to commence take-off. As the engines roared and we were pressed

271

down in the seats for the rumbling headlong rush out along the runway and then up into the night air, I squeezed Sam's hand and she turned to look at me. 'It's OK. We're out. Ish'll be on the next flight,' I promised her, and myself.

At least the tape was safe, tightly wrapped in its plastic bag and secured with black insulating tape to make sure that it didn't rattle when it was slotted into the battery compartment of the SLR's flash gun, hidden from view by the top and bottom section of batteries that I had carefully chopped to size with the axe to fit the remaining gap, making them just long enough so that they had to be compressed into the compartment and popped up realistically when the lid was taken off.

It had been enough, just, to foil the security man. Thank God I had remembered last thing last night to throw the spare batteries out of the camera bag. If he had found them and suggested that we change the flat batteries in the flash, I would have been sunk.

But he hadn't, so I could go on breathing again, Gerry and Khan or no Gerry and Khan.

Epilogue

March, England

It was two months since the genocide and the outbreak of civil war. I had sat down at his invitation in the pleasant if anonymous interview room. Bright early Spring sunlight streamed in through a row of windows set high in the wall, solid bars of white gold slanting down to pierce the room architecturally. The air conditioning was cool, discreet and quiet, the metal-legged table had a wood-effect Formica top, the chairs were standard office issue. They were neat, nothing shabby, I noticed. Business like. That was reassuring.

Much like him, his clothes, his approach, his slightly old-fashioned formal professionalism.

We sat facing each other across the desk, the bundle of printed pages in the centre between us.

'Well,' I said breaking the silence. 'This is it. This is the whole story.'

'Yes. Thank you.'

Pushing back in his chair and bending slightly to his left he lifted an antiquated soft brown leather briefcase on to his lap and opened it with a snap. With his half-moon rimless spectacles balanced birdlike on the end of his slightly podgy nose, he delved into the bag.

He was slightly balding and carried with him the reassuring air of an elderly family doctor. Behind him, there was a dancing flash of brilliance as a mote of dust sparkled in a shaft of sunlight. And then it was gone.

I felt strangely peaceful and distanced now that I had unburdened myself.

He half-pulled a folder from between the dividers of his briefcase, squinted at it for a moment before rejecting it, letting it slip back into the depths of his bag and peering in again in search of the right one.

Relaxed now that it was done I carried on talking.

'It's a pretty odd one,' I smiled.

He nodded encouragingly as he carried on searching.

'Funnily enough, I'm not sure that I really know all of it myself.'

He pulled out an envelope and laid it on the table. Then he was back rummaging in his briefcase as I spoke as much to myself as to him, 'I'm not sure where it all actually started.'

Now some wax appeared.

'In my blacker moments I even have doubts about the whole thing.'

'Aha,' he said, pulling out the right piece of paper.

'But I suppose as a lawyer, I shouldn't really be telling you that, should I?'

He was nodding absentmindedly.

He clicked shut his bag and surveyed the table as if silently checking that he had everything.

But no.

'The tape please.'

'Of course,' I reached inside my jacket and drew out a small white bundle. 'Do you need to see it?'

'Ah, yes please.'

I had the cassette wrapped in an unsealed envelope. I pulled the tape clear and held it out just long enough for him to register what it was and to nod before I slid it back inside.

'So if you could put that on top of the papers please,' he said, as I sealed the envelope.

'Of course.'

His short fat fingers spun the piece of paper round on top of the table and pushed it towards me. There was a moment of confusion as I hadn't brought anything to write with. Now it was his turn to put a hand inside his suit jacket. He pulled out a fountain pen and a yellow plastic biro with a black cap.

'The biro will do fine,' I said, taking the proffered cheap Bic. As I pulled off the lid I saw that it obviously hadn't been used for some time and semi-congealed ink had seeped to form a sticky, black, glutinous blob around the tip.

I looked down at the clean white sheet of paper with its neatly typed and formulaic wording and declarations. I knew that I would be smearing the clotted ink across it as soon as I touched the pen to it but it felt somehow appropriate; almost as though I would be writing in blood.

I could feel an element of panic start to rise so I shut my eyes and drew a deep breath to calm my nerves. As I did so just for an instant it felt as though I was trapped in a bubble of silent time.

I might have unburdened myself of the story but not of the knowing. I could still see and hear and feel and smell and taste the scorched rubber at the back of my throat. I knew that every time I closed my eyes in the darkness I would be back. Back with that

274

helpless feeling as I looked at the list of the drowned; distraught in a ditch hemmed in by the metallic stench of the burnt out car; horrified at the oozing thickness of the congealing blood; hearing the crackle of the all consuming flames; and that morning afterwards experience of the warm dry gritty texture of the concealing ashes between my fingertips. I had written both to ensure I had an exact reminder but also to forget. But I knew that I could never really wipe it from my mind. I would always know.

I felt no guilt, I reminded myself suddenly, angrily snapping my eyes open to the light as I did so. It had all just happened. It had all just been necessary.

'Right,' I said, taking another deep breath and asking, 'Where do I sign?'

But really I wanted to ask myself, Where had it all started?

And was I right?

I scrawled my name against the pencilled cross and then printed it underneath, together with my address against the typed heading. I could feel him watching me as I did so.

I paused for a moment, scanning the page momentarily, just to check nothing else was required, before putting the pen down on top of the paper and sliding both back across the table.

My signature was appalling, a big scrawled capital P and a horizontal zigzagging line trailing off towards the middle of the page. The curse of the professional and cases needing hundreds of letters to employees, creditors, customers that all need signing in a rush.

I sat back as he squiggled his mark above the typed details on the form.

'Right,' he exclaimed, as he put his pen down. He pocketed the biro again and pulled the lid off his fountain pen. 'Now we just need to seal it.'

He pushed his glasses back up his nose and looked up at me. On the desk he had a little handheld seal, a small set of pliers which were two round metal discs, about two inches across and a quarter of an inch apart instead of jaws. He slid the paper into the gap between the discs, making sure that they covered his signature under the typewritten notice and carefully squeezed the handles, crushing the paper between the jaws. As he released his grip the spring loaded dies opened and as he pulled the paper away I could see his raised seal embossed across the page.

'So that's it. That's now notarised, witnessing that you have

275

provided me with these papers today.'

While I had been signing he had placed the bundle into a large gusseted manila envelope, he slipped the declaration of the date of delivery in on top and closed the self-seal flap. He looped thick red ribbon around the middle of the envelope, half knotted and then looped it at right angles around the length, quickly tying a neat small bow in the middle of the front. It was incongruously like a Christmas present. The ribbon was about three-eighths of an inch across and looked good and tough.

'So, it's a sort of memoir is it?' he asked as he worked.

'Yes, sort of.' More of an aide mémoire I thought to myself.

'There's quite a lot of it,' he said. 'Did you type it all yourself?'

'No, a friend helped me.'

'Must have taken an awfully long time.'

'Yeah, quite a while, there's a lot in there.'

'Yes,' he said. 'There must be.' He picked the envelope up in his hands as he was turning it over to tie the knot on the front. He held it still for a moment as though judging its weight. 'That must be a couple of hundred pages, it's a weighty tome. I've always admired people who can write. I've always thought it must be very difficult. How do you remember sufficient to be able to write something of that length and have all the detail?'

'Well, sometimes it just comes,' I said. 'You remember one thing and as you're writing about it you remember more and more detail about that particular thing. But some of it is based on papers and notes and newsletters that we had at the time.'

'You've only just come back haven't you?' he said.

'Yes, we flew home at the end of January.'

'So I guess it must be all pretty fresh in your mind?'

'Yes, very, very fresh, very...' I searched for the right word, 'very vivid.'

'It must have been horrific.'

I let that one pass in silence.

He changed the subject. 'So how do you do it?'

'What, the writing?'

'Yes.'

'Well, I just put it all on to tape.'

'Yes, I can see that,' he said. 'Tape is obviously the best, isn't it?'

'Yes,' I agreed.

'I find them really useful myself,' he said. 'Everything important goes on the Dictaphone. It just makes life so much easier.'

'Yes they do, don't they.'

'Right,' he said, again, at length. A blob of red wax had gone over the knot, to be imprinted with a seal and my details were written in the top left-hand corner of the outside of the envelope. 'Now, that's fine,' he finished, admiring his handiwork. 'We'll put that in our secure storage as you requested. Only you, or your executors, have access to it, as you have instructed and there it will stay until we hear otherwise from you.'

He looked up at me again. 'So there it'll be for ever,' he smiled, 'or until you decide you want to publish your memoirs.'

'Oh, I don't think I'll be wanting to do that,' I said dismissively. 'I think they're a bit too painful for that.'

We shook hands and he agreed that he would forward me his invoice.

'Thank you very much,' I said.

The interview room opened into the main reception. We shook hands again at the entrance.

'Goodbye,' he said.

'Goodbye,' I replied.

The dark tinted glass doors opened suddenly and anticlimactically as I walked towards them. The change was a shock and for a moment the glare caught me and I screwed my eyes shut against the brightness.

In the darkness, Africa, the years in Jijenga swirled as a bubble of hot bright vivid fleeting memory on a strong black current. The bubble was a revolving sparkling sphere of sunshine and primary colours. Jijenga's sky, billboards and sands. And as I looked, I could see the bubble floating, floating away backwards, back down the black stream of memory, a brilliant beacon that I knew would never fade, but only become more and more distant and remote as the years went by, becoming smaller and vaguer as it did so.

Mkate? I felt no guilt. He wasn't kith, wasn't kin.

Now where had I come across that before?

I was sorry, however, that Ish was dead, killed for his story, the story I could have given him. Sorry that I encouraged Sam to let him go looking for it in the first place. Sorry for having got Sam involved in the first place and sorry all the ways I had failed her, and them both ever since. Sorry for the way we were compromised by the death of Mkate, sorry that we could not start to tell Ish's story for fear that our murder would come out. I had killed someone in cold blood and disposed of their body and how could I ever hope to explain that one away? That I just had to do it? That, because he was an African policeman, it didn't matter so much? Is that what I would be saying?

Nothing remained of what Ish had managed to achieve in such a short space of time. Nothing that would enable his name to survive, to achieve at least the immortality that he had sought and had been on the brink of, not even his photographs, which had come back from the developers fogged and unusable, as though the film had been put next to an X-ray machine said the man in the photography shop.

Which of course, with Dave's cassette in the case it probably had.

I walked out of the door into the bright warm, soft, gentle, English spring sunshine.

I wondered for a moment what I would do next.

But there was one thing that I did know I had to do, to start to get on with my life again.

And I just had to hope to God that Colin was right.

Lightning Source UK Ltd.
Milton Keynes UK
25 November 2009

146714UK00001BA/64/P